Secrets and Whispers

a novel exploring love and family dynamics

by

Robert Luis Rabello

This book is a work of fiction. All of the names, characters and incidences are either a product of the author's imagination, or are used fictitiously. Any resemblance to actual events, locales or persons, living or dead, is strictly coincidental.

© 2018 by Robert Luis Rabello.
All rights reserved.

No part of this book may be reproduced, stored in a retrieval system, or transmitted by any means, electronic, mechanical, photocopying, recording or otherwise, without written permission from the author.

ISBN - 13: 978-0-9878298-8-7

Cover art by Robert Luis Rabello

Dedicated to the glory of God, to my beloved cousin,
Sandra

May love follow in your footsteps and laughter fill your heart

and in loving memory of
Magdalena, my saintly mother-in-law

You rest from your labor, and your deeds will follow you.

Robert Luis Rabello

Summerland, British Columbia

November 2018

Choosing Life Over Death

A few hours before she drew her last breath, Frieda Bergen summoned Algernon – First Priest of the Holy Order of Ravenwood – to deliver the Ordinance of Final Rites. She did not articulate a motive for this request. She never discussed her reasoning with anyone, but smiled weakly before slipping out of consciousness, just as Algernon scurried into her room.

The troubled priest wondered if this dying woman's gesture signaled a desire for reconciliation. Her labored breathing, pallid skin, chapped lips and dry, sticky tongue foretold of her imminent departure from the physical world into unity with The Great God. Maybe Mrs. Bergen, who'd always maintained a harsh, critical attitude toward him, sensed his doubt about spiritual uncertainties of this kind and understood his longing for personal connection. Maybe calling him to her deathbed affirmed her unspoken belief in his sincerity.

Whatever her intent may have been, moody insecurities arose in Algernon's soul, forcing him to avert his gaze. Across the darkened room sat his twin sister, Kira, whose grey eyes projected hopelessness. With the help of a cane she arose, greeting him with a sibling kiss.

"She's been asking for you," Kira whispered.

Arising from a chair on the near side of the bed, Volker Pfaff – Mrs. Bergen's elderly brother and former high priest of the sacred Temple Elsbireth – stood to embrace Algernon. His voice quavered and his face reflected the pain of imminent loss. "My son!" he exclaimed, though the two men were not related. "How good of you to come!" Then, grasping the younger man's strong upper arms he added, "Are you up to this?"

Algernon nodded. "I am."

Secrets and Whispers: *Choosing Life Over Death*

However, the young priest appraised the elderly woman with mixed feelings. She'd been powerful in her day. Mrs. Bergen was one of very few people who inspired Algernon's fear. Many times her sharply-worded phrases had wrenched asunder the thin veil concealing a wretched truth: Algernon felt desperately unworthy of his calling. Unlike her priestly brother, Frieda Bergen discerned no virtue in a young man whom she considered violent and irredeemably inveterate. Her captious language echoed in Algernon's memory, rousing indignation that he'd long struggled to control. His brow furrowed, his nostrils flared, his flesh flushed and his lips tightened.

Evaluating the change in her twin brother's expression, Kira squeezed his shoulder. "It's okay," she encouraged, her solidarity diffusing his emotion. "She can't hurt you anymore. Forgive, and let her depart in peace."

With his anger melting beneath his sister's gentle consolation, Algernon took a deep breath. He'd found courage to come here only after praying to release his bitterness, only after letting go of what he considered righteous resentment. The persistence of his spiritual struggles, the internal strife fraught with misgivings and the awareness of his own shortcomings had long ago shattered his pride. Knowing his own need of forgiveness, Algernon preferred to err on the side of mercy, lest he also come under judgment. This truth transformed him into an effective priest, despite his self-doubt.

Glancing again at Mrs. Bergen's enfeebled form, Algernon reached for her forehead, gently touching the woman's thin, grey hair and tenderly caressing her sweaty skin with his thumb. "May the Great God hear my prayer," he began, reciting the liturgy from memory. "May his mercy cover all wrongdoing and preserve the soul of Frieda Bergen, beloved of her brother, her late husband, and all who have known her.

Secrets and Whispers: *Choosing Life Over Death*

"By the authority of my holy office, invested by the One who is forever faithful in forgiveness, I absolve this woman and release her soul into eternity . . ."

***

While the ceremony itself took only a short time, in harmony with Tamarian customs, Algernon – as presiding priest – lingered with Mrs. Bergen as long as her breath remained. He sat in awkward silence with Volker Pfaff and Kira, his thoughts a personal storm of strife, listening to the dying woman desperately clinging to her last moments.

When the telephone rang, Kira felt relieved that she had an excuse to leave the room. Although she'd been undertaking intensive physiotherapy to recover from a gunshot wound to her right leg several weeks earlier, the young woman still couldn't walk without the aid of her cane. The phone – a candlestick design not quite as old as the house, itself – stood on a small table at the end of the upstairs hallway. Kira fumbled for the receiver just before the operator on the other end gave up on the call.

"Bronwyn for Kira," the operator said.

"This is she," the crippled girl replied.

"Please go ahead," the operator encouraged curtly, connecting the call.

Bronwyn, Kira's best friend and Algernon's fianceé, sounded anxious over the noisy crowd on the other end of the line. "The train's here," she announced. "I can't deal with my mother without your help. Can you come?"

Hearing the tension in her friend's voice, knowing that Bronwyn had been waiting at the station for her parents and other family members to arrive, Kira decided to honor the living over the dying woman in the nearby bedroom. "Mrs. Bergen is still with us, but I'll take my leave and meet you at the hotel," she promised.

Secrets and Whispers: *Choosing Life Over Death*

Kira could hear disappointment in Bronwyn's voice. Her mother strongly disapproved of her engagement, and Algernon's absence would likely amplify their displeasure.

"Please don't be late!" Bronwyn urged. "This is going to look really bad . . ."

After assuring the anxious young woman that she'd soon meet her at the hotel, Kira hung up the phone and called her eldest brother, Garrick, and his wife, Brenna, suspecting – by virtue of her warrior brother's breathlessness when he finally answered the line – that she'd interrupted the amorous couple again. Kira expected an impatient response, as he'd become rather intemperate since his last deployment, yet Garrick retained his composure and spoke to her gently.

"We won't keep you waiting," he pledged.

Kira didn't question his sincerity, but didn't believe he'd fulfill that promise. Punctuality made for good manners among Tamarians; however, Garrick's Lithian wife did not share in his culture's perception of time, and she'd not appreciate cutting short their private contact. Kira understood Garrick's longing to linger in Brenna's passionate embrace, as their obvious devotion and frequent intimacy inspired her unspoken envy.

She hobbled to Mrs. Bergen's room, pausing at the doorway, listening to her twin brother's eloquent, intercessory prayer. He had a way with words, she thought. Kira quietly turned toward the bedroom where she'd been staying since Mrs. Bergen fell critically ill.

The young Tamarian woman hadn't focused on her personal history in this house since returning here a few weeks earlier. Caring for the old woman and making a myriad of social and practical arrangements for her brother's wedding had consumed Kira's attention. She'd neglected her own interests – including her garden – for the sake of the wedding. But for a fleeting moment, as her left

Secrets and Whispers: *Choosing Life Over Death*

hand rested on the walnut wainscoting, Kira's mind drifted back to a place of personal pain, of suffering rooted in addiction and slavery. Violence and miscarriage whispered from these walls.

Kira forced these memories into their prison, as the dismal circumstances that plagued her past no longer held sway over her present. Her future and her family depended on making wise choices now. With a muttered, half-earnest prayer, she slipped out of her casual clothes, opened the wardrobe and wrestled into a beautiful dress that she'd bought while shopping with Brenna a few days earlier.

Admiring her slim, athletic figure in a mirror, Kira smiled. This imported gown – with its fitted, button-down bodice and daring, scoop-cut back – featured a knee-length ruffle skirt in a pretty, pastel floral fabric.

Not long ago she'd have balked at its price, but Kira had learned how to make money in the investment markets and wanted Bronwyn's family to know that their daughter was not marrying into poverty. Kira put on a matching set of carefully selected jewelry, intending to address that particular objection with casual displays of affluence.

There were other issues with both families she knew she'd face, but Kira had carefully planned this first meeting with Bronwyn's parents to develop a positive impression of her and her brothers. That's why she'd bought the dress. That's why she'd paid for dinner at the hotel in advance. Everything had to be perfect.

After fixing her hair and donning a red sweater, Kira picked up her shoes and straggled back to Mrs. Bergen's room. She made just enough noise while entering to encourage her brother to finish his prayer.

Algernon raised his eyes and turned toward her. "They've arrived?" he inquired, making no effort to mask the dread in his voice.

Secrets and Whispers: *Choosing Life Over Death*

Kira nodded. "Don't worry," she assured him. "I'll run interference for you." The young woman offered her twin another kiss, bade a final farewell to Mrs. Bergen, then gave Volker Pfaff the traditional priestly blessing, which the old man returned graciously. She breathed in relief tempered by a thread of regret as she turned away from the somber scene, knowing she'd never see Mrs. Bergen again.

Downstairs, Freya Pfaff, the widowed daughter of the former high priest, solemnly prepared a meal with her mother, Erika. As other family members would soon gather in the parlor, ascend the stairs and pay their last respects, the women made beet soup and fresh bread in advance. They'd head upstairs to wash and prepare Mrs. Bergen's body as soon the elderly woman passed away.

Kira poked her head into the kitchen, interrupting the women's work. "I'm sorry, but I have to leave now," she announced. "I'll come back for my things."

Erika smiled weakly. "Thank you for being here," she said. "It meant a lot to Frieda and the entire family that you were willing to care for her."

"It's a small matter," Kira replied. That wasn't true, but the lie served to conceal an uncomfortable reality. Mrs. Bergen thought the world of Kira, who tolerated the old woman's acrid wit without complaining. For that reason, Kira had stepped into a role typically handled by a relative or a palliative care nurse, despite having grown weary of the responsibility.

"Go on," Freya urged. "Your task here is done. It's the living who need you."

With emotion rising in her eyes, Kira nodded and turned away, relief washing over her soul. Inwardly happy to be rid of Mrs. Bergen, while concurrently experiencing guilt for feeling that way, the young woman left the house and carefully descended the well-worn stairs from its covered back porch to retrieved her hydraulic bike.

Secrets and Whispers: *Choosing Life Over Death*

In stock form, this machine lacked sprockets, chains and friction brakes. The power and stopping functions of conventional bicycles were handled by a pedal driven hydraulic pump and handlebar-mounted controls.

Now – courtesy of Tembe, the smolderingly handsome Abelscinnian who'd taken a fancy to Kira at Garrick and Brenna's wedding last year – Kira's bike featured a battery and electric pump, which enabled her to ride without using its pedals. She unplugged the device, looped her cane into a holder and sped down Mrs. Bergen's gravel driveway.

Kira loved the raw power of her electric bicycle. She didn't ride on the street because the cobblestone pavers rattled her body and stirred pain in her leg. Instead, she glided along the city's gravel walking paths, winding her way through the quiet, leafy neighborhood, over curved stone bridges spanning the steamy, braided streams of the River Honeywater.

She felt relieved to get outside, relieved to have her life back. The freedom inspired by speed renewed the young woman's appreciation of her youth and vigor. Kira smiled and waved at young children playing in their yards as an unseasonably cool breeze and the wind of her passage swept over her skin, flinging the long locks of her platinum blonde hair into the wake of her passage.

***

Although Kira attributed her eldest brother's breathlessness over the phone to interrupted sex, had she actually witnessed the truth, she would have burst out laughing. After visiting the royal library and checking out a book on fitness exercises for couples, Garrick and his lovely bride decided to try out some of the routines in the privacy of their home – a hidden music manse located at the northern edge of the palace complex.

Secrets and Whispers: *Choosing Life Over Death*

This effort harmonized with the treatment regimen that the regimental psychologist, Dr. Bauer, had prescribed for Garrick in an effort to help the young officer cope with the lingering impact of combat trauma. "Your brain chemistry will change with regular exercise," Dr. Bauer advised, "and further, you will find sleep both easier and more restful."

Although the newlywed couple held many interests and core values in common, they'd struggled to find mutually-enjoyable fitness activities. Brenna, who loved running, easily outpaced Garrick on the cross-country trail she used for early morning exercise. Her relentless stride, strong legs, lightweight body and excellent stamina endowed the petite woman with an astonishing ability to run with great speed over long distances.

Garrick preferred swimming. Exercising in the water gave him a full-body workout without sweating, yet while Brenna also appreciated that attribute, he needed motivation – some form of competition to inspire greater effort – but she could not match him in the pool. Also, being married had cemented her bond to him, which meant that Brenna didn't like being seen in public wearing a swimming suit. She reserved her beauty for his exclusive benefit and resented the leering men, gawking teenagers and envious women who glared at her at the pool, leaving reticent Brenna feeling guilty for attracting attention.

They'd set up a frame and crossbar behind her piano, near their lower floor patio doors. The first exercise they tried involved Brenna wrapping her legs around her husband's waist, while they both reached to do a set of pull-ups. His arms and torso, however, were longer than hers, mandating that he keep his arms flexed so that she could reach the bar. Worse, with her legs wrapped around him, he also found his breathing restricted.

Secrets and Whispers: *Choosing Life Over Death*

Unable to hold on, Garrick let go. With his weight added to hers, Brenna's pianist fingers lacked the strength to maintain her grip. With a shriek, they tumbled to the mat below, their mirth resounding in the overhead dome.

Push-ups proved a little easier. With Garrick lying face-down, Brenna put her toes on his shoulder blades and her hands around his ankles. They could sustain this position and alternate as they did their push-ups, provided they stayed in sync. Yet in a playful manner, Garrick tried to disrupt his wife's rhythm, changing the cadence and intensity of his exercise like a horse trying to rid a rider from its back.

Brenna, who had an excellent sense of balance, returned the favor by putting her lips on her husband's calf and blowing against his skin to make a rather loud, obscene-sounding noise. He began laughing – partly from the rude sound and partly because her fluttering lips tickled him – and eventually flopped onto the floor. She rolled away, pretending to glower at him, until he made a silly face and she sputtered into a spasm of giggling.

Crawling forward, Garrick planted little kisses on his wife's right leg, moving up to her thigh, her arm and then her neck. In response, Brenna pulled him close, sliding her hands across his broad back and leaning her forehead against his shoulder. She held him with trembling arms as a tear traced down her cheek, landing on Garrick's flesh.

"What's wrong?" he inquired, the playfulness in his demeanor vanquished by concern.

Turning her head to the side, the Lithian woman wiped her eyes dry. "I can't remember the last time I saw you so happy," she replied. Brenna leaned back and took his chin into her hands. "I've been worried about losing you. I've prayed in desperate hope that you'd come back to me, and now, just for a moment, you have."

Secrets and Whispers: *Choosing Life Over Death*

Bewildered by her words, Garrick paused to think before responding. "I'm trying, Brenna. I know it hasn't been easy, but I'm doing the best I can."

Brenna shook her head. "You can't help what you're going through," she sniffed. "It's not your fault. This is my burden to bear, my issue to cope with."

Garrick wiped her tears away and drew close enough to kiss her soft lips. "Maybe you need to talk to someone about this."

With a sigh, the Lithian woman let her focus wander to the dome high overhead. "Nobody understands what it's like for me to watch you spiral downward like this. Combat has driven the real you away, and nothing I do seems to help bring you back."

He didn't think that was true. From his perspective, the same dreams and longings he'd shared with her when then first met still stirred his heart. "You are helping, Brenna. If it weren't for your love and patience, I wouldn't be able to cope. I'd have given up without you at my side."

Brenna gazed at him longingly, then looked away. How could she help him understand without sounding selfish? "I'm happy that you feel that way," she stated. "This has been hard for me. Nobody really gets what I'm going through, watching you struggle. Kira tries, but she's got her hands full with wedding plans and caring for Mrs. Bergen. I can't lean on her right now."

Pausing before broaching a delicate subject, Garrick affectionately caressed his wife's hair. Its thick, black strands felt silky and soft to his touch. "There's the MSA," he suggested, referring to the Military Spouses' Association. "They have a support group for people whose partners have combat trauma. If anyone can sympathize with what you're going through, it's them."

Secrets and Whispers: *Choosing Life Over Death*

Brenna's eyes brightened with simmering anger. "What makes you think they're going to welcome a foreigner with open arms?"

"You haven't set foot in one of their meetings," he reminded her, keeping his tone gentle in the hope of avoiding an argument. "The trouble you're facing with me is a common problem among combat vets. These are military people, you're a Heroine of the Republic, and I'm sure you'd find a warm welcome among them."

"I know enough about your people to know better," she replied, her voice sharpening.

Garrick pulled away, feeling defeated. "I'm only trying to help," he stated. Then, thinking about another Lithian woman who was living at Kira's house, he added,"What about Ileana?"

"I hardly know her," Brenna replied. "It's not right to confide in a stranger. Besides, every time we visit your sister, all Ileana wants to talk about is Woodwind . . ."

Brenna's lifelong friend, Woodwind, served in the Tamarian Special Forces. He'd been sent on a secret military mission to a foreign country, and though Garrick knew about the operation, he could not discuss its details, even with his wife.

Pausing to think of a way he could tactfully redirect the conversation, Garrick pulled his beloved close again. "I'm sad that you're suffering and I want nothing more than to help you feel better."

Brenna patted his back. "I know," she replied. "But what can you do beyond what you're already doing? If I knew how to handle this, I'd be doing it."

"You could go back to Dr. Bauer," he suggested.

"Stop trying to fix everything, Garrick!" she snapped. "You need to focus on your recovery. Once you get over your trauma everything will get better for me."

Secrets and Whispers: *Choosing Life Over Death*

"You can't have it both ways," he insisted. "You're right when you say that I can't help how I feel, but you're also putting the burden back on me when you insist that your mental health is linked to an improvement in mine.

"I'm doing what Dr. Bauer tells me," Garrick reminded her. "I'm making an effort to heal. You, of all people, should know that the scars never really go away. The best we can hope for is a different kind of normal, and I'm doing everything I can to get there, not just for my sake, but for yours as well."

Brenna, who'd struggled with combat trauma of her own, knew the truth of his claim. Her belief that faith gave her an advantage over her secular-minded husband blinded her to his progress. This contrast in perspective often served as a fault-line for conflict between them, so Brenna kept her thoughts on this matter unspoken.

Instead, she leaned into Garrick's shoulder and let his affection wash over her soul as he held her close. "What are you going to do about Bronwyn's brothers?" she asked, changing the subject.

Most of the inter-service rivalry between the Tamarian Defense Force, the Inland Navy and the Expeditionary Force – the recently activated branch in which Garrick served – remained fairly friendly. Given that nearly all of the officers in the Tamarian Expeditionary Force, Garrick included, had also served in the TDF, Expeditionary officers usually extended due respect without question.

But it didn't always work the other way around. Bronwyn's three brothers were all TDF veterans. Darren, the eldest, had risen to the rank of Staff Sergeant, while Harold served as a Field Sergeant and Willem – whom everyone called Willi – made it to Lance Corporal. Through Bronwyn, Garrick had heard that these men held the TEF in low esteem. Knowing that the decision to marry Algernon

Secrets and Whispers: *Choosing Life Over Death*

stirred controversy in Bronwyn's family, Brenna worried that her man might not deal with their criticism very well.

"I rank them," Garrick stated. "They have to respect that, if nothing else, so I don't think they'd say anything rude to my face. If they do, they run the risk of being reported for disrespecting an officer.

"Besides, Bronwyn told me that Willi served with a TDF unit on the Saradon before I was deployed last summer. She says his unit was ambushed by the Tanarak, so we have combat experience in common."

Brenna's expression darkened. She'd heard her husband's harrowing stories of the intense brutality and terror inflicted by Tanarak warriors. He'd told her they were the most formidable cavalry the Tamarians had ever faced, and the suffering he experienced after encountering them had shaken the young soldier to the core.

"How are they going to know you're an officer?" she asked. "Are you going to wear your dress uniform?"

Garrick shook his head. "Kira wants us to favorably impress Bronwyn's family, so I'll wear my Queen's Honor lapel and rank pins." Then he hedged, knowing the sensitive nature of his follow-up statement. "I think it's a good idea for you to wear yours, too . . ."

"No!" the Lithian woman replied flatly.

He'd ventured into dangerous territory. Brenna, who'd been honored as a Heroine of the Republic for her actions in battle, hated the recognition that came along with the title. Many soldiers coveted Garrick's pin, but no other living veteran held the title given to Brenna. "We don't need to make a big deal about it," he soothed.

She glowered at him. "They'll make it a big deal. Everyone does."

"Just be polite and tell them you earned it for action in Kameron. They're military people. They won't pry."

Secrets and Whispers: *Choosing Life Over Death*

Brenna put her head into her hands. "I don't see why we have to bother with this dinner," she complained. "Bronwyn's family needs to meet Kira and Algernon. There's no point in us being there."

"It's what Kira wants," he replied. "If she thinks it's a good idea, we should respect her decision."

Kira, despite being the youngest of the Ravenwood siblings, had the right to make reasonable demands of her brothers by cultural convention. Brenna had long advocated that Garrick make room for his little sister's autonomy, and only in recent weeks had he acquiesced to his wife's wishes. In addition, Brenna hoped that socializing would help restore a sense of normalcy in her husband.

"Okay," she conceded. "We'll go."

"You'll wear the pin?"

Brenna scowled, opening her lips just enough to reply. "Yes. I'll wear the stupid pin."

Garrick brightened, scooping his lightweight bride into his arms. "That's my girl!" he proclaimed, twirling her around as if they were dancing.

Brenna laughed, holding on as he swayed across the tiled floor. As the phone rang, she feigned protest while he hastily carried her upstairs and playfully dropped her on their bed. Garrick breathlessly reached for the phone just before it stopped ringing . . .

***

Bronwyn's mother, Irena, earnestly believed that her only daughter was making a grave mistake. She'd agreed to visit and meet the rebel priest whom the foolish girl had promised to marry, but Irena fully intended to discourage the union. With that end in mind, she'd asked her sister, Marla – a psychologist and champion distance runner – to accompany her and evaluate the young prospect.

Secrets and Whispers: *Choosing Life Over Death*

Irena's trump card – the legal right to deny permission for Bronwyn to marry this man – could be wielded if all else failed, but she didn't think that would be necessary. Bronwyn had always been a good girl, she adored her father, and had never before crossed either of her parents. Irena felt confident that Bronwyn would yield to reason, abandon this silly obsession with the priest, his reformed whore of a sister, along with their public service to strippers, prostitutes and other degenerates.

At the train station, the fearful look in Bronwyn's brown eyes confirmed that she understood her family's opposition. Arvid, Bronwyn's father, embraced his daughter with deep and lingering affection. "I'm very proud of you," he told her. "I'm sure this will be a time of happiness for all of us."

But Bronwyn didn't believe him.

The young woman feigned happiness, greeting her brothers nervously. Darren treated her like a small child, Harold seemed distracted – like he had more important things to do than waste time on his little sister – while Willem smelled of beer. Bronwyn had been a gangly girl before leaving home for a new life at the Temple, which cemented sibling opinions long before she'd grown into womanhood. Thus, they could not comprehend the value of her gentle character, nor appreciate her practical mind. Additionally, no one in the family understood the difficulties surrounding her unfair dismissal from the Sacred Community. Everyone presumed she'd been at fault.

Sikki, Darren's wife, leaned forward to grab Bronwyn's shoulders – avoiding an embrace – while pressing her cheek against the heavyset girl's face and kissing into the air. Her insincere salutation and the sneer-like smile that formed on Sikki's lips hinted at the hidden contempt she'd long felt for the younger woman.

Secrets and Whispers: *Choosing Life Over Death*

Irena felt her jaw tightening while watching the scene. Although she'd made an effort to accept Sikki into the family and love her as her own, the cold way the woman treated Darren, and her transparently hostile attitude toward Bronwyn, quickened Irena's pulse.

Heidelinde, Harold's bride – whose fading beauty and seductive charm had once served as formidable social weapons – improved slightly on Sikki's performance. But it wasn't much. Heidelinde appraised her sister-in-law with palpable condescension, tugging on the fabric of Bronwyn's plain dress with a wrinkled brow and a slight frown on her ageing lips. "We should do some shopping," she said. "Let me buy you some pretty clothes."

Vega, Willem's wife – who also happened to be Sikki's cousin – looked both uncomfortable and unhappy. She'd not uttered a word concerning the Ravenwoods, staying silent and sipping wine while her sisters-in-law gossiped on the train. Ignoring her husband, Vega jumped down from the coach, pulling Bronwyn into a tight embrace with a sad smile and whispered words of affirmation. Her emotions arose, staining Bronwyn's dress with a solitary tear.

Irena tightened her lips knowingly.

When Tante Marla stepped onto the platform and opened her slender arms, Bronwyn turned to her mother in surprise. "You didn't say she'd be coming . . ."

"You didn't ask, dear," Irena replied. "But aren't you happy to see your favorite auntie?"

Catching herself, Bronwyn drew the slender, athletic woman near and held her tightly. "I'm so glad you came!" she said, sniffling as she struggled to compose herself.

Marla, who held doctorate degrees in developmental and educational psychology, correctly interpreted the reason for Bronwyn's edgy demeanor and spoke reassuringly. "Don't be afraid," she whispered. "I'm here for you. Everything will work out."

Secrets and Whispers: *Choosing Life Over Death*

Porters arrived to haul the family's baggage downstairs, where an electric van awaited. When Irena asked Bronwyn about this, the young woman replied, "Kira made all the arrangements. You don't have to worry about a thing."

Though he should have known better, at the mention of Kira's name, Harold quipped, "She's the friend who hangs out with *strichmadchen* and strippers, right?"

"It's ministry," Bronwyn replied, defensively.

"Don't be upset," Heidelinde replied. "If it's true, he's just stating fact."

Bronwyn shook her head. "You don't understand. She helps exploited women take control of their lives again."

"Ministry? That sounds shady to me," Darren stated.

Noting the tears forming in her daughter's eyes, Irena ended the banter. "Stop it!" she warned. "We're here to meet Algernon and his family. Hold your tongues if you have nothing good to say!"

While her wisdom silenced the critical remarks concerning Kira, Arvid knew that Irena had already made up her mind about the Ravenwoods. She'd omitted any mention of their daughter's pending marriage because she didn't support Bronwyn's decision. He made eye contact with his wife, his displeasure evident in an expression she knew him well enough to understand. Arvid didn't view his daughter as a third-rate prospect and trusted her judgment.

He sat next to Bronwyn in the van and patted her knee reassuringly. "Your brothers speak in ignorance and folly," he told her. "Your choices are not theirs to make."

"Then why is everyone so hostile?" she asked.

Arvid gathered his thoughts for a moment. "Have patience and pray, my dear. I will advocate for you."

Marvic, Tamaria's capital, ranked as the most modern city any of the family had ever seen. Its broad main avenues branched into a maze of narrow, tree-shaded

Secrets and Whispers: *Choosing Life Over Death*

streets lined with little shops and row houses that towered four or five storeys overhead. Slender parkland fringed the streams of the steaming Honeywater, the mineral-laden river whose many branches surged swiftly through the city and plunged over the precipice beyond its walls.

Light rain began falling as the van followed Victory Street, with its well manicured central divider and marble war monuments, downhill toward the palace complex. Just before Memorial Stadium, the driver turned north into the University District where expensive apartments mingled with cafes and trendy, boutique vendors displaying their wares in large windows. Near the edge of the Dragon's Lair military base, the van stopped beneath the portico of the venerable Gold Leaf Hotel, Marvic's oldest luxury resort.

A pretty, platinum-haired girl wearing a lovely dress and a red sweater leaned on a cane while she waited at the entrance. She directed a team of hotel porters to help unload the van and smiled broadly as Bronwyn's family approached, greeting each one of them by name. "I'm Kira, Algernon's twin sister," she announced. "Welcome to Marvic. We're pleased that you've come."

***

Irena frowned. Bronwyn paled in comparison with this very attractive, highly charismatic young woman. Darren and Harold blushed under the fire of her attention. Even Arvid appeared to have fallen under the young woman's spell. Heidelinde's face, flushed in frustration, revealed the hidden terror of suddenly being displaced by a younger, prettier center of all masculine attention.

Kira wore expensive clothes, high-end shoes and just enough makeup to accentuate her natural beauty. She smiled easily, inspiring trust with delicate charm, and her witty sense of humor hinted at formidable intelligence.

Secrets and Whispers: *Choosing Life Over Death*

Irena noted how quickly Kira calmed Bronwyn's nervous demeanor with encouraging words, hand-holding and close proximity. While Bronwyn looked homely and heavy standing near comely and slender Kira, the blonde girl held Bronwyn in high esteem and treated her with the deep respect of faithful friendship.

Kira's demeanor and attitude favorably impressed Irena and her keenly-observant sister, Marla. But how had this young woman, whose provincial accent whispered of the poverty-stricken southeast, come into wealth that enabled her to dress like a princess, arrange private transportation to this high end resort, and then pay for all the accommodations Bronwyn's family members required? In Irena's eyes, this pretty young thing seemed to be trying a little too hard to impress everyone.

"Algernon is attending to a dying woman right now," Kira stated, interrupting Irena's reverie. "I don't know when to expect him, but we'll gather in the Panorama Room for dinner in 30 minutes. Our brother, Garrick, and his wife, Brenna, will be joining us for the meal."

***

A loud explosion rocked the palace gate and rumbled through the ground. Garrick instinctively dropped and covered the back of his head. His heart raced, but within moments, a familiar calm arose in his soul as he lay on the damp cobblestones, listening.

Brenna, pushing herself up to her knees, unconsciously reached for her boot knife. But palace compound bylaws prohibited weapons on this side of the wall, and she didn't have the hyper-sharp Lithian blade strapped to her leg. She waited, her senses on high alert.

Secrets and Whispers: *Choosing Life Over Death*

Two Defenders, members of the elite palace guard, burst through the gate with carbines leveled. "Stay down!" one of them warned.

Garrick heard shouting and the dull clatter of many booted feet scurrying about inside the checkpoint. He could feel the fallen rain soaking through his clothes as order gradually prevailed over the chaos inside.

Sergeant Fallon came out a few moments later. "Lady Brenna!" he called. "We have injuries. We need you."

When Garrick arose, the sergeant stopped him from following her. "Please go home, sir. We'll send your wife back when she's done."

Despite the fact that he ranked the sergeant, Garrick understood the need for the local commander to assert control of the situation. "Very well, sergeant," he replied.

Brenna whispered, "I love you," in Lithian to her husband as he departed. She followed Sergeant Fallon into the security area at the gate, dismayed that moisture from laying on the wet pavement had soaked through her blouse and skirt. Before being married this wouldn't have bothered her at all, but now, the immodesty brought heat to her cheeks and an urgent desire to cover up.

But no one else cared. Amid the dust and shouting, teams of Defenders were busy removing debris. Sergeant Fallon led Brenna through the secure area into a room off its entrance. Windows had been blown in, spraying the area with shards of glass. Bits of shattered stone littered the ground. Dangling pipe and loose wire hung from the ceiling. The smell of concrete dust lingered in the air.

Triage had been set up in the holding area just off the interrogation room, where brave men screamed in pain and a pair of medics desperately worked to save their lives. Brenna stepped over a pool of blood and knelt at the side of a Defender whose torso looked like it had been torn open by a giant cat.

Secrets and Whispers: *Choosing Life Over Death*

"It's okay," she reassured. "I'm here to help."

Evidence of blast overpressure on the tissue, coupled with secondary contusions from stone and bomb fragments had done a lot of damage. Brenna closed her eyes for a moment, praying for power in her native tongue until she could feel a familiar strength surging through her flesh. She removed her sweater, rolled up the sleeves of her blouse, kissed her fingers and set to work.

The attending medic, who was applying pressure on a severed artery to staunch bleeding, watched with astonishment as this petite, foreign woman inserted her small hand into the open abdominal cavity. "What are you doing?" he snapped. "We need a clamp!"

Her patient lurched and screamed as Brenna's slender fingers explored the injury. "Be still!" she ordered. A moment later, she felt the broken blood vessel fuse together and let go. "Got it!" she announced.

Brenna worked backwards, feeling for bits of stone, steel and cloth, removing these and healing damage. As her fingers returned to the skin, the bewildered medic saw the flesh fully restored, with no evidence of injury.

Terror overtook him and he swore at her. "Who are you?" he stated fearfully. "How do you do that?"

Brenna ignored the query. "Can you please hold him down?" she asked, examining the next wound. She repeated her procedure on every one of his injuries until her patient lay still, weak, but breathing normally.

"Ambulance is on the way!" a Defender announced.

"When they get here, tell them this man needs plasma, platelets and RBC," Brenna stated authoritatively. She acted like a doctor, not a medic.

The medic looked at her as if in shock.

"If you don't write it down, they won't be able to tell just by looking at him," she insisted.

Secrets and Whispers: *Choosing Life Over Death*

***

Garrick changed his clothes and called the Gold Leaf, leaving a warning message for Kira. He felt listless, wishing he could do something more productive than pacing across their modest upper-floor apartment. The explosion revived a hyper-awareness of being alive that he'd often experienced in combat, an oddly gratifying sensation, a thrill he'd genuinely missed in the months since his return home, where his life's experience often felt dull.

Waiting for Brenna only increased his frustration. He'd known about her uncanny healing skills since very early in their relationship, and though she attributed her awe-inspiring ability to faith in a deity she called Allfather, Garrick had never been able to rationalize an explanation for her curative proficiency any more satisfying than her personal superstition offered. It shook the foundations of his worldview to the extent that he simply accepted it as reality, rather than trying to explain how it worked. Whatever the reason, he knew the Defenders needed her.

Daylight ebbed beyond the redwood grove that rose to the south. Kira would, no doubt, feel unhappy that her perfect plan to impress the Traugott family would be spoiled by his tardiness. But Garrick felt confident that his little sister could handle them. Kira was queen in the social domain. No one could match her in that realm.

Sergeant Fallon phoned thirty minutes later, using the direct line from security checkpoint rather than the operator. Agitation resonated in his voice as he spoke. "Lady Brenna has gone to the hospital with the wounded," he told Garrick. "She asked me to tell you that she'd meet you for dinner afterward."

"Thank you, Sergeant," Garrick replied. "Is the outbound gate open yet?"

"Come on up, sir. We'll let you through."

Secrets and Whispers: *Choosing Life Over Death*

While Garrick crossed the bridge isolating the manse where he lived with Brenna from the rest of the palace complex, the phone rang again. But the din of falling water drowned out the sound, and he did not return home to answer it.

***

Ileana, the Lithian refugee who lived with Kira and Algernon on Superstition Mesa, expected a quiet night of relaxation, listening to music on Kira's record player; however, a telephone call that interrupted her solitude inspired anxiety. She needed to notify Algernon in town, but remembered warnings against leaving the homestead after dark. Like all Lithians, Illeana's tetrachromatic vision allowed her to see fairly well at night; yet with no weapon to wield when facing a threat, she could only run, rather than fight. Also, she could speak very little Tamarian, and the language barrier limited her ability to communicate.

She managed to place a call to Garrick, but nobody answered. That left her with no other choice in response to the urgent message from a vulgate-speaking official from the Royal Penitentiary. Ileana had to find Algernon at the Gold Leaf Hotel. She dressed for rainy weather and departed, knowing that Lithians were typically not welcome in public places.

***

Garrick took an elevator up to the Panorama Room, which offered an expansive view of the University District. With the Traugott family and Kira already enjoying their second course, he offered an apology for arriving late.

Secrets and Whispers: *Choosing Life Over Death*

"We heard the explosion from here," Bronwyn stated. "It rattled the whole building. We're glad you and Brenna weren't hurt. Do you know what happened?"

"Apparently, it was a homemade chemical bomb in the back of a delivery truck," Garrick replied. "A forensic team's investigating, so they won't tell me anything, but quite a few Defenders were injured in the blast."

Vega shook her head. "Who would do such a thing?"

Kira offered Garrick a kiss on the cheek before he sat down at one of the empty chairs. Noting that his brother was not present, he inquired, "Where's Algernon?"

"He's still with Mrs. Bergen," said Kira, her nerves silky smooth, indicating that she remained in control despite their brother's absence. "He'll be here soon."

"Brenna sends her regards," Garrick stated. "She'll join us after her work at the hospital is done."

Bronwyn proceeded with introductions, after which conversation temporarily drifted into stilted silence. Garrick, who began eating without offering a blessing on his food, noticed that Willem drained his beer stein and called for another, while Vega fiddled with her wine glass.

"So your wife is a nurse?" Arvid inquired at length.

"No sir," Garrick replied. "But she has specialized combat medic skills, and we were just on the other side of the palace wall during the attack. She went in to help with the wounded."

Intrigued, as something stirred in his memory, Darren added to the questioning. "If she's not a nurse, where did she take her medic training?"

Why was Bronwyn's oldest brother asking this? What did it matter to him? "She didn't train in a formal sense," Garrick stated. "Her healing ability is a natural talent that's been refined in combat with the TDF and the TEF."

Darren leaned forward, his eyes widening. "Where has she served?"

Secrets and Whispers: *Choosing Life Over Death*

Garrick put his fork down. Knowing his wife didn't like attention, displeasure crept into his tone. "Why does that matter?"

"My sister said your wife is Lithian," Darren explained. "I served with the 5th Division, First Infantry at Kicking Horse Gap. We fought the invading Azgar and suffered heavy casualties in that engagement . . ."

Garrick felt his mouth going dry. He and his Junior Scout troupe had been the first Tamarians to encounter an Azgar unit during that conflict. The young officer's heart raced, knowing the likely outcome of Darren's story.

"Their artillery was terrifying. We got pounded until they nearly wiped us out. I got hit by shrapnel and was in such bad shape the medics sent me to Dead Hand Ridge.

"My face, my neck and my chest were a mess. I've never felt so much pain in my life, and I was sure I wouldn't make it, but I remember this nurse, a little Lithian girl with skin like porcelain, beautiful blue eyes and long, dark hair. She saved me. Was that your wife?"

Slowly, Garrick nodded. "Yes, that was her."

Darren swore, partly in stunned shock and partly in triumph. He turned to his brother, Harold. "You didn't believe me! You said I was shell-shocked and imagining things. You said I couldn't have been injured that badly!"

"You have no scars!" Harold retorted. "Your face is still as ugly as it was when we were little!"

"That's how it works," Garrick interjected, trying to diffuse the conflict between brothers. "When she served as a medic in my unit, I watched her heal wounds many times. When she's done working on an injury, it looks like nothing ever happened."

Harold shook his head. "How the hell does that work? It makes no sense!"

"She prays!" Kira stated. "That's how she does it."

Garrick rolled his eyes. "Oh, here we go . . ."

Secrets and Whispers: *Choosing Life Over Death*

"Stop it!" Kira commanded. "You know it's true!"

Marla watched the animated banter between the siblings with interest, noting well-dressed Garrick's deep skepticism and Kira's acceptance of what she considered facts at face value. But this talk about Brenna piqued her curiosity. Who was this mysterious Lithian woman?

Algernon arrived in the midst of the discussion. He looked tired, winded and his shoulder-length hair, dampened by rain and tousled by the wind, needed attention. Why hadn't he checked the mirror before coming in? Kira turned to him as her heart pounded. He was going to wreck everything by making a poor impression . . .

But Algernon moved around the table, greeting the Traugott family members warmly and thanking them for making the journey. Bronwyn pulled him toward an empty seat next to her parents. He declined the wine selection, as Garrick had done, but Bronwyn poured herself a third glass to calm her nerves, saddened by the unwarranted belligerence of her brothers.

Irena leaned toward her daughter's ear and with a smile whispered, "He's really handsome!"

"He's much more than that," Bronwyn assured. "You and Pappa will love him once you get to know him."

Irena raised her brow. "We'll see," she said.

Although he hadn't eaten since breakfast, Algernon declined the first two courses of the meal, thanking the waiter for the spinach and pine nut salad that everyone else was enjoying at the moment. He wanted to hold hands with Bronwyn, but she kept pushing him away.

"So, Algernon. Tell us about this ministry of yours," Tante Marla suggested.

Bronwyn's eyes widened. Why would she ask such a thing in front of the entire family?

Secrets and Whispers: *Choosing Life Over Death*

Algernon wiped his lips with a napkin to buy a little thinking time. "I support my sister's outreach to exploited women, primarily by teaching their children."

That was a very safe answer. "These women live on Superstition Mesa with you?" Marla queried.

"That's how we started," Algernon replied.

"You're the only man involved in this . . ." Harold asked, his tone suggesting something inappropriate in the ministerial arrangement.

"What are you getting at?" Garrick growled.

Harold deflected. "It was just a question."

Algernon, who discerned lies easily, knew that Garrick was right and appreciated his support. But Algernon had more to lose than did his brother and decided it wiser to dignify the tactless question with a response. "Do you have children?" he inquired.

"Yes," Harold replied, taking Heidelinde by the hand as if seeking an ally. "Our daughter is married now."

"So you have grandchildren?" Algernon continued.

"Yes. We have three grandchildren."

"When they come to visit you, I would never presume that any impropriety occurred under your roof."

Growing defensive, Harold spat, "What do you mean? I would never . . !"

"Neither would I," the priest replied calmly. "A real gentleman should naturally extend the same courtesy of presumed innocense to me."

"Algernon!" Kira exclaimed.

"No, he's right," Arvid stated sternly. "My son is totally out of line right now."

The paternal rebuke stunned Harold. He stood and nearly stalked away from the table in anger, but Irena intervened. "Don't you dare!" she warned. "That reckless innuendo was rude, and you owe Algernon an apology."

Secrets and Whispers: *Choosing Life Over Death*

Heidelinde felt embarrassed, nudging her husband to comply. Harold swallowed his pride and sat again. "My parents are right," he said insincerely. "I regret my words."

Algernon extended grace immediately. "I forgive you," he said. "But you can be confident that your sister would never tolerate misbehavior from me."

"Neither would I!" Kira added in a peevish tone.

Tante Marla suppressed the urge to titter, but when Irena sputtered her wine, she, Heidelinde and Sikki burst out laughing. Under his breath, Willem muttered, "Spank me, baby girl!" which earned him a smack from Vega.

Moments later, Brenna walked in. Her damp sweater hung heavily on her shoulders and rivulets of rain that dripped from her dark hair ran down her cheeks. Staff members had initially denied her entrance, forcing her to stand in the rain, until her service pin convinced a reluctant manager to let her in, provided she used the staff elevator with an escort. Brenna crossed her arms as the terror of meeting new people radiated from her face.

Their laughter ended abruptly. Garrick arose and beckoned for his wife, who'd now become the fixation of everyone's focus. That made everything worse for her.

Darren, recognizing Brenna's lovely face and noting the pin on her lapel, stood in her honor. "Get up!" he ordered in a snarling whisper, knocking Harold in the shoulder. He reached for Willem, grabbed a fistful of shirt and yanked his inebriated brother to his feet. "Stand, you idiot!" he spat. "She's a Heroine of the Republic!"

Brenna hated the attention. That was why she'd not wanted to wear her honorific pin, but now she felt trapped, and Garrick had been seated at the far end of a long table.

Noting her distress, Kira pulled herself upright. "Please excuse us," she announced. Taking Brenna by the hand, Kira led her to a ladies' washroom and handed her a cloth hand towel. "Here you go. Dry yourself off."

Secrets and Whispers: *Choosing Life Over Death*

"I didn't have time to go home first," Brenna complained, wrestling out of her sweater. "I was afraid that I'd miss the dinner."

Blood stained Brenna's blouse. Her skirt was dark enough to hide the gore, but her top looked like she'd been performing surgery. "Take this off," Kira suggested. "Make your camisole opaque and wear my sweater."

Brenna shook her head. "Your clothes don't fit and my cleavage will stick out for everyone to see. It's immodest! All the men will stare!"

"Just try it on," Kira urged. "Boobs are better than blood when people are eating, and besides, Heidelinde could use a little competition tonight . . ."

Not certain what she meant by that, Brenna continued to hedge.

"Trust me!" Kira urged. "Bron really needs you now."

Reluctantly, Brenna caved into Kira's pressure. She dried her hair with a towel, willed her filmy Lithian camisole to thicken and turn burgundy red – a desire to which it mysteriously conformed on demand – then donned Kira's sweater, buttoning it all the way up. Appraising herself Brenna grimaced, "I look ridiculous!"

"Let me clean your skirt while you fix your hair," Kira suggested, handing Brenna the brush from her purse. She scrubbed the stains on the fabric with a cold, damp towel to remove them, but standing back and looking at her sister-in-law with a critical eye, didn't like her overall appearance. "That won't do," she said, unfastening the top buttons of the borrowed sweater.

"Kira!" Brenna moaned. "I don't want to show off!"

"I know," Kira stated. "But you look way better when it's not buttoned all the way up." She leaned against the counter, her grey eyes alive with sincerity. "Don't worry, Brenna. Everyone respects you. Bron's parents will quash any leering. They don't tolerate nonsense."

Secrets and Whispers: *Choosing Life Over Death*

"How can anyone respect me when they don't know me?" Brenna demanded, scowling at the mirror. "This is the wrong way to make a favorable impression."

Kira smiled prettily, picking up the discarded blouse, rolling it into the wet sweater and giving it back to her sister-in-law. She put her hand on the Lithian woman's shoulder and urged her out of the bathroom. "Your reputation precedes you. Darren says he was one of your patients at Dead Hand Ridge. You saved his life."

"I'm not comfortable with this!" Brenna complained.

"Don't worry. I'll deflect their attention. After I introduce you to everybody, you can sit down, enjoy your meal, and let me handle everything else."

***

But Kira's plan unraveled within a single footfall past the threshold of the Panorama Room. The two women walked into an agitated discussion between Garrick and Willem, whose alcohol-fueled volatility inspired furrowed brows and knowing glances around the table.

"They screwed us so your precious Expeditionary Force could sweep in and take all the glory for defeating the Tanarak. If we'd been reinforced like we should have been, the plainsmen would never have won a battle."

Garrick shook his head. "There's no conspiracy to make the Defense Force look bad," he replied. "Nobody has ever suggested that you and your men didn't fight with honor out there, but units that are designed for defense are not trained to battle on the enemy's ground. That's never been the mission of the TDF . . ."

"See!" Willem erupted triumphantly. "You even admit it! You said we were set up to fail!"

"No, that's not what I said," Garrick corrected, far more patiently than Brenna and any of his siblings had

Secrets and Whispers: *Choosing Life Over Death*

heard him argue since returning from his last tour of duty a few months earlier. "The Defense Force has a different role, a different mission. That's all. The Expeditionary Force deployed to drive the enemy away from our frontier and defeat them on the Saradon, and that's what we did.

"But our success has nothing to do with the training, equipping, combat readiness, troop size, effectiveness or funding of the TDF. I've personally testified in a Senate inquest after that conflict, and nobody remotely suggested or implied that the Defense Force did not fight with distinction."

Willem pounded the table and swore at Garrick. In fury he arose, confident that this Expeditionary Force officer distorted the truth to conceal a conspiracy. In a pleading voice Vega tried to calm her husband, but Willem shoved her away so forcefully she tumbled to the floor.

That was enough. While Sikki darted to her cousin's rescue, Darren and Harold restrained their brother, wrestling him out into the hall where sharp words and the timely arrival of security staff quickly diffused the volatile situation. Willem's older brothers promised to take him up to his room where he wouldn't disturb any other guests.

Vega fled in shame. Sikki went after her, and the two women did not return to finish dinner.

Garrick felt awful. He'd not intended to create a scene. As Brenna skulked into her seat, he turned to her and suggested, "Maybe we should go."

"Please don't," Irena implored, putting her hand on Garrick's forearm. "The son we raised isn't like this. He was a good boy and an excellent soldier, but he changed after his deployment on the Saradon. Something unspeakably horrible happened out there.

"Vega says he has nightmares. He's become sullen and won't talk to her. He's drinking too much. He's angry all the time and he's looking for someone to blame."

Secrets and Whispers: *Choosing Life Over Death*

Garrick understood this problem in an intimate way. He glanced at Brenna, read the anxiety in her expression, and suddenly felt very fortunate that she'd not given up on him. Turning back to Irena, he said, "Has Willem undertaken mental health treatment?"

Arvid shook his head. "He believes that will make matters worse. Apparently, his commanding officer doesn't think highly of soldiers who seek help of that kind."

"Well, his commanding officer is wrong," Garrick stated flatly. "The help is there because people need it."

"We've encouraged him to visit a private psychologist," Irena added. "But he won't go."

"Give me his commanding officer's name," Garrick suggested. "I'll see what I can do on my end."

"We would be grateful," Arvid concluded.

Conversation gradually turned normal as the staff brought out the main course. As Kira explained the story behind her ministry, Tante Marla tried to engage reticent Brenna about her interests.

When Marla heard that Brenna enjoyed running, she smiled in a slightly condescending manner. "I've not seen you at any of my events. Do you run competitively?" the older woman asked, her eyes lowering and lingering on Brenna's burgeoning cleavage.

"No," the Lithian woman replied. "I enjoy running for fitness, but there are a lot of athletes who train on the university's cross-country track. It's a very demanding course. If you're willing to join me, I'd love to have a running partner."

Marla raised her brow, having already drawn the wrong conclusion. "Do you honestly think you can keep up with me?"

"You'll be the one to struggle," quipped Garrick. "Don't let her size fool you. My wife can outrun a horse."

Secrets and Whispers: *Choosing Life Over Death*

"I'm a champion distance runner," Marla warned. It wasn't a boast, but a statement of fact. She didn't believe that this little slip of a Lithian girl could be serious about maintaining a world-class pace. "But if it would please you, we can meet on the track on the morning."

Brenna beamed, delighted at the prospect that Marla would partner with her. "That's great, but you should give yourself a few days to acclimate to the altitude."

Marla's skepticism continued. "That's not necessary. I'm in excellent condition. How long is the circuit?"

"It's three miles," Garrick interjected. "It also has an elevation change of 500 feet."

"Oh, so you run as well?" Marla queried.

"Not if I can help it," he replied. "And not with her!"

Tante Marla smiled, trying to sound gracious. She tapped Brenna on the hand. "Tomorrow morning at the university track, then?"

Brenna's brow raised. "You're sure you don't want to get used to the altitude, first?"

"No, my dear. I'll be fine."

Garrick felt sorry for Marla, but thought he'd stirred enough drama for one night and said nothing further.

***

Bronwyn, who loved her family, felt so embarrassed by the evening's events she couldn't wait for the ordeal to end. Annoyed that Algernon kept caressing her back, or reaching for her hand, she leaned toward him and stridently whispered, "Stop it!"

He didn't feel that he'd done anything to deserve that treatment, but given that he didn't want to make matters worse with her mother – whom he knew objected to his union with Bronwyn – the young man suppressed his hurt and didn't take his fianceé to task.

Secrets and Whispers: *Choosing Life Over Death*

"We'll talk about this later," he warned, quietly.

Heidelinde, noting that Bronwyn was ignoring her betrothed, took the seat on Algernon's right. At first, she seemed innocent, asking questions about his interests and why he'd become a priest. But after a few minutes of less than enthusiastic listening, her queries became personal.

"So I take it you didn't take a vow of celibacy," she cooed, tipping her wineglass toward her lips in a slightly suggestive manner.

"There's no point in uttering an oath you don't intend to fulfill," Algernon replied, thinking that the woman might have already had a bit too much to drink.

"Well then, tell me," Heidelinde continued, "Why would a handsome kid like you look twice at Bronwyn? What could she have possibly done to stir your interest?"

Beneath the veneer of honest questioning, Algernon discerned many expectations shattered by his interest in a young woman whose family members clearly disliked her. Controlling the urge to lash out in her defense, he said, "If you can't see her value, then you don't know her."

Heidelinde wasn't expecting a response like that. She nosed into Algernon's personal space and lowered her voice. "Everybody knows she's got nothing going for her. She's far from pretty. She's already fat. What do you think she's going to look like ten years from now?"

Algernon retreated, backing against Bronwyn. His close proximity initially inspired her irritation, but when the young woman recognized what her sister-in-law was doing, Bronwyn slipped her arm around Algernon's shoulder and looked at Kira for support.

Kira, noting this from the other side of the table, abruptly dropped out of her conversation with Bronwyn's parents. Her redirected attention caused a shift in Irena and Arvid's focus, but Heidelinde didn't notice that she'd suddenly stepped into the social spotlight.

Secrets and Whispers: *Choosing Life Over Death*

"Charm is rooted in lies and beauty withers away," Algernon replied. "But good character endures forever."

Heidelinde leaned into more suitable adjacency as she let another mouthful of wine linger seductively on her tongue. "So you're serious about my sister-in-law," she stated, rather than asked. "This is a long-term commitment, even if someone better suited comes along?"

Algernon nodded slowly, his expression edging toward something volatile and dangerous. "Otherwise, there's no point in making a vow, is there?"

"I suppose not," Heidelinde agreed, her lips curling into an artificial smile. "That makes you a man of great integrity. You are, no doubt, the perfect priest . . ."

The blade of that insult slipped into Algernon's soul. Heidelinde's keen perception cut through the cloak of priestly prevarications that concealed confused and often contradictory motives. Algernon blushed, far too aware of his personal flaws to lash back.

Heidelinde, pleased that she'd won that contest of wits, rose from her seat. "I'm off to check on the men," she announced. "I've revealed enough truth for one night."

Bronwyn struggled with her emotions. She took in a deep breath and wiped her eyes as her lips trembled. "Why does everyone have to be so mean?" she rasped.

Arvid took his daughter into his arms. "Small minds often have big agendas," he soothed.

Algernon felt like he'd been exposed as a fraud. Kira hobbled over and sat in the seat Heidelinde had warmed. She took her brother's hand in her own, leaned forward and affectionately kissed his cheek. "Pay no mind to her," Kira whispered into his ear. "She's a wrinkled hag with sagging tits and bad breath."

"This is not how I imagined the evening would turn out," he told his sister quietly. "I'd hoped for better."

Secrets and Whispers: *Choosing Life Over Death*

Kira would have responded, but she heard commotion in the hall. Stern male voices mingled with a feminine outcry, calling Brenna's name in a vaguely familiar language that she didn't understand.

"How did you get in?" one of the male voices demanded. "We don't serve your kind here!"

Brenna dashed from her seat. The agility and speed of her departure startled the Traugotts. Garrick – with Algernon responding a moment later – bolted behind her. Arguing ensued beyond the dining room.

"I'm so sorry," Kira said to Bronwyn's parents as she reached for her cane and rose from her seat. "Let me find out what's going on."

By the time she'd shuffled into the hallway, Garrick had taken control of the situation. He was quite skilled at that, Kira thought. Standing in the midst of a circle of four security men, slender, snow-haired Ileana spoke to Brenna with urgency in her voice.

"What's going on?" Kira inquired.

Brenna turned as Garrick further diffused the agitated security team. "Ileana came to fetch Algernon," she said. "But she had to sneak into the hotel because the reception staff wouldn't let her in. That's why the security people are so upset.

"Ileana told me that someone called the homestead from the Royal Prison. *The Shadow* needs a priest. She says he's facing imminent execution."

Analysis

An hour after the dinner ended, Irena and Marla sipped herbal tea in the Gold Leaf Hotel's lounge. Arvid decided to take a hot bath and retire early. Because she was not tired, his wife took the opportunity to discuss the evening's events with her sister, in private. Irena, upset by the conduct of her sons and their wives, would deal with them later. At the moment, she wanted to focus her attention on the Ravenwood siblings.

"Let's start with Kira," Irena suggested, "since she's the once financing everything. What do you think of her?"

Marla's brow arched high. "Most young women who are that attractive project an expectation of preferential treatment from others. I don't see that with Kira. Behind her distingué demeanor is a clenched fist. I suspect she's had to fight for whatever she has."

"So where do you think her money comes from? For a girl whose accent sounds like she's a hick from the wrong side of Broken Wing Lake, she wears clothes and jewelry that send a very different message. The fact that she paid for porters, the van transport, the dinner, our drinks, and accommodations in a high-end hotel like this has me worried."

"You're suggesting she's come into money illegally?" Marla inquired. "Could she live in the same house with a priest and get away with that?"

Irena scowled. "I'm not so sure about Algernon's priestly credentials."

"Why would you doubt them?"

"I've read unflattering editorials about him," Irena stated. "He spends time with questionable people, like that man who's been scheduled for execution tonight . . ."

"Well, if he's a priest, that's part of his job," Marla countered. "You can't hold that against him."

Secrets and Whispers: *Analysis*

"Yes, but it's a cumulative thing. He's bad news. That young man has killed people with his bare hands."

Again, Marla corrected her sister. "I read that, too. But his life was being threatened by a criminal gang from Kameron. Those people are totally ruthless. The fact that the police never leveled charges against him means Algernon acted appropriately.

"The priesthood trains in martial arts precisely because they minister among the unsavory. Those men he killed were importing opium into the country. It's likely that the outcome would have been very different if he'd not been so capable of defending himself."

"Whose side are you on?" Irena snapped.

"It's not a matter of taking sides," Marla replied. "You asked me to come so I can offer my objective opinion. I'm not here to rubber stamp your disapproval."

That wasn't the response Irena wanted to hear. Irena picked up her tea and looked to the side. "You may be right, but it still doesn't address the issue of where the girl gets all her money."

"Well, either it's legitimate or it's not, but at this point, how can we tell?"

Irena returned her gaze to her sister. "What's the most likely source of her income? She says her public service is done out of a desire to save vulnerable women from being exploited. I believe that puts her in a position to gain their trust, and then exploit them, herself."

"That's pure speculation," Marla concluded.

"Do you have a better explanation?"

"I have no evidence either way," Marla replied.

"But it's plausible that she's doing something shady. For all we know, she's running a brothel out of that place up on Superstition Mesa."

Marla shook her head. "Do you believe that Bronwyn would associate with someone like that?"

Secrets and Whispers: *Analysis*

"I believe my daughter is sweet, but naive," Irena stated. "Kira's pretty. She's charming and she makes Bronwyn feel important."

"Or," Marla interjected, "they're actually close friends and the Ravenwood girl values Bronwyn for her character, her committed friendship and her work ethic. Why are you immediately presuming the worst?

"If you're really concerned about where she's getting her money, why don't you ask? I'm sure Bronwyn knows. Or, better yet, ask the girl, herself!"

Irena, who'd been hoping for affirmation, began feeling annoyed. "So, you think Kira's trustworthy?"

Marla shrugged. "She has a Kamerese slave brand on her left arm. Did you see it?"

Irena nodded. "Of course. She showed us when she was telling her story."

"Getting branded like that is a painful and disgraceful procedure, one that proves she was a common whore. That's not something women do for the sake of credibility – especially when they're pretty – yet Kira didn't cover it up and speaks openly about her experience.

"The brand aligns with her story in a way that makes it compelling. The evidence that she's telling the truth is strong in this case."

"But it still doesn't explain where she's getting all her money," Irena remarked.

"No, but that doesn't mean she's dishonest, either."

"Well then, where does a girl like her get the kind of resources to put up our whole family in a place like this for days on end?"

Marla shook her head. "I don't know. Maybe she's come into an inheritance. Maybe she's made good on her investments. Maybe the source of her income is actually Brenna. There's no way of knowing without asking."

Irena scoffed. "You really think Brenna's wealthy?"

Secrets and Whispers: *Analysis*

"Absolutely. Look at how she and her husband were dressed. That cute little camisole of hers costs more than 20 sterlings. I've seen them in high-end lingerie stores. She wore a designer skirt, and those knee high boots of hers were probably five times what the camisole is worth. Her entire outfit looked like it belonged to a princess.

"Garrick wore a tailor-made shirt and slacks. His cufflink gems had perfect color and sharp faces. I'm sure they're authentic, and I'll bet his shoes were Vatheran leather, too. Your sons can't afford to dress that well."

"He's an officer," Irena remarked.

"Yes, but officer pay is not significantly higher."

"Well, his little wifey didn't wear a stitch of make up and no jewelry, either."

"True," Marla replied. "But she's Lithian, and from what Kira told us, the woman is deeply devout. I saw her pray over her food before she started eating. Maybe she doesn't wear jewelry as a way of honoring her god. I've heard that conservative Lithians are weird that way."

Irena returned to her tea. "Well, she looks like she's just put her dolls down. I think she's far too young to be married. And did you see that ghastly scar on her neck? Darren says she saved his life, but when he came home after the war we couldn't tell he'd been wounded.

"If she could heal him so well that there's no visible sign of what he reports was a life-threatening injury, why is she walking around with a big, ugly scar? Aside from that she's a lovely little thing. It's clear she values her appearance, given that she looked totally embarrassed while Kira marched her to the ladies' room to dry off. If I'm right, how did she get that horrid gash, and why couldn't she heal it?"

"I'll ask her about it, tomorrow," Marla replied, confident that Brenna would never be able to keep up with her on the track. "I'm sure we'll have time to talk."

Secrets and Whispers: *Analysis*

Irena finished her tea and poured another cup for herself. "There's something about that family that I don't trust. They act like they've got something to hide."

"Why do you say that?" Marla inquired.

"Did you notice the way they're always teaming up whenever one of them gets asked an uncomfortable question? They close ranks immediately."

"That shows they're close and loyal to each other. You're reading more into that behavior than is warranted."

Annoyed now, Irena put her tea cup down. "All right," she quipped. "What's your analysis, then?"

Marla had been thinking about this as dinner progressed, and believed she had a pretty good idea of the dynamic among the Ravenwood siblings. "First off, Garrick is the undisputed leader. He's all about control. He doesn't touch his wife, and she doesn't touch him."

"Well," Irena interrupted, "the dreamy way they looked at one another made me think they needed a quiet room . . . They're sticky with mutual attraction."

"I saw that, too," Marla smirked. "It looks like they try to suppress that smouldering sensuality in public, but they're not fooling anyone."

"Married couples normally show affection, or speak to each other using terms of endearment," Irena remarked. "Yet these two never did. Not once."

"Perhaps their contact avoidance in public is rooted in societal taboo," Marla speculated.

"Because she's Lithian?"

"Quite possibly," Marla suggested. "While Brenna is a Heroine of the Republic – that's not something anyone can fake – her facial expressions and body language prove that she hates the notoriety that comes with the title. Notice how quickly her honorific pin disappeared after she and Kira went to the ladies' room. The respect she deserves for that decoration makes her uncomfortable,

Secrets and Whispers: *Analysis*

which suggests she's not been treated well among our people. The price that Brenna and Garrick pay for their mutual devotion is not expressing affection in public.

"So Garrick is happy to give Kira the stage. She's attractive, she's comfortable in that role, and she deflects attention from Brenna. That allows him to observe and evaluate, like a military tactician. Should anyone challenge his sister or brother, Garrick charges in to support them."

"Algernon doesn't need a defender," Irena added. "That young man is both clever and fearless."

"Yes, but only on the surface," Marla remarked. "Patterns of behavior among siblings are set in early childhood. Kira was probably favored in her family. I'd say that Algernon's mother neglected him and he's starving for Bronwyn's affection. Whenever he reached for her and she rebuffed him – something I saw several times – he always looked hurt. He never insisted on requited touch because he's vulnerable to rejection. I suspect that beneath his confident demeanor, Algernon is emotionally fragile.

"Garrick knows this and habitually protects his brother. He defends Kira, too, but the dynamic between them is different. Garrick tolerates her. He doesn't approve of what she does and how she thinks – rolling his eyes and openly scoffing at some of the things she says – but Kira knows he has her back, and he makes sure everyone else is aware of that, too. He's like a father in that family, and he's unlikely to give up the power that goes with it."

"You say Algernon needs affection because he was rejected by his mother, but I saw that Bronwyn didn't appreciate his advances, no matter how gentle they were."

Marla poured another cup of tea, nodding at her sister's observation. "Bronwyn is desperate for your affirmation. She's not herself because she's worried,

Secrets and Whispers: *Analysis*

knowing that you don't approve of her engagement. She's sensitive to your attitude, and nearly every interaction she's had with her siblings and their spouses on this trip has been negative. All of this confirms her fear of family rejection. I'm sure she wanted to impress everyone tonight. That's why she left Kira in charge of the evening."

"So you think Algernon is looking for a mommy replacement . . ." Irena concluded.

"Bronwyn is kindly and gentle," Marla stated. "She's big, soft and kindhearted. If he's looking for comfort in a woman's arms, she's ideal for him."

"My daughter is not therapy for someone else's childhood dysfunction," Irena snapped. "I can't have her dragged down by a boy who needs a wet nurse!"

Marla shook her head. "We all have needs, but needs don't make us dysfunctional. Brenna's a busty little thing, too, and Garrick dotes on her. If Algernon's found a match in Bronwyn, what's wrong with that?"

Irena sighed. "Darren made a poor choice with Sikki. Harold was totally smitten with Heidelinde the Horrible. Both of those marriages are deeply unhappy. I don't want my daughter making the same kind of mistake."

"Well, Bronwyn isn't like her brothers," Marla stated. "You and the boys openly wonder what Algernon sees in her, but why not focus on what it is she sees in him?"

"She's totally irrational," Irena began. "I can see that he's handsome, strong and smart. She tells me that he's hard-working, self-disciplined and makes her feel pretty. But I worry that he'll tire of her and walk out after she's had children, after she's put on even more weight."

Marla nodded. "That's possible in every committed relationship. There are no guarantees. But consider what

Secrets and Whispers: *Analysis*

I've told you. What does Bronwyn see in Algernon that gives her confidence he won't behave that way?

"They've been an item for two years, they live in the same house – and she's admitted to me that they sleep in the same room – but she's not pregnant. You know it's not easy for men to resist. What does that say about Algernon's integrity? Is a man with such a high degree of self-control when he's young and easily aroused likely to abandon his commitments when he's older?"

"It's possible," Irena replied.

"Yes, but is it likely? Algernon is serious about his vows. He abandoned his fiancée and her family at a carefully-arranged get-acquainted dinner for the sake of ministering to a condemned criminal. That's commitment. And, despite some atrocious choices on Kira's part, she and he remain very close. Is a boy who willingly risked his life on a dangerous trek through a war zone to save his wayward sister likely to turn his back on his wife?"

Irena sighed. Kira's story had been compelling, and the considerate way the Ravenwood twins treated one another supported Marla's view. "You have a point."

"Very well then. Keep your mind open. Arvid says that Bronwyn has good judgment. I know what's been written in the editorials, but bear in mind that controversy sells papers. People love dirt, so editors live for scandal.

"Think about this and answer honestly: Does the actual Algernon you've now met match the caricature of him that's portrayed in the papers?"

"Not really," Irena admitted.

"Then give your daughter the benefit of the doubt until you have strong evidence to the contrary."

***

Secrets and Whispers: *Analysis*

Before dawn broke the next morning, Algernon trudged through the quiet streets of Marvic. He stopped at a bakery, bought a breakfast sandwich and tea – which he devoured quickly – then caught a streetcar for the city gate. Emotionally drained and physically exhausted, the tired priest quickly fell asleep. The streetcar driver had to waken him at the end of the line.

He could have gone back to the Gold Leaf Hotel, where Kira, Bronwyn and Ileana had stayed overnight, but after his beloved's frequent rejection the previous evening, he felt sullen and decided to return home. The pressure of being on display for her family hadn't helped. Neither had the ugly scene with wicked Heidelinde.

What was wrong with that woman? Why did Bronwyn's family insist on making this hard on her?

Losing confidence that he'd ever be able to impress his fianceé's highly critical mother, Algernon's withdrawal from social contact allowed him to evaluate the situation and process his raw emotion alone, without interference.

Amplified security at the city gate slowed his progress through the checkpoint. Algernon, who'd still been attending Mrs. Bergen's bedside when the explosion at the palace entrance occurred, knew nothing about the reason behind the delay. Distracted by worry over his future with Bronwyn, he absent-mindedly imagined the best course of action to take.

Should he break off the engagement? If Bronwyn could not bring herself to show even a minimal amount of physical affection in front of her family now, was this an indication of her future attitude? Was she just playing with his devotion, secretly intending to leave him before making her commitment?

That was a frightening thought. Algernon had been rejected many times before, and each time a young woman wounded his heart, he'd felt himself growing

Secrets and Whispers: *Analysis*

colder and angrier. Would Bronwyn, who'd been so gentle, so warm, so increasingly amorous, really turn away after being willing to share herself with him?

Had he been wrong to stop her? Would she be acting this way right now if they'd already had sex?

After passing through the gate, Algernon turned northward. Weak daylight painted the distant mountain peaks, still heavily laden with winter snow, and the air clung to the cool moisture of last evening's rain. Descending the track down to Wounded Heart Creek, noting the bright green of early leaves turning toward the light, Algernon felt strangely conflicted.

He'd been with *The Shadow* during the assassin's last hours. Agitated, fearful and angry, the man ranted about life and his misfortune. "Nothing matters," he complained. "There's no good, no evil, no right, no wrong. In the end, we're all food for worms. Life is meaningless!"

"The issue of evil and good matters a lot to the living," Algernon replied. "It certainly matters to the innocent. In the final analysis, what we do makes a rather significant difference to those we love."

"Don't preach at me, boy!" the assassin roared. "I cleaned up this town so that decent people could walk the streets. What thanks did I get for that?"

"I'm not here to judge you," Algernon countered. "I'm not here to affirm your choices, either."

"Well I don't need your comforting words! And I don't need your make-believe god's forgiveness, either!"

Algernon didn't agree, but he held his tongue.

The Shadow's end was not brave. As the hour drew near he sobbed like a child and heaped curses on Algernon for priestly powerlessness.

"You're worse than useless!" he'd screamed. "Why did you even bother coming here?"

Secrets and Whispers: *Analysis*

When the time arrived to march to the gallows, *The Shadow* refused to come out of his cell. Algernon, backed into a corner, watched the thin man fight off three guards before two very burly prison officers bearing truncheons, arrived. All five men, working together, finally subdued the prisoner, tying his hands and feet like a roped calf.

The guards loaded *The Shadow* onto a stretcher. Algernon listened to the condemned killer's muffled sniffling, watched him shudder in anguish and desperately beg for his life as the men carried him to the platform. They placed a hood over his head, followed by a noose.

"Holy man! Don't live in vain!" the notorious killer shouted just before the trap door flew open and the man's neck snapped clean at the end of the swinging rope.

It was the most horrible sight Algernon had ever witnessed. Nobody stood in the breach to ask for clemency. Nobody in authority offered mercy. Algernon turned away, struck by the finality of the sentence.

Then he raced to the bathroom and threw up.

Now, an awareness of his beating heart, his breathing, his sense of self – fully alive in the brightening dawn – awakened his mind to Bronwyn's perspective. He knew her family's disapproval wounded and saddened her. She'd been terrified to see them again. The condescending contempt expressed by her siblings affirmed her fears.

They didn't know how efficiently she managed Kira's household, keeping expenses low and comfort high. They'd never tasted meals made with love and creative flair. They didn't understand how she delighted in making others happy, working hard to ensure success in a home she would never inherit.

He remembered her warm lips, her soft body, the desire in her brown eyes and the comfort she willingly extended to him. Bronwyn wiped away the ache of rejection, healing scars wrought by years of scorn and

Secrets and Whispers: *Analysis*

repudiation. Algernon valued the depth of her noble and selfless character. He knew he could be the faithful partner she needed, encouraging her best to blossom under his care. He knew he could help her shine, serve as her strength, defend her honor and fill her life with love as long as he drew breath.

But did she need him like he needed her? Would she become bitter and spiteful, like her brothers?

Walking away now would consign both of them to pain and loneliness. Walking away now would ruin Kira's already fragile ministry, driving a wedge between his sister and her best friend. Staying with Bronwyn meant working in harmony to serve others, as he earnestly believed he'd been called to do. Staying with Bronwyn would allow them to build a beautiful life together.

But did she want all of that as badly as he did? Could she cope with her family's repudiation? Would she remain firm in her conviction that she wanted him?

Algernon arrived at the summit of Superstition Mesa feeling breathless and a little dizzy from the climb. Bright daylight burst over the distant mountain peaks, revealing a verdant landscape teeming with life.

Superstition Mesa was gradually reverting into its natural state. Every passing year, new trees arose along the edges of meadows, where farmers had once planted barley and hay. Vines and tall weeds now engulfed the derelict homesteads, where old dreams had perished in winter chimney fires, withered crops and hunger.

As Algernon moved out of the forest, a grazing musk deer raised its head, turning its large ears toward the source of the sound. The solitary creature paused for a moment, frozen still, then trotted into the deep forest growing along the mesa's western edge.

"You scared it off!" a woman's voice complained.

Secrets and Whispers: *Analysis*

Startled, but unafraid, Algernon turned. He recognized the Wildlife Officer from his less-than-cordial encounter with her several weeks earlier. What was her name again?

"You shouldn't be using this trail," she stated, approaching the solitary priest more confidently than warranted. "This area is off-limits."

"Unlike you, I actually live here," Algernon replied, trying to catch his breath. "You already know that, and I don't appreciate your sanctimonious attitude."

The blonde-haired woman smiled without showing any teeth. "Just doing my job," she stated.

"Which doesn't involve harassing me," he reminded her. "What are you doing here so early in the morning?"

"I'm looking for gwynling," she replied, referring to a family of diminutive, winged humanoids who'd taken up residence in the abandoned military fort at Lookout Point, on the southern tip of the mesa. "Have you seen them?"

Algernon shook his head. "Not since winter."

"Did you see them very often before that?"

"You don't know much about gwynling, do you?" he remarked, continuing his homeward journey.

"And you do?" she challenged, following him.

"Clearly. Gwynling are reclusive creatures. If they don't want to be seen, they won't be."

"I'm only trying to protect them," she countered, her voice edgy and defensive as she tried to match his pace.

Algernon stopped, turning to face the young woman. "They're feral and they're perfectly capable of taking care of themselves. They don't need your protection any more than the musk deer do."

"Ugh!" she groaned in frustration. "There's been no trace of any gwynling on the refuge for weeks now. I've been coming up here at all hours of the day and night trying to figure out what happened to them."

Secrets and Whispers: *Analysis*

Turning away, Algernon kept walking. "They have legs, and they have wings. Maybe they've moved on."

"Or maybe the giants got them all," the Wildlife Officer stammered in desperation, chasing after him.

"No," Algernon replied, shaking his head. "There were gwynling here after the army put up the palisade wall last winter."

"So, you saw them!" she exclaimed, triumphantly.

"I saw a mother with her baby," Algernon stated, telling an incomplete truth that grated against his vow to speak honestly. The mother in question was Jhiran Vell, a gwynling whom he'd befriended years earlier. But he didn't want to complicate matters by admitting this to the Wildlife Officer.

"When was this?" she demanded.

"I don't know!" Algernon admitted. "I focus on spiritual problems with human people. I don't concern myself with babysitting a family of gwynling."

"Don't dismiss me!. I'm doing research." she argued.

"And I'm not stopping you," Algernon retorted. "Get on with it and leave me alone!"

Thinking that he'd finally be rid of her, Algernon turned away again. Tired and irritable, he desperately needed sleep. But she didn't let him walk away.

"Wait!" she pleaded. "I've been up here since before dawn, but I didn't bring anything to drink. Can I trouble you for some water?"

Tamarians considered refusing to offer refreshment, even to an annoying stranger, the high point of rude behavior. With a sigh, Algernon beckoned. "Alright," he conceded. "Come along."

The blonde woman smiled, but he'd already turned his back and didn't notice. He didn't care, either, but she didn't take the hint. "How long have you lived here?"

Secrets and Whispers: *Analysis*

"If you must know, this is my fourth summer on the mesa," he replied impatiently. "But my sister's house is three years old."

"So you built it together?" she asked, struggling to keep up with his deliberately lengthening stride.

Algernon shook his head, not wanting to lie. "I had help. Friends with strong backs gave me a hand."

She'd always thought the house looked imposing, but said nothing as they followed the trail beneath a ridge line that eventually opened into another meadow. A crew of military engineers busily loaded trucks with scrap left behind by an army detachment deployed here during the winter. They'd set up the defensive palisade that divided Superstition Mesa into northern and southern sections.

"It's about time!" Algernon muttered. He felt relieved that the army was cleaning up its own mess, as he didn't have the resources to do it himself.

"I sent them here," the Wildlife Officer claimed. "I wrote a complaint that they were in violation of the Refuge Protection Act."

Algernon bounded up the stairs. "I suppose I should thank you, then," he remarked, removing his shoes and holding the vestibule door open for his guest.

She'd never been inside this place before. Huge beams, chained together to form a bird's mouth just below the central cupola, must have taken a large crew or a crane to erect. The homestead was much more spacious than she expected.

"Anyone home?" she asked.

"I am," Algernon replied, stuffing an armful of sticks into the kitchen's masonry stove, activating its fan and lighting a fire. "My sister, our house guest and my fianceé are in town right now."

"You're getting married? I didn't know."

Secrets and Whispers: *Analysis*

"Yes. Young men tend to do that," he stated, filling a tea kettle and placing it on the stove, wishing she'd stop asking so many questions. "In the priesthood, holy matrimony is prerequisite to starting a family . . ."

"Will you live here after the wedding, or are you going to live with your bride's family?"

Ignoring the question for a moment, Algernon continued preparing tea. "What's it to you?"

"I'm just making conversation," she replied.

"Look, I've been up all night and I'm really tired," he warned. "You can make yourself some tea and show yourself out when you're done. I'm going to sleep now."

The Wildlife Officer watched him head into a room. Because he didn't shut the door all the way, she crept to the side and peeked at a mirror visible in the opening, watching, wide-eyed as the young man undressed.

She stifled a gasp. He had a strong, well-defined form to go along with that handsome face. Since no one else was around, a wicked, seductive fantasy arose in her mind. She felt confident in her sensuality and could have acted on her desire – believing that he'd not be able to resist her – but out of respect for his bride-to-be, she suppressed the thought.

After making and quietly enjoying her tea, the Wildlife Officer left her lipstick-marked mug in the sink and spent several minutes quietly exploring the big house. She peered in on the sleeping monk, wistfully admiring him again, before slipping out of the vestibule and going on her way.

***

Brenna raced to the broad staircase above the university's main entrance, worried that she'd be late for her meeting with Bronwyn's aunt. She knew that

Secrets and Whispers: *Analysis*

Tamarians valued punctuality, but intimacy with Garrick ranked higher in value to Brenna than did impressing an acquaintance. Nonetheless, she'd raced from the palace to arrive on time.

The Lithian woman paused at the top of the stairs to catch her breath, gazing at the familiar, undulating landscape stretching to the south. As dawn spread across the city, windows and metal rooftops shedding the remnants of last night's rain, glinted in the strengthening daylight. Brenna felt warm inside, remembering the strength and passion of her husband's amorous embrace. Gentle, yet urgent and persistent, he relished stirring her delight, coaxing repeated peaks of pleasure in her strong, athletic body that demonstrated his love for her. Brenna prayed in gratitude for him, contented by his affection, greatly relieved by his gradually improving mental health.

Approaching footsteps startled her back into the moment as Marla bounded up the stairs. "There you are," she said. "I hope I haven't kept you waiting long."

Marla boasted a perfect runner's build. She stood a full four inches taller than Brenna, with a very lean frame and little body fat. Her resting heart rate, strengthened by years of training, averaged only 50 beats per minute, but climbing the stairs at this altitude had already taxed her and she breathed heavily. The woman wore lightweight running shoes, silky shorts and a loose tank top, exposing enough skin in the early morning cool to produce gooseflesh on her arms and legs.

Brenna, on the other hand, concealed her body beneath a zippered track suit with long sleeves. The outfit completely covered her muscular legs and veiled her strong shoulders. She also wore a pair of knitted gloves to protect her piano-player fingers from the cold. With her black hair tied into a ponytail, she looked cute, rather than serious.

Secrets and Whispers: *Analysis*

"Where's the track?" Marla inquired.

"Follow me," Brenna replied, tilting her head and then bounding lightly up the stairs.

The Tamarian woman didn't expect Brenna to begin running right away, but Marla complied, surprised that the dainty girl set a strong pace. Could she sustain the speed? As Brenna's lissom limbs effortlessly propelled her bantam body up another set of long stairs leading to the crest of University Hill, Marla labored to match her tempo. Winded and suffering from side cramps as she arrived at the summit, the Tamarian woman noted in shock that the girl wasn't even breathing hard. Brenna had to be hiding huge lungs in that little frame of hers . . .

"On the other side of the athletic field, the trail follows the contour of that ridge," Brenna stated, pointing to the nearby geographic feature. "I usually sprint across the track. It helps me warm up."

"You go ahead," Marla replied, gesturing with her hand as she struggled to breathe in the thin air.

Other athletes on the field noted the two women with only passing interest. Brenna burst into a sprint that didn't draw a second glance from anyone else. Marla wondered how long the Lithian girl could keep that up.

On the far side of the track, Brenna once again waited for her companion. Concern furrowed her brow as Marla slowed to a stop. "Are you okay?" she inquired.

Breathing hard, Marla put her head back, filling her lungs with air, astonishingly unable to sate her need for oxygen. How could this wee little thing run so fast? "Just give me a moment," she urged between breaths. "You were right about the altitude."

Brenna nodded. "I struggled for a few days when we first moved here, but you'll get used to it."

Secrets and Whispers: *Analysis*

Marla's eyes scanned Brenna's womanly form between breaths. "Can I ask a personal question? Isn't it uncomfortable to run with a body like yours?"

What a rude and inappropriate thing to say! "No," Brenna replied tersely, offering no further explanation.

"Are you going to run like that the whole way?" Marla asked, a little worried that she might.

Brenna shook her head. "It's too far for sprinting, but I usually cover three miles in about 12 minutes. Will that be okay with you?"

How could this little slip of a girl maintain a tempo like that? "Why don't we take it easier today," Marla suggested, swallowing her pride. "I didn't realize how thin the air is here, and I don't want to get altitude sickness."

Knowing that Marla should have listened to her advice at dinner, Brenna nodded, holding her tongue from expressing criticism. "I'll let you set the pace."

But that didn't help. Cramps plagued Marla's legs and side within the first third of the trail. Climbing what the runners grudgingly referred to as Heartbreak Hill taxed her stamina. Marla staggered to the summit before collapsing in the verge at the side of the trail.

"You should stand," Brenna encouraged. "Will you let me help you?" She offered her hand, pulling the Tamarian woman to her feet. "Are you feeling sick?"

Marla, pale and gasping, leaned on the Lithian woman's shoulders and shook her head. "I'm sorry," she panted. "I just can't keep up. I'm normally not like this."

"I'm sure it's the elevation," Brenna soothed. "Give yourself some time and you'll feel better."

And thus, the run turned into a stroll, permitting the women an opportunity to talk. As the conversation settled upon the previous evening's dinner, Brenna expressed irritation at the boorish behavior of Bronwyn's relatives. "Why is your family so hostile to Algernon?"

Secrets and Whispers: *Analysis*

Marla hadn't expected such a question, but she honored the request with care. "There are two reasons," she began. "The first is that Algernon's taken a priestly vow of poverty. My sister doesn't want to support him with an inheritance that is rightly Bronwyn's.

"The second concerns his reputation. Everything our family has heard about Algernon involves violence, the illicit sex trade, and opposition to important institutions, like the Temple. My sister and Arvid are conservative people. These things chafe against their values."

Brenna frowned. "Central to Algernon's poverty vow is a commitment to communal living. His spiritual values demand that he refrain from a focus on material things. It's not about living in want, nor does it mean he's lazy and needs charity. Once you know him, you'll learn that he shoulders a manly share of the workload around the homestead without complaint."

Uncertain about sharing too much of her family's dynamic with the Lithian woman, Marla chose her words carefully. "My sister has only one daughter. If Bronwyn marries Algernon, Irena will disinherit her, and Sikki will be next in line. The only person who wants to see that happen is Sikki, herself."

"But Irena doesn't have to disinherit her daughter," Brenna argued. "No one is forcing her hand. Leaving Bronwyn a legacy will mean that she can pass it on to her own daughter in time. What's wrong with that?"

"Marrying a poor priest means that children will be born into poverty," Marla countered. "Irena doesn't want her grandchildren growing up in a cold, dark hovel."

Brenna laughed. She pointed at Lookout Point, the stone fortress looming at the summit of a high scarp face. "That's Superstition Mesa. Once you've been up to Kira's homestead, you'll understand how silly that sounds. Her

Secrets and Whispers: *Analysis*

place is spacious, warm, and filled with light. The mesa would be a wonderful place to experience childhood."

"With *strichmadchen* living under the same roof?"

Brenna replied, "The women who come to shelter at Superstition Mesa are trying to turn their lives around. They're leaving the sex trade, not participating in it."

"Yes," Marla agreed. "But they don't necessarily leave behind the destructive habits they've picked up along the way. Irena is concerned about the influence these women may have on her grandchildren."

"Then she should talk to Bronwyn and Algernon about that," Brenna suggested.

"Oh, she will!" Marla promised.

Annoyed, Brenna pressed her on this. "Why does that sound like a threat? What's the root of this animosity? This is supposed to be a happy time, but most of Bronwyn's family has been rude to her thus far."

Marla hadn't liked the dynamic around the dinner table, either. "They're just concerned. Nobody wants Bronwyn to make a mistake."

"A mistake?" Brenna repeated, growing angrier. "Why would any of you think getting married to Algernon is a mistake? You people don't even know him!"

For a reticent woman, Brenna had a strident streak. "Don't misunderstand me," Marla cautioned. "I'm here to advocate for my niece. You're right that we don't know Algernon, but in addition to the distasteful news accounts we've read, he openly supports Kira's ministry."

"You and the news writers know nothing about the twins," Brenna stated. "But I do. Kira's faced a relentless smear campaign and threats to her life from hired killers, all financed by blood money from the Temple. Algernon stood strong by her side the whole time. Yet never once did either of them speak out against the priesthood."

Secrets and Whispers: *Analysis*

Shocked to hear this, Marla stopped in her tracks. "What are you talking about?"

"Maybe you should visit the Ministry of Justice while you're in town," Brenna suggested. "Look up the recent case against High Priest Abelard. You'll find an impartial account in the public record confirming that corrupt police and Temple officials conspired to kill Kira."

"I'll do that," Marla promised, taken aback by the news. "But there are other problems. For example, we've heard rumors that Kira's a lesbian. Is that true?"

Brenna shook her head. "She's bisexual."

"Are you okay with that?" Marla inquired, expecting a pious girl to oppose behavior of that kind on principle.

"My views are irrelevant," Brenna replied. "She's my sister-in-law. My obligation is to love Kira, not judge her."

"So she's never made a move on you?"

"Of course not!" Brenna said flatly. "Nor would she. I belong to Garrick, and he belongs to me."

"What about the rumors of a sexual liaison between her and Bronwyn?"

"I know nothing about that," Brenna replied.

"Do you know where Kira gets her money?"

Brenna put her hands on her hips. "Every question you've asked me is underlain with suspicion that somehow Kira and Algernon are living an elaborate lie.

"But without blushing Kira will tell you that she's shared her intimate gifts with both men and women. Algernon admits to his violent past without making excuses for it, either, but since he's been with Bronwyn he's done a lot of growing up. I've known the twins long enough to affirm they're precisely whom they claim to be."

That response, delivered in a sharp tone, sounded more defensive than warranted. "I don't mean to offend you," Marla assuaged. "It's just that sometimes people are skilled at manipulation and deception . . ."

Secrets and Whispers: *Analysis*

"By saying that you presume that I'm some ingenue whose inexperience disqualifies me to judge the integrity of other people. But I'm 29 years old, I've lived through two major wars in three different countries and I'm far from naive!"

Astonished, Marla couldn't reply. She thought Brenna looked no older than 14 . . .

The Lithian woman put her hand on her heart. "You Tamarians only see my bosom, not my brain. Kira and Algernon are as genuine as two young people can be. I know their strengths and I know their flaws. I also know that Bronwyn is good-hearted and sincere. She wouldn't associate with people of poor character."

Taken aback by Brenna's spirited defense, Marla felt a little intimidated. The girl carried herself like a warrior. "You didn't answer my question about Kira's money . . ."

Brenna turned to continue walking. "Read the verdict of Abelard's case at the Ministry of Justice. That will explain a lot. Anything else is Kira's business to reveal, not mine."

"So it's all honest?"

"Yes," Brenna replied. "If your sister allows Bronwyn and Algernon to marry, their children will never want for anything. Kira will see to that."

Embarrassed, Marla fell silent for a long time. As the trail wound along the ridge, into a vale and over a bridge, then turned west and climbed again, she finally found the courage to broach another question.

"Where did you get the scar on your neck?"

Brenna hated talking about this. "I was captured by insurgents when I served with the Expeditionary Force in Kameron. They beat me to break my will and steal my virtue. They made me watch unspeakable things, tormenting other prisoners in my cell. When that didn't work, a rebel soldier tried to sever my head."

Secrets and Whispers: *Analysis*

"That's horrible!" Marla gasped. She glanced at the scar again, the only visible flaw in Brenna's otherwise perfect complection. "But Darren says you can heal wounds. Why didn't you heal that one?"

"I am only the vessel through which Allfather pours his power," Brenna replied cryptically. "How he chooses to manifest his will is not mine to decide. My scar proves that I need grace." Brenna, knowing the awful truth of her own vengeful spirit, still struggled to accept the permanence of that fact.

What was that supposed to mean? "So, you persist in serving the god who didn't heal you?"

"With every thought, with every breath and every beat of my heart," Brenna stated, speaking with sincere conviction, her expression intense and earnest.

"I don't get it," Marla replied, shaking her head. "You're loyal to a being whom you say heals others, but won't do the same on your behalf. That makes no sense."

Hearing Marla say this, Brenna concluded that Bronwyn's aunt did not share the pious perspective of her sister. That realization came as a bit of a surprise. "Love is not about keeping score," she said. "Allfather is not a divine exchange into which I deposit adoration and withdraw favor. He leaves room for everyone to make their own decisions, including choices for evil.

"As a little girl I didn't always comprehend what my parents did. Likewise, as an adult I don't always apprehend the purpose of Allfather's will. Faith is about trusting in the holy character of the creator, who lavishes life and prosperity on all people – not just those who serve him. The fact that I'm alive at all has made that clear to me. I wish I didn't have this ugly scar. I'd love to be whole and pretty again, but I know that I am loved, and that matters a lot more to me than how I look."

Secrets and Whispers: *Analysis*

Marla fell silent. Her shattered view of Brenna as a shapely little love toy for Garrick transformed into appreciation for the young woman's integrity. The Lithian woman fiercely defended her husband's family, spoke with unquestionable intelligence and expressed deep devotion to her faith. The psychologist hadn't expected any of this.

Glancing at the steadily rising Daystar, Brenna frowned. "I don't want to be late for work," she said. "I hope I haven't offended you, but I have to go."

"I'm not offended in the least," Marla replied. "It's been good to talk to you. I've learned a lot and look forward to seeing you tonight."

Brenna smiled. She turned away and raced up the trail, her ponytail swishing back and forth in a steady rhythm. Marla, watching the young woman's rapid stride, marveled that such a small woman could run so fast.

***

"What a mess!" Captain Mariel Hougen remarked. Shattered glass crunched beneath her booted feet as she examined blast damage and burn marks at the palace gate. Dark stains that spread across the concrete floor told a grim tale.

"We're waiting for the investigation to finish before we clean and rebuild," said Colonel Andrea Scheer, the commander of the palace gate detail, who'd also been assigned to uncover the truth behind the attack.

"I read your preliminary report this morning," Captain Hougen stated, wondering why she, as a member of the Expeditionary Force Intelligence Service, had been invited to tour the scene. "I understand you're looking into the sources of the ammonium nitrate and trigger explosives used to make the bomb. What would you like me to do on your behalf?"

Secrets and Whispers: *Analysis*

The colonel paused at the charred remnant of a desk. "I understand you're a linguist," she stated, watching the copper-haired captain nod in response. "We recovered pamphlets from inside the truck. These appear to be printed in the Kurian language, which no one on my staff knows how to read."

Mariel took the papers from the colonel's hand and glanced at them. "Yes ma'am, I can read this," she said, scrunching her brow into a scowl.

"What does it say?" the colonel inquired.

"It's written in riddles," Mariel replied. "I'd have to analyze it in detail to understand what it means."

Colonel Scheer tightened her lips. "My investigation is time sensitive," she warned. "On behalf of the Defenders' CID, I thank the TEF for its cooperation. I'm confident you'll report to me in an expedient manner."

"Count on me!" Captain Hougen replied.

***

Garrick waited in the quiet lobby of the Gold Leaf Hotel, wishing he could join his sister for breakfast upstairs. Judging from the aromas coming out of the nearby kitchen, it likely would have been a hearty meal. While he earnestly adored Brenna, she'd grown up in a wealthy household, where servants cleaned and did most of the cooking. As a result, she'd never developed an interest in preparing food, and her culinary creations lacked both flavor and imagination. The one envy he secretly harbored against his brother was that Bronwyn's skills in the kitchen rivaled those of a professional chef.

Despite this, Garrick never held Brenna's indifference to cooking against her. Being married involved a host of compromises – including the need to leave ample room for her faith – that often required him to give up or

Secrets and Whispers: *Analysis*

defer things he wanted. He loved his wife enough to accept her imperfections without complaint, but that meant their meals were often brought in from bakeries and high-end restaurants behind the palace wall. Brenna's fruit and bread breakfasts served as the singular exception to that practice.

He'd eaten bread and cheese, with a little fruit she'd cut, just before daylight. Thinking about his beloved singing in the kitchen while she prepared her simple meal inspired a smile. When he slipped off the shoulder strap of her camisole, the smooth, soft texture of her skin stirred his desire. She responded with sweet affection, and their rising passion nearly made both of them late.

With his heart pounding again, Garrick willed his mind back into the present. As the opening of a nearby elevator door drew his attention, Garrick made eye contact with Bronwyn's brother, Willi.

Believing that an ugly confrontation might quickly ensue, Garrick steeled his nerves. But hints in Willi's demeanor, his shuffling gait and guilty facial expression, suggested reluctant contrition.

"Good morning," Willi began.

Garrick nodded, wishing that he'd not been thinking about Brenna a moment earlier. He remained seated, watching the corporal struggle to decide whether to remain standing or take a seat.

"I, uh . . . I guess I was out of line last night," he confessed, casting his glance to the side.

"You guess?" replied Garrick, his tone a bit sharper than necessary. Willi already looked defeated.

"Well, that's what Darren and Mother told me . . ."

Garrick let tension build before speaking. "They sent you down here to make things right? Don't bother unless you have something of your own to say."

Secrets and Whispers: *Analysis*

Willem slouched into a nearby chair. "I had too much to drink," he admitted. "I wasn't thinking."

"That much is obvious," Garrick affirmed. "Your life and beer make for a bad mix right now. Not only did you insult my honorable service and accuse me of being a liar without any supporting evidence, but you also raised your hand to your wife.

"Now, you don't know me, and if you want to shovel dirt in my direction, I might overlook your stupidity once. But I have no use for any man who mistreats his woman. Your behavior was appalling!"

Willi's emotions, already close to the surface, spilled out of his eyes. He swore, shaking his head and sniffing. "I know!" he confessed. "I screwed up this time! I didn't mean to, and now I've ruined everything!"

Memories of his own father's frequent contrition screamed from Garrick's memory. Willi's tearful regret only hardened his resolve and increased his disdain. "Don't cry on my shoulder!" the young officer warned. "Go and make things right with your woman."

"She won't talk to me," Willi stated.

"Oh?" Garrick inquired, knowingly. "So this has happened before?"

Willi glared at Garrick, but couldn't sustain his gaze. "What would you know about that?"

"Enough to recognize a serious problem when I see it. Enough to understand that you won't find the solution to your trouble in the bottom of a glass. Enough to warn you that every time you stagger back to the cess pit you're trying to crawl out of this morning, you'll find the sewage gets a little deeper."

"Well, what the hell am I supposed to do?" Willi demanded, growing angry. "Who are you to give me advice on how to run my life, anyway?"

Secrets and Whispers: *Analysis*

"Don't raise your voice at me, Corporal," Garrick warned. "If you want control over your life, if you want to stop making things worse, quit the drinking right now. Then go and make things right with your wife."

Willem shook his head in disgust. "I just had a bit much, that's all. It's not a problem . . ."

"This is not the first time," Garrick reminded him.

"Look, you know nothing about me," Willem retorted. "You have no idea what I've been through!"

"Try me," Garrick responded. "You think you have a lock on loss and trauma? You've lost friends in battle? Welcome to the club, soldier. Anyone who's been in the line of fire knows that story very well."

Willi put his head into his hands, forcing fingertips into his own scalp. He dared not admit the secret problem he was facing. "Damn it all!" he muttered.

Thinking that Willem was referring to the terror of the Tanarak, the words found resonance in an angry, vengeful desire that Garrick had been battling to overcome for many weeks. Quietly taking a deep breath, he leaned forward and lowered his voice. "I wouldn't let a soldier in my platoon anywhere near a gun if I heard talk like that," Garrick stated.

"What's that supposed to mean?" Willem inquired, paranoid that Garrick might have found him out.

"It means you need help."

"What? Are you a shrink now?" Willem mocked. "You think therapy's gonna help me?"

"You'd prefer to beat your wife?" Garrick replied. "Is that working for you?"

Though he wanted to lash out in anger, somewhere in his heart Willem understood the hard truth that Garrick's analysis had just revealed. But his pride rose like a towering rampart, preventing conciliation. "Damn you, too!" Willi muttered, standing and storming away.

Secrets and Whispers: *Analysis*

***

"I think that will do," Heidelinde stated.

Kira had to admit that while she disliked Bronwyn's sister-in-law, the woman had excellent taste in clothing. The long-sleeved crossover blouse she'd chosen featured a soft lace floral pattern and a silk sash that added length to the overall look. On a heavy girl, its vertical lines looked slimming. It's deep V-neck served a similar purpose, and when paired with a matching camisole for the sake of modesty, the shirt flattered an hourglass figure nicely.

While Bronwyn liked the look, she furrowed her brow while appraising herself in the mirror. "It's really expensive," she complained. "It's not right for me to spend your money like this."

"Price isn't a problem unless you're poor," Heidelinde replied with a condescending smile. "You're shopping with me, not your boyfriend."

Bronwyn looked hurt, and immediately Kira rose to her rescue. "What a wicked thing to say!"

Heidelinde feigned offense. "Is what I said untrue?" she cooed. "Your brother told me he doesn't take a vow he can't keep. Hasn't he taken a vow of perpetual poverty?"

Kira struggled against the urge to beat the woman with her cane. "You've not said one nice thing to Bronwyn since you arrived, and now you're insinuating that my brother is a beggar. Where do you get off thinking it's okay to behave like this?"

With her eyes widened and brows raised, Heidelinde shrugged in feigned disbelief. "I don't understand why you're upset. I'm just stating fact. And as far as being nice is concerned, I brought Bronwyn here to get her out of those frumpy rags she's wearing. How is that not nice?"

Secrets and Whispers: *Analysis*

Bronwyn felt her loyalties being torn in two different directions. "Can we just get along?" she pleaded. "If this is going to be a problem, I'll just put everything back."

Kira snatched the pile of clothes occupying a chair by the dressing room. "Not a chance!" she replied.

"What are you doing?" Bronwyn asked, her voice growing desperate. She didn't want another public scene involving her family, and wished that everyone could just be happy that she'd found someone who loved her.

"Proving that we're not Temple mice!" Kira retorted. "If you want to dress in expensive stuff, that's fine with me. Now, if you want that blouse and camisole, take them off and I'll run everything up to the till."

Heidelinde shook her head, confident that a hick like Kira couldn't afford to pay over 160 sterlings for this collection of new clothes. She smiled as the crippled girl hobbled to the register, triumphant when Kira realized she wasn't carrying enough money to pay for everything.

But Heidelinde watched in astonishment as Kira offered a deposit and persuaded the cashier to put the purchase balance on her personal account.

Bronwyn sulked as she followed Kira back onto the street. This disharmony developing between her relatives and Algernon's family had to stop, but she felt powerless to influence Kira, and Heidelinde had a wicked way of twisting things to her favor. Bronwyn wanted to go home.

"Do you shop there frequently?" Heidelinde asked as the three women waited in queue for the trolley to arrive.

"Not unless I'm with Brenna," Kira replied. "I don't have the tits for clothes like that."

Heidelinde raised her brow at Kira's vulgarity. "Why haven't you taken Bronwyn there before? Why do you let her dress in dowdy hand-me-downs that look like they came out of her *grossmutti's* wardrobe?"

Secrets and Whispers: *Analysis*

"Can you say anything nice?" Kira snapped. "Every time you open your mouth, you're putting someone down. I don't know where you get the idea that it's okay to treat other people like that, but it really needs to stop!"

"How rude!" Heidelinde retorted, genuinely shocked at Kira's temerity. "I have a good mind to . . ."

"To what?" Kira replied. "I can't be bought, and I can't be bullied, either."

Angrily, Heidelinde slapped Kira across the face for her impertinence, a move which wrought swift retribution. In a reptile-quick response, Kira snapped a two-knuckled hook punch into the side of the older woman's neck. The hard, left-handed blow knocked Heidelinde to the ground.

"Kira!" Bronwyn cried.

Heidelinde choked, gasped and soiled herself. She'd never been hit before, never known pain before, and had never struggled to draw a breath before, either. Fearfully, she rose to her feet, backing away from the stern-faced crippled girl and into her sister-in-law's gentle embrace.

With memories of the taunting rich girls from Deception Creek echoing in her memory, Kira shook her head. "Don't cry, Bron. I didn't hit her nearly as hard as she deserved . . ."

***

After the streetcar arrived near the entrance of the Gold Leaf Hotel, Heidelinde scurried inside and hastened to the elevator with fleet steps. She stank, but said nothing to either of the younger women during the tense trolley ride from their shopping excursion, leaving Bronwyn certain that Kira had ruined everything.

Before the streetcar arrived at the hotel, the red mark on Kira's cheek had turned puffy and her eye was swelling shut. Stewing angrily, Kira glared at Bronwyn,

Secrets and Whispers: *Analysis*

who'd sat alone, with her arms and legs crossed, staring out the window. Kira could read unhappiness in Bronwyn's face as she rose to exit, but didn't want to make matters even worse by saying anything.

Alone in the elevator, Bronwyn mustered courage to speak. "I can't believe you hit Heidelinde," she rasped.

Kira shook her head. "You think it's okay for her to constantly insult you, and then insinuate that you don't wear nice clothes because Algernon's vow of poverty extends vicariously to you?"

"It's not about that, and you know it!" Bronwyn seethed. "I'm not Brenna. Wearing fancy clothes is not important to me."

"Then why didn't you tell her that?" Kira snapped. "You let that woman strut around like she's the grand judge of everyone she meets, and never call her into accountability. Then you get sullen with me for defending myself after she hit me without reason."

"You didn't have to hit her back," Bronwyn retorted. "How do you think this is going to look to my parents?"

Kira rolled her eyes and sighed. "Why doesn't your mother put that woman in her place? She's enabling this poisonous behavior by not putting a stop to it."

"What if she can't?" Bronwyn snapped. "Heidelinde always gets what she wants. She's beautiful, she's an only child who inherited a fortune, Harold is blind to her faults, and my mother has no leverage over her."

"That makes it okay for her to treat you like dirt?"

The elevator door opened and Bronwyn strode out, leaving limping Kira behind. She didn't want to cry. She didn't want to argue with her best friend, either. With her emotions rising, Bronwyn opened their room door and slammed it shut behind her. Fighting back tears, she pulled out her travel bag and stuffed her belongings inside without bothering to fold her clothes.

Secrets and Whispers: *Analysis*

Kira opened the door just as Bronwyn reached for the knob. Noting the bag in her friend's right hand, she asked, "Where are you going?"

"I don't know," Bronwyn replied, shaking her head. "Anywhere but here." She pushed past Kira and hurried to the elevator.

"What about the dinner play tonight?" Kira inquired. "I've already made all the arrangements."

"I'm not going," Bronwyn replied.

"How's that going to look to your parents?"

"It doesn't matter!"

Kira retreated toward the elevator. "It's going to be rather awkward to explain why you're not there . . ."

"You deal with it," Bronwyn snapped. "I'm done!"

"How can you say that? You're getting married in a few days."

Bronwyn shook her head as the elevator opened. "Maybe not!" she warned.

Kira didn't make it to the elevator in time to stop her. She swore in a very unladylike manner, just as the door for the second car opened.

Irena, Bronwyn's mother, stepped out. "It's you!" she said. "Just the girl I need to see . . ."

***

A dozen conflicting desires arose in Bronwyn's mind. Chief among these, she felt undeserving of the trouble brewing between her family and the Ravenwoods. How could she explain to Kira that she'd only been trying to keep a lid on the conflict by agreeing to go shopping with Heidelinde? Of course she hadn't wanted to go! Brenna had offered to take her to that particular store on more than one occasion, but Bronwyn couldn't reconcile

Secrets and Whispers: *Analysis*

spending lavishly on a wardrobe while people suffered in poverty on the streets.

Stupid Harold made a scene with Algernon, Willi spewed anger at Garrick during dinner, and now Kira felt justified in knocking Heidelinde to the pavement. For a fleeting moment, Bronwyn let a smile curve the corner of her lips, but she suppressed the thought. How was she going to get out of this mess, now?

For her entire journey home, Bronwyn stewed about her upcoming marriage. Was all of this opposition and trouble a warning from the Great God that she ought not marry Algernon? Had she blinded herself to the legitimate worries of her parents about Kira and Algernon, just like Harold had done with Heidelinde?

Yet as she ascended the gravel track leading up to Superstition Mesa from the Augury Creek Service Road, Bronwyn felt her body longing for Algernon's comfort. In his arms she always felt safe. His love helped her feel confident. He made her feel pretty, and she needed him.

Quiet prevailed inside the homestead. "Algernon?" she called, hoping he was there.

When he didn't answer, Bronwyn took off her shoes, removed her coat and entered. The blinds were open and the tea kettle hadn't been put back. Was Ileana home?

Bronwyn tiptoed to the room she shared with Algernon and pushed the door open. He was sleeping soundly on his mat, curled up with a pillow in a manner that she found endearing. After creeping inside and leaving her bag on the bed, Bronwyn went back into the great room where she noticed a mug in the sink.

It wasn't like Algernon to leave dishes unwashed.

But when she lifted the mug to wash it for him, Bronwyn's heart began to pound. Mistrust pervaded her frame of mind, leading her a very uncharitable analysis.

Whose lipstick was this?

Hard Lines

Arvid Traugott wrinkled his brow in deep and sustained concentration as he evaluated a graduate student's paper. Knowing the likely outcome of his family's journey to Marvic, the professor had brought work along to distract his attention from the reality that Irena intended to derail their only daughter's engagement.

Years earlier, before Bronwyn entered womanhood, he'd stridently opposed Irena's decision to allow the girl's admission to the Temple Elsbireth. He'd lost that battle with his wife, creating persistent, negative tension that rippled through their relationship and required years of work to heal. Arvid knew the extent of unhappiness in his sons' marriages – which he'd felt duty-bound to support at the time – so he didn't want to cross his wife again.

He and Bronwyn sustained an enviable degree of trust and affection. Arvid recognized his wife's compassion in their daughter, her practicality and good sense. These traits endeared Bronwyn to him, even though the young woman lacked her mother's slender beauty. He also understood that these characteristics gave his beloved daughter value that only a wise young man could discern. No matter how strongly his sons asserted that heavyset Bronwyn could never attract a decent man, Arvid knew that her loyal nature would make her a faithful wife.

The room door opened, pulling him away from his reverie. Irena walked in, sat on the bed and took off her shoes. "How's the evaluation going?" she asked.

Arvid put his pen down. "In truth, I'm finding it a little hard to concentrate right now." When his beloved didn't reply, he asked, "How was your talk with Kira?"

Irena forced a smile, shaking her head. "My sister was right about that girl. She's a fighter."

"She admits to hitting Heidelinde?"

Secrets and Whispers: *Hard Lines*

"Without any hesitation, and not a hint of regret," Irena replied. "But she told me that Heidelinde slapped her first, and she's got a red mark on her cheek to prove it. I suspect that's going to bruise by tomorrow."

Arvid sighed. "What does Bronwyn have to say?"

"I don't know," Irena admitted. "Kira told me that she packed her things and took off. The Ravenwood girl is worried that Bronwyn wants to call the wedding off."

Sensing something sad in his wife's demeanor, Arvid arose and sat next to her on the bed. He turned her chin toward his and kissed her. "Isn't that what you've wanted? Isn't that what you came here to do?"

"Not like this," Irena admitted, her eyes dampening. "I'm trying to talk sense into the girl, but the rest of our family seems determined to tear out Bronwyn's heart and trample all over it."

"Well then, we need to stop them," he suggested.

"It's a little late for that," Irena said, wiping away her brimming tears. "Harold and Heidelinde checked out after I spoke to Kira. Willi says they're going home."

Arvid shook his head. "We shouldn't be surprised. Heidelinde has never been willing to admit fault."

"It takes two, my dear. I don't think Kira would express contrition, either. That girl has an iron spine to go with that fist of hers. She took a very hard line with me.

"There's more going on here than we think. Brenna's not the dainty, porcelain doll she appears to be. Marla noticed a battle knife on the Lithian girl's leg while they were running this morning and decided to check Brenna's combat citations in the National Archives."

"Heroine of the Republic is an honorable title," Arvid replied, not surprised about the knife, as women often needed protection, even in Tamaria. "Why is that a problem? Shouldn't we affirm the woman's heroism?"

Secrets and Whispers: *Hard Lines*

"She killed 19 Kamerese rebels in a single combat action, wielding only a recurve bow and a sword . . ."

Arvid raised his brow.

"That's right," Irena continued. "Marla discovered that Kamerese rebels captured Brenna on a raid. They tortured and tried to kill her in captivity, but she escaped. Later, Brenna led the assault to rescue other prisoners and destroy the compound where she'd been held."

"That's impressive," Arvid remarked.

"It's violent," Irena insisted. "The whole family is violent. Kira hits people when she's angry and Algernon's killed people with his bare hands. Like his adorable little wife, Garrick has several citations for valor in action, but Marla suspects he's mentally unstable. A few weeks ago, he killed four people in a gunfight not far from here."

"Did he face any charges?" Arvid inquired.

"No," Irena admitted, "but that's not the point. Our daughter is mixed up with people who rely on brutality to get their way. The more I hear about the Ravenwood family, the more I worry for Bronwyn."

As Arvid put his arm around his wife, she turned into his embrace. "You don't think she knows about this?"

"What does it matter what Bronwyn knows? She's in love, she thinks the world of Algernon, and she's not alone in her admiration. Marla told me that Brenna defended the young priest like they were related by blood. She insists that Bronwyn made a wise choice with him."

After thinking about that long enough to formulate a wise response, Arvid stroked his wife's hair. "That's your decision," he encouraged. "The foreign girl doesn't matter."

Irena sighed. "Kira wants to put the dinner play plans on hold until she can persuade Bronwyn to change her mind. But I'd like to talk about all of this with our daughter before anyone else gets to her."

Secrets and Whispers: *Hard Lines*

***

Hours of research in the Royal Library finally revealed an important thread lurking in obscure historical documents, history books and contemporary news reports from small town papers on the northwestern coast. With her notes growing in volume, Captain Mariel Hougen's analysis cast light on a shadowy organization whose roots reached back at least 500 years.

Centuries before the Nord islanders ventured across the sea and colonized Kurian territory, this heavily forested region had been ruled by paladins who took their orders from monastic priests living in hidden temples that lay high in the eastern mountains.

Mariel learned that these groups, though culturally and linguistically different, merged in a futile effort to defend their lands from Nordan raids, calling themselves the Iron Order of Mist and Soil. An entire mythos developed around them that made it hard for Mariel to tell fact from fantasy in the documents. But their rule didn't last long, as they were soon outclassed by superior Nordan weapons and leadership.

Initially, the Nordans governed fairly and were welcomed as liberators. The Order of Mist and Soil faded into irrelevance, but the brief memory of its glory days remained alive in the hearts of fanatics and the disaffected, who adopted language and iconography that appeared in the burnt pamphlet the Defenders recovered after the truck bomb attack on Marvic's palace.

Among these, Mariel recognized a double dragon and sword, an image appropriated by a group calling itself the Old Order. Mariel chain-referenced that name in the periodical index and found recent newspaper accounts attributing responsibility for political assassinations and bombings to this organization. Next, she cross-checked

Secrets and Whispers: *Hard Lines*

Old Order in an index of political publications and found a manifesto that promoted violently overthrowing the Nordans, expelling all foreigners, and returning to what the society called "Kurian values."

The linguist's dark eyes widened. "Really?" she muttered to herself. "What nonsense!"

Reading through their poorly-written newsletters and recruitment posters, Mariel learned some of the code language she'd seen in the recovered pamphlet. These documents referred to the Nordans as *slakchen* (slimy ones), the Kamerese as *fetlikchen* (greasy ones), the Vatherans as *kwijlen* (damned ones), and in a borrowing from the Tamarian tongue, her own people as *kritschen*, whose root was a vulgar word for male genitalia.

The Old Order leadership championed ideas related to thunder, soil, mist and iron in the newsletters, but without additional references Mariel had no way of knowing what these terms meant. She suspected that these ideas were rooted in ethnic nationalism

Mariel arranged her notes several times, but no clue revealed the answer she sought. Why would a Kurian terrorist group attack Tamaria's palace?

***

Bronwyn angrily burst into the bedroom she shared with Algernon. "What is this?" she shouted.

Roused from deep slumber, Algernon focused his groggy mind on a mug she held in her hand. "You woke me up to ask me about a tea cup?"

"Don't be stupid!" she spat accusingly. "Whose lipstick is this?"

Algernon sat up. "Well, it's not mine."

"Don't play games with me!" Bronwyn warned. "Who else has been here?"

Secrets and Whispers: *Hard Lines*

"Our local Wildlife Officer," he told her, sitting up. "She followed me home this morning."

"And you let her in?"

"Of course. Is she still here?"

"She'd better not be!" the young woman threatened.

"Stop yelling, Bronwyn," he replied. "I got no sleep last night and came home exhausted. The woman met me on the trail and said she was thirsty. I put on water for tea, told her to show herself out, then went to bed and fell asleep. What's the big deal?"

"You were alone with another woman in here, and you think I have no reason to be upset?"

"No," he stated, shaking his head. "I'm not the least bit interested in her."

Stunned by his reply, Bronwyn's eyes widened and her jaw dropped. "That's all you have to say?"

Algernon rubbed his eyes and ran his fingers through his shoulder-length hair. "What do you want me to tell you?"

"The truth!" she insisted.

"I have," he stated. "But that doesn't seem to be working for you right now."

Bronwyn shook her head. "Unbelievable!" She discarded the mug, opened the travel bag on her bed and began stuffing more of her belongings into it. She looked a lot more hurt than angry.

"What are you doing?" he asked, bewildered by her inexplicable behavior.

"I'm leaving!" she stated, sniffing, hurting, regretting.

After thinking for a moment, Algernon inquired, "Where do you want to go?"

"I don't know," she replied. "Far away!"

Hearing this, Algernon arose, dressed and pulled out a bag of his own, into which he hastily dumped all of his clothes. He assembled toiletries in the bathroom, then,

Secrets and Whispers: *Hard Lines*

remembering that he likely needed money, recovered a pouch from its hiding place as Bronwyn slammed the front door and stomped down the outside stairs.

Algernon raced down the path after her, as soldiers working in the meadow paused to laugh and mock him for being rejected by the husky, brown-haired girl.

"What are you doing?" Bronwyn demanded when he caught up with her.

"I'm going with you," he announced, breathlessly.

"No, you're not!"

"Are you going to stop me?"

Bronwyn didn't really want to push him away. Despite her anger, the young woman's integrity did not permit her to attack him verbally. "Ugh!" she moaned. "You're impossible!"

"No," he corrected. "I love you. If you insist on running away, then I'm going, too."

"I don't want you to follow me!" she asserted, lying. "I want you to leave me alone!"

"Then give me a good reason. Tell me what I've done to deserve this . . . Go on!"

"My family doesn't like you!" she spat.

Algernon shrugged. "Well, from what I've seen, your family doesn't like you, either!"

Bronwyn's face reddened. "How can you say such an awful thing?"

"Easily," he replied. "You've repeatedly told me that your brothers treat you like you're a small child. Last night I saw this with my own eyes and heard it with my own ears. They're not interested in your happiness. They criticize and run you down every chance they get.

"Your sisters-in-law are no better. Vega's nice to your face, but won't utter a word in your defense when Willi says something nasty. Sikki has a lofty opinion of herself, and Heidelinde needs a broom to fly around on!"

Secrets and Whispers: *Hard Lines*

Trying to suppress a smile – the remark was not only funny, but fitting – Bronwyn turned away. "My parents love me!" she insisted.

"That's true of your father," Algernon said. "But if it's true of your mother, she has a strange way of expressing it. She hasn't done a thing to end the hateful nonsense from your siblings."

Bronwyn turned to walk away, but Algernon went after her. "Why are you following me?" she demanded.

"I'm not letting you leave me," he stated.

"Why can't you just let me go?" she asked, her voice growing desperate, knowing how tenacious he could be.

"Because you're holding a knife to my heart right now," he admitted. "I've committed myself to you. Had I actually done something that merited your leaving, I'd be sad, but I'd be man enough to let you go."

"You had another girl in the house," she retorted. "That's not a good reason?"

"No, it isn't," he insisted. "It was cold this morning, and she was thirsty. Do you think I'm so hard-hearted that I'd not show courtesy to someone in need? I started a fire, boiled water for her and went to bed, nothing more.

"But this isn't about me. It's about the ugly fact that your relatives have been flogging your self-esteem since the last time you went home to visit. It's about their belief that you somehow deserve to be lonely and miserable.

"Well, I don't buy any of that. I know you're a good woman. I know you're kindly and generous. I know how deeply you care about the people you love. I know you're a woman of high principle. None of that is on their list. None of that matters to them, but all of it matters to me, and that's why I want you.

"They sneer about how unattractive they think you are, while I find you absolutely beautiful. They scoff at

Secrets and Whispers: *Hard Lines*

your intelligence and treat you badly, but I know you're smart, I know how hard you work around here, and I know you deserve to be valued as a treasure. Their perceptions are rooted in lies, Bronwyn, and I'm begging you to stop believing them!"

Bronwyn felt the walls of her resistance crumbling, knowing that everything Algernon told her was true. The pain in her soul arose until she couldn't stop its expression. She dropped her bag to the ground, sat on it, and cried.

A moment later, she felt Algernon's hand resting gently on her back. She sensed his nearness, his solidarity, his willingness to support and reached to pull him close. Bronwyn held him tightly as the frustration, betrayal and hopelessness she'd felt washed away in a hurricane of heaving breath, a flood of tears, trembling hands and helpless weeping.

Algernon said nothing, offering no advice. He held her until his knees ached from the gravel and her strong embrace softened. Then he wiped her tears away with his thumbs and reached to kiss her, greatly relieved to feel her willing lips press against his and her tongue teasing in unspoken promise.

He stood, offering his hand, which she accepted as she rose to her feet. "Where do you want to go?" he asked.

With a sniff and a brief, little smile emerging through her sadness, Bronwyn said, "To the cabin."

***

Garrick's well-intended plans to tour the town with Bronwyn's brothers dissolved as their relational conflicts intensified. Darren claimed that Harold had already seen Marvic on a previous visit – which Garrick later learned

Secrets and Whispers: *Hard Lines*

was a lie – and after Willi stalked back to his room, the young officer concluded that he'd not be attending, either.

Darren's weathered skin, thin, greying hair and the wrinkled lines on his face suggested that he'd lived a hard life and probably drank heavily. Like all of his siblings, Darren inherited the husky, barrel-chested physique of their father. Despite his age the man maintained enviable fitness, and his gruff demeanor reminded Garrick of the late Sergeant Ringer.

The older man couldn't conceive why anyone would follow Garrick into combat, yet he secretly envied the officer's relationship with beautiful Brenna. However, his skepticism remained muted because Garrick ranked him, and that merited respect. Darren also noticed that Garrick carried a concealed weapon. Why was that necessary?

After deciding to focus their tour on the capital city's history, the two men visited various military installations around town, starting with one of the artillery revetments placed in strategic locations along the city wall. These nine inch guns, the largest permanently installed artillery in the Republic, could hit targets nearly 30 000 yards away.

"We could have used these on the Saradon," Darren said wistfully. "We'd have kept the Tanarak at a respectful distance that way."

Garrick tightened his lips as the memory of a terrible artillery strike that killed Tanarak women and children mocked from deep within his consciousness. That action, that one error in judgment, had cost Captain Engels his career.

Next, the men stopped at the Dragon's Lair Training Compound, the base where Garrick had once attended officer's training school. Listening to his tour guide explain the various facilities on base, Darren grew curious. "Are you still on active duty?" he inquired.

Secrets and Whispers: *Hard Lines*

"No, I've taken leave," Garrick replied. "My brother needs me right now."

That seemed strange. In Darren's experience, the army essentially owned a soldier's time until discharge. "Is that the way things are done in the Expeditionary Force these days?" he asked.

Garrick didn't dignify that question with a response.

After this, the men went to Memorial Stadium, the largest and most elegant sporting arena in the country. It featured a first-of-its-kind retracting roof, modern facilities and a rubberized track surface purported to reduce strain on runners' joints. Because Darren didn't seem interested in the stadium, Garrick cut their visit short.

"What else would you like to see?" Garrick asked.

Darren mused on that question for several moments. "How about your garrison?" he suggested.

Suspecting that Darren had an ulterior motive for the request, Garrick narrowed his gaze. "Why do you want to go there?"

"Just curious," Darren replied with a shrug.

"Maybe another time," Garrick said, his refusal spoken firmly enough to communicate the idea that he had no intention of ever guiding a tour of Fort Aeolus.

For the next hour, the men used the streetcar network to see some of the notable buildings in Marvic, including the city's library, its municipal hall, a massive, indoor shopping plaza and one of several hydroelectric power stations. After this, they stopped for tea at a little shop that featured outdoor seating.

Darren ventured a question between a bite of bread. "What do you think of this wedding business?"

"I'm happy for my brother," Garrick replied.

Darren suppressed a scowl. "Why do you say that?"

"Because Bronwyn's a terrific woman. I think she's an excellent match for him."

Secrets and Whispers: *Hard Lines*

"Why would you say such a stupid thing?" Darren mused. "Bronwyn's a starry-eyed, naive girl looking for her mother's approval."

"Supporting your sister is hardly stupid. Bronwyn needs your mother's assent in order to marry. That fact doesn't make her worthy of your derision."

Darren overlooked the insult. "What has she seen in life that makes her think she's ready for serious commitment? She was still playing with dolls when she left for the Temple, and she's been sheltered in that place for years. Bronwyn doesn't know the first thing about the reality of adult experience."

Garrick stopped him. "You don't know your sister very well, nor have you any idea what it's been like for young women in that unholy place."

"Unholy? What are you talking about?" Darren demanded, expressing righteous anger. "Your brother's a priest! How dare you speak ill of the Temple!"

"Why shouldn't I?" Garrick retorted. "It's been a nest of debauchery and a sanctum for pedophiles. The former high priest would have lost his head for it, too, had my sister not pleaded with Her Grace to show him mercy."

Darren, who knew nothing about the case and had no concept of Kira's moral integrity, didn't believe him. "My brother's right," he spat. "You're a damn liar!"

"You weren't there," Garrick replied, firmly. "But I was. Everything I've told you is public record now. I suggest you get your facts straight before you speak.

"And it would help if you showed interest in your sister and paid attention to what she has to say, rather than presuming you already know everything about her life over the past ten years Maybe then you'd understand that she has unquestionably excellent character. Everyone in your family should be immensely proud of the woman

Secrets and Whispers: *Hard Lines*

she's become. A loving brother would applaud her outstanding contribution to our community."

"You and your arrogant siblings strut around waiting for accolades and get upset when you don't get them," Darren complained. "You act like your dookie don't stink, but the rest of us recognize that stench. And you're so full of it the smell doesn't bother you anymore.

"So let me tell you something I already know. This whole charade is going to end badly. My mother is never going to allow Bronwyn to marry your worthless brother. They'll have to run off to Kameron, like I heard you had to do, and she'll be disowned by the entire family the minute she does that.

"I don't know how you forged invitations from the palace, what strings your slutty sister pulled, or who she slept with to get it done. I don't care, either . . ."

Garrick stood, his anger rising. "Watch your mouth!"

The older man leaned back in his chair with his palms up. "She admits to being a whore. Why do you object? Can't bear to hear the truth, lieutenant?"

"My sister's past is none of your concern," he replied. "You have no right to judge her. You have no right to undermine my brother's happiness, either."

Summoning all the self-control he could muster, Garrick reached into his pocket for change and slapped coins onto the table to pay for his drink. "Don't choke on your tea, sergeant," he said. "I presume you can find your own way back . . ."

***

"I don't know what to do!" Kira complained.

Aside from the formal recitations she performed with Bronwyn and Algernon every morning and evening, Kira very seldom found herself in prayer. This instance seemed

Secrets and Whispers: *Hard Lines*

less like a petition to the Great God and a lot more like a rant, but with her emotions running high and no willing ears available for listening, venting her frustration in a less-than-humble petition seemed the most appropriate course of action. She paced back and forth in her hotel room, grateful that Ileana – her Lithian house guest – had gone straight to work and didn't know about all the trouble with Bronwyn's family.

"These people are supposed to be devout, but their hearts are hard. They know nothing about mercy. They delight in making Bronwyn miserable. They twist everything to suit their belief that I'm unworthy of Bronwyn's friendship – and okay, maybe I am – but that's her choice to make, not theirs!

"And why do they hate Algernon so much? What did he ever do to them? After all he's been through, he finally finds someone who's willing to share herself with him, and all of them act like he's defective, somehow. It's so unfair! I know Bron loves him, and he loves her, too . . .

"Algernon needs her. She's good for him, too. If he can't marry Bron he'll go back to being angry all the time. He respects her virtue, and what's his reward? He gets the prize he craves and the comfort he needs yanked from under his nose at the last possible moment.

"What good does it do to frustrate him like this? Would you prefer that he just bonk the daylights out of her without a commitment? Does his faithfulness mean nothing to you? It sure doesn't matter to Bron's family."

Interrupted by a knock on her door, Kira sniffled and wiped her tears away. "Who is it?" she called.

Behind the door answered Vega. "I'm sorry for bothering you," she said. "I'll come back later if you like."

Kira opened the door. "What do you want?" she asked, rather less politely than etiquette demanded.

Secrets and Whispers: *Hard Lines*

Vega's brow raised in pity. "She really did hit you!" the older woman said, noting the puffy redness around Kira's left eye. "I'm so sorry!"

"Well, she got it worse than she gave out," Kira stated. "But she didn't get what she deserved."

"She soiled herself," Vega said quietly, her eyes averted. Wasn't that shameful enough? "She had to shower and wash her panties before she and Harold left."

"Is that what you wanted to tell me?" Kira asked.

"No," Vega replied, shaking her head. "Irena told me that Bronwyn took off. I came here 'cause I want to help."

Uncertain of the woman's trustworthiness, Kira felt reluctant to invite her in. "Help? How?"

"It's a personal matter," the older woman replied, glancing at other guests in the hall. "I can come back at another time if you're busy."

Kira shook her head. "No, that's okay. I don't mean to be rude. I'm just upset. Come on in."

Glancing around the room and noting it was empty, Vega asked, "Were you on the phone?"

"I was talking to a friend," Kira replied, lying. With her deceit wrapped in warm charisma, the lie turned invisible. She gestured toward the window with her left hand. "Have a seat and tell me what's on your mind."

Vega, only a few years older than Brenna, clung to her youth with a form-fitting sweater, a short skirt and excessive makeup. She chose one of the two chairs near the window and looked at the courtyard, below. "I know you're doing your best to impress my in-laws," she stated. "I can see that you're well-intended."

Accurately judging Vega's vulnerable demeanor, Kira sat on the bed – close enough to telegraph trust. "Bronwyn is my best friend," she said quietly. "I'd do anything for her and my brother."

Secrets and Whispers: *Hard Lines*

"I'm not sure that matters," Vega replied. "My cousin and Darren are ruining everything."

"Why?" Kira asked. "Bron's such a sweet girl . . ."

Vega swallowed. "My family comes from Starvation Overlook," she admitted, referring to a tiny northern town. "We're not wealthy people. Sikki married Darren to get away from there. She doesn't love him. She never has. All Sikki wants is the Traugott's money. That's why she and Darren are working so hard to make Bronwyn miserable."

Kira shook her head. "That doesn't make sense. If Bronwyn doesn't marry my brother, she remains the heir of her mother's property."

"Oh, they want them to get married," Vega admitted. "They're trying to make Bronwyn feel that her family is against her. If she has no support from home, they're convinced she'll run away with your brother. Once that happens, Irena will disinherit Bronwyn and Sikki will divide the property and investments among us. Everything was fine until you clobbered Heidelinde. Now she's too ashamed to show her face. She and Harold ran home."

"You're a part of this?" Kira clarified, trying to stifle her growing anger. "You'd betray Bronwyn for money?"

Vega shook her head fearfully. "They wanted me in on it, too, but I just can't do this to Bronwyn. She's so sweet! Everyone knows she loves Algernon. She can't stop talking about him and has confidence none of us has ever seen before. Her brothers realize this is a chance to get their greedy fingers into Irena's investment accounts."

"Let them have it," Kira insisted. "We don't need it."

"Well, maybe you don't," Vega stated. "But I'd rather see Bronwyn get what's rightfully hers than live with the fact that Sikki and Heidelinde get away with this."

"So you'd betray your own cousin?"

With her eyes downcast, Vega nodded. "I have my reasons," she said quietly.

Secrets and Whispers: *Hard Lines*

"What about Willem? Is he in on this, too?"

"He has bigger problems than money to worry about," Vega said.

"Well, what about your children?" Kira inquired. "If this is such a great opportunity to spread the family wealth around, why aren't you involved in the plot?"

"We have no children," Vega stated. "We will never have children."

Kira's eyes widened, knowing that Brenna and Garrick had been struggling with infertility. After experiencing two miscarriages, the Lithian woman quietly wrestled with spiritual doubt and feelings of inferiority.

Noting Kira's response, Vega continued, "It's not that I can't. It's that Willem won't."

Kira sensed pain in Vega's expression and it softened her heart. "I don't mean to be untoward, but does he prefer men?"

Vega shrugged. "I've suspected as much for a long time." The older woman's tone saddened as she glanced at Kira. "If so, he's really good at hiding it, and the family doesn't talk about it. He's never touched me, except in anger. That's something I figure you'd understand."

"What do you mean?" Kira asked, puzzled.

"I've heard talk about you," Vega continued quietly. "There are rumors . . . well, I've heard you like girls."

"Yeah, but I like boys, too. People are people. Love is love. Body parts are only a means to an end."

Scowling at that statement, Vega paused to muster courage before continuing. "Irena had a contact at the Temple who reported that you and Bronwyn were found together in a compromised position."

"Old news," Kira said in response. "Bron doesn't want me that way. She never did."

"So it's true? You had sex with her?"

Secrets and Whispers: *Hard Lines*

"Once," Kira admitted. "It was a set-up to get me into Brother Abelard's harem. He threatened to tell your family that he'd caught us if I didn't comply with his demands. He used a girl already under his control to spy on me. She was watching when I took Bron to my secret place, and then he and another priest walked in on us.

"Bron felt completely humiliated. They stared at us like gawking schoolboys and wouldn't let us get dressed. That incident not only cost Bron her ordination, she also complained that she'd felt pressured to let me have my way. It took her a long time to forgive me for that."

"Do you still . . . want her?" Vega asked, her tone slightly accusatory.

Kira shook her head. "Bron's my friend, nothing more. She's my ally in ministry, a great help in our household, and I won't jeopardize our friendship for anything as transitory as a romp in bed. Besides, Algernon needs her a lot more than I do."

"But what if both of you could have what you need from her?" Vega offered.

"What are you suggesting?" Kira asked, a bit of menace rising in her voice. "I'm not sure I like what I think you're saying right now."

"Hear me out," Vega said, nervously. "What if your brother and Bronwyn called the wedding off, but stayed together. They could start a family. He gets what he needs from her, and you keep doing your ministry thing."

Kira found that suggestion so ridiculous she laughed. "What kind of credibility do you think we'd have if my brother had children without being married?"

"Well, it's not like you're ministering to virgins . . ."

Kira rolled her eyes. "You don't understand what we're trying to do," she said. "We work closely with citizen groups and government agencies to integrate isolated

Secrets and Whispers: *Hard Lines*

women back into society. We need community support to do that. What you're suggesting runs counter to our goals.

"Besides, an ordained priest having children out of wedlock puts Algernon into the same category as the creepy men who kept personal harems and ran a sex ring at the Temple. He would never consent to that."

"What are you talking about?" Vega demanded.

"I'm saying that my brother is an honorable man. He loves Bronwyn and wants to start a family. If he can't trust her integrity now, then what kind of girl is she?"

"Well, she had sex with you. That doesn't put her into a very favorable light . . ."

"Bron wasn't exactly willing," recalled Kira. "She was terrified and shaking. Nearly all the girls in the cloister were having sex, and Bron was afraid of being cornered. Sister Alba picked on anyone who she thought was vulnerable, and a lot of girls were teasing Bron for being a prude. She never wanted me to bonk her – she's not that kind of girl – but she consented to my seduction because I could protect her from more aggressive women."

This version of events included details that added complexity and nuance to the story Vega learned from the family's Temple source. "You protected her?"

"Of course," Kira stated. "Lucky for Bron, the male priests preferred skinny and fair-skinned girls like me. Otherwise, she'd have been forced into blow jobs, orgies, bondage parties, or worse . . ."

Vega's eyes widened. "That happened to you?"

Kira nodded, her countenance darkening as she considered the unpleasant memory. "It was awful. After I left the Temple, Bron forgave me for what I did to her. But she made me swear that I would never make a move on her again, and she's been a faithful friend ever since."

Speechless for a moment, Vega's eyes brimmed with emotion. "I'm sorry. I didn't know."

Secrets and Whispers: *Hard Lines*

"That's why I'm impatient with your opposition to Bron's engagement. She and Algernon are doing this the right way. Why don't any of you see that?"

"I do!" Vega replied.

"Then why even contemplate that they not marry?" Kira countered. "I know Bron. Her desire for my brother is pure. She wants her family at her side. She wants her mother to help me tie the knot at the wedding ceremony. She wants harmony and joy. That's who Bronwyn is.

"Besides, how do you think her very conservative mother is going to react if she hears that my brother and Bron are bonking when they're not married?"

"She told us they're sleeping in the same room," Vega stated. "How do you know they're not having sex?"

"You sleep in the same room with Willi. Maybe you even share the same bed. You should know that proximity doesn't mean the two of them are going at it. Bronwyn sleeps in a single bed, while Algernon has a mat on the floor. They always leave the door open. My room is right next to theirs. If they were having sex, I'd hear it."

"But they might be very discreet. You can't know that for sure."

"She's just had her period," Kira stated. "I know for a fact that Bron and Algernon aren't having sex. The real issue here shouldn't be trying to keep the two of them from getting married. What needs to happen is for Bronwyn's mother to back away from her hard line, give her blessing and put an end to all this stupid intrigue about inheritance."

Vega stood. "I wish I could do something about that," she said wistfully. "But I don't see how. Irena knows that her sons are unhappily married, and she doesn't want the same thing happening to Bronwyn."

***

Secrets and Whispers: *Hard Lines*

Algernon and Bronwyn took the farm service road to Wounded Heart Creek and followed the narrow trail back up to mesa in order to avoid being observed and possibly followed by the soldiers cleaning up the meadow.

Along the way, Bronwyn told Algernon about the confrontation between Heidelinde and Kira. "I'm angry at your sister right now!" she complained.

Laboring up the hill for the second time that day, Algernon tightened his lips. Kira had been bullied by the rich town girls many years earlier and didn't tolerate nonsense anymore. Although he believed that his sister knocked down haughty Heidelinde for good reason, Algernon felt so worried that Bronwyn would leave him, he said nothing in his sister's defense. "Do you want me to talk to her?"

"What good will that do?" Bronwyn complained. "What's done is done. Now I have to figure out how to clean up the mess!"

Not knowing what to say, Algernon remained silent. His heart pounded with anticipation as they climbed the hidden, overgrown track to the abandoned cabin. Once inside, Bronwyn's desire sprang to life in passionate kissing, and caressing. He had a tough time restraining her urgent sensuality.

As their contact pushed previously accepted limits, he honored his word to be patient, praising her beauty and her worthiness of his affection. "It's okay," he soothed, calming her. "I want you, but I can wait."

Bronwyn felt conflicted, torn between wanting to give her virtue to him and respect for the restraint he consistently exhibited when they were alone. "I want you, too," she whispered, pulling him close. "I want you badly."

He quickly fell asleep in her arms. Bronwyn reflected on the reality that Algernon inspired her longing in large part because she felt safe with him. He stirred

Secrets and Whispers: *Hard Lines*

her desire, yet never imposed his will on her. Nobody else knew how he behaved when they were alone, and nobody ever would. His endearing manner, his delight in her feminine form and the gentle touch of his hands, lips and tongue roused a craving within her that Bronwyn felt powerless to control. Had he behaved in a less principled and careful manner, she'd have already given herself to him, no matter what her parents might have thought.

If he treated her this well before they were married, she felt confident that he would remain gentle after their hands had been tied together. If he supported her emotionally now – willing to run off and leave his beloved twin sister behind – Bronwyn believed he'd be loyal to the end of his days.

She'd not wanted to abandon him. That's why she hadn't left while he slept. Bronwyn knew that she'd awakened him to rouse a response, fully expecting that he'd fight for her. With her instincts proven right, the young woman resolved to marry Algernon no matter what her family said or did.

Despite this determination, she still felt hurt that her brothers were being so mean, that Sikki and Heidelinde were nasty, and that her own mother refused to bless her union. Bronwyn didn't understand why her family couldn't see Algernon's value and rejoice.

Something else had to be going on. Something else was happening that she couldn't see. Some hidden desire drove this destructive behavior, but what could it be?

Bronwyn ran her fingers through Algernon's hair, frustrated because she couldn't imagine any course of action that would unite her family. "If only they would love," she murmured prayerfully. "Then they would understand. Then we could all be happy . . ."

Secrets and Whispers: *Hard Lines*

Her movement awakened Algernon from his slumber. He arose with his head pounding and hunger rumbling in his belly. "I need to eat," he told her.

Their lips met and lingered for a moment. "Okay," she agreed. "Let's go home."

***

Music teased from beyond the stone bridge leading to the circular manse Garrick shared with Brenna. He passed through the ever-present mist rising from the warm current of the River Honeywater, a veil that kept his home in perpetual seclusion. This beauty of this place inspired feelings of safety in a world fraught with danger, of sanctuary filled with peace and love.

Garrick heard a boy's voice and Brenna's piano on the other side of the door. Yet the first pair of eyes he met when entering the airlock were bruised from a fight and grey, not blue; brimming with regret, not desire.

"Kira? What happened?" he asked with concern.

The young woman embraced her brother and kissed his cheek. "We need to talk," she said quietly.

"I'll meet you upstairs," he told her, taking off his jacket and slipping out of his shoes.

As Garrick entered the main room, Brenna paused from her teaching. Her smile lightened his heart. Rune, her 11-year-old star student, turned on his heels, straightened his back and saluted like a soldier. From the couch, Rune's stern-faced grandmother watched Garrick return the gesture and scoffed. The levity ended one moment later, as Brenna called the boy's attention back to his lesson and Garrick ascended the stairs.

Kira waited in the upstairs living area, an open space with a single bathroom, a modern kitchen – that Brenna, who didn't bother with cooking, never used to its

Secrets and Whispers: *Hard Lines*

potential – and a small patch of tile with a table and chairs reserved for dining. The room featured a couch, a sitting area near a window, and a neatly-made bed.

This second floor apartment provided a comfortable space for the young couple, despite its diminutive size. Kira always found the view from up here breathtaking, as its northeast-facing windows overlooked the sheer scarp of Wounded Heart Canyon, revealing the vast expanse of Fallen Moon Lake far below and distant, snow-clad mountains rising to the east. On its southern side, a misty redwood grove and the lovely cascade of the River Honeywater lent a primeval feel to the view.

Kira gestured toward the kitchen, where dirty dishes awaited attention. "You wash, I'll dry," she offered.

Since the noise from cleaning dishes would likely mute the sound of their discussion, Garrick agreed. "What's going on?" he asked.

After she outlined the events with her shopping excursion, the conflict with Heidelinde, the strained conversation with Irena, and Vega's revelations, Kira expressed exasperation. "What Vega told me makes sense, but how do we counter a conspiracy like that? Bronwyn doesn't deserve mistreatment, and neither does Algernon."

Garrick didn't share his interactions with Willem and Darren, but his sister had a point. "What Bronwyn's brothers do won't change anything," he offered. "The only power they have is to make Bronwyn feel miserable, and we counter that by fully supporting her.

"You shouldn't feel bad about Heidelinde. Anyone who's met her knows she needed a lesson in manners. By taking her and Harold out of play, you've strengthened Bronwyn's hand and dealt her siblings a setback."

"Well, Bron wasn't happy with me," Kira admitted.

Garrick shrugged. "She'll get over it. Bronwyn's marital prospects have never been favorable. She isn't pretty, and she's heavy. What she's got going for her is character, and not everyone's smart enough to see that."

"Bron used to worry that he couldn't see past her tits," Kira added. "He worked hard to build her trust."

"Oh? So men recognize your brains right away?" Garrick teased, bumping her hip to the side with his.

"Ha!" she replied, leaning on her cane to bump him back. "As if the way Brenna fills a blouse doesn't turn your head . . . We all adore a good rack, don't we?"

"Nothing wrong with that," Garrick admitted. "But honestly, Bronwyn has a lot more going for her than all those self-absorbed, macromastic wonders who caught his eye in the past. He's done well to keep her, and we both know that she can could do a lot worse than him."

Kira understood that most people agreed with these unpleasant sentiments. Bronwyn and Algernon matched well for many reasons – especially in the alignment of their personal values, which promised a long-term impact far more lasting than physical attraction could sustain. Algernon's life had been littered with unrequited romances, while Bronwyn had never attracted interest from anyone.

Kira understood more intimately than most how desperately the young couple needed one another. "So you don't think she's going to call off the wedding?"

"Not a chance," he replied. "If the story you heard from Vega is true, Bronwyn's brothers know her well enough to count on it."

"But what can she do if Irena doesn't give consent?"

Garrick shook his head. "I'm sure there are ways around that problem. Once the queen sanctioned Bronwyn's marriage, that changed everything. I suspect it will be nigh well impossible for Bronwyn's mother to disapprove when the wedding day arrives."

Secrets and Whispers: *Hard Lines*

Kira's eyes widened, her mind blossoming with relief until she realized that if she did nothing, Sikki and Heidelinde might still make off with Bronwyn's inheritance. "Okay, but we need to do damage control with Bron and stop her wicked sisters-in-law."

"How do you plan on doing that?" Garrick asked.

"It's probably not a good idea to tell Bron or her mother about the inheritance plot," Kira concluded. "The only evidence I have is Vega's testimony, which she could easily deny, making me look like a fool."

Garrick agreed. "Then it's wiser to say nothing. If you stay silent, you protect your position. Brenna told me that Marla hinted something about Bronwyn's mother digging up dirt on us. She's looking to dissuade her daughter, but Bronwyn knows that you've supported her decision to marry more than anyone else."

Kira set her dish down and scrunched her brow.

Noting this, Garrick paused. "Given what's going on with her family, what's the best outcome you can expect?"

"Bron doesn't need Irena's money," Kira stated, slowly shaking her head. "She's a modest and frugal woman. I can easily take care of her."

"But you don't want to see her siblings making off with a legacy that's rightly hers," Garrick added.

"Absolutely not!" she replied, returning to the task of wiping the dish dry. "I don't want to see Bronwyn and Algernon get heartbroken over this either."

"Honestly, Kira, it wouldn't hurt Algernon to worry a little about losing her. He needs to remember how good he has it, and she needs to see that he cares enough to contend for her."

"Okay," Kira assented. "But Bron was really upset when she stormed off this morning. It's thrown my plans for the dinner play out the window."

Secrets and Whispers: *Hard Lines*

Garrick rinsed his final dish and pulled the drain plug. "You want my advice? Go home. Be the friend that Bronwyn needs and convince Algernon to impress Arvid. He's the only one with any influence on Irena."

Kira nodded, understanding the wisdom of her brother's counsel. "What about the dinner play?"

"I'll take Brenna," he said, smiling. "It might help me get lucky tonight."

Kira rolled her eyes and took the final plate from his hands. "Is that all you think about?"

"These days, pretty much," he replied.

***

As Algernon and Bronwyn approached the meadow where their homestead stood, he noticed a pair of figures sitting on the porch. "Are those your parents?" he asked.

Bronwyn peered over her fiancé's shoulder. "What are they doing here?"

"Likely waiting for you," he replied. "They're going to ask where we've been, and why we're carrying our stuff."

"We can't just let them sit there!" she complained.

Algernon turned toward her. "You'd prefer to tell them what we were doing at the cabin? How well would that go over?"

She scowled in response. "Our private conduct is no one else's business."

Regretting his tone, Algernon took her hand in his. "No, it isn't. So let's figure out how to keep it that way."

"You're hungry," she reminded him. "Maybe they are too. I can put a meal together."

"I'm more concerned about their disapproval than I am about hospitality. If we tell them where we've been, they'll think we were having sex. You don't need criticism from your family right now, and I've sworn an oath . . ."

Secrets and Whispers: *Hard Lines*

Thinking quickly, Bronwyn came up with a plan. "Okay, here's what we'll do. We'll go around the back way. You stop at the hot spring and have a dip. I'll go through the laundry room door and put our bags in the closet.

"Then I'll invite my parents in and make lunch for you. Give me about twenty minutes, and then you can come home."

Algernon nodded. He smiled and kissed her. "I'd be happier if you'd join me," he teased.

"You're incorrigible!"

"What's wrong with wanting you?" he replied.

Bronwyn detected something in his voice that she couldn't quite identify, a vulnerability in his tone warning her to pay close attention. His unwillingness to talk about what was troubling him began to worry her as the young couple retreated to the cabin. She followed Algernon up the hill, breathing hard as she labored to climb a slope still laden with last autumn's decaying leaves.

Surefooted and fit, Algernon paused, offering to carry her bag. While she knew he was well-intended, Bronwyn shook her head. "I'm okay," she asserted.

At the summit, he turned north and worked his way between mature fir and hemlock trees. Damage to their lower branches, flattened saplings and trampled ferns littering the understory testified that giants had used this footpath while hunting the resident gwynling last winter. Algernon led Bronwyn along the descending trail, their breathing punctuated by footfalls and the sound of his bag bouncing against his back.

After walking for a few minutes in silence, Bronwyn asked, "How did it go with *The Shadow* last night?"

Algernon shook his head. "It was ugly and didn't end well. I don't want to go through that again.

"I'm more concerned about your brothers and their wives acting like idiots. You deserve more respect than

Secrets and Whispers: *Hard Lines*

they give you." After a pause to gather courage he added, "I also wasn't happy that you kept pushing me away."

Shocked to hear him say this, Bronwyn's initial reaction was denial. "I wasn't pushing you away!" she insisted. "I sat next to you the whole time."

He shook his head. "Every time I put my arm around you, or tried to hold your hand, you brushed me off. One time, you even told me to stop, and you weren't very nice about it, either.

"Now, I don't think I was doing anything wrong. It's not unreasonable for people who are planning to marry in a few days to show discreet affection in public. It wasn't like I was fondling you in front of them."

Realizing that he was right, Bronwyn hedged. "We were sitting with my parents," she responded. "I didn't want them to get the wrong idea."

He didn't let her cling to that excuse. "What does that mean? What idea could they get wrong?"

"Well . . . I don't know. I guess I didn't want them to think that your interest was purely physical."

Exasperated, Algernon threw his arms to the side. "Our relationship is far from platonic. Are you so ashamed of me that the only time we can touch is when nobody in your family can see it?"

"No!" she insisted. "It's not like that."

"I'd have a hard time knowing that based on the way you were treating me last night. You sent a very clear signal that you're not as interested in me as I am in you, while we are both aware that I'm the one respecting boundaries when no one else is watching."

"That's not fair!" she cried, her voice cracking. "I'm under a lot of pressure and everything's going wrong! I just don't want to make things worse . . ."

Secrets and Whispers: *Hard Lines*

Terrified of pushing too far, Algernon paused. His expression and body language softened. "I'll grant that," he offered. "But can you see my point?"

Bronwyn dropped her bag and crossed her arms.

Since she wasn't moving, Algernon took that as an indication that he should continue to negotiate. "When you refuse modest, discreet affection, I feel like you're not serious. When your mother sees your reluctance to let me touch you, she's naturally going to think that you're not confident about your future with me. I'll bet your Tante Marla sees your behavior as telegraphing second thoughts about our engagement."

"That wasn't what I intended!" she insisted, sadness washing over her face. "Never!" Bronwyn opened her arms and stepped into his embrace.

The reassuring comfort of her soft body inspired relief. Algernon, grateful for her commitment, stroked her hair as she kissed his neck. "I'm not going to embarrass you in front of your loved ones," he promised. "What I need is public affirmation of my affection. I don't think I'm asking for much. Please don't push me away again."

"Okay," she agreed. "Just keep your hands off my boobs and my butt when my parents are around."

Hearing this, Algernon sighed. "You've been in control of where my hands are allowed to go from the very beginning," he reminded her. "That's not going to change. I only touch your soft parts when you want me to, and you know that. Nothing I did last night was remotely inappropriate in public."

Bronwyn rested her forehead against his. "You're right," she affirmed. "I'm sorry, Algernon. I wasn't thinking and I didn't mean to hurt you."

One kiss later, he forgave her and they continued on their way. At the terminus of the north-south ridge they'd been following, the trail descended steeply into a

Secrets and Whispers: *Hard Lines*

natural fold in the rock. Because of the narrow passage and uncertain footing, Bronwyn let Algernon carry her bag to the bottom before she followed.

Just to the west of this formation lay the only hot spring on the mesa suitable for bathing. In order to make their plan work, Algernon pulled a towel from his travel bag just before bidding Bronwyn goodbye. She scurried down the trail, but he didn't go into the water. Instead, knowing that his beloved would be facing her parents all by herself, he looked into the heavens and earnestly prayed, "Help her!"

The hot spring lay only a short distance from the homestead, and as she turned a corner, Bronwyn realized that her plan had already unraveled. Both of her parents were wandering around the back side of Kira's house, where the wind turbine tower stood. Algernon had set the machine up in a strategic high spot where westerly winds funneled between a pair of intersecting ridges. Bronwyn imagined her father pointing out that the tower stood on unobstructed ground just in front of this natural funnel.

It didn't take long for Irena and Arvid to notice her approach. They paused, as if uncertain of their right to be on someone's property without permission, but soon Irena lifted her skirts and ran toward her daughter.

"Oh, honey!" she exclaimed as Bronwyn dropped her bag and the two women embraced. "We were so worried about you! What happened?"

Stifling a snippy response, Bronwyn let her mother go and picked up her bag again. "I'm angry," she replied. "I was going to run away with Algernon, but he talked me out of it."

That response took Irena by surprise. "Run away? Where would you go?"

"What does that matter, *Mutti?* I'm here now." The young woman collected courage and strode purposefully

Secrets and Whispers: *Hard Lines*

toward the house. She'd never argued with her mother before, and doing so now felt uncomfortable. Yet the sense of injustice she'd been experiencing with her family compelled the young woman to maintain a hard line.

"Where's Algernon?" Irena asked.

"He stopped at the hot spring for a dip," Bronwyn replied over her shoulder, letting the implication that she could have joined him settle in her mother's mind. "I came home to get some food ready. Are you hungry?"

Perplexed, Irena offered, "Let me help you."

Arvid followed his wife and daughter to the back door of the huge, polyhedronal home, noting that the raised garden beds showed evidence of tender care. His eyes lingered on the scene as Bronwyn led them into the pantry and laundry area.

Observing the paucity of the pantry stores, Irena's brow wrinkled. "Is this all the food you have?"

"For now," Bronwyn replied. "There was a lot more a few weeks ago."

Alarmed now, Irena put her hand on her daughter's arm. "Darling, if you're going hungry, you can tell me."

Bronwyn shook her head as she opened the inner door. "*Mutti,* no one goes hungry here."

Arvid had never witnessed his only daughter speak in such a terse manner, especially to her mother. The professor held his counsel as they entered the house, but as he beheld the beautiful, massive beams overhead and the spacious interior they enclosed, he let out a low whistle. This place was both huge and lovely!

"Have a seat, Pappa," Bronwyn encouraged, tossing her bag into her room. "The cushions in the living room are comfortable."

While her daughter pulled out cookware and utensils, Irena glanced around the sprawling kitchen. Bronwyn had far more room to prepare meals here than

Secrets and Whispers: *Hard Lines*

Irena had in her own house. She recognized high quality in the neatly hung pots, pans and cooking tools her daughter used. Also, Bronwyn had a set of very expensive Lithian knives on the counter.

"How did the Ravenwoods find this place?" Irena asked while her daughter lit the stove.

In between breaths to catch the kindling on fire, Bronwyn replied, "Algernon designed and built it for Kira."

"By himself?"

"No. He had help from neighbors and friends."

Why was she so short with her responses? Bronwyn typically prattled. This unusual behavior concerned Irena enough to risk an outright inquiry. "Honey, why are you so upset?"

Bronwyn looked at her mother with teary eyes. "I'm getting married in a few days, but nobody in my family seems the least bit interested in my happiness. Why would you think that fact wouldn't bother me?"

"Honey, we're just concerned, that's all."

"Concerned about what? Concerned for whom?"

Irena tried to be patient. "We've been over this," she stated. "I don't think Algernon is a suitable match."

"*Mutti,* you don't even know him," Bronwyn moaned. "You make judgments on my behalf as if I'm a small child with no experience, no discernment and no capacity to recognize him as a good partner, even after spending years in his company. Have you even talked to him yet?"

"Well, I spoke to Kira this morning," Irena said. "It was not a pleasant conversation."

"Why is that? Did you expect her to be happy after Heidelinde repeatedly put me down, treated Kira with contempt and then slapped her for sticking up for me?"

"Heidelinde and Harold have gone home," Irena stated. "They've seen enough to form their own view."

Secrets and Whispers: *Hard Lines*

Bronwyn shook her head. Noting that the gasification process had already begun, she lowered the flame on the cook top with a dial that controlled its fan speed. "They'd made up their minds before ever stepping off the train. Everyone has, including you."

In the ensuing silence, the young woman reached into the refrigerator, pulled out some vegetables and set them on a cutting board. She also retrieved a container of cooked rice, which she placed near the stove top.

Mustering courage, Irena continued. "These people you're mixed up with are deeply violent. That worries me. Everyone in our family is rightly concerned for you."

Bronwyn shook her head. "All three of my brothers are soldiers. They've all seen combat, and they've all taken life. Should you be concerned about me being with them?"

"There's a context to their experience," Irena said, defending her sons from what she considered a pointless attack. "They're not mindlessly looking for trouble."

Selecting her favorite knife, Bronwyn began cutting the vegetables for her stir fry. "Are you listening to what you're saying?" she asked. "You imply that Algernon and his family thoughtlessly wander about seeking danger. That's highly offensive, *Mutti*. It's also untrue."

Irena held her ground. "This so-called public service that Kira started – this ministry to street urchins, strippers and *strichmadchen* – puts her into contact with the worst kind of people. Associating with that kind of crowd naturally exposes you to needless danger."

After collecting and discarding the unwanted parts of her vegetables into a compost bin, Bronwyn scraped her cuttings into a skillet and stirred it. "We've had less trouble from the people you think are dangerous than we've had from the Temple," Bronwyn stated flatly.

"That's ridiculous!" Irena countered. "I understand that you're upset about the denial of your ordination, but

Secrets and Whispers: *Hard Lines*

I've heard it was your inappropriate liaison with Kira that led to your expulsion."

Bronwyn felt hurt every time anyone brought up that incident, but this time her resolve hardened. "I wasn't expelled," Bronwyn replied. "I left on my own accord, more than two years after the incident with Kira. Besides, my sex life isn't anyone else's business, including yours. I don't know who you've been talking to, but it hurts that you're willing to listen to everyone but me."

"Honey, it's not a matter of trying to shame you, or prove you wrong," Irena said in a soothing voice. "I'm just trying to protect you from making a big mistake.

"The Ravenwoods are bad news. I know you admire Kira – she's pretty and charismatic. You say you love Algernon, too. But honey, everywhere these people go they leave behind a trail of violence and bloodshed. That's not who you are. You're so much better than this . . ."

Bronwyn left her stir-fry to simmer, took her mother's hand and led her toward the laundry room. "I want to show you something," she said. "Have a look at the flooring over here . . ."

Irena saw burn marks, a spray pattern of holes and gouges in the floorboards. The nearby wall and the bathroom door showed similar damage. "What's this?"

"We had a young girl named Solace staying with us," Bronwyn began. "She'd been an opium runner who picked up drug payments for a criminal guild at the strip clubs. The guild targets pre-teen girls for that job because they're too young to face charges for trafficking.

"Solace was terrified and in trouble, but Kira saved her from that life. She defended a girl who was too weak and too fragile to defend herself. That's the essence of our public service, and as a devout woman you ought to be more sympathetic to the plight of disconnected young ones who become the prey of wicked men.

Secrets and Whispers: *Hard Lines*

"Up here, Solace was safe from the Opium Guild. She had time to heal from her physical and emotional wounds. Like me, she's the heir of her family's property, but she'd run away from home to escape physical abuse.

"Her departure didn't sit well with her two older brothers. They tracked her down, intending to return her to a life of mistreatment and shame, but we protected Solace from them. That's what we do."

"I'm not following you," Irena said impatiently. "What does this have to do with your floor?"

"In the final act in his campaign against Kira, High Priest Abelard gave these young men weapons, a map to the homestead and paid them to come up here and kill us. They brought shotguns. One of them went to the front, while the other one busted through the back door and headed inside. He knocked down our canning, breaking glass, tipping bins and scattering our food stores all over the floor. That's why we don't have very much right now."

Fearfully, Irena asked, "Then what happened?"

"Someone had to stop him from hurting Solace. It wasn't Algernon. It wasn't Kira. It was me. I threw a pan full of hot coals into his face and beat him for all I was worth. He fired the gun before he dropped it, ruining our floor, but I was too close for him to hit me. By the time I finished, he'd curled up, crying and begging me to stop!"

Bronwyn's reddened cheeks burned. Her eyes brimmed with emotion, remembering the terror of that moment. Seeing this, Irena put her hand to her breast and shook her head. "What happened to you, honey? You're talking like a monster, not my sweet little girl."

"I'm not a little girl, *Mutti*. I'm a grown woman, and I know that every one of us has a monster inside. We all need repentance. We all need forgiveness. Even saintly

Secrets and Whispers: *Hard Lines*

Brenna – the most devout woman I've ever met – learned that lesson the hard way. I've had to learn it, too."

Hearing this, Irena confirmed that Bronwyn knew about the horrible deeds Brenna had done. Her eyes followed her daughter as Bronwyn strode back into the kitchen and attended to her stir fry with a wooden spoon.

"Look at what your association with these people has done to you," Irena urged. "This is not who you are."

Bronwyn paused from her task. "*Mutti*, it's obvious that you don't know who I am. You don't know Algernon, either. If you did, you'd understand why I love him. But I don't believe you're interested in how I feel. You've come up here determined to derail my engagement."

"Honey, that's not true!" Irena insisted.

"It's not?" Bronwyn countered. "I see no evidence of your mind being open. I've faced nothing but criticism from you, my brothers and their wives the whole time!

"What other conclusion do you expect me to draw? You've been desperately trying to prove that Algernon is deficient. You're highlighting his problems, blinded by your opposition to the point of not being able to see any good in him. That's wrong on many levels . . ."

Something in Irena's heart longed to believe her daughter, but worry about Bronwyn's ultimate and certain unhappiness hardened the older woman's perspective. "Look at your brothers," she argued. "Darren married Sikki against our advice, and he's deeply unhappy."

"Algernon is not Darren," Bronwyn countered. "My brother had no self control. We all know that Sikki was four months pregnant with their first child when they married. She seduced him to get away from desperate poverty, and now she's licking her lips knowing you intend to disinherit me."

An expression of shock erupted on Irena's face. "What a rude thing to say!"

Secrets and Whispers: *Hard Lines*

"We only need to look at a calendar to know it's true," Bronwyn stated. "Sikki's a gold digger who's never loved Darren, Heidelinde's a manipulative witch who's cast a spell on Harold, and poor Vega's just a pretty screen to hide Willem's homosexuality."

"Bronwyn!" Irena stammered, stunned by her daughter's temerity. "How can you talk like this?"

"What's the point of hiding our family secrets?" Bronwyn asked. "You think I don't know about my brothers? You've been happy to treat Algernon like he's inferior, but he has twice the integrity of all of them, combined. We sleep in the same room and spend a lot of time alone, but I'm still a virgin. Algernon treats me with more respect than I'm getting from my own family, yet everyone presumes that either I'm too naive, or too fat and ugly to attract a decent partner."

"Honey, that's not true!" Irena insisted. "I have your best interest at heart, and I would never think such horrible things of you!"

Bronwyn pulled four bowls out of the cupboard. "If you really have my interest at heart, then don't just hear what I say, think about it and understand. I'm not looking for a trophy, like Harold. I'm not hiding anything, like Willem. I want someone with whom I can build a life. I want someone of good character, a man who is smart, loyal and trustworthy, a man who treats me well and knows how to work. Algernon is all of those things."

"Honey, listen to me," Irena pleaded. "His flaws are serious. He's got a long history of violent behavior, and there are whispers of sexual impropriety at the Temple."

"He's no more violent than any other man," Bronwyn replied. "He's a gifted martial artist, for sure – and you don't want to mess with him – but he's never raised his hand to me like Willi did to Vega last night."

"That doesn't mean he won't," Irena interjected.

Secrets and Whispers: *Hard Lines*

"Nor does it mean he will. You're afraid for me. I get that, but I'm telling you from experience that your fear is unfounded. Aside from sparring practice, I've never seen Algernon hit Kira. The two of them argue all the time, but she's not afraid of him at all. They're committed to each other. They talk through their problems, even when their emotions are high. He treats me the same way.

"You base your judgement on what other people have told you, on secrets and whispers, but I actually know him. I know what he's like when we're all alone. Nobody else does – especially your source from the Temple. I've experienced his restraint, and he's had many opportunities to take advantage of the naivete that so worries you. I know all of this first-hand. So when I tell you he's a man of self-control, why won't you believe me?"

Irena offered no response, losing herself in deep introspection. Was she so blinded by what everyone else had told her that she'd not given Algernon a chance to reveal himself? If so, why were her maternal instincts on such high alert?

She watched Bronwyn add spices to her stir fry before setting the table. "What will you do if I don't approve?" Irena asked.

Exasperated, Bronwyn raised her voice. "*Mutti*, why are you not listening to me? Have you heard nothing I've said this whole time?"

"Answer my question," Irena ordered sternly.

Bronwyn felt like crying. Why was her mother being so cold? "I love you," she countered. "I honor and respect you, and I don't want to take a hard line stance,but you're wrong about Algernon. I've thought this through very carefully and I've made up my mind. I'm getting married to him whether you approve or not."

Pillow Talk

Brenna sensed tension in her husband's demeanor. With unspoken concern she'd watched him slip back into silence, uncomfortably aware of his terse response to anyone attempting to engage in small talk. He wasn't rude, nor did he express impatience, but his reluctance to interact often resulted in single-word responses that shut down all efforts to sustain conversation.

He dared to slip his right foot between hers beneath the table at dinner, and even held her hand after the lights dimmed for the evening's entertainment. Brenna half expected him to kiss her during a few moments of total darkness between scenes, but he didn't.

After the play, he didn't want to take the streetcar back to the palace complex. "It's a pleasant evening," he noted. "Why don't we walk?"

Brenna agreed, but he didn't use their time together for talking. Instead, he reached for her hand and strolled along the darkened streets in a leisurely manner. Her husband's unusual behavior inspired a strange blend mixing mild anxiety – as the couple habitually avoided touching in public – and delight in his quiet affection and close proximity.

He'd been making a lot of progress in recent days. Brenna noticed his return to voracious reading, an uptick in the overall tidiness of their apartment on the days when Solace wasn't scheduled to clean, and the delightful restoration of laughter long suppressed by the crushing burden of combat trauma. Garrick had recently decided to learn how to play the trumpet. For at least two weeks, he'd slept through the night. His appetite had also returned. With Dr. Bauer's treatment regimen working so well, Brenna felt dismayed to witness the current setback.

Secrets and Whispers: *Pillow Talk*

After an uneventful excursion through the exclusive neighborhood near the university, the young couple walked through Equality Park and entered the damaged security gate guarding the palace entrance.

"Any news on the attack investigation?" Garrick asked the duty sergeant as he surrendered his sidearm.

The middle-aged non-com didn't even look up from her form as she accepted Garrick's weapon. "Nothing yet, sir," the woman replied.

At the cul-de-sac where the road ended and the trail to their home began its winding path through the redwoods, Brenna took his hand again while they walked. This was partly from necessity, as he could not see as well as she could, but the strength of his grip telegraphed his need of her comfort, a desire reinforced by a languid embrace at their front door.

"Did you like the play?" she asked.

He shrugged to express his indifference. "Being with you has been the best part of the evening," he replied. "I'm happy in your company."

Upstairs, Garrick unbuttoned his shirt and tossed it into the laundry hamper. He decided that he could wear this pair of trousers again, but consigned his socks to the hamper and grabbed a hanger for his slacks.

Brenna hummed a hymn in the kitchen, her melodious voice integral to the pleasant tapestry of his quiet life behind the palace wall. She moved a footstool toward the counter and stood on it to open a cupboard. Garrick heard her pouring water for herself and turned to catch her gaze. "Would you like some?" she asked.

Although it would have taken very little effort for him to fetch his own drink, Garrick recognized the countless courtesies his wife extended to him and smiled in admiration. His gratitude for her thoughtfulness strengthened his appreciation of her good character, and

Secrets and Whispers: *Pillow Talk*

he hoped that she felt similarly blessed by his kindness to her. "Thank you," he replied.

She, still wearing her evening gown, glided from the kitchen bearing a glass and a smile for her husband. After offering him the drink, Brenna slithered out of her slinky dress and discarded it on the nearby couch, but didn't take off her Lithian camisole, knowing that a little tease could be effective in stirring her husband's interest.

But he set the water on his night stand, arranged his pillows for sitting, then shut off the light. Garrick slipped into bed, rather than beckoning for his bride while he could still see her.

Brenna frowned as her eyes adjusted to the gloom. "Don't you want to see *The Twins*?" she asked quietly. "They've been wanting you all day long."

Garrick pulled the covers back for her. "Yes, I want them," he promised, "but we need to talk, first."

With a sigh, the Lithian woman willed her camisole to loosen, pulled it overhead and carelessly flung it aside. She curled up next to her beloved, resting her head on his right shoulder. "What's on your mind?" she asked.

Garrick took a drink of his water, then set the glass down. "Why do you love me?"

Brenna sat up, her bright eyes alive with alarm. "What kind of a question is that?"

At first, the pale gleam of Brenna's tetrachromatic vision in low light had seemed a little spooky. Now, however, Garrick found the sight reassuring. "I'm not questioning your devotion," he said, caressing her cheek. "I'm thinking about your father. When I first met him I remember feeling intimidated. I had to be careful about everything I said because he was listening. I had to be careful about the way I treated you because he was watching how you responded to me."

Secrets and Whispers: *Pillow Talk*

"You must have done something right," she replied. "He loves you, now."

"Not at first. He disapproved of your interest in an unbeliever, but somehow, you changed his mind."

Brenna leaned against his shoulder again, her memory alive as she absent-mindedly played with her husband's chest hair. "Did I, or did he find you impressive once he had the chance to evaluate your character?"

Garrick shook his head. "I don't know. Your mother accepted me right away, but from my point of view, it seemed clear that your father wanted you to marry someone of faith among your own people."

"If I'd met anyone of your integrity, intelligence and good looks among my own people, I might have," Brenna replied. "But my sister Cassie's prettier and she's the one all the worthy suitors wanted. No decent man found me intriguing until you came along."

That seemed hard to believe. "But your father changed his mind about me. How did that happen?"

"I told him the story of how we met, how brave you were in battle, and how patient you'd been when it came to getting under my blouse . . ."

"You actually said that to him?"

"Of course!" she responded. "He was well aware of how I'd struggled to attract the right kind of attention. Respectable men found me too devoted – either to Allfather, or to music – not slender enough for their liking, too muscular for the academic, and too smart for the athletic. The rest of them just wanted to get their hands on *The Twins*."

"Well, *The Twins* are magnificent," he stated quietly, nuzzling her ear, sliding his fingers down her shoulders and lovingly caressing her soft flesh. "Who wouldn't want to get their hands on them?"

Secrets and Whispers: *Pillow Talk*

"Hmm," she mused. "Maybe so, but they distract everyone I meet." Brenna pressed her bosom close, her desire igniting his. "I'm happy that you wanted me, but you weren't like the others. I'd never met anyone as self-disciplined. Your patience and gentle touch made me feel safe. I quickly felt confident that you sincerely loved me.

"My father went through this while courting my mother, so he understood. After he learned why I found you trustworthy, his opposition softened.

"And on top of that, I told him about your amazing mind. You're very well-read. You can talk about anything, and unlike every other man I'd met before you came along, you knew how to listen. You made me believe that my thoughts and feelings mattered to you."

"Well, they do," he stated. "You're interesting and clever in the way you apply morality to life. Everything matters to you. Every situation gives you an opportunity to shine. I admire the way you think . . ."

"Even where we disagree?" she interrupted, pulling away, leaving him a little disappointed.

The young couple usually avoided the dangerous contrast between his secular view and her piety, as that topic frequently spiraled into dissension. Garrick believed she was trying to support him in her uniquely spiritual manner, but he feared getting into a pointless argument and chose his words with care. "Our differences give us room to grow," he stated. "We're always learning and changing, but you allow me to be myself. That's one of many things I love about you."

"So why did you bring this up?" she queried, still a little worried that he hadn't addressed the unspoken issue motivating his moody disposition that evening. Instead of leaning against him again, Brenna crossed her arms and sat against her pillows.

Secrets and Whispers: *Pillow Talk*

Garrick scowled. "It's about all this strident opposition to Algernon. Bronwyn's family is supposed to be devout and close-knit, but that's an elaborate veneer. They're hiding dark secrets beneath the surface.

"Something's wrong with Willem. It's more than combat trauma, and it's more than too much drinking. I phoned his commanding officer today and learned that he's been recommended for mental health services on four occasions, but he's turned the help down every time."

"Maybe he's ashamed," Brenna remarked.

Garrick shook his head. "Perhaps, but this Lieutenant Isenberg I spoke to is no dumb woman. She told me, off the record, that family pressure is preventing the corporal from seeking treatment."

"What's that supposed to mean?"

"It's code language for, 'There's more to this than I'm at liberty to discuss.' It's linked to a hint about an internal investigation into immoral conduct. If Willem is convicted of something like that, he's facing prison."

"Poor Vega!" Brenna muttered. "She seems like the nicest of the bunch."

"She'll get his pension," Garrick stated. "That's the way it works. The army will even relocate her to a different region if she wants, and she'll qualify for subsidized housing, too. In Tamaria, we don't penalize a spouse when a soldier misbehaves."

Brenna thought about this for a moment. "What does this have to do with Algernon?"

"I wouldn't want to be in his shoes right now." Garrick snuggled closer to Brenna, enjoying the sensation of her soft skin against his. "In my case, your father gave me a chance to prove myself. It was uncomfortable at times, but he was fair with me. I don't feel like Bronwyn's family is giving my brother that courtesy."

Secrets and Whispers: *Pillow Talk*

"Marla said as much," Brenna offered. "She had a laundry list of reasons that disqualify Algernon from their consideration. She acted surprised when I defended him."

"Did it sound scripted to you?"

"Now that you mention it, I think so," she agreed.

Garrick controlled his rising anger. "Kira told me that Vega admits they'd made up their minds to oppose the engagement before any of them arrived. I suspect they've rehearsed their discussion points so that no matter how well we treat them, no matter how nice their accommodations, or how impressive Algernon may be, they fall back on a pre-written script."

"The only way to combat a narrative like that is to replace is with a more compelling one," Brenna replied. "I think that what your sister and brother have become, given the circumstances of your upbringing, shows not only remarkable resiliency, but also an unmistakably powerful spiritual and moral transformation."

He'd expected her to say something along those lines. "I agree, but the Traugotts already know where we've come from, and for a group of supposedly pious people, every one of them remained unmoved when Kira told them how that loser Marco got her hooked on opium and sold her as a slave. They didn't bat an eye when she related Algernon's harrowing rescue, either.

"They're so rigid about this that at lunch today, Darren called my sister a whore and suggested that she'd spread her legs to get wedding invites from the palace."

Astonished, Brenna sat up again. "What a completely ignorant and rude thing to say!"

"That's what I'm getting at," Garrick continued. "No matter what truth we tell, they have a counter-narrative. There's no context to anything they say, and they seem to know far more about us than they should."

Secrets and Whispers: *Pillow Talk*

"You're suggesting that they have a source on the inside?" Brenna queried. "You believe all of this intimate knowledge about Kira and Algernon is coming from someone at the Temple, someone with a vendetta?"

"Absolutely," Garrick replied. "Whether that person is still there remains an open question."

Brenna folded her hands and leaned back against her pillow, momentarily lost in thought. "It doesn't matter what they think of us," she concluded, her tone revealing more anger than resignation. "If they're determined to oppose the wedding, we can't change their minds . . ."

While Garrick suspected that Irena would eventually offer her assent, he resented the power that her family possessed to make Bronwyn and Algernon miserable. Reluctant to discuss that problem further, he changed the subject, confident that Brenna would never dismiss or ridicule the reason behind his moody silence that evening.

"I got a phone call from Talon just before your lessons finished this afternoon," Garrick explained. "He said that someone who matches Darren's description came nosing around the base, asking about me."

Knowing her husband well, Brenna's eyes shone with sympathy. "You think he's looking for dirt on you?"

Garrick nodded. "It fits the Traugott family pattern. During our tour this morning, he asked me why I wasn't working, but I didn't want to tell him."

"That's none of his business," Brenna replied.

"True, but if he finds out I'm on mental health leave, that'll be one more strike against Algernon. Willi believes I'm part of a vast conspiracy to dishonor the Defense Force, and Darren called me a liar for telling him about Kira's case against the Temple. He said we're all arrogant and looking for approval." Garrick watched his wife's bright eyes narrow. "I wasn't impressed."

Secrets and Whispers: *Pillow Talk*

Brenna tightened her lips. Her husband felt sensitive about his mental health leave, yet she'd been an eyewitness to his bravery and knew his leadership skills firsthand. "It's meaningless talk," she soothed. "He's ignorant – perhaps willfully so – but I know who you are and I'm well aware of why you struggle. If he had a fraction of your integrity, he'd hold his tongue in shame.

"I don't know where Bronwyn gets her loveable disposition. No one else in her family shares that trait. Every word and every action we've seen from her brothers proves they aren't worthy to stand in your shadow."

"You're so sweet," Garrick said quietly, pulling her near until her lips met his. A soft, lingering kiss, a firm embrace and her deepening breath fluttering rhythmically over his skin fanned the coals of his desire. He nuzzled her neck, nibbling gently on her smooth skin, moving his right hand down her bare back while his left hand traced down her collarbone.

Brenna shut her eyes, losing herself in the warmth of her husband's amorous attention. She took in a long breath and began to pray in gratitude.

***

After evening prayers in the living area with Kira and Bronwyn, exhausted Algernon brushed his teeth and went to bed. Much to Bronwyn's dismay, he'd fallen asleep within moments of lying down. She'd stood in the doorway wanting to confide in him, and draw strength from his confidence, but she didn't have the heart to awaken him.

Wistfully, Bronwyn pulled the door closed, glanced at Ileana – who often spent her evenings writing letters at the kitchen table – then tiptoed towards Kira's room and quietly knocked on the door.

Secrets and Whispers: *Pillow Talk*

Kira, who'd been expecting – and believed she partly deserved – a diatribe for hitting Heidelinde, held her breath. Yet Bronwyn's expression revealed sorrow, not anger, and the emotion brimming in the young woman's eyes stirred Kira's sympathy. She reached for her cane, rose from her bed, and wordlessly opened her arms.

"I'm so sad!" Bronwyn lamented, stepping into Kira's embrace and weeping into the smaller woman's hair. "Why is everyone against me?"

"Shh," Kira soothed quietly, holding her friend close. "You know that isn't true."

With her emotions running high, Bronwyn vented a litany of frustrations. "My brothers hate me! Their wives are horrible, and my mother says I'm a fool!

"Everything I do is wrong. Everything I say is wrong. Every time I try to fix things and make my people feel better, they turn on me!

"Why are they treating me like this? What have I done to make them so nasty? Why can't they just be happy for me?"

Kira shook her head. "You don't deserve this, Bron. You're a good woman, a faithful friend and my formidable ally. I couldn't serve like I do without your help."

Unable to respond, Bronwyn leaned on Kira's shoulder and sobbed. As the two women sat on the bed, Kira rocked Bronwyn gently and let her cry. Knowing she needed affection, not advice, Kira held her tongue.

A moment later, Ileana abandoned her writing and appeared in the doorway. The Lithian woman placed her hand on Bronwyn's shoulder, closed her eyes and began to pray in her alliterative native tongue. Neither of the other women could understand her words – though Kira had heard Brenna pray like this many times – but they fully understood her intent.

Secrets and Whispers: *Pillow Talk*

Affirmed by the feminine solidarity, Bronwyn slowly regained her composure. Kira handed her a handkerchief, with which Bronwyn dried her eyes, and into which she blew her nose. Ileana offered an affectionate squeeze of her shoulder before quietly leaving the room.

Bronwyn smiled weakly and watched the slender, snow-haired Lithian woman go. Returning her attention to Kira she asked, "What am I going to do?"

"You start with the relationships that are least damaged, and build from there," Kira suggested. "From what you've been telling me, your dad should be first."

Bronwyn nodded. "He would listen," she agreed.

"Tell him how you're feeling about all of this. I'm sure he already has an idea how hurtful the last couple of days have been for you."

"Then what?" Bronwyn queried. "It's not like I need his permission to marry."

Remembering Garrick's advice, Kira continued. "That's true, but he's probably got more influence with your mom than anyone else."

Hearing this, Bronwyn shook her head. "Why is it that you and Algernon want to strengthen my bonds with family, while my brothers and my mom want to tear them apart? If it were the other way around, I'd be concerned that you were trying to isolate and manipulate me."

"My only agenda is loyalty to you and my brother," Kira promised. "I support you because I love you."

"They're supposed to love me too!" Bronwyn cried. "It's ironic that I'm getting encouragement and wisdom from the people my mother thinks are degenerate thugs. Why can't she see in you what's so obvious to me?"

"She's afraid, Bron. That's what she's been saying all along. Your brothers have dysfunctional marriages. She doesn't want that for you, so she's focused on our flaws."

Secrets and Whispers: *Pillow Talk*

Bronwyn sighed in frustration. "It's not like she's warning me about stuff I don't already know! In fact, I could tell her racy things about you and Algernon that she's never heard . . ."

"But she doesn't trust that you're thinking straight right now," Kira said calmly.

Bronwyn shook her head. "I can't convince my mother of anything. It's like she's already made up her mind. Just before she left this afternoon, she warned that she's not only willing to disinherit me, she'd try to nullify my marriage in court. My own mother threatened me with legal action. She's completely irrational!"

Kira thought for a moment. "There's a way around that," she suggested. "You won't like it, but we could stop your mom from having any legal grounds against you."

Suspecting what Kira was going to say, Bronwyn crossed her arms and tightened her lips. "Tell me."

"I know it's not what you want, but we could get Astrid to sanction the wedding. She'd do it if I asked her."

Bronwyn shook her head, still struggling to forgive the newly promoted High Priestess for the way she'd behaved while they lived at the Temple. "I'd go to Kameron first. She's the last person I want at my wedding!"

"I understand," Kira replied, though she felt mildly annoyed that Bronwyn wouldn't let go of her ill will. "But as High Priestess, her consent has higher legal standing than your mother's. That would be the easiest way to overcome your mom's opposition."

After a deep sigh, Bronwyn's eyes brimmed with tears again. She stared at the ceiling, trying to avoid another bout of weeping. "I don't want to fight with anyone," she sniffed. "I want *Mutti* to help you tie my hand to Algernon's. Why can't she let me make my own choices? Why is she treating me like a child?"

Secrets and Whispers: *Pillow Talk*

"I know," Kira soothed, rubbing Bronwyn's broad back and pulling her into an embrace again. "I'm really sorry that you're going through such pain right now. I know you wanted this to be a happy time."

Bronwyn pulled away after a few moments and sniffed. "*Mutti* asked me to delay the wedding for six months. She said I needed time to think."

Kira held her breath. She'd spent a lot of money on the celebration thus far and didn't want to see that going to waste. "Can you wait that long?"

Slowly shaking her head from side to side, Bronwyn gazed at Kira with sadness. "I have this hunger inside me," she admitted. "I want to be Algernon's wife. I want to give him everything he needs. I want him to be satisfied and happy with me."

"Is he unhappy with you now?" Kira asked.

Averting her eyes, Bronwyn tightened her lips again. "You know what I mean," she said quietly.

"Oh . . ." replied Kira, who had a hard time thinking about her brother in an amorous context. She knew he'd been badly hurt by their mother's rejection, and that his emotional neediness frightened other girls who'd caught his eye. Algernon could be assertive and persistent if he didn't get what he wanted, prompting Kira to inquire, "Is he pressuring you into having sex? Do you want me to talk to him?"

"No!" Bronwyn insisted, trying to avoid a discussion concerning physical intimacy. "It's me. It's not him."

Kira squeezed her friend's hand. "You've been around my brother long enough to know who he is. You know his strengths, and you know his flaws . . ."

"Much better than my mother does," Bronwyn interrupted. "She thinks he's prone to violence, and she's worried that he'll start hurting me."

Secrets and Whispers: *Pillow Talk*

Flashing a pretty smile, Kira cupped her own bosom in her hands and shook them. "Put your pillows in his face, and he'll be putty in your fingers."

Bronwyn tried and failed to suppress a grin. She sputtered, and then the two young women began laughing out loud. Kira thought it was wonderful to hear Bronwyn's laughter again.

***

Mariel Hougen sat in bed, reading through the draft of her report. Immersed in her analysis, she muttered aloud without worry that someone might overhear.

"Why would Old Order carry out an attack on our palace?" she mused. "What do they gain?"

She'd visited a military intelligence archive that afternoon and read every paper she could find mentioning the Kurian nationalist group. Although they'd organized many violent demonstrations, their terror attacks in the Nordan coastal colony had been poorly coordinated and unprofessional – typically involving a small group of minimally-trained activists using handheld weapons, or bombs no bigger than a grenade. Their reputation for successful assassinations seemed inflated, at best.

If Old Order planned and carried out the attack on Tamaria's palace, this represented an order-of-magnitude increase in coordination, sophistication and lethality. Being able to conduct an operation involving the acquisition of materials and assembly of a powerful bomb in a foreign country represented an incredible advance in the group's capabilities.

But these people could barely construct a sentence. How were they able to successfully pull off a lethal strike deep in Tamaria's heartland? And what was their motive?

Secrets and Whispers: *Pillow Talk*

Mariel wrote "prestige" in the margin of her draft. An operation on foreign soil would likely raise the credibility of the group as a viable threat against the ruling power, but the only reason Mariel could imagine they'd chosen Tamaria and not the Nord Islands was because the Old Order lacked the means to challenge the Nordans' powerful navy.

This explanation didn't resolve the question of why Tamaria had been selected as a target, nor did it address how the group managed to evolve its capabilities so quickly. That brought up an entirely different possibility.

"What if it's not you people at all? What if someone wants us to think it's you when it's not?"

Mariel scrunched her brow and sat up, reaching for a goblet of red wine she'd poured before going to bed. If this was an elaborate set-up, whose political agenda would be advanced? She took a drink, swished it to the back of her tongue and set the wine back down. Picking up her notebook, she began brainstorming anew.

She didn't think the Nordans needed an ally to crush a minor insurrection. After all, their navy rivaled the Kamerese navy in power, and no one could stop them from enacting a blockade or quarantine of every port. They could supply their ground forces with impunity with no one, other than the Kamerese, able to interdict their shipping. Their firm control over the coast assured that any support for groups like the Old Order had to come from inland nations – either the Vatherans in the north, Tamaria to the east, or Kameron to the south.

If someone in Tamaria happened to be supplying weapons or expertise to rebel groups, Mariel knew nothing about it. While there were elements of elite Tamarian Special Forces operating in the mountainous frontier region, their mission involved reconnaissance, not combat. They'd been ordered to avoid confrontations that might

Secrets and Whispers: *Pillow Talk*

provoke the Nordans, and as far as Mariel knew, they'd been successful.

So if weapons or training had been funneled through Tamaria, it couldn't have been a government-sanctioned action. That not only limited the potential scope of a weapons supply operation to the level of smuggling, it also made the palace an unlikely target. After all, conducting an act of war over a minor issue like gun running seemed ham-fisted, at best. Captain Hougen didn't think the Nordans were that stupid.

That left two possibilities. Either Old Order had new leadership and significantly better training, or Tamaria's Kamerese allies were complicit . . .

Mariel shuddered. "You wouldn't betray us, would you?" she queried rhetorically in Kamerese, one of seven languages she spoke fluently. "But if you did, who'd plan something like this, and why?"

Tamaria, a landlocked nation, could not participate in a maritime conflict. Thus, Kameron gained nothing in its naval rivalry with the Nordans by provoking their allies into a fight on the Kurian coast. Additionally, the Kamerese had a large, modern and capably commanded land army at their disposal. Official Kamerese involvement made no sense.

But that's when Mariel remembered Brenna's sister, Cassie. She and her boyfriend had been the guests of Kamerese King Alejo at the palace during the civil war in that country. Hadn't she talked about terror groups using bombs? Hadn't there been an attack on the palace there?

That last thought quickened Mariel's pulse. Instinctively she reached for her phone, but noting the time, reconsidered. "The lieutenant retires early," she mused. "I wouldn't want to interrupt his pillow talk."

***

Secrets and Whispers: *Pillow Talk*

Although she tried reading as a means of distracting her mind from maternal worry, Irena couldn't focus on her novel. She'd read the same paragraph four times before abandoning the book in frustration. Impatiently, she waited for Arvid to finish in the bathroom.

"Are you nearly done, dear?" she asked.

Arvid, his lips foaming with toothpaste, appeared in the bathroom doorway and nodded. He vanished for a few moments, turned on the water to rinse his mouth, then wiped his face with a towel and shut off the bathroom light. "Doesn't the book interest you?"

Irena glowered at her husband. "How can you pretend that nothing's wrong?"

Arvid slipped out of his robe. His broad chest and strong arms, now graced with grey hair, still captivated his wife's interest. "I'm pretending no such thing," he replied, climbing into bed. "Bronwyn refused to come with us this evening, Harold and Heidelinde have left, while neither Sikki nor Vega bothered to attend.

"Willi's acting like a scared cat. Darren squirmed like a guilty schoolboy all night, while Lieutenant Ravenwood – with his pretty little Lithian wife – sat at their own table as if they'd never met our acquaintance. I'm sure your sister could write another dissertation on the deep dysfunction in our family right now."

Irena crossed her arms. "The root of this issue is that our daughter is being unreasonable and stubborn!"

"So you're happy with the outcome of your conversation this afternoon?"

He'd hit a nerve. Irena abandoned her book and swallowed hard, fighting back tears. "Bronwyn won't listen to reason," Irena rasped.

Arvid drew near, reaching for his wife's hand and squeezing it affectionately. "She's in love," he stated quietly. "Since when has love been rational?"

Secrets and Whispers: *Pillow Talk*

Irena glared at her husband, annoyed that he'd fallen into the habit of taking Bronwyn's side.

When she didn't reply, Arvid continued. "I know you feel disrespected right now," he soothed.

"Disrespected?" Irena spat, withdrawing her hand. "She was downright rude to me! I've never heard such insolence from her. This is the fruit of her ill-considered association with those . . . with those people!

"After all this time, she should know that I love her. After raising her and supporting her, giving her a decent home and moral instruction, she should know that all I want is her success and happiness!"

Arvid raised his brow. "Step out of your own concern for a moment and consider Bronwyn's point of view. Like it or not, she loves Algernon. How does your strident disapproval of that reality show support?"

"Why are you taking her side in this? Can't you see how dangerous these people are? Or have you fallen under Kira's charismatic spell?"

"That's foolish talk!" Arvid replied sternly. "Don't dishonor my fidelity by insisting I approve of everything you do. I love you enough to be honest, even when it hurts. There are no sides here. Bronwyn is my daughter as much as she is yours. Why would anyone, especially her own mother, expect me to refrain from defending her? Your strong opposition to Bronwyn's marriage is breaking both her heart and yours."

Irena shook her head. "Our little girl is making the worst decision of her life. Her choice is going to lead into poverty, squalor and abject misery! That boy is violent. That whole family is nothing but bad news . . ."

Arvid scoffed. "From what we've witnessed, he's very gentle with her, even when he's disappointed. Have you seen so much as a single bruise on Bronwyn?"

"No," Irena admitted.

Secrets and Whispers: *Pillow Talk*

"She'd been alone with Algernon, possibly for hours, before we arrived. He'd been dishonored by Harold and Heidelinde the night before, and she was upset over all the disharmony in our family, yet she boldly paraded around the kitchen in a daredevil, spaghetti-strapped tank top without showing so much as a single mark of mistreatment on her body. You keep insisting that he's going to harm her, but you've seen nothing to indicate that he's ever done so."

"That doesn't mean he won't," Irena countered. "Look at what Willi did to Vega . . ."

"Willi was drunk. Did you notice that neither Algernon nor his brother touched the beer and wine?"

"No, I didn't notice," Irena admitted. "But what does that matter?"

"It illustrates that you're seeing what you want to see, not necessarily what's really there. That's why you can't comprehend Bronwyn's interest in that young man.

"Last night Kira had only one drink with her meal. Brenna had wine with dinner, but didn't finish her glass. Both she and Garrick drank only water at the dinner play this evening. That's no second-hand anecdote. We can see that the Ravenwood men don't drink."

After being married to Arvid for nearly 50 years, Irena felt confident that he wouldn't cross her without good reason. She trusted him to speak truthfully, even when she didn't like hearing what he had to say. Although this felt very uncomfortable for her, she was woman enough to listen. Fighting back tears again, she asked, "I am really being irrational?"

He nodded.

Irena let out a deep sigh. "Okay, beloved husband. What do you see that I'm missing?"

Arvid arranged his pillows so he could lean against them while he spoke. Before he continued, he took her

Secrets and Whispers: *Pillow Talk*

hand in his again. "You spoke to Kira and then Vega for nearly an hour after Bronwyn's departure this morning. By the time our taxi arrived at the homestead, the soldiers working there said they'd seen her leave with Algernon."

"Okay," Irena agreed. "What's your point?"

"The porch had been swept clean. Bronwyn didn't know we were coming, so no one could have cleaned the place to impress us in anticipation of our arrival . . ."

Irena didn't respond.

"When we walked around the property, did you notice the abundance in the garden beds, the excellent repair of their fencing, and their weed control? All their tools had been hung in a shed. Everything about that homestead reflects thought, loving care and attention to detail. Is this what you expect from thugs?"

"It was tidy up there, but that doesn't detract from Algernon's violent history," Irena contended.

"We're missing the context to his past. If violence is his preferred problem-solving method, we'd see evidence of that propensity now. But you know that Bronwyn isn't hiding bruises. You've admitted that the Ravenwoods have no alcohol problem. You've witnessed the affection in their family – a tenderness and respect that they also extend to Bronwyn. You've heard them defend one another. All of these things point to a functional, mutually-supportive family. Why wouldn't you want Bronwyn involved with people who treat each other like this?"

"What if it's all an elaborate show?" Irena asked. "What if they're just acting this way to impress us?"

"Is that what Marla thinks?" Arvid countered, knowing his sister-in-law had been favorably impressed after her morning run with Brenna. "You invited her along for that reason."

Irena shook her head. "It's absurd to grant such weight to the testimony of a Lithian witch who heals

Secrets and Whispers: *Pillow Talk*

wounds with a kiss. I'll grant that Brenna is an adorable little thing – despite that scar on her neck – but why is she more credible than my source at the Temple?"

Arvid shrugged. "You won't tell me who your contact is, yet you insist that this person is above reproach. Have you wondered why you're getting so many negative stories? Is it possible there's an old score being settled?"

Although Irena didn't answer, her cheeks burned and she couldn't maintain eye contact.

"You heard Kira tell a moving tale about how she was hooked on opium and lured to Kameron by a wealthy, smooth-talking drug dealer. Vega says the Ravenwood girl ran away from abuse at the Temple, believing this fellow would give her a better life, but he led her into a war zone and then sold her as a slave.

"Yet Algernon, whom you believe is inveterate, refused to give up on her. You're worried about the violence associated with that story, but overlook the fact that this young man loves his sister deeply enough to travel into very dangerous territory, risking his own life for hers. This is not the behavior of a man who takes what he wants by force and turns away in apathy. Algernon cares for his loved ones and defends them when they're vulnerable. Why wouldn't you want that kind of devotion for Bronwyn?"

"It's inevitable that he's going to hurt her!" Irena insisted. "A violent disposition is central to his character. That fact rightfully worries me."

Patiently, Arvid continued. "We've received respect in deed and in word from him in every instance. Aside from Kira's incident with Heidelinde – which, knowing her as well as we do, she likely deserved – they've treated us better than our family has been treating them.

"After enduring insults from our son and having his character publically smeared by Heidelinde, Algernon

Secrets and Whispers: *Pillow Talk*

uttered not a word in his own defense. He didn't get angry, nor did he retaliate. Bronwyn didn't show any fear that he might lash out against her. She's not afraid of him, and that should mean something to you."

"She's in love, Arvid. Our little girl is totally smitten by this handsome boy and his beautiful, charming, seductive sister. Bronwyn can't think straight. She's even admitted to participating in violence, herself!"

"You heard the story, my dear. She was defending her home against an armed intruder. She believes she had an obligation to protect the young girl whom they'd rescued. There's a context to her behavior."

Irena shook her head. "Our daughter is not violent! If she's become that way, it's because her friendship with these Ravenwood people has warped her character."

"Let me remind you that neither Kira nor Algernon taught Bronwyn how to fight. That's a skill she learned while studying at the Temple. You know that ministering to the downtrodden brings risk. As part of her spiritual training, Bronwyn learned the skills she needed to survive an encounter with violent people – in this case, a man who went to the homestead with a shotgun and ill intent.

"Do you think that if she'd politely asked him to leave the premises, he would have done so? We all agree that she did something terrible that day. She admits as much herself, but her decisive action is the reason she's still alive with her virtue intact.

"She's not a little girl anymore, my darling. Bronwyn is a grown woman, with adult thoughts and adult needs. She's found someone with whom she can build a life, and they've made a great deal of progress already. They have an active ministry that inspires our concern, but is ministry nonetheless. They live in a beautiful area, in a spacious home that's already well-established and comfortable. It will be a great place to raise children."

Secrets and Whispers: *Pillow Talk*

Irena shook her head. "He's taken a vow of poverty. There is no way he can provide for them, especially when the babies come along."

"How can you say that? Think about the impressive size of Kira's house, the abundance you witnessed in their garden, and the modernity of their lifestyle. His vow of poverty is about a commitment to living in community, not promise of perpetual misery."

"That's Kira's place, not Bronwyn's," Irena stated.

"Why is that a problem?" Arvid countered.

"Because she'll always be living at Kira's mercy. She'll always be an underling in that household. What Kira wants she'll get, and Bronwyn will defer to her.

"Remember what Vega told us. Kira admits to seducing Bronwyn at the Temple. My source was right about her. That girl is manipulative, and any environment where she has control is not an ideal situation for our daughter, especially when children come along."

Arvid drew near, pausing to let the tension rise. "If that's really a concern, why are you threatening to withhold her dowry and disinherit her?"

"I don't want to see those people benefitting from the wealth we've spent our whole lives building," Irena replied. "I don't want her to partner with a lazy leech who will drain her resources dry and then leave her in squalor to raise children all alone."

"Nothing in their household had its origin with us," Arvid countered. "Their home on Superstition Mesa is bigger and more comfortable than ours. They've built everything there without our help."

"Only because Kira's rich . . ."

Arvid raised his brow and leaned back against his pillow. "Your premises are conflicting," he corrected. "You can't complain on one hand that Bronwyn is marrying a

Secrets and Whispers: *Pillow Talk*

poor priest, while on the other insisting that the source of their comfort is his twin sister's wealth.

"While I share your concern about Kira's power over Bronwyn, Vega also told us that the seduction incident was a one-time event. Let me remind you that when we first met, you were involved in similar experimentation. We know that Willem has propensities along those lines, yet he and Vega remain committed."

"So then, why are you insisting that I'm not seeing the whole picture?" Irena asked, a little hurt that her husband so rightly pointed out her own flaws.

"Because your intransigence is damaging both you and Bronwyn. The more stridently you insist that she lacks good judgment, the harder you're pushing her away. Threatening her with lawsuits and disinheritance only strengthens her opposition . . ."

"Well what would you have me do?" Irena shouted. "I have good reasons to oppose this marriage. It's my right as her mother to insist that Bronwyn think this through!"

"Have you not spoken your piece?"

"I have. She's not listening."

"No, my darling. That isn't true. Don't mistake her lack of compliance with lack of comprehension. She's heard everything you've said and she fully understands your opposition. The problem here is that Bronwyn disagrees with you."

Irena grew more impatient. "I have the final say in this matter," she insisted. "Bronwyn must obey me!"

"So this is about power?" Arvid queried. "You love Bronwyn, but your need for control over her is an idol to which you are sacrificing your relationship with her."

Stunned by her husband's accusation, Irena fell silent. Her eyes widened as the truth of his testimony burned in her breast. Her emotions rose and spilled down her eyes in streams of regret. Although she tried to

Secrets and Whispers: *Pillow Talk*

control herself, something profoundly spiritual moved in her soul and she began to weep bitterly.

"What have I done?" she lamented. "I love my little girl! I never wanted to hurt her!"

Arvid wrapped his wife in a compassionate embrace. "I know," he reassured. "I believe you."

***

Willem heard the hotel room door open and watched his wife walk in. "You're late," he stated.

Vega glanced at the bed where her husband lay in his underwear and a t-shirt, noting the empty beer bottles on his night stand. "You're drunk," she replied.

He glared at Vega as she sauntered across the room, the sensuous movement of her hips and trembling of her barely-contained bosom accentuated by high-heeled shoes. None of that mattered to him, but Willem felt betrayed that she'd left him alone that evening.

"So, where'd you go?"

"Out," she replied disinterestedly, setting her purse on the dresser. Vega hung her 3/4 sleeve bolero in the room's closet and removed her shoes. "My cousin is much better company than you are right now."

"Well, you stink of smoke and you look like a slut!"

Unwilling to dignify that remark with a response, Vega retrieved her purse, went into the bathroom and shut the door. Glancing at her aging reflection in the mirror, she breathed nervously. Willi could be dangerous after he'd been drinking. Should she go somewhere else?

Sikki and Darren would want privacy. Irena and Arvid might take her in, but they always sided with Willem. That left Marla, who'd ask uncomfortable questions while faithfully defending her nephew.

Secrets and Whispers: *Pillow Talk*

Vega opened her purse, revealing the .25 caliber revolver she'd bought that afternoon as a deterrent against further abuse. The vendor had warned that the weapon was too small to do any real damage. "You're unlikely to stop a determined attacker with this thing," he'd argued.

But Vega didn't really want to hurt anyone. She just wanted to make sure that Willi would stop hitting her.

Willem heard the sound of her urinating, closely followed by the toilet flushing. He staggered to his feet and waited in front of the bathroom door with a half empty beer in hand, listening until she activated the shower. He tried the doorknob, but found it locked.

"Come on!" he complained, pounding the door with his flattened hand. "We need to talk!"

"You said that I smell like smoke," she replied. "I'm just washing my hair. I'll be out shortly."

That was a lie. She didn't want to deal with him. Vega waited for him to respond, hearing nothing for nearly a minute before she hurriedly undressed and stepped under the water. What was she going to do?

Hoping that he'd fall asleep, Vega showered slowly, lingering under the hot water, letting her imagination wander until he pounded on the door again. Shocked back into her unpleasant reality, she shut the water off.

"What are you doing in there?" he shouted.

"I'll be out soon," she promised.

"Why did you desert me?" he complained through the door. "We had a deal. You act like the dutiful wife to make us look good, and you'll get part of the estate in the end. Leaving me to attend that stupid dinner function by myself was not part of the plan."

"You're drunk again!" she complained. "You've got a better relationship with the bottle than you do with me. Your behavior is the problem here, not mine!"

Secrets and Whispers: *Pillow Talk*

He hated the fact that she kept calling out his drinking. "It's your fault!" he shouted. "You're discarding me when I need you."

"I'm not responsible for your choices!" she replied.

"You've driven me to this!"

"Not true! We have a sham of a marriage, and you know it! You're just using me to make yourself look good."

Willem leaned against the door. "Oh, come on, baby! It's not forever. We've just got to get through this wedding business with my stupid cow of a sister. Once she bonks that boy of hers, Mother will do the right thing."

"This has nothing to do with me!"

"The hell it doesn't!" Willem argued. "I needed you, but you weren't there. Everyone else at the dinner had a date. Even Lieutenant Ravenwood showed up with his little tart of a wife – all tits and no brains! It's not fair you made me go by myself. People talk. They're gonna figure it out sooner or later."

At that moment, hotel security knocked on the main door. "Is everything all right in there?" a man's voice demanded sternly.

"Yeah, we're just talking," Willem insisted.

"You need to keep it down, sir. Other guests are complaining about your frequent shouting."

Willem put his beer down, his mind racing. "Yeah, okay. No more shouting. I got it. You can go away now."

"Ma'am, can you hear me?" the male voice inquired.

"Yes," Vega replied.

"Are you safe?"

Trembling, Vega feared making a scene. "Yes," she said, her voice desperately trying to cover the lie.

"Very well, ma'am. If you have any trouble, please call the desk right away."

"Okay, I will," she promised.

Secrets and Whispers: *Pillow Talk*

Waiting for the security team to depart, Willem drained his bottle, leaned against the wall and belched.

"I'm waiting," he said, trying to speak just loud enough for his wife to hear, but not so loud to alert anyone else's attention.

Before she opened the door, Vega put her purse into her right hand, holding it behind her back. The moment she unlocked the bathroom door, Willem charged forward. He grabbed the top of the towel she'd girded herself with, his momentum shoving her backward, and as she fell he snapped the towel off.

"You stupid slut!" he spat. "Your fuss made them come here. You're gonna pay for this!"

Vega fell naked to the tile and slammed into the bathtub. Her purse slid beside the toilet as he grabbed hold of her left leg, intending to drag her out of the bathroom. It hurt. There was nothing sexual about his behavior. He wanted to humiliate her now.

She squirmed, desperate to get away from the violence she knew would be forthcoming. Because her leg was still wet, she managed to wriggle free. With singular, purposeful focus, Vega reached for her gun, twisting to face her husband and pointing the weapon at his chest. "Get away from me!" she screamed.

Although he'd been under fire before, Willem had never faced a gun in such close quarters. Despite its small size, the tiny weapon had its intended effect. He slowly retreated with his hands held aloft. "Aw come on, baby! You don't mean it . . ."

"Get out!" she warned, slowly rising to her feet.

"Where am I supposed to go?" he complained.

"I don't care. Just get out of the room now!" As she stood, Vega held her weapon steady, her steps a mirror of his as she directed him into the hall. Another guest

Secrets and Whispers: *Pillow Talk*

paused in terror as Willem retreated. Once he was outside, Vega slammed the door shut and locked it.

***

Sikki pursed her lips as she sat on the hotel bed, her irritation further evident in crossed arms and a scowl that lined her face. After enduring several moments of her husband's silence, she shook her head. "So, what did you do with your deadbeat brother?"

Darren began to undress for the second time that evening. "I put him in a cab and sent him to Bronwyn."

"What a stupid idea," Sikki mocked. "He's drunk. What if he tells her about the plan?"

"What else could I do?" Darren groused. "If security found him wandering the halls in his underwear, there'd be a scandal. Mother's already been on my back about protecting the family's reputation.

"You probably shouldn't have gone out with Vega tonight. From what Willi says, that's what got him drinking in the first place."

"So this is my fault?" she countered defensively. "I don't control his addiction. He made the choice to get wasted tonight, not me."

After laying his trousers on the back of a chair, Darren sat on the bed to remove his socks. "We need to be patient and unified through this. Just a few days of working together until my desperate sister does the right thing, and the dowry and inheritance come to us.

"But you and Vega decided to go off on your own, leaving us looking like a pair of lonely old bachelors. Willi starts to drink, and then Vega threatens him with a gun the two of you bought this afternoon. Tell me how you had no influence over what happened this evening . . ."

Secrets and Whispers: *Pillow Talk*

"Look," Sikki snapped. "Your wastrel brother has been abusing my cousin for years, and it's getting worse. She's finally had enough, and I don't blame her.

"After the scene at dinner last night, she tried to make up with him, like she always does. And again, he was full of tears and promises. But Vega's heard all this before. He'll never change, and she knows better than to trust him anymore. He would've hurt her badly tonight if she hadn't bought the gun for protection, so don't shift the blame for your brother's bad behavior onto me!"

Stifling a snarky retort, Darren removed his socks and tossed them near the window seat. "I'm not blaming you for my brother's drinking problem," he insisted. "I'm saying that if you'd stuck with the plan, he'd not have been alone in the room with nothing to do except get himself plastered. We should have stayed together. That way we could have set limits to his consumption."

"The plan is falling apart," Sikki snapped. "You can't manage your brothers. They've not done what they'd agreed to do, and that puts our plan in peril. Harold ran after Heidelinde after that brainless bimbo hit her. Willi is totally out of control. He shows up here in his underwear, stupidly drunk, and you see no problem with giving him a set of your clothes and sending him off to Bronwyn!"

Darren shook his head. "You need to relax. We've got plenty of dirt on these Ravenwood people, and more keeps turning up. I found out this afternoon that our war hero, Lieutenant Ravenwood, is on mental health leave."

Sikki raised her brow. "How do you know?"

"I went to Fort Aeolus this afternoon and asked around. I went to a club where the men drink and met a soldier named Luther, who happens to be in the lieutenant's platoon. He had plenty to say."

"Go on," Sikki encouraged, a hint of hope rising in her voice.

Secrets and Whispers: *Pillow Talk*

"Luther told me that Lieutenant Ravenwood didn't have what it takes to pass Officer Training School. The Expeditionary Force commanders were so desperate for combat leaders, they gave him a battlefield promotion before they deployed to Kameron. Luther says he's been on the ragged edge of disaster ever since. Everyone hates having him as XO in garrison because he's young and full of self-importance."

"None of that is helpful to us," Sikki interrupted.

Darren corrected her in a mild tone motivated by longstanding love. "I'm not done, my dear. It turns out that LT Ravenwood's been on mental health leave for a couple of months. He had a gunfight in the street, followed by an incident where he threatened the high priest. The kid is unstable."

That accusation raised Sikki's brow. Everyone in the Traugott family had high regard for the Temple. "But that has nothing to do with Algernon," she stated. "The older brother's behavior is no more a reflection of Algernon's character than Willi's bottle binges reflect on yours."

"It matters to my mother," Darren countered. "That's what counts. When she does her investing, she looks at the way company leaders get along with their staff. She says that strong relationships build good character, especially in the formative years, and that's why it's important to evaluate family dynamics. She didn't criticize you at all until after she'd spent time with your parents."

Sikki remembered. Irena had been very hard to persuade. "Still, she gave her consent in the end."

"Yes, but your family isn't as screwed up as these Ravenwoods are. It's only a matter of time before they reveal their true colors. We've got Sergeant Sigvald's youngest brother on the inside – that kid who's Algernon's friend – plus what we know of Lieutenant Ravenwood, straight from the mouth of someone who serves under

Secrets and Whispers: *Pillow Talk*

him. Once mother learns of this, there's no way she'll ever agree to let my little sister marry Algernon."

"But if Willem blurts out the truth in one of his famous moments of regret, your sister may call the whole thing off just to spite us," Sikki replied, pointing out what she thought should be obvious and frustrated that Darren didn't get it. "Your brothers don't know how to shut up. They're impulsive and they always react in the moment."

Darren slid under the covers, drawing near and lowering his voice. "Bronwyn is not beautiful, like you," he murmured. "She's an overweight heifer whose got nothing going for her. She's found this defective family and they're the best she can do. The only reason Algernon's interested in my sister is because he's so damaged no one else will give him a second look. There's no way she'll ever turn the eye of a normal man. She's too ugly, too heavy and too stupid to attract anyone decent.

"This is Bronwyn's one chance to get married and everyone knows it. She's totally smitten with this pariah priest, but Mother will never approve of her union with a thug like him. As long as we stay calm and stick to our plan, we'll get what's rightfully ours."

Sikki reached for the lamp on her bedside table, switched it off and rolled over. She'd had enough for one evening. "You'd better be right," she warned.

Darren slid his hand across her belly and up to her breast, kissing her shoulder. He loved Sikki. After more than 30 years of marriage, he still found her attractive. "You'll see, honey," he whispered.

Sikki felt his arousal, but his touch annoyed her. "Stop it!" she insisted. "I'm not in the mood right now."

***

Secrets and Whispers: *Pillow Talk*

Ileana put her hand on Kira's shoulder and gently shook her hostess. "Wake up!" she urged in vulgate. "There's a man at the door."

Kira stirred from a sound slumber and glanced at her bedside clock. She heard the urgent sound of a male voice calling for Bronwyn and reached for her cane. "Get dressed," she urged. "It can't be good news at this hour."

As Ileana retreated, Kira hobbled to her dresser and pulled out the .32 caliber handgun Garrick had once insisted she take for protection. Calmly, she loaded the weapon, limped over to the hook on the back of her door and slipped into her robe.

"Come on, Bronwyn!" the male voice shouted. "It's cold and dark out here!"

Kira flipped on the outside light switch, opened the door and steadied herself to use the weapon.

Momentarily blinded, Willem took a step back and swore as he focused on the barrel of yet another handgun. "Don't shoot me!" he pleaded. "I won't hurt you!"

"Yeah, right!" Kira muttered, recognizing the odor and behavior of a drunkard. She lowered her gun. "You couldn't piss your way out of a paper bag right now."

"Look, I'm sorry for bugging you, but can I talk to my sister?"

Kira scowled. "You can wait." She shut and locked the front door, ignoring Willem's protests as she limped over to the room Bronwyn shared with Algernon, muttering foul words in irritation for being awakened.

"What's going on?" Algernon asked, stopping his sister before she entered the room.

"It's Bron's brother, Willem," Kira replied. "He showed up at the door smelling like he's taken a bath in Dad's fermentation vat . . ."

Algernon kissed her forehead. "Go back to bed," he recommended. "I'll deal with him."

Secrets and Whispers: *Pillow Talk*

"You're actually gonna let him in while he's plastered?" Kira asked, incredulously.

"He's our brother," Algernon replied quietly. "We can't leave him outside."

Kira rolled her eyes. "Fine!" she whispered. "Do whatever you want. He's your problem . . ." The young woman hobbled back to her bedroom and shut the door.

Outside, Willem continued to wail for Bronwyn. In desperation, he began to bang on the door again. Annoyed with this behavior, Algernon confronted him on the porch. "What are you doing here?" the monk demanded.

"Where's my sister?" Willem replied, trying to push past Algernon, yet finding the smaller man impossible to move out of the way.

Calmly, Algernon responded, "She's sleeping. Now answer me. What are you doing here at this hour?"

"Come on!" Willem moaned, growing angry. "Just get out of my way and let me in!"

"Don't be stupid," Algernon warned menacingly.

Willem, partly due to his diminishing intoxication, sensed something very dangerous in Algernon's demeanor. In the first wise decision he made that evening, Bronwyn's wayward brother backed off. "I had a fight with Vega," he admitted, his voice brimming with remorse. "She kicked me out and I have nowhere else to go."

Algernon resisted the urge to criticize. He watched as Willem slumped into sobbing against one of the porch posts, struggling to suppress disgust. Because he'd seen this sort of remorse in his own father, finding even a pittance of pity proved difficult. Waiting for the older man to regain control, Algernon held his tongue. "You can sleep in the living room tonight," he offered at length. "But you have to be quiet. If you make a fuss, I'll call the sheriff and you can spend the night in lockup."

"Okay," Willi promised.

Secrets and Whispers: *Pillow Talk*

"And there is no alcohol in this house, so don't go looking for the hair of the dog when you're hung over. Once you're sober, we'll talk. But for now, leave your shoes out here and wash up in the bathroom. I'll get you a blanket."

Willem complied meekly, astonished at the homestead's massive beams and spacious interior as he stepped inside. Following Algernon's directions to the bathroom, he washed his face and used the toilet.

"I'm obliged," he mumbled as he returned to the living area, glancing about in curiosity, wondering where his little sister slept.

Algernon tossed him a pillow. "Go to bed. You can work on relational mending tomorrow morning."

Missing Pieces

An unusual and unpleasant noise awakened Bronwyn in the pre-dawn light. The air in the house felt cold as she lay very still, listening to Algernon's rhythmic breathing on the floor for a moment. Someone began coughing, and then retching. The sound, originating in the living area, stirred the husky young woman's curiosity. She arose and scurried quietly to the door.

The smell of vomit assailed her senses. Wrinkling her nose and holding her breath, Bronwyn stepped into the kitchen and flipped on the light switch. Her eyes widened. "Willi? What are you doing here?"

He cursed the bright light, arose and staggered to the bathroom with his head pounding. Bronwyn heard the tap running as he rinsed out his mouth.

Annoyed that he'd not replied, the young woman scowled at the sight in the living area. Her brother had emptied his dinner all over the floor, soiling three cushions used by the family for sitting. Bronwyn gathered the pillows and tossed them outside. Then she went into the laundry area to fetch a bucket, a mop and towels.

Willem wandered over to her, a bit shocked to see his little sister looking very grown-up in a filmy purple nightgown. After clearing his throat he said, "I'm really sorry about the mess."

Bronwyn shut off the hot water tap and mixed a bit of vinegar into the bucket. "You couldn't make it to the toilet?" she asked in a pleading voice.

"I was sleeping," he told her. "I couldn't help it."

Pushing past her brother, Bronwyn added, "Yet you know how to find the bathroom without asking . . ."

"Aw, come on, Bronwyn! Not you too!" Willem lamented. "Why is everyone on my back all of a sudden? I feel awful right now . . ."

Secrets and Whispers: *Missing Pieces*

"You poor thing!" she mocked, carrying the bucket and mop through the kitchen. "It must be really hard to be you right now . . ."

Willem didn't like his little sister speaking to him in such a tone. He grabbed her left arm in warning, but she easily twisted away and shoved him hard.

"I'm not Vega," she warned. "Mess with me and I'll hurt you!"

Holding up his hands, Willem backed away. She'd become quite strong since leaving home and he was in no shape to contend with her. "Okay!" he acquiesced. "Since when have you been so touchy?"

Bronwyn set her bucket down and immersed the mop. "What kind of entitled life do you live? You come in here in the middle of the night while I'm sleeping, barf all over my floor and expect me to feel happy about it? I love you, but I'm not your servant girl!"

Willem felt guilty as he watched his sister wring out the mop. Though his head felt ready to explode he offered, "Maybe I should do that."

"You'll only make a muck of it," she spat. "You can barely stand on your own feet right now. I live here and I don't want to smell your vomit for weeks on end."

"I didn't mean to hurl!" Willem said defensively, leaning against the kitchen counter. "Things just got out of hand with Vega, and I had a drink or two. That's all."

The siblings' raised voices roused Algernon, who appeared from the bedroom with Bronwyn's robe in hand. He offered her the garment, wordlessly reached for the mop and began cleaning the floor.

As Bronwyn donned her robe Willem stopped her. "I'm sorry about the mess. I swear it won't happen again."

Algernon, who'd heard vows like this as a child, scoffed. He used the mop skillfully, the lean muscles in his back and shoulders flexing rhythmically as he worked.

Secrets and Whispers: *Missing Pieces*

Willem noted that the young man had a very defined physique. The musculature of his upper body looked like strong rope when contrasted with the delicate strands of blonde hair that danced across his upper back. At the very least, Bronwyn had drawn the interest of someone far fitter than herself. A moment later, when he realized that his sister noticed his admiration with scowling disapproval, Willem looked away.

With less than 30 minutes remaining until their typical waking time, Bronwyn lit a fire and put a kettle on for tea. Algernon finished washing the floor and went to the bathroom after dumping out the dirty water and drying the floor with an old towel.

"He's better-looking than you are," Willem admitted.

"Keep your eyes to yourself, brother," Bronwyn warned. "He's mine."

Willem smirked. "I'm not standing in your way," he replied. "If you want to marry that boy, it's your concern. I have no say in it."

"Then why all the opposition?" Bronwyn inquired. "Why is everyone being so mean to me? Ever since I showed up to announce my engagement, you and Harold and Darren have been nothing but nasty."

"No one but Mom cares about who you marry," Willi stated. "We're just deferring to her in this."

"Since when have you decided to play the role of a dutiful son?" Bronwyn scoffed, detecting the lie. "What have I ever done to deserve the way you're treating me?"

With her words cutting his soul, Willem sighed. "You're right. We've been pretty awful."

Ileana emerged from her room wearing a pretty bathrobe. She kissed Bronwyn on the cheek and lingered quietly in the kitchen until Algernon emerged from the bathroom. Kira, whose bruise at the hand of Heidelinde had blossomed overnight, awakened last.

Secrets and Whispers: *Missing Pieces*

Bronwyn began making porridge while Algernon raised the window quilts, checked on the homestead's battery voltage and peered at the cistern's water level. Ileana disappeared into her room while Kira sat at the table, sipping tea and eyeing Willem with sullen suspicion.

Rather than gathering in the living room, as was the family custom, Algernon conducted morning prayers at the dining room table. He read from a leather bound copy of *Gottslena* writings that Garrick had given him, reciting the rest of the day's liturgy from memory.

Willem, despite his professed devotion to the traditional Tamarian religion, didn't pay much attention to the spiritual content of Algernon's recitation. Instead, he focused on the way his sister interacted with the handsome priest, permitting constant touch that edged toward the erotic. No one else seemed to notice that Algernon always had his hands on her, nuzzling her neck, letting his gaze wander to her bosom, and that he paid very little attention to Ileana, who was much prettier. He also listened attentively when Bronwyn spoke, smiling at her appreciatively and praising her during his prayer. The young man clearly found her fascinating.

At breakfast Bronwyn and Algernon fed one another, a traditional Tamarian gesture of servitude. Their kindness penetrated Willem's headache, broke through his sibling intolerance and inspired guilt for his participation in the disinheritance and dowry plot.

He watched his sister brew a pot of analgesic tea after Ileana left for the boutique dress shop where she worked. Algernon stretched near the front door. Kira, who'd already completed her stretching routine, nursed her second cup of tea at the table.

"So, is it true what they say about you?" Willem asked his hostess. "The stories I've heard about you at the Temple are downright scandalous."

Secrets and Whispers: *Missing Pieces*

Kira's grey eyes glared over her mug. She took a sip before setting her drink down. "I don't give a steaming pile of donkey dung about your concern for my reputation."

"So, it's true?"

"What's true?" she asked.

Algernon paused, not appreciating where this conversation might be heading.

"Well, one person says you're into girls, but someone else says you're a suction queen. Which is it?"

Kira didn't take the bait. "Do you ever go down on your wife?"

"What's that supposed to mean?" he retorted.

"The way your eyes linger on my brother makes me wonder," she stated, enjoying the sight of Willem's discomfort. Kira hadn't actually witnessed what Bronwyn had seen, but she remembered Vega's testimony. "When was the last time you made Vega cry out in pleasure, rather than in pain?"

"My relationship with my wife is none of your business," Willem retorted.

"Just as my sex life is none of yours," Kira replied with a sweet smile.

"But you're in ministry," Willem continued. "Isn't it hypocritical to have your, uh, proclivities?"

Kira shook her head. "I'm not running from my past. I'm not leading a double life, pretending to be someone I've never been . . ." She paused, her expression hardening as the truth of her words penetrated Willem's hangover. "Don't judge me by standards that you can't personally uphold, and don't presume that my past defines my future any more than yours does you."

"I don't get it," Willem stated, shaking his head. "People don't change. If you were a slut with itchy thighs at the Temple, then that's who you are . . ."

"Willem!" Bronwyn snapped. "How rude!"

Secrets and Whispers: *Missing Pieces*

"It's okay," Kira assured her friend. "He's not saying anything new." Turning back to Willem, Kira continued, "I'm not denying my biology. Your belief that no one can change comes from ignorant people who insist that if you're not like them, you're wrong; that you have a choice in the matter, and that it's immoral to act on your desire.

"So you married Vega to cover it all up, hoping that your problem would go away, but it hasn't. You can't help yourself and presume that everyone else is the same."

Willem stood to his feet and slammed his hands on the table. "Who are you to judge me?" he demanded.

Algernon arose, ready to defend his sister.

Bronwyn brought the tea over and gently pressed her brother back into his seat. "Don't be angry, Willi," she soothed. "The way you feel right now is what it's been like for me ever since I announced my engagement. "You don't need to hide who you are from us," she continued, gently. "We're not here to judge or condemn you. We're your family, not your enemy."

Willem glowered at his sister. "You have no idea what's really going on," he warned. "None of you do."

"Try me," Kira insisted. "Your bumbling intrigue is transparent as a window."

Presuming that Kira's past precluded her from having deductive skills, Willem leaned back in his chair and scoffed. "Go ahead. If you think you're so smart . . ."

Having spoken to Vega the previous afternoon and Brenna over the phone before Willem arrived, Kira had been brooding over the details and developed a compelling theory. "It starts with your mother. She attended school with a woman who used to run the women's cloister at the Temple. When the Supreme Council found out she was a pedophile – preying on girls like me – they defrocked and removed her. She's the one who's been feeding your mother dirty stories about me and Algernon.

Secrets and Whispers: *Missing Pieces*

"Your brother, Darren, knows someone who's related to Gunnar Vinkholdt. Sadly, Gunnar can describe my fondness for fellatio because I wasted my skills on his pathetic, little-boy flesh."

Taken aback, Willem cleared his throat. "What are you talking about?"

"A child could put this together," Kira said, knowing from Willem's expression that she'd uncovered truth. "Your family has heard about things that happened to us inside the Sacred Enclosure – very specific events twisted to make us look bad. But it's all old news, and because it's so old, it could only have come from one source – the former Priestess Alba – who cornered and fondled me as soon as she noticed I had tits."

"I don't know what you're talking about!" Willem insisted. His eyes revealed a litany of long-concealed lies, as he was too hung over to cover up the truth.

"You do, and your mother does too," Kira replied.

"My mom knows Sister Alba?" Bronwyn asked. "How do you figure?"

"Your mother's opposition started well after you wrote to announce your engagement. She routinely runs background checks on company officers in her work as an investment agent. It would have taken her time to contact someone from the Temple, and nearly two months after you first wrote to her about your engagement, she sent a train ticket for you to come home.

"Brenna told me the stories your Tante Marla related to her. The personal stuff is all from years ago – most of which only Sister Alba would know. Also, at dinner your mother mentioned that she'd graduated from Lakeview University in Burning Tree, the same school Alba attended. She and Alba are the same age. The rest of the stuff she's been complaining about came from reading unflattering newspaper editorials about us."

Secrets and Whispers: *Missing Pieces*

Turning back to Willem, Kira continued. "Now the only person at the Temple who ever called me a suction queen was Gunnar. He used to brag about his brave older brother serving in battle against the Azgar near Kicking Horse. Your brother Darren and my brother Garrick were also involved in that conflict.

"That's how Darren knows Brenna. He was injured in battle and sent to Burning Tree, where Brenna was working as a nurse. So Darren must have served with Gunnar's brave older brother. I didn't know who your source of dirt was until you told me."

Hearing this, Algernon grew angry. He stalked outside and slammed the door. Bronwyn arose. "Drink your tea," she urged her brother. "You'll feel better." Then she followed her betrothed to the porch.

Willem turned, but Kira stopped him. "I'm not done," she said. "Your brother Darren married Sikki because she's beautiful, but he thinks with his prick, not his head. She's never had money and Darren can't satisfy her on a sergeant's salary. They're looking at Bronwyn's dowry and family inheritance with big eyes. To get it, they've conspired with you and Harold to make Bron feel miserable and ensure your mother stops her marriage."

"That makes no sense!" Willem stated. "Nobody else gets a thing if Bronwyn doesn't get married."

He'd just confirmed the truth of Vega's tale without realizing he'd done so. Kira smiled in triumph. "Bron loves my brother and he loves her. You, Harold and Darren are playing a wretched game to isolate your sister and make her feel miserable. You're destroying the bond between her and your mother, hoping that Bron will abandon the dowry and give up the inheritance that's rightfully hers. I despise what you're doing."

Willem shook his head. "You're wrong."

"Am I?" Kira questioned.

Secrets and Whispers: *Missing Pieces*

"Nobody gets what he sees in her," Willem stated. "Except that maybe your brothers have a thing for stupid girls with big tits."

Kira felt like hitting him for disrespecting the two most important women in her life. She paused, gathering self-control. "If you weren't Bron's brother, I'd snap you like a twig!" she warned. "Brenna has more brains in her toenail clippings than you do in that fat head of yours. I'd tell you to write this down, but I doubt you know how. Get your crayons out and draw a picture so you'll always remember what I'm about to say. If I ever hear you speak badly about Bronwyn again, I'll hit you so hard you'll choke on your teeth.

"Your life is a mess because your heart is dark and cold. You need to quit drinking and fix the deplorable way you treat your wife. Even if you don't want her for sex, there's no reason for you to mistreat her!"

***

"Why didn't you sit with us at the dinner play?" Marla asked a little later that morning, her tone suggesting she'd been hurt rather than offended.

"Darren didn't tell you about his conflict with my husband?" Brenna inquired.

Marla shook her head. She felt cold and wanted to get started on the trail. "No. What happened?"

Still miffed at Darren's rude behavior, Brenna tried to remain cordial. "He and Garrick had an argument at lunch. Darren said some rather uncharitable things about Kira, insinuating she'd behaved inappropriately so that Bronwyn's wedding could be held at the palace.

"Garrick and I wanted to spend a romantic evening together. We thought that sitting with your family might put our plans at risk, so we chose a different table."

Secrets and Whispers: *Missing Pieces*

Marla had noticed that other guests refused to join the amorous couple. She suspected that Brenna's Lithian heritage informed that choice, but held her tongue. "Was it a successfully romantic evening?" she asked.

While that remark bordered on excessively personal for polite conversation, true to her culture and upbringing, Brenna didn't blush. "Without doubt."

Having heard about Garrick's condition from Darren and suspecting Brenna would be reluctant to admit it, Marla continued, "You don't have to say if it wasn't."

Understanding Marla's intent, Brenna replied, "Garrick doesn't need to woo me into bed. I don't need wine and dinner to want him. Why do you ask?"

"It's not my intention to pry," Marla clarified, taking on a professional tone. "But combat veterans often struggle with social re-integration when they return home. Regular intimacy is an important component of recovery."

Hearing this, Brenna felt confident that Darren's snooping around at Fort Aeolus had revealed the truth of Garrick's mental health leave. There was no other good reason for Marla to say this. "He's under the care of Dr. Bauer," Brenna replied. "I assure you that he's receiving appropriate counsel."

Marla smiled sincerely. "I'm pleased to hear it, and I'm confident that you're a source of great comfort and strength for your husband." She paused, gathering her thoughts for a moment. "But let me encourage you to likewise seek support. Dealing with a loved one's combat trauma can be an isolating experience. Other spouses walk that path. There is no need for you to feel alone."

She meant well, didn't she? "I'm never alone," the Lithian woman responded. "Allfather strengthens me wherever I go, whatever I do, and whatever I face."

"How does faith help you in your current situation?" Marla asked. "How are you coping?"

Secrets and Whispers: *Missing Pieces*

"It's not easy," Brenna admitted. "I pray and I cry a lot, but Garrick's getting better."

Despite her personal skepticism and disbelief, Marla didn't want to offend the younger woman. Yet she couldn't bring herself to accept the idea that Brenna's faith made a material difference in Garrick's progress. "How can you attribute this to the influence of your deity when your husband is under the care of a professional?"

"Why can't Allfather use Dr. Bauer to improve my husband's condition?" Brenna countered.

Marla shrugged. "If I accept that God exists and cares about a solider's mental health, then that's a reasonable conclusion to draw. But you've already told me that your God doesn't always answer prayers for healing. Why do you believe that he's involved in the lieutenant's care when the direct cause of his recovery can be linked to Dr. Bauer's treatment?"

Brenna shook her head. "From your perspective faith makes no sense."

Surprised at such honesty, Marla's brow furrowed with concern. "So why do you bother to pray?"

"I can't perceive the purpose in suffering," Brenna stated. "I don't know how my pain will resolve when I'm in the midst of turmoil, but I'm confident that Allfather loves me. Whenever I feel anger or despair about my circumstances, I trust in his good character and persist in my petitions for my own sake, for my own sanity."

Marla had heard her say something similar before, but she had to admit that Brenna's spiritual perspective featured a consistent and functional logic. She smirked, not in contempt of Brenna's faith, but not in agreement with it, either. "Well, if your prayers help you cope and maintain healthy relationships, then I affirm you."

"Does Garrick's need for counseling reduce your regard for him?" Brenna asked.

Secrets and Whispers: *Missing Pieces*

"No, not at all," Marla replied. "Soldiers routinely experience unspeakable horror. It's the decent ones who struggle with combat trauma. In a way it's good that they do, as we don't want psychopaths running around the battlefield with loaded weapons."

"Is that what you've said to Willem?" Brenna queried in a slightly accusative tone.

Caught off guard, Marla held her breath. "What do you know about Willem?"

Brenna turned and ascended the stairs, walking at a brisk pace that she expected Marla to maintain. "I know that he's repeatedly refused mental health treatment. People in the armed forces are tight-knit and don't share with outsiders, but they talk freely among themselves."

"I see," Marla stated. How did Brenna know this?

"Darren learned about Garrick's leave because he's a member of the brotherhood," Brenna continued. "Other soldiers trust him because he shares the blood bond of combat veterans. If he'd not gone to Fort Aeolus and stopped at a bar to drink with other soldiers, you wouldn't have known about my husband's combat trauma."

The psychologist hadn't realized that Brenna knew about this, too. "I suspect that there's something going on with my nephews to which I am not privy," she replied, struggling to keep pace with the smaller woman. "I'm sorry that Darren invaded Garrick's privacy. If you want, I'll have a word with him about that."

Brenna paused. "Garrick is fine," she stated. "My concern is for Bronwyn. I think Darren, Harold and Willem want to sabotage their sister's wedding. Bronwyn needs her family's support. All of you owe her that much."

Marla put her right hand on Brenna's shoulder. She knew about the Lithian custom of placing a hand on the heart as a means of showing complete sincerity, but didn't know Brenna well enough to risk that gesture. "I promise

Secrets and Whispers: *Missing Pieces*

you, I'm here to support my niece. If there's anything nefarious going on, I'll find out and put a stop to it."

Brenna nodded, her eyes widened and her brows raised trustingly. "I'll leave that to you," she offered.

Not long after they began a warm-up lap around the track, Marla found herself falling further and further behind the tireless Lithian woman. Still unaccustomed to the altitude, Marla pushed herself to the verge of nausea before slowing to a walk.

Brenna's clarity of mind encouraged Marla to think. She considered her family's recent behavior with a critical view, first pondering the stridency of Irena's opposition to Algernon. Something about it seemed out of character. Irena typically treated everyone she met with an automatic kindness that bordered on the naive. She'd always been sweet and gentle-spirited. Why wasn't she extending the same grace to Bronwyn's fiancé?

And why had Darren so vigorously investigated and breathlessly revealed Lieutenant Ravenwood's personal struggle with combat trauma? As a veteran, he should have honored the lieutenant's privacy, and maybe as a sergeant, he also should have respected Garrick's superior rank – even if the officer was young enough to be his son.

Both Willem and Vega had missed breakfast at the hotel. Sikki had been particularly snippy, while Darren remained evasive about his brother's whereabouts.

Marla didn't believe he was speaking truthfully, and Brenna's comments about Darren, Harold and Willem hit close to home.

Willem had been battling a drinking problem, the roots of which extended into his struggle with homosexuality and the facade he maintained in order to protect his career. Marla understood that his marriage to Vega would never produce children, and that she, with increasing frequency, concealed bruises on her body.

Secrets and Whispers: *Missing Pieces*

Both of his older brothers had taken him to task about this in the past, but festering dysfunction was destroying that marriage. So why take it out on Bronwyn?

Harold's angry diatribe against Kira and his sudden departure from the city had a lot to do with Heidelinde's shame. She'd never been one to admit culpability in social wrongdoing, and being put into her place by a younger, prettier and more assertive woman certainly would have been too much for Heidelinde to handle. That much made sense. Harold also tended to follow her lead, but oddly, she'd never before expressed the blatantly condescending attitude toward Bronwyn she'd exhibited during her brief stay. Why had she been acting this way? Why would Harold want to make Bronwyn feel bad about herself?

And what was the point of their behavior? The young woman obviously loved her family and craved their support. What did it matter to Darren, Harold and Willem that Bronwyn had chosen Algernon to be her partner?

Marla believed that only Arvid had been true to himself and supportive of Bronwyn since she announced her engagement. In a conversation on the train journey to Marvic, he'd told Marla, "I want to meet this young Algernon before I pass judgment on him." And that's what he'd done thus far.

Arvid would reveal his thoughts to Irena in private, but would never cross her in public. They'd disagreed on supporting Darren's marriage to Sikki, and Harold's union to Heidelinde – the latter causing friction between them. The singular time they'd agreed in this area was with Willem and Vega – a marriage in significant peril.

For Bronwyn's sake, Marla tried to keep an open mind and counsel her sister wisely. While she'd agreed with Irena's concerns and affirmed her opposition, after meeting Brenna – whom she'd found delightfully intelligent and quite persuasive – her perspective had changed.

Secrets and Whispers: *Missing Pieces*

While she'd never thought much of Lithian people, influenced – to her private chagrin – by the prejudices of her culture, Marla discarded her previous view in light of this devout woman's refreshing honesty. Ironically, it had been Darren's high regard of Brenna that paved the way to this newly suspended judgment, allowing the psychologist to change her mind and accept the Lithian woman's testimony about Kira and Algernon.

Brenna's obvious and fervent devotion didn't mix well with the wretched stories about the Ravenwoods the Traugott family had been hearing. Further, her positive testimony concerning the twins' spiritual maturity harmonized with their actual behavior. Marla felt confident that the Lithian woman spoke with integrity.

As Brenna turned the corner and sprinted toward her, Marla – fighting another rush of nausea that swelled in her gut – sat on the cold grass. Moments later, Brenna's soft hands lifted her chin as a worried expression appeared on the younger woman's face.

"Are you okay?" Brenna asked.

Marla shook her head. "I feel like throwing up," she admitted. "And I'm cold."

Brenna took off her zippered track top and draped it on Marla's shoulders. "The altitude is hard on everyone," she said, though she'd already recovered her breath. "But it's easier to breathe if you stand."

"I'm not sure I can," Marla admitted, feeling weak.

"I can help you if you'd like," Brenna offered, bending her knees, putting the taller woman's hands on her shoulders as she took hold of Marla's upper arms.

With Brenna's assistance, Marla stood to her feet again. She leaned on the smaller woman until the momentary nausea passed, noting the sculpted musculature of Brenna's shoulders and upper arms. Maintaining a physique like hers required effort.

Secrets and Whispers: *Missing Pieces*

"You're very fit," Marla remarked. "I'll bet the boys lined up to court you before Garrick came along."

While she didn't want to talk about this, silence in Lithian culture implied agreement. Brenna cleared her throat. "Most of the men who were interested in me found my will and my intelligence intimidating. They wanted me for carnal reasons and cared nothing for my character. Courting wasn't easy for me.

"But Garrick was like a cool breeze on a hot day. He's never been afraid of my mind. He encourages the best in me and always wants me to excel. He's a caring and supportive partner. I'm fortunate to have found him."

Marla stood to her full height, concurring with a nod. "I can relate. My family thought I'd never marry." She smiled at the smaller woman, remembering wistfully. "But like you, I also found someone who appreciated me."

"I didn't realize you were married," Brenna stated. "Where's your husband?"

Marla's expression quieted. She pursed her lips as a far-away look evolved on her face. "I'm a widow. My Franzel was a good man, but he fell ill a few years ago and never recovered."

Brenna bowed her head. "May you find comfort in his memory."

"I do," Marla replied, nodding. "My experience gives me insight into what my niece must be feeling right now. I imagine she's convinced that no one will love her like Algernon does."

Brenna, however, remembered Algernon's interest in Thea, one of her younger sisters. Cynthia had no viable prospects on the isolated Velez estate in Kameron, and later admitted to their father that she'd deliberately ignited Algernon's interest. She'd followed him on a hike and turned his head by skinny-dipping in a hot spring, feigning indignation when she caught him gazing at her.

Secrets and Whispers: *Missing Pieces*

Algernon, captivated by her bountiful form, nearly abandoned Bronwyn in favor of Thea; but after spending time in her company, he realized they had little – other than mutual attraction – in common. While Cynthia was undeniably beautiful, he couldn't imagine a viable future with her and returned home.

Bronwyn had forgiven him, and since that incident with Thea, he'd been unquestionably faithful. Nonetheless, Bronwyn felt hurt by the betrayal, she had an excellent memory and remained sensitive to any discussion of Brenna's *not-so-little* sister. Thinking it wiser to avoid discussing this subject and potentially creating more trouble for Bronwyn, Brenna replied, "May it be so."

Moments later, Marla changed the subject. "I don't feel well enough to run. I hope you're not disappointed."

Brenna shook her head. "I know a place where we can get you some medicinal tea. It'll help you with the altitude sickness."

***

"Notice the way she's turned her cane backwards," Bronwyn commented to her brother. "She does that so the support leans into her body rather than away from it. When you see that, you know the person holding the cane understands how to use it as a weapon."

Willem scowled. He'd never thought of his little sister as a martial arts expert, but her commentary made sense. He watched Kira stand on both feet, holding the cane behind her left arm with its length resting on her back. She faced Algernon intently, waiting for his attack.

When he leaped forward, she twisted her upper body, stepped forward and extended her left arm in response. The cane snapped into an arc, whistling through the air with terrifying speed.

Secrets and Whispers: *Missing Pieces*

Willem felt sure that blow would split Algernon's skull, but the priest had anticipated the move and deflected his sister's arm with his right hand as he thrust his left palm toward her face.

Kira wrenched her torso into the opposite direction, turning her head away so quickly that Algernon's palm merely glanced off the top of her head. As her foot circled backward, she twisted the cane beneath her arm and heaved it that direction, forcing her brother to step his left foot away to avoid her hard, rearward thrust. She'd have badly hurt a lesser opponent, but his response to her attack put him into a perfect position . . .

He followed with a right-footed roundhouse kick aimed at Kira's abdomen. She met the force of his blow with a right-handed downward block, matching her strength against his – a contest she couldn't win. His kick landed hard, she groaned and tumbled backward, rolling over her left shoulder and sweeping the cane in a swift frontal arc to prevent him from following up.

Willem grimaced. "It's hardly fair," he remarked. "Even I can see that he's better at this than she is."

"They were more evenly matched before she'd been shot," Bronwyn said. "Not being able to use her right foot very well puts her at a significant disadvantage.

"Had she not been hurt, she could have matched his roundhouse with one of her own. But her kick would have hit him in the back, which is a lot harder to block."

"Does he ever practice on you?" Willem asked.

Bronwyn shook her head. "It wouldn't help," she admitted. "Kira's much better than I am. She can hold her own with him, and he needs the challenge."

"What about the older brother?"

"Garrick?" Bronwyn inquired, raising her brow. "Fighting like this is not his thing. Give him a rifle or a handgun and that's a different matter."

Secrets and Whispers: *Missing Pieces*

"That figures," Willem smirked. "He probably can't handle his little sister, either."

"Garrick's expertise is in combat leadership," Bronwyn stated. "He's got the medals to prove it."

"Yeah, and Darren says that Brenna's a Heroine of the Republic. They probably give away combat citations like candy in the Expeditionary Force."

"Watch Brenna with a sword and you wouldn't be talking that way," Bronwyn replied.

Willem pointed at Algernon. "How would she do against him?"

"With a weapon, she beats him easily."

"That wee little thing?" Willem exclaimed in disbelief. "She's so top heavy she'd fall over trying to fight . . ."

Bronwyn smirked at his ignorance. "She's been working with a sword for more than twenty-five years. Don't misjudge her just because she's delicate and pretty."

Willem, who thought Brenna looked no older than thirteen, dismissed that remark as an exaggeration. He returned his attention to Algernon, who went after Kira while she was still on the grass, trying to grab hold of her and grapple. Repeatedly, she fought him off with her cane while struggling to stand up.

"Why doesn't he back off?" Willem asked. "She's down again. Doesn't that mean he's won?"

"Do you think a thug is going to let up just because he's knocked her down? She trains like this to survive. If she didn't, some nut job would have killed her long ago."

"Is she really in that much danger?" Willem asked, his skepticism evident in a slightly sarcastic tone.

Bronwyn grimaced, watching Algernon land a front kick against Kira's shoulder. "You have no idea . . ."

Willem shook his head. Despite his sister's tea dulling the impact of his hangover, he still craved a drink. "If their ministry is so dangerous, why are you involved?"

Secrets and Whispers: *Missing Pieces*

Bronwyn narrowed her brow. "What's that supposed to mean?"

Was she really that dumb? "Well, if you're under such a big threat, why aren't you out there?"

She paused for a moment, hurt by her brother's insinuation that she couldn't defend herself. "Most of my work now is here at home," Bronwyn explained. "I'd been going to the train station with Helga, but since Astrid became High Priestess, we've had acolyte volunteers from the Temple take my place.

"But Kira goes into the strip clubs and hotels where exploited girls work. She also visits them in jail. Algernon deals with the pimps, the handlers and the muscle men that try to keep the girls in line."

"So, you're just a lowly *hausfrau*," Willem stated.

Bronwyn stood, annoyed with his relentless insults. "We'll see how long you can last with me!" she challenged, muttering under her breath as she stood and stalked toward the door.

Willem turned back to the action, watching Algernon execute a sweep that knocked Kira's cane away as she tried to stand. She tumbled to the grass, swearing in an unladylike manner, earning the exchange of a few terse words that Willem couldn't quite make out. At length, Algernon extended a hand to help his sister back on her feet. They embraced briefly, but his anger still simmered.

"Gunnar's a shard-born, cretinous dandy prat!" Algernon complained. "He'd better hope that I never lay eyes on him again!"

"Save your outrage for the dish boy," she countered. "No need for you to take out your frustration on me."

Sulking back to the porch, Algernon wordlessly offered Kira one of the towels hanging on the porch rail. She smacked hands with him and wiped her face, but didn't thank him.

Secrets and Whispers: *Missing Pieces*

He wordlessly reached for the other towel. A few minutes later, Bronwyn came through the front door. She'd changed into workout clothes and carried the padded gloves, headgear and body armor they used for full-contact sparring.

"Here!" she said to her brother, dumping the armor at his side. "Put this stuff on . . ."

Kira, noting the complete lack of movement in her friend's bosom realized that Bronwyn had put on a Lithian halter – a gift from Brenna's mother – who'd designed the garment to provide three-dimensional support during athletic activities. The halter had other properties that were controlled by the will of the wearer, but Kira knew that Bronwyn had worn it because she meant business.

"She's gonna kick your butt all the way back to Feral Springs," the pretty blonde woman warned.

"Never!" Willem growled. As a soldier, he'd done well in training and his combat experience instilled confidence that he'd prevail. He towered over his sister, possessed far greater physical strength and had always dominated Vega. He had no idea how well Bronwyn could fight.

After donning the headgear, gloves and body armor, he put his hands out to the side. "What about you?"

"I don't need protection," Bronwyn promised.

"Look, I don't want to hurt you," Willem replied condescendingly, following his sister onto the large grassy patch where the twins had just finished sparring.

"You won't," Kira smirked.

Algernon, under his breath, warned, "He'd better not, if he knows what's good for him . . ."

Willem adopted a fighting pose, bouncing on the balls of his feet, while Bronwyn circled to his left, staying on the outside of his elbows. When he playfully jabbed at her with his left glove, she turned sideways – just enough to avoid getting hit – shuffle stepped forward and delivered

Secrets and Whispers: *Missing Pieces*

a hard fist beneath his extended arm, followed in rapid succession by a left-handed corkscrew punch to his chest and elbow into his cheek. She grabbed his neck and slammed her left knee into his abdomen twice, delivering every blow so quickly, Willem had no chance to retaliate.

Bronwyn hooked her left foot behind his legs and shoved him forcefully. He dropped backward, landing hard, stunned by her strength. What Bronwyn lacked in speed and agility she more than made up for in power, fighting in a simple, yet brutally effective style. She slid back into a martial stance. "That's once. Now get up!"

"So you want to play rough?" he taunted angrily, panting hard in the thin air. "We can do that!"

He lunged at her aggressively, but Bronwyn didn't flinch. She stepped into a side kick that thundered into his gut, stopping him cold. The husky woman twisted into a left-footed roundhouse that snapped into the side of his head with such force, Willem nearly blacked out. He dropped to his knees, cowering beneath his right hand, dizzy and coughing as breakfast rose in his throat.

"That's twice. Get up!" she demanded.

He staggered to his feet, but she offered no respite, snapping a right-footed front kick to his thigh, followed by a double hook that hit his shoulder and the opposite side of his head hard enough to knock him down a third time.

"That's three," she taunted. "You couldn't even hit me once! Don't ever call me a lowly *hausfrau* again!"

***

After taking a shower, Algernon accompanied Bronwyn's brother back to Marvic. They walked down the path to the Augury Creek Service Road in uncomfortable silence until Willem began complaining about his only sister. "It's like I don't know her anymore," he groused.

Secrets and Whispers: *Missing Pieces*

Algernon shrugged. "That's true. You don't. She's lived apart from your family longer than she lived at home. Bronwyn isn't the little girl you remember. She's a smart and capable adult who deserves your respect. It's pathetic that all she's getting from you is scorn."

Willem tightened his lips. He really needed a drink and didn't want to talk about his sister's maturity. "Have you banged her yet?"

What a rude question! "No," Algernon replied flatly.

"Well, the way you've got your hands all over her, I find that hard to believe."

Algernon, who'd spent many years longing for a woman's affection, needed the reassurance of Bronwyn's proximity and the promise of her desire. He felt he'd been discreet about physical contact in the company of her family and resented the dishonesty of Willem's remark.

"After all," Willem continued, "the way you caress her in front of me makes me think you must be doing a lot more than that when I'm not around."

"Just shut up!" Algernon warned. "You have a habit of saying things best left unspoken, and your pointless criticism is irritating. I don't care if you don't like me, but you have an obligation to love your sister. That's what real men do. Unless you're willing to express affirmation, unless you're offering sincere support, your commentary is both inappropriate and unwelcome."

After watching Algernon's ruthless martial skill and being humiliated by Bronwyn, Willem felt intimidated. "Sorry," he muttered.

But Willem's regrets and promises failed to impress Algernon, whose personal experience affirmed the wisdom of mistrusting a drunkard. "Don't give me any more reason to think that Kira's right about you. As much as I'd like to give you the benefit of the doubt, nothing you've done inspires my confidence."

Secrets and Whispers: *Missing Pieces*

The rebuke burned in Willem's soul. "What is it with your family?" he complained angrily. "You, your brother and your sister act like you're high and mighty, like you have no flaws, when I know better!"

"This denial of yours is working?" Algernon asked.

"I'm not denying anything," Willem countered.

"If that was true, why did you show up at my house in the middle of the night, thick-tongued and stinking of beer?" Algernon argued. "Why weren't you snuggled up in bed with your pretty wife? Is your head pounding right now? You've been shaking and craving a drink since the first thing this morning. Is that my fault?

"If you think you're perfectly okay and everyone else has problems, then you're in cold water and deep trouble. You're like a drowning man complaining that other people don't know how to swim!"

Willem gritted his teeth. "Damn you!" he muttered. "I know you're no better than I am!"

Algernon nodded. "That's the first truthful thing I've heard from you all morning . . ."

A steel gate, painted white, controlled access where the path to Superstition Mesa met the Augury Creek Service Road. Willem followed Algernon around it, noting a scowl on the monk's face at the sight of a Wildlife Office truck parked on the road. What was that about?

Most of the fields to the west of Superstition Mesa had already been planted. The aromas of living soil and fresh verdure, carried on a light breeze from the west, leant a calming influence to the tension between the men. At length, as they walked along the tree-crowned rock face of the mesa, Willem relaxed enough to resume talking.

"Okay, I've got problems," he admitted. "My wife's a nag. She complains that we can't afford the stuff she wants, and she's always spending money on new clothes, new shoes – you name it.

Secrets and Whispers: *Missing Pieces*

"She's borrowed money from Heidelinde and Harold's after me to pay it back. But I'm a soldier on a soldier's pay. I can't afford what she wants.

"What am I supposed to do about that? I can't support the kind of lifestyle she demands. It's relentless. She wants to dress in fancy clothes like Brenna. She wants to strut around wearing the latest fashion, but I'm not rich. They don't pay me like they pay your brother."

Brenna had her own source of income. She certainly had expensive taste and a particular style to her wardrobe, but she always bought her own clothes. "Garrick's an officer," Algernon replied. "Salary goes up with rank in every branch of military service."

"The Senate lavishes funding on the Expeditionary Force," Willem retorted. "Everything they have is the best money can buy, but what do they have to show for it? They failed in Kameron and failed against the Tanarak last year. But we didn't get airships and armored vehicles. We had to hunt down those savages on foot!"

Having listened to Garrick testify at a recent Senate inquest, he knew that in combat, the Expeditionary Force had been effective against a more numerous, well-armed and tactically clever adversary. Willem had no evidence to back up his accusation, but Algernon tried to keep the conversation from escalating into an argument and replied with care. "You're on the same side," he stated. "My brother says the Tanarak fielded the finest light cavalry he'd ever seen. No one believes the TDF didn't fight well. There's no dishonor in needing reinforcements."

Willem shook his head as the city wall, with its multiple entrances, loomed ahead. "Give us their budget, their weapons and their logistical support and we'd have made those Tanarak dogs beg for mercy!"

"Garrick already told you that the Expeditionary Force has a different mandate and mission . . ."

Secrets and Whispers: *Missing Pieces*

"The hell with the TEF!" Willem thundered, drawing the attention of Defenders at the gate. "They're a drain on resources. They've never defeated anyone, yet they strut around like their pricks are bigger than everyone else's!"

An amiable, inter-service rivalry existed among all branches of the Tamarian military. The Inland Navy, the Defense and Expeditionary Forces, Defenders and Special Forces each maintained a certain degree of swagger. Algernon knew that his brother often shrugged off the banter of Defenders guarding the palace. But Willem's complaining sounded different. His venomous tone lacked any semblance of humor, as if his evaluation of the Expeditionary Force was grounded in actual fact.

"Don't make a scene," Algernon warned.

In the presence of Defenders, Willem exerted control. He listened as a soldier named Schiller – a man well acquainted with Algernon – asked cordial questions about the priest's ministerial duties for the day. Willem's reception proved far less friendly. Schiller grilled him when Willem couldn't produce any identification.

Sensing the shame that Willem felt when being forced to confess that he'd had a fight with his wife the previous evening, Algernon came to his rescue. "I'll vouch for him," the young priest said. "He's harmless."

As they walked down the grand stone steps on the far side of the gate, Algernon expected some form of gratitude and felt annoyed that Willem extended no such courtesy. Instead, the older man made a point to grouse about nearly everything in his life.

He complained that Darren treated everyone else in the family as if they were soldiers in his squad. He called Harold a lickspittle for his incessant and irritating tendency to fawn over Heidelinde – the only person among the siblings and their spouses whose independent wealth enabled her to spend without limit.

Secrets and Whispers: *Missing Pieces*

Stating that fact hinted at Willem's debt again, leading Algernon to conclude that Kira had been right about a conspiracy to deprive Bronwyn of her dowry and inheritance. Nearly everything Willem complained about had its root in lack of money.

When Willem lamented that he never seemed able to please his father, Algernon held his tongue. He didn't want to talk about the terrors of his childhood, leading Willem to conclude that the priest had nothing else to say.

After boarding the Victory Street trolley and accepting the blessings of several people, Algernon sat on a bench with Willem and inquired, "What are you going to do about Vega?"

Willem shook his head. "I don't know. I've really wrecked it this time. I don't think she'll take me back."

Pausing to consider that remark, Algernon nodded slowly. "You really need to quit the drinking."

Impatiently, Willem huffed, "Everybody wants me to change! Nobody accepts me for who I am!"

"There are a lot of things in life that you can't control," Algernon replied. "But drinking is one thing you have the power to overcome. What you lack is the will."

"I can quit any time!" Willem contended. "But why should I? Who are you to give me advice, and what business of it is yours to nose into my relationship with Vega? Quit your preaching and leave me alone!"

Algernon shrugged. "As long as you cling to the delusion that you're doing fine, things will only get worse. It would be far easier for me to not care and let you flounder than to help you pick up the shattered pieces of your life. But I love your sister, and right now, that's just about the only thing you've got going for you . . ."

***

Secrets and Whispers: *Missing Pieces*

Marla noticed that Lillian, the young baker working at Isadora's Tummy Yummies, didn't like Brenna. She actively ignored the Lithian woman until it became socially awkward to continue doing so, then spoke to her with sneering lips and a voice dripping with contempt, using as few words as possible to accomplish her task.

The hot drink, specially formulated to ease altitude sickness, featured a pleasant, peppery flavor. "You know that girl?" Marla asked, fighting a blossoming headache.

Brenna nodded. "Lili was one of Kira's clients. She was her first real success story."

Marla glanced over her shoulder. Lillian, a slender blonde with her hair pulled back into a ponytail, looked rather ordinary in her white smock and apron. "You're telling me she was a sex worker?"

Brenna nodded. "If it hadn't been for Kira, she'd have been stuck in that life. But Lili's got an excellent business ethic. She runs the shop for Isadora now."

After drinking more of her tea, Marla lowered her voice. "Why does she treat you so badly?"

Raising her brows and smirking, Brenna replied, "She's no worse than anyone else around here. When Garrick's not around, this kind of behavior is typical."

"But you're a Heroine of the Republic. You deserve respect! The least she could do is mind her manners . . ."

Brenna shrugged. "I've been dealing with this since I first arrived in Tamaria. Men either leer at me or fall all over themselves to attract my attention. Women simmer with envy, flirt with Garrick and whisper vitriol just loud enough for me to hear. Children mock and call me names, and old people make no effort to hide their contempt. Lili is just reflecting the values of her culture."

That was the first socially-critical remark Brenna uttered in Marla's presence, and while worded gently, its truth stung. In a moment of self-reflection, Marla realized

Secrets and Whispers: *Missing Pieces*

that she'd also felt reluctant to take Brenna seriously, judging the Lithian woman by her appearance, rather than waiting to learn of her character.

Glancing at the clock, Brenna pursed her lips. "I'm sorry, but I need to go. Are you going to be okay?"

Marla removed Brenna's track top and returned it to her. "I think so," she replied. "But I'll stick around here for a few minutes to make sure."

After watching Brenna leave, Marla decided she wanted to learn more about Lillian. The psychologist stood with her mug in hand and leaned against the counter that Lili was wiping with a wet towel. She began by making a positive comment about the tea, the clean condition of the storefront and encouraged Lillian to open up about herself by asking how long she'd been working for Isadora.

Once she'd successfully established rapport, Marla steered to the topic to her intended destination. "I'm visiting town for a wedding," she stated. "And I understand you know the sister of the bridegroom."

"You're talking about Kira?" Lili asked.

"Yes," Marla replied. "I'm the bride's aunt."

Lili smiled. "Bronwyn's a really nice girl. She's lucky to have Algernon."

"Oh?" Marla probed. "Why is that?"

A little blush appeared on Lili's cheeks. "He's really handsome!" she gushed. "He's super smart, too. I wouldn't have known how to work the till and do sums if he'd not taught me."

"Did you live at Kira's house?" When Lili nodded, Marla continued. "What's it like up there?"

"Well, it's really big and it's nice inside," Lili began. "I had my own room. Bronwyn's a good cook. She always made sure I had enough to eat. I'm grateful for the way they helped me when I was in trouble. They showed me how to turn my life around. "

Secrets and Whispers: *Missing Pieces*

The young woman appeared eager to talk about the experience that led her to meeting Kira. "I didn't know anyone in the city when I first came here," she explained. "Bronwyn met me at the train station and tried to save me from the man who'd promised me a job. Algernon would have protected me from him, too, but I didn't know any better. The man promised glamorous work for me, but he lied. He only wanted me to take my clothes off."

She related a sad tale about debt, exploitation and opium abuse that eventually led to jail, where she met Kira. "I just wanted to die," Lili admitted. "I felt alone and I was afraid. I thought the only thing I could do for the rest of my life was let some ugly, sweaty man grind me into a mattress. It was awful!

"But Kira went to the jail and found me. She told me that her brother would represent me in court and protect me from my pimp. I left that life behind and never went back!"

Moved by Lillian's testimony, Marla's mind began to wander. It had been easy to conclude that Kira's ministry was an inappropriate outreach for a woman of faith, yet she'd reached into a dark world and rescued Lili from enduring exploitation. Marla could no longer deny both the need and the efficacy of Kira's unusual public service.

And it sounded like Algernon had been integral to the process as well. "I imagine you were frightened when you first went to the homestead. How did you feel about Algernon? Were you ever afraid of him?"

Lili shook her head and smiled. "He's always been nice to me."

At that moment the shop door opened, its bell tinged, and in walked Arvid. Surprised to see Marla at the counter, he smiled. "I wasn't expecting you to be here," the older man said.

"You came without Irena?" Marla inquired.

Secrets and Whispers: *Missing Pieces*

Arvid shook his head. "Bronwyn phoned the hotel this morning. She wants to meet with me alone. Did she phone you as well?"

Marla shook her head. "Brenna brought me here for tea after I got sick on the track," she admitted. "Maybe I should go . . ."

"Perhaps we should ask my daughter when she arrives," he stated. "Besides, I could use the company while I wait."

***

Garrick hurried down the stairs. Anyone who needed to use the bell so early in the morning had to be the bearer of bad news, which didn't bode well.

To his surprise, Captain Mariel Hougen stood at the door. "Good morning, lieutenant," she said with an admiring smile.

He saw nothing urgent in her expression, but her appearance made him feel self-conscious for not having showered yet. "Good morning, captain. What brings you here at this hour?"

"I need to see Brenna," she stated, peering over his shoulder in anticipation of being invited in.

Garrick hedged. "She's not back from her morning run, but I expect her soon . . ."

After a moment of awkward silence, Mariel widened her eyes. "Aren't you going to let me in?"

"I told you. Brenna isn't home," he restated, reluctant to let the attractive woman enter.

Mariel put her hands on her hips. "It's a national security matter, lieutenant This is not about seduction."

Because she ranked him and he wasn't the least bit interested in her, Garrick stepped aside and let her in. "I have tea if you'd like some."

Secrets and Whispers: *Missing Pieces*

"That would be lovely," she replied, walking into the tiled, semi-circular studio where a grand piano stood. She noted that the manse looked far tidier than it had the last time she'd visited and wondered if Garrick had hired someone to clean the place. Mariel, who'd roomed with Brenna for a few months, knew that the Lithian woman had grown up in a household with personal servants. She'd never had to clean anything, generated clutter in her path, and felt no urgency to reorder the chaos of her creating. Mariel had long felt that Brenna's proclivity for making messes amplified work for everyone else.

Garrick returned with the promised tea, offering Mariel a mug as she sat on the practice room sofa. The music manse did not lend itself well to entertaining, but the young couple seldom attracted visitors anyway and its isolation suited them.

"What's this national security matter that demands my wife's attention?" Garrick asked.

"I need to contact her sister, Cassie," Mariel replied. "I remember Brenna saying something about a terrorist group detonating a bomb near the Kamerese palace, and I want to verify the source before contacting our allies to discuss a theory I'm developing."

Garrick nodded, remembering. "They wanted to reverse the economic and social reforms King Alejo enacted during the civil war." Then, drawing his own conclusion Garrick continued, "You think radical Kamerese are connected with the palace gate bombing?"

"I didn't say that," Mariel responded, "but I'm not denying it, either."

"The Defenders told me some Kurian separatist group carried out the attack. What makes you think the Kamerese were involved?"

"I didn't say they were," Mariel reiterated. "It's just a possibility I'm investigating."

Secrets and Whispers: *Missing Pieces*

An uncomfortable silence followed. Garrick sat in a chair by the piano, glancing at the clock. Brenna had to show up soon, or she'd be late for work.

Mariel rescued him from the social awkwardness. "I could have phoned Brenna about this, but there's actually something I think I should tell you . . ."

The way she phrased that statement sent a chill down Garrick's back. "What's on your mind?"

"A personnel file came across my desk a few days ago. I'm not at liberty to offer specifics, but I can tell you that a private who transferred into the Expeditionary Force from the 1st Army 3rd Battalion, TDF alleges he did so because a certain corporal, soon to be related to you by marriage, made repeated advances on him."

"You're talking about one of Bronwyn's brothers?" Garrick clarified.

Mariel nodded. "Corporal Willem Soehn . . ."

"Well, that explains a thing or two," he stated. "How do you know about this?"

"It's routine," Mariel said. "Every soldier who transfers in goes through an evaluation. We check the psychological profile, school records, medical history, combat notes, and disciplinary incidents for everyone who gets into the Expeditionary Force. I did yours, too."

"You looked into my background?" Garrick asked, his tone a bit more demanding than prudent.

"Of course," said Mariel calmly. "You came highly recommended by everyone in your unit, but there were concerns about your obvious youth, inexperience and family history. Your father's reputation as a drunkard, your mother's well-known promiscuity and your siblings' notoriety as troublemakers raised concern among senior officers about your suitability for transfer. There was also a girl who accused you of rape. She dropped the charges soon afterward, but the accusation is still on record."

Secrets and Whispers: *Missing Pieces*

Garrick fell silent. The girl to whom Mariel referred was Gudrun, a distant cousin who'd lived at his great uncle's ranch on the Saradon. Her son was probably old enough for school already.

"We do these background checks to avoid getting the cast-offs from other service branches. It's been part of my job since the early days of the Expeditionary Force.

"I'd been assigned to have a look at you and assess your relationship with Brenna," Mariel continued. "Because of her Lithian heritage, she presented a security risk. Additionally, everyone made certain assumptions about the nature of your relationship with her, and part of my tasking involved finding out if you were – to put it politely – honoring her virtue.

"It turned out that you were nothing like your mother. You also don't drink, which alleviated the concerns about your father, and with the exception of that incident where you allegedly threatened the former high priest, you've also shown more maturity than either of your siblings."

Desperate to change the subject, Garrick returned to Mariel's initial revelation. "So your background check uncovered the internal investigation into the corporal's conduct for immorality?"

If that statement surprised Mariel, she concealed it skillfully. "I never told you he was under investigation. I merely stated that an allegation had been made."

But Garrick, having spoken to Lieutenant Isenberg, Willem's commanding officer, suspected the investigation she'd hinted had its roots in the incident Mariel revealed.

"I've brought this to your attention because a certain Sergeant Soehn – same last name, which is odd – showed up at Fort Aeolus asking questions about you."

"That's Bronwyn's oldest brother," Garrick told her. "Their wives are cousins. Talon already told me about it."

Secrets and Whispers: *Missing Pieces*

The front door opened and Brenna breezed in, slipping out of her shoes and unzipping her track top as she and Mariel exchanged greetings that reflected the warmth of long-term friendship.

"I'm sorry to bother you so early," Mariel said. "But I'm working on the bombing and I need some help."

Brenna smiled, her eyes glancing at Garrick and reflecting promise that made his pulse quicken. She pulled off her socks, dropping them, along with her track top, near the front door while she explained the reason for her tardiness to Mariel. "I don't have a lot of time right now," she admitted. "We can talk while I shower."

Garrick remained in the studio while the women went upstairs. Mariel's revelation about Willem explained his strident complaining about the Expeditionary Force. His grousing had nothing to do with taking over the fight against the Tanarak. As Garrick had already suspected, Willem had bigger problems than just his drinking . . .

But were the allegations about his behavior true? Did Bronwyn's family know anything about it? Was this score settling? How did this play into the family's opposition to Algernon's marriage? The puzzle remained frustratingly incomplete.

Evidence

Colonel Scheer slowly and carefully read through Mariel's report, taking her time, absorbing the nuance of its conclusions and writing notes to herself. The woman had short-cropped grey hair and pale eyes that locked onto Captain Hougen's face like a predator. "What proof do you have that any of this is true?" she asked.

Mariel cleared her throat. She'd taken care to compose her report in a way that avoided unsupported conjecture, but hard evidence eluded her. "It's more a matter of who has the capability to launch an attack of this scale and daring," she replied. "In my view, the Kurian nationalists lack the requisite sophistication. They've done nothing like this in the past, and we're an unlikely target for them."

The colonel set Mariel's report down and leaned back in her chair. Her wrinkled brow furrowed as skepticism arose in her expression. "You've come to us highly recommended," the colonel began. "This document is detailed and comprehensive in scope, but I struggle to grasp how a group like *Guardas de la Raza* benefits from carrying out a terror attack on behalf of the Kurians."

"I believe they're acting for their own benefit," Mariel clarified. "Leaving evidence that the Old Order is responsible deflects the investigative trail away from them. After attacking the Kamerese palace, loyalist forces in that country cracked down on the group, leaving them fragmented and leaderless. Bombing our palace either demonstrates their resurgence, or is a copycat action."

Colonel Scheer raised her brow. "I admire the depth of your analysis, captain, but I simply don't see evidence implicating the Kamerese in this attack. What we have here is speculation. There is nothing that directly ties any Kamerese terrorist group to the palace attack."

Secrets and Whispers: *Evidence*

"It's more the absence of clues that concerns me," Mariel replied. "The only linkage between bombing and the Old Order is a collection of poorly-written pamphlets found in the wreckage."

"The transport company who owned the truck had been hired through Kjelvik, in Norda," the colonel countered, shaking her head. "You admit yourself that the money for the rental was wired from that town. Further, we've identified the truck driver as a Kurian national who, from the interviews we conducted with the transport company, struggled with our language. They also told us that they were concerned about his driving skills. Kameron has more mature transportation infrastructure than the Nordan coast, which fits his profile nicely. "

"That's true," Mariel admitted, "but it's not the complete story. Kjelvik is very close to the Kamerese border. The driver entered Tamaria through Desperado Falls several days before the attack. Because there are no direct routes from the Nordan coast to that point of entry, it would have been more direct, and a lot faster, to come by train from the west. So why did the driver came through Kameron?

"We've learned that the bomb-making materials were sourced locally and everything was paid in cash. Without a paper trail, we can't track the source of the funds.

"I've looked into the Old Order's banking records. They're teetering on financial ruin because the Nordans have frozen assets and imposed an import embargo.

"But the *Gardas de la Raza* has members deeply networked in the banking system. We know they're associated with multiple business accounts in Tamaria. They have the expertise to hide their transactions. The Old Order has nothing like that here."

Secrets and Whispers: *Evidence*

Colonel Scheer shook her head. "I understand what you're saying, but this is all circumstantial. I need actual facts, captain."

"This was a meticulously planned attack," Mariel stated. "We have limited evidence because the people who carried out this bombing have a great deal of experience in executing terror. They have both the means and the motive to carry this out."

Somewhat impatiently, Colonel Scheer asked, "Okay, so what do the Kamerese gain by attacking us?"

"It furthers the organization's agenda by retaliating against their government's ally. The attack strengthens their support among those who are unhappy with reform in Kameron; people convinced that loyalist forces were unfairly bolstered by our participation in their civil war."

"So you're telling me that the gain for them is purely ideological in scope?"

Mariel nodded. "They can't take us on militarily. This is the best they can do."

"Why not take credit for it, then? Why the elaborate ruse of making is look like Old Order is responsible?"

"Because their own government would crush them," Mariel stated. She opened her briefcase, pulled out a recent Kamerese newspaper and pointed to a story. "Last month, someone detonated a bomb at a Tamarian dock facility in the port city of *Huéscar*, near the mouth of the Angry Bear River. Our Kamerese allies investigated and arrested suspected members of the *Gardas de la Raza*.

"Here's another," she continued, referring to an older article in a different paper. "This one's from *El Torno La Barca*, a smaller town on the northern Kamerese coast. Its target was a fish oil processing plant, a joint venture between Kamerese and Tamarian investors. The fish oil from this plant is processed to remove glycerin, which we use in the manufacture of explosives.

Secrets and Whispers: *Evidence*

"Both targets were directed at our commercial interests, and in both cases, Kamerese authorities traced the crime to the *Gardas de la Raza*. They want to rattle our alliance, but when that didn't work, the radicals attacked our palace, using a Kurian driver."

"That would represent a significant escalation," the colonel remarked. "What you've outlined is compelling, but I hesitate to endorse your conclusions. There are too many assumptions in this analysis for my comfort.

"I can't take this report any further, unless you can provide me with hard evidence that this Kamerese terror group you've identified is responsible. At this stage in my career, I'm not in a position to rely on speculation."

That remark felt like a slap in the face. Mariel had spent many hours translating documents, researching all avenues and carefully analyzing the threat.

She maintained her cool until dismissed from the colonel's office, but stalked out of the Defenders' headquarters building with strong emotion rising in her soul. Why were people in authority so unwilling to listen?

***

Under a beautiful clear sky, Kira worked on weeding her garden beds. She loved the aroma of healthy soil and the sensation of her fingers working in the dirt. This task gave her time alone, time to think, and sometimes to pray. On this occasion, it simply felt good to shut her mind off.

Plants had a less invasive way of communicating. Certain weeds quietly suggested that her soil was too acidic or alkaline, too dry or too wet. The leaves of her flowers and vegetables added their testimony to the tale. Beneficial insects, along with the occasional pest, offered hope or caution, allowing the young woman to adapt her horticultural methods to suit the garden's needs.

Secrets and Whispers: *Evidence*

Thinking about adaptability brought a very different subject to mind. Years earlier, Algernon had befriended a gwynling thief named Jhiran, a strange little woman with a childlike mind. Wild gwynling – diminutive, winged humanoids who lived high in tree canopies in small troupes – were typically reclusive creatures. Giants considered gwynling a delicacy and had hunted them to extinction in many regions, but a solitary family group survived in the sheltered redwood forest of Wounded Heart Canyon, which separated Superstition Mesa from the vast promontory upon which the city of Marvic stood.

Jhiran, however, did not behave like a typical gwynling. She'd developed a mysterious ability to read minds, or put her own thoughts in the minds of others. This capability made her an uncanny judge of character. Jhiran survived in human society by thievery, a lifestyle which presented no moral conflict for her. The gwynling woman followed Algernon home after his long excursion to the Velez estate in Kameron, promptly joined the local gwynling troupe, and mated with one of its members. Jhiran convinced the family to leave the redwood forest and live in the derelict stone fort at Lookout Point on the southern tip of Superstition Mesa.

She'd rightly believed they'd be safe there, but that decision attracted hunting parties of local giants, violating an agreement Algernon had negotiated with them.

He'd desperately – but unsuccessfully – tried to manage the ensuing conflict. Garrick, who'd arrived in the midst of a violent altercation, shot and killed three warriors from the Clan of Broken Bones with his .45 caliber handgun. Later, a Tamarian army battalion set up camp to the south of Kira's homestead, erected a defensive palisade wall that crossed the entire mesa, and conducted operations to seek and destroy the giants.

Secrets and Whispers: *Evidence*

All residents in the Augury Creek region – including Kira, Bronwyn, Algernon and the women who lived with them – had been evacuated to the city for their safety. After Kira finally returned home she spoke to Jhiran one last time, learning that the gwynling woman intended to go back to Kameron with her newborn baby to escape the brutal Tamarian winters.

During that conversation, Jhiran told Kira that she'd seen "a bad lady" from the Wildlife Office roaming near the old fort. Having experienced Jhiran's spooky mind-reading ability, Kira took note of the warning.

But no one had seen Jhiran since. Had she returned to the Velez estate? Perhaps Tembe, the handsome Abelscinnian engineer whose family lived with Brenna's parents, would know. Kira decided to inquire when he returned with the Velez family to attend Bronwyn and Algernon's wedding.

With the Great Eye Nebula – the ghostly, glowing remnant of a distant, dead star – inching below the horizon, Kira moved her three-legged stool over to the next garden bed. Inclining her ear toward the house, she paused, scrunching her brow at the sound of a woman's voice. Bronwyn had gone to visit her father more than an hour earlier and Ileana typically did not return until very late in the afternoon. Abandoning the stool and retrieving her cane, Kira hobbled toward the front door.

A blonde woman with a pear-shaped backside was peering through one of the front windows. She wore a Wildlife Service uniform, had a 30 caliber rifle slung over her shoulder, and carried a duffel bag. What was she doing snooping around here?

Kira cleared her throat. "Excuse me!" she said.

The woman turned around, red-faced for having been caught peeking through the window. "Um, I'm uh,

Secrets and Whispers: *Evidence*

just looking for Algernon," the woman stammered. "I knocked, but no one answered."

She was far too slim to be his type, but Kira thought she looked cute. "He's not here."

The Wildlife Officer smiled and reached for Kira's hand in the universal gesture of peace. She recognized this attractive woman's strong resemblance to Algernon, but she'd already made a social blunder and didn't want to make another, so she chose her words with care. "I'm Karin," she said. "I'm the gwynling case manager for the Wildlife Office."

Kira liked the woman's perky smile and friendly demeanor. Her blundering effort to bounce back after making a fool of herself was endearing. "What do you want with my brother?"

"I need to talk to him about a development in the case of the missing gwynling troupe," she stated. "I've found abandoned nesting sites and uncovered clues that might shed light on their whereabouts."

The expression on Kira's face morphed from interest to suspicion and she crossed her arms, finding it odd that she'd been thinking about Jhiran just before this woman's arrival. What an intriguing coincidence . . . "How does this involve my brother?" she asked.

Why the change? Why the sudden hostility? "I've just come back from the old fort at Lookout Point," Karin explained. "It's been locked up for years, but the army gave me permission and a key so I could have a look inside. I found several gwynling nests and additional evidence that I thought maybe you, or your brother, might be able to explain."

Her slightly accusatory tone warned Kira to respond carefully. "You're mistaken. I know nothing about that place and I'm sure my brother doesn't, either."

Secrets and Whispers: *Evidence*

Karin knelt down to set her rifle on the porch. She unzipped the duffel bag and pulled out a hand-cranked flashlight, an axe whose blade had been damaged by contact with concrete, a folding saw, several items of children's winter clothing – nearly all soiled – remnants of a military surplus survival kit, several rations wrappers, food tins and some fire starter sticks. "Most of this hasn't been used," she explained. "These things couldn't have been left behind when the fort was mothballed."

Kira scrunched her brow. She thought the duffel bag looked newl. "You found all of that inside the fort?"

"Yes," Karin replied. "The entrance was secure. In fact, it was rusted and tough to open, but all this stuff was scattered around in several different rooms. Someone had left a well-used tin can stove behind, and nearby I also found dried orange peels and a lot of chicken bones."

Karin stood to full height and her demeanor hardened. "As you know, gwynling have no means to produce these things," she said. "Therefore, someone supplied them, in contravention of the Wildlife Act."

"Or they were stolen," Kira replied.

"Stolen by whom?" Karin countered, amplifying her hostile tone. "And stolen where? Gwynling are wild creatures. They don't build tin can stoves, raise poultry and grow fruit. They don't live in cities, and don't have access to military supplies and manufactured goods.

"It's far more likely that you, your brother, or one of the disreputable women who live with you provided these items to the resident troupe. Their familiarity with humans may also explain why they've disappeared."

"That's a stretch," Kira stated. "I think it's far more likely your department isn't pleased that you're ignorant of the gwynling's itinerant nature, their nesting and migratory habits. So you've been snooping around, spying on my brother and spinning wild stories.

Secrets and Whispers: *Evidence*

"You have no idea what you're talking about. If you think we're responsible for the gwynling's disappearance, that thought had a long a lonely trip through your desolate, impoverished mind."

Astonished, Karin bristled. "How dare you insult me like that!"

Kira moved into the woman's space, her eyes alive with anger. "How dare you accuse us of wrongdoing. How dare you set foot on my homestead and spy like some sick voyeur. Do that again and I'll have the sheriff up here to charge you with lewd conduct!"

Intimidated by Kira's assertive tone, Karin backed away. "You've not heard the end of this!" she warned.

Kira glared at the woman, wordlessly watching her descend the stairs and trot down the path to the farm service road. "I'll bet we haven't," she muttered in reply.

***

"Kira thinks that Darren, Harold and Willem are after my dowry and inheritance," Bronwyn complained, tearing at the pastry her father had ordered for her, but not eating it.

Arvid raised his brow, taken aback. "That's a serious allegation," he replied. He sipped his tea as a thoughtful expression arose on his face. "Why would she think such a thing?"

Bronwyn shook her head. "It doesn't matter. I don't care about the money. We don't need it . . ."

Arvid reached for his daughter's hand. "Darling, we've worked long and hard to ensure that you and the children you will have one day can count on a viable future. The dowry is yours to set up a household or invest as you wish. This is our legacy, and it's important to both me and your mother that it goes to you."

Secrets and Whispers: *Evidence*

"Not at the expense of our relationships," Bronwyn countered. "I don't want to sacrifice the love of my brothers over money. It's not worth it. If they're being mean to isolate me and guarantee that I go against *Mutti's* wishes, then they can have it all."

"Now, that's foolish talk," Arvid stated, letting go of Bronwyn and returning to his tea. "This is not a zero-sum game. Your brothers are not your enemies."

"Then why are they being so mean to me?" the young woman pleaded. "I've been nothing but nice to them, yet they're running me down at every opportunity. Not only has their behavior been hurtful, it also reflects badly on our family. What do you think Algernon's brother and sister think of us now? What about saintly Brenna? How well is our faith being represented by their conduct?"

"We men were going to have a talk about that before Harold took off with Heidelinde," Arvid said. "But your friend, Kira, derailed my plans . . ."

Bronwyn bristled – disliking the implication that Kira was culpable in the conflict – but she didn't explain how awful Heidelinde had been that day. "Kira's my friend. She was only defending me."

"You're a grown woman, yet you need someone else to defend you?" Arvid queried. He disapproved of how Kira handled that situation as Kira's behavior reinforced Irena's belief that the Ravenwood family was impulsive, domineering and prone to violence.

Responding to the hurt look on his daughter's face, Arvid changed the subject. "Let's set that aside for now," he suggested. "I want to talk about your mother."

Bronwyn's eyes brimmed with tears. She didn't want to cry in public, especially in front of Lilian – who was working behind the counter and paying more attention than was polite – so she willed her emotions into check. "I can't talk to her. She's totally unreasonable."

Secrets and Whispers: *Evidence*

"I have spoken to her on your behalf," Arvid assured his daughter calmly. "Your Tante Marla is also advocating for you. I don't believe your mother's position is as rigid as you may believe it to be."

"She threatened to have my marriage annulled in court!" Bronwyn replied in a hoarse whisper. "That doesn't sound very flexible to me!"

"That statement was unfortunate," Arvid admitted. "She responded in fear and was thinking out loud. Now that her emotions have cooled, you'll find her less strident than she was when we visited you at Kira's homestead."

Hope blossomed in Bronwyn's heart. "So she's not going to oppose my wedding plans?"

"She still has concerns," Arvid cautioned. "You'll need to discuss them with her, and I trust you'll do so in a rational and respectful manner."

Bronwyn looked away. No matter how legitimately upset she'd felt, arguing with her mother had neither felt right in the moment, nor did it resolve the issue. "I love *Mutti*. I don't want to ruin my relationship with her."

"She feels the same way," Arvid promised. "This breakdown in trust has been difficult for her."

A surge of indignation arose in Bronwyn's mind that she suppressed before responding. "The breakdown in trust is not my doing. I've been honest with *Mutti*, but she was opposed to Algernon before they'd even met."

Arvid shrugged. "Your mother has reasons."

"Kira thinks *Mutti* heard all the dirt on her and Algernon from that pedophile, Sister Alba," Bronwyn stated. Noting the shock evolving on her father's face, she pressed her point. "You know something about that?"

Reluctant to admit an uncomfortable truth, Arvid tightened his lips. "You're an adult now, and maybe it's time you learned why we agreed to let you leave home and live at the Temple . . .

Secrets and Whispers: *Evidence*

"When I first met your mother, she was romantically involved with a woman name Hiltrud. It was an experimental fling with no lasting value, but it created a scandal at the college. According to policy, both your mother and Hiltrud should have been dismissed for misconduct, but some backdoor deal went down and Hiltrud quietly departed, promising to never return.

"The discipline committee put your mother on behavioral probation. In time, her relationship with me ended all talk of impropriety."

Bronwyn remembered Kira's unflattering account of the story between Irena and Sister Alba. While she'd long felt terrible about the intimacies Kira had compelled her to share, Bronwyn felt powerless to articulate the sense of betrayal inspired by this revelation. A solitary tear spilled from her eye, revealing soul-crushing sorrow.

"When you expressed interest in the Temple, your mother assured me you'd be safe there," Arvid continued. "She said she had a friend in the cloister who promised to look after you, but she never admitted who this woman was. I've since learned that Hiltrud changed her name to Alba when she joined the Sacred Community. She was the one who protected you during your early years there."

Kira had been right, but a more complex understanding of the truth weighed heavily on Bronwyn's heart. Despite the fact that she'd blossomed into womanhood early, Bronwyn had never been part of the widespread sexual abuse at the Temple in those days. Many young woman in her cohort had been pressured to participate, but Alba's harem strictly excluded Bronwyn.

She'd attributed this to being unattractive and heavy, as Sister Alba and the men involved tended to prefer the prettier, blonde-haired and slender girls moving through the ranks. But Astrid had once complained to Bronwyn that she had a defender in the priestly ranks.

Secrets and Whispers: *Evidence*

"You have immunity from all this," the skinny priestess accused. "Nobody will ever mistreat you here. Nobody will ever force themselves on you, so be grateful for your protection and stay away from my Kira!"

Astrid later found the courage to expose Sister Alba, an act that sidelined her career long before High Priest Abelard's tenure. After Sister Alba was defrocked, Astrid used newly acquired power to adjust the acolyte chore schedule, making life miserable for Bronwyn. Astrid assigned her the dirtiest, most miserable tasks available as punishment for her friendship with Kira.

"You've known about this all along, and you never said anything to me?" Bronwyn sniffed, her voice cracking.

"No," Arvid insisted. "Tante Marla pieced the story together from certain things that Kira told Vega, and that Vega subsequently passed on to her. Marla wanted to make sure the story was true, so she phoned the Temple yesterday and spoke to the High Priestess. Your auntie explained it all to me just before you arrived."

The fact that Astrid knew about this only made matters worse for Bronwyn. She glanced at her pastry and shook her head. "None of what you've told me changes anything," she said.

"I understand where your heart is," Arvid reassured. "Your mother knows what it's like to be manipulated by a powerful woman, and she's worried that Kira will dominate you like Hiltrud did her."

"I'm not sleeping with Kira," Bronwyn hissed, drawing approval from Lilian as she added pastries a display case. "She's my friend. There's nothing more to it."

"No one is accusing you of impropriety," Arvid replied reassuringly. "The issue is that you're living in her house and participating in her ministry. Those two things alone give her considerable control over you.

Secrets and Whispers: *Evidence*

"As long as you're getting along, it's not going to be a problem. But the moment there's a conflict, you're going to find yourself at a significant disadvantage. Even with Algernon on your side, your mother's concerned that household decisions – issues that potentially impact the way you choose to raise your children, for example – may not align with your wants and values."

Bronwyn loved her father enough to hear him out and ponder his counsel. "I committed myself to communal living when I entered the Temple," she began. "So did Kira, and so did Algernon. All three of us have been doing this since we were children.

"We're all aware that communal living creates a set of unique challenges. Learning how to work those out is integral to our household ethic. It's also central to Algernon's priestly vows. Kira loves him. She respects him, and she's not going to put his values, his happiness, or his children at risk. Neither you, nor *Mutti* can deny that he and Kira are very close. Algernon has already risked his life for her, and I'm sure she'd do the same for him.

"As his partner, and Kira's friend, that commitment to communal living, and the grace that goes with it, extends to me. I've been part of Kira's household for years, and she's never pushed me around – not once."

Arvid wrinkled his brow and steepled his fingers in concern. "That may be true, but Kira's homestead is not the Temple. You have no Supreme Council to enforce equity and advocate for you there."

Bronwyn held her tongue. She didn't want to argue with her father, but she knew from experience that corruption plagued the Supreme Council during her time at the Temple. In fact, the senior priesthood had unfairly ruled against her ordination, questioning her fitness for service because she remained close friends with Kira and had been fully involved in her ministry.

Secrets and Whispers: *Evidence*

That betrayal left a lingering wound, inspiring unspoken resentment she reserved for private prayers that she'd never shared with anyone – not even Algernon. But now that Astrid had been appointed to the role of High Priestess, Bronwyn's mistrust in the Temple as an impartial institution increased significantly. Entreating the Great God for humility and grace hadn't helped, as Bronwyn secretly clung to her animosity and still struggled to honestly forgive Astrid.

"I'm not compelled by an oath to live under Kira's roof, even after Algernon marries me," she stated. "I have a right to start my own household whenever I want."

"You'd have Algernon choose between you and his twin sister?"

"He already has," Bronwyn replied. "The fact that he didn't take a vow of celibacy proves it. Kira has known all along that he intended to marry."

"What about his vow of perpetual poverty?" Arvid asked. "If he left his ministerial work with Kira, he would leave communal living behind and betray that sacred vow, would he not?"

Bronwyn shook her head. "Former High Priest Volker gave Algernon his own order to protect him from the corruption of the Supreme Council. His community is centered wherever he lives."

Arvid clicked his tongue, his brow raising in an understanding manner. "And I understand that Kira's not ordained. So if they part ways, she'll lose financial support in the business community and will have to fund her public service out of pocket."

"Yes," Bronwyn affirmed. "Not to mention the loss of credibility that would entail. Algernon not only offers a spiritual authority to her ministry, he also advocates in court for Kira's clients, where she has no right to speak for anyone other than herself.

Secrets and Whispers: *Evidence*

"The girls are safe in public because their pimps and strongmen won't mess with Algernon. They're terrified of what he can do to them. Losing him would make Kira's work with exploited women nigh-well impossible."

Arvid had not considered these factors before. He now realized that his daughter's position in Kira's household would actually strengthen once she married. This novel understanding softened his heart and increased his belief that Bronwyn had chosen her partner wisely. "In the ultimate sense, decisions about your future are yours to make," he told her. "Your mother and I both want you to be happy and successful."

Bronwyn smiled, but her happiness lasted for only a moment. The shop door opened and Darren charged in, his face flushed, his lungs heaving from exertion.

"There you are!" he panted. "Where's Willem?"

"He came in with Algernon early this morning," Bronwyn replied, distressed by the insinuation that she should be responsible for her brother's whereabouts.

Darren leaned against a table, rolled his eyes and shook his head. "You stupid girl!"

Arvid stood to his feet. "Son!" he warned. "Show some respect. Don't speak to your sister that way!"

Ignoring his father, Darren focused his attention on Bronwyn. "You were supposed to stay with him, not let him wander off to a bar, somewhere!"

Mildly annoyed at Darren's behavior, Arvid patted Bronwyn's shoulder in a reassuring manner and moved between her and her eldest brother. "Tell me," he ordered sternly, but quietly. "What's going on with Willem?"

Noting her brother's labored breathing and need to steady his balance on a nearby table, Bronwyn turned and reached for his hand. "Come, sit with us," she encouraged. "You'll get sick trying to exert yourself."

Secrets and Whispers: *Evidence*

Something in Bronwyn's mild response calmed Darren enough to comply. He felt dizzy, and somewhere in the back of his head an ache began clamoring for attention as Bronwyn asked Lilian for altitude tea.

Lili, intrigued by all the choice gossip she was overhearing, smiled sweetly and reached for a pot already steeping on the back counter. A local specialty, altitude sickness tea – brewed from dried coca leaves and other herbs mixed with almond milk and honey – sold briskly among tourists during the spring and summer.

When Arvid returned to his seat, Darren gave an account of the previous evening's conflict between Vega and Willem that painted his brother in a more favorable light than was warranted under the actual circumstances.

Arvid tightened his lips in displeasure. "So you sent him, without any warning, all the way to see your sister in the middle of the night?"

Listening to his father phrase that question made Darren feel foolish. He rubbed his temples and squinted. "What else was I supposed to do? Vega had security ready to throw him out of the hotel. I couldn't let him wander about in the cold. We have a reputation to protect."

Turning to Bronwyn, Arvid asked, "At what time, and in what condition did he arrive at Kira's house?"

Bronwyn shook her head. "I don't know. I didn't wake up. Kira answered the door, and Algernon made him a bed in the living area. I learned he was with us after I heard him throwing up on our pillows. He was so sick he couldn't make it to the bathroom!"

"So, he'd been drinking to excess again," Arvid concluded in disgust. "I hope he was apologetic."

"Are you kidding me?" she replied. "Willem was hung over, shaking and strung out. He was pining for a drink before we'd gathered for prayers, but Kira honors Algernon's vow and keeps no alcohol in the house.

Secrets and Whispers: *Evidence*

"Willi was nothing but rude. We tried to help him. Algernon talked to him about making things right with Vega, but Willi thinks he's done nothing wrong."

Arvid, weary of the conflict among his children, addressed Darren sharply. "I don't know what's in your head, son, but you, your brothers and your wives have treated your only sister to a tirade of constant scorn and relentless criticism since our arrival here.

"This will stop now. You will use your influence for good, not evil, and you will begin acting like a brother worthy of Bronwyn's admiration. If you don't know what that means, I can spell it out for you."

"It's okay, sir. I get it," Darren replied meekly.

"Good! We're a family who sticks together, even when we disagree with one another. We've come here to affirm and support your sister in her decisions, not to create drama and trouble for her."

Darren nearly choked on his tea. "You agree with her choice to marry this . . . this thug? Come on, father!"

That impulsive statement raised Arvid's brow. "From where I sit, Algernon has acted with greater care and wisdom in Willem's case than you have. He's not yet a member of our family, but he's been a better brother to Willi than either you or Harold have been."

"Father, how can you say that?" Darren scoffed. "We don't know where Willi is, or what Algernon's done with him. For all we know, he's left him bleeding in a ditch!"

Arvid shook his head. "You will not engage in speculation with me. It's completely inappropriate to make wild accusations and smear someone else's character.

"Whether you like it or not, Algernon is an ordained member of the priesthood, and as such, he deserves your respect. That is the very least of courtesies you should extend to him."

"But father . . ."

Secrets and Whispers: *Evidence*

"Am I clear, son?" Arvid asked in a warning tone. Darren nodded. "Yes sir."

"Good. Now, finish your tea. When you're done, you and I will look for Willi. We'll uncover the root of his trouble, even if that means admitting him into rehab for treatment. We will honor his dignity and care for him with patience and love. That's what families do."

***

One thing that struck Irena as impressive about the city of Marvic was that its streets lacked litter. The detritus typical of human habitation – garbage, sewage, refuse and the unpleasant odors that went along with them – simply didn't exist. She saw no vagrants, derelict drunks, scruffy orphans, prostitutes or beggars, either.

As she walked through the university neighborhood with Marla, Irena glanced down back alleys and into gutters looking for trash and evidence of human tragedy, but saw nothing of the kind. Not a single wall sported graffiti, political polemics or damage due to vandalism.

Smiling street vendors and shop owners offered friendly greetings. The aromas of fresh bread, brewed coffee and the sounds of lively conversation wafted from storefronts with open doors and welcoming decor.

"Doesn't this place seem unnaturally clean to you?" she asked her sister.

Marla shrugged. "We're staying in a wealthy area. Maybe if we wandered into a poor part of town things might look different."

Irena scrunched her brow. "I've been to Burning Tree, Vengeance, Kameron City and a host of smaller towns. The veneer of wealth in those places can't cover the smell of poverty. You don't have to look hard to find it. But here, I see no evidence of squalor anywhere I look."

Secrets and Whispers: *Evidence*

"Well, it can't be paradise," Marla replied, ignorant of the irony in that statement. "Kira works with strippers and *strichmadchen*. They have to ply their trade somewhere – likely nowhere near the places we've been."

Irena nodded, her feet slapping on the paving stones as she walked downhill. The sisters angled toward Victory Street, the main thoroughfare that led from Marvic's gate to Equality Park, where the Senate building stood and beyond which the walled palace compound lay. They chatted about everything other than family matters, particularly Bronwyn's imminent marriage, as they descended into Marvic's bustling government district.

Large clusters of busy citizens crowded the walkways. Tourists waded carefully across Victory Street and hurried in and out of many shops. At a prominent corner, a massive, marble staircase led from the street to the courthouse entrance. A huge, rectangular portico lay beneath the shelter of a triangular pediment held high overhead by slender stone pillars. By the time the sisters ascended the stairs, Irena felt breathless and dizzy.

"Take it easy," Marla warned, "or you'll get sick."

The Victory District Court House featured marble floors and huge paintings portraying peace, justice and societal order stemming from the rule of law. Its frescoed foyer ceilings continued the theme. The sheer size and scope of this building inspired awe in Irena's mind as indistinct conversations and the footfalls of well-dressed people striding purposefully to their destinations echoed off its stone walls.

Amid the lawyers, support staff, families and interested citizens milling about, it didn't take long for Irena to spot Algernon's clerical robe. An animated conversation rose between him and a heavyset, balding man in an expensive suit. Irena could see frustration on the monk's face as the older man scolded him.

Secrets and Whispers: *Evidence*

Neither she nor Marla caught the gist of the argument. Algernon stalked away, disappearing into a nearby courtroom just before a security guard shut the door. The burly man pointed to a court office where the sisters could obtain passes to attend the proceedings.

On the docket for the morning, three cases involving women showed Algernon as priest advocate. All of these had been scheduled in a courtroom with Judge Gertie Schraum presiding. After showing their security passes and entering, Irena and Marla took seats in a sloping gallery that faced the empty jury box on the opposite wall, watching the Crown Counsel greet Algernon using the traditional gesture of honor merited by his priestly office.

Irena scowled. She'd come here to personally witness this aspect of Kira's public service, hoping to find evidence that Algernon wasn't engaged in legitimate ministry. Watching educated law professionals – like the Crown Prosecutors – respecting him and chatting amiably together didn't fit her preconceived narrative.

Everyone stood and bowed their heads when the bailiff announced that Judge Schraum would be presiding. The pale-skinned, gray haired senior woman projected a no-nonsense demeanor as she entered and took her seat in an elevated dais beneath a marble and jade panel, where a portrait of Queen Tamar hung. Her powerful voice called the court to order as the proceedings began.

The first case involved a round-faced teenager who came down from the gallery and stood next to her priestly advocate at the defense table. They exchanged whispered words while Judge Schraum reviewed her notes.

"Kathryn Uberoff," the judge began. "I'm pleased to see that your police record has been clear since you appeared before me six months ago. Your counseling officer reports that you've maintained regular contact and that you've landed a job. What do you say?"

Secrets and Whispers: *Evidence*

"If it pleases the court," Algernon responded.

"Yes, Brother Algernon," Judge Schraum stated. "You may continue."

"Thank you, your honor. Miss Kathryn completed a telephone operator's training course and has been working for City Telecom ever since. She is also attending classes at Meridian Remedial College in an effort to complete her high school diploma."

The judge wrinkled her brow. "And what about the addiction counseling?"

Without missing a beat, Algernon described the young woman's struggle in frank terms. "After a lengthy and painful withdrawal, Miss Kathryn reports that she's not used opium for nearly five months. Her counseling therapy is ongoing and she's attending a support group with other opium addicts, as indicated in my report.

"She has also reconnected with her estranged mother and has been seeing her children under supervision since she last appeared before this court."

This young thing had children? Irena glanced at Marla, who didn't seem the least bit surprised.

The judge nodded. "That sounds like progress. I'm pleased. I also understand your client wishes to rescind my supervision order. On what grounds does she make that request?"

"Miss Kathryn is now gainfully employed, she's been drug-free for ten weeks and believes supervised visitation strains relations with her children."

Judge Schaum shook her head. "From where I sit, that's not enough time. I would like to see at least a year pass without drug use before I rescind that order. However, I will temporarily remove the restriction on the boundaries of visitation rights and enable your client to spend time with her children in public spaces to the north of Victory Street, provided these visits remain supervised."

Secrets and Whispers: *Evidence*

"As it pleases the court," Algernon replied.

Irena noted the disappointment on the young woman's face and wondered why Algernon didn't press for concessions from the judge.

"Brother Algernon, do you have any additional recommendations on behalf of your client?"

"Yes, your honor. I do. Given the track record of progress Miss Kathryn has made to date, I request an upgrade to her housing subsidy. This would enable my client to find accommodation in a quieter neighborhood, as evening rail traffic often interrupts her sleep."

Another skeptical expression passed over Gertie Schraum's face, but she nodded. "I see no reason to deny that request. Your client is on the path to recovery and has made good progress to date. This court will authorize a ten-sterling-per-month increase in the housing subsidy, effective immediately.

"Crown counsel, do you have anything to add?"

A tall, blonde haired woman wearing a court robe rose to her feet. "The Crown is satisfied with this citizen's rehabilitation. We have no concerns at this time."

Judge Schraum turned to address Kathryn directly. The young woman stood nervously, swallowing hard as the judge spoke to her. She looked terrified.

"Don't be discouraged, young lady," Judge Schraum said in a gentle manner. "I've seen many in your situation make far less progress down this road. You're doing well. Keep it up!"

Kathryn nodded unhappily.

"Next!" the judge announced, banging her gavel.

Irena watched the young woman fight back tears as she climbed back into the gallery. The heavyset man who wore the fine suit entered as Kathryn sat down again. With her attention returning to Algernon, Irena saw him smile broadly when the judge called the next defendant.

Secrets and Whispers: *Evidence*

"In the case of the Crown versus Tabea Pabst," Judge Schraum began, "We have arrived at the assigned date for determining the final disposition of this matter."

The young woman in question scurried to Algernon's side. She'd dressed in a floral-patterned gown, had her long blonde hair in twin braids and couldn't stop smiling.

"Crown Counsel," the judge continued, "are you fully satisfied with this citizen's rehabilitation?"

The tall woman in the courtly robe stood again. "We are, Your Honor. If it pleases the court, we apply to remove all constraints and limitations on Miss Tabea's citizen rights."

Marla raised her brow. She'd never heard that happen in a court before.

"Brother Algernon, I presume you are speaking on behalf of this client?"

"As it pleases the court, Your Honor."

"In your view, is she ready to rejoin society?"

"Yes, Your Honor. Miss Tabea turned her design skill into a successful business that has shown profit in its first year of operation. She's also involved in the Temple's poverty outreach ministry and is serving as a weekend Resident Assistant at the Angel Arms Shelter for Battered Women. In addition to this consistent, significant re-connection with our community, she's been drug-free for over a year."

Judge Schraum raised her brows and nodded. "The purpose of sentencing in Tamarian law is, at its heart, an effort to re-integrate the wayward into society. Your work, Brother Algernon – in conjunction with the efforts of your twin sister – has been essential in the rehabilitation of many exploited women. I had my doubts about you at first," she admitted, "but I'm favorably impressed."

Secrets and Whispers: *Evidence*

Turning toward the defendant, Judge Schraum continued, "Tabea Pabst, I hereby rescind all restrictions on your citizen rights. You are free to go."

Tabea squealed with delight. She hugged Algernon, who turned red-faced and appeared thoroughly embarrassed, then she danced over to the Crown Prosecutor, who accepted Tabea's embrace appreciatively.

"Thank you!" Tabea announced to the judge as she twirled toward the exit. Even after the guard closed the door in the wake of her departure, everyone in the courtroom could hear her joy echoing through the foyer.

Judge Schraum shook her head. "If only all cases ended that well," she sighed, glancing at her notes. "Next up, we have Gisela Saudek . . ."

"Your Honor," Algernon called. "May I approach with Crown Counsel?"

The heavyset man in the business suit stood as a very beautiful, blonde-haired woman made her way to the defendant's table. He followed her and set a briefcase at the spot where Algernon had been standing.

Irena watched the exchange between Algernon, the judge and the two Crown Prosecutors carefully. While their conversation was too quiet to hear from the gallery, it soon became clear that no one was happy.

"Mr. Stennitz," the judge called. "Why are you darkening my courtroom today?"

The heavyset man cleared his throat and pulled a document from his briefcase. "Your Honor, I have a petition on behalf of my client. She wishes to change counsel and revise her previous plea."

"Approach," the judge ordered, dismissing Algernon and the Crown Counsel. She reached for the document, reading it with a deepening scowl. Judge Schraum shook her head. "This appears to be in order."

Secrets and Whispers: *Evidence*

"Your Honor, the Crown stridently objects," the tall prosecutor said. "This is highly irregular!"

"Perhaps, if Crown Counsel would focus on doing its job instead of adoring a renegade priest, we could continue," Mr. Stennitz replied.

Ignoring the banter, the judge banged her gavel down. "I will have order in my court," she warned. "Mr. Stennitz, you will take your seat at the defendant's table. Gisela Saudek, you will approach."

Algernon glared at the bigger man, but said nothing as the judge conversed quietly with the beautiful defendant. A moment later, the younger woman turned away, refusing to make eye contact with Algernon as she returned to her seat.

"Brother Algernon, I will grant Miss Saudek the requested change in counsel. You will step down."

Algernon scurried out of the courtroom over the continued objections of Crown Counsel. Irena followed him outside, with Marla trailing close behind.

"Wait for us!" Irena called as the courtroom door closed. She and Marla scurried to Algernon's side. "What was that all about?" she asked.

"It's brute intimidation," Algernon replied. "Gisela's been forced to rescind her plea while that thug lawyer attacks the Crown's case."

"Why would the court allow that?" she asked.

Algernon shook his head. "It's all legal maneuvering. Gisela works in a high-end strip club. She makes huge money for her pimp doing private shows – and likely a lot more – to entertain rich men, but she was caught buying opium on the street. That's why she wound up in court.

"Kira had been working with her for months, building trust. Gisela only agreed to let me represent her under the condition that we'd help her establish a new life with her daughter. She knows this is what we do, and I'd

Secrets and Whispers: *Evidence*

warned her that working with us would involve cooperation with the authorities. She said she was okay with that, as long as she could get a fresh start.

"This morning, along comes Fat Man, threatening legal action if I interfere in his new client's case. Gisela's pimp hired him to represent her, and there's nothing I can do because she's consented to this."

Irena shook her head. "But if she wants to start a new life, why would she agree to that?"

Algernon paused. Irena caught a glimpse of his anger and it frightened her. "Gisela's pimp is holding her daughter hostage. She's most likely been threatened with harm to the child if she doesn't cooperate."

"That's horrible!" Irena replied.

"That's what we're up against," he complained. "I explained this to the judge, and the Crown Prosecutors agreed with me, but the ruling has to be in harmony with the law – not on what we believe is true – and everything that sleazy Mr. Stennitz did today is perfectly legal.

"He'll attack the Crown's case, find something weak in it and claim that Gisele was set up. Then, they'll move her to another city with a new identity, and the process will start over until she's no longer profitable to them."

"And this is legitimate?" Irena asked.

"No, it's not." Algernon admitted. "But what evidence can I present to prove she's being intimidated?"

***

Later that afternoon, Brenna arrived home from work to the sound of her husband struggling to produce a pleasant tone on his new trumpet. She'd bought it for him as a gift, after he expressed interest in learning music, and taught him a rudimentary lesson on how brass instruments worked. He'd taken it from there.

Secrets and Whispers: *Evidence*

But he sounded awful, sputtering, straining to create sound, and sometimes fruitlessly blowing air into the mouthpiece to produce absolutely no tone at all. Nonetheless he persisted, determined to triumph.

Brenna swayed into the practice room, leaning against the door frame and sliding her hip to the side, seductively. She smiled when he stopped, noting the small circle of redness in the center of his mouth that evidenced his effort and self-discipline. "You know what they say about trumpet players . . ." she cooed.

Garrick set the instrument down and beckoned for her, his heart racing as she leaned forward to kiss him. "Enlighten me," he requested.

The Lithian woman smiled as she draped herself onto his lap, caressing his face with her warm hand. "Finest lips in the world."

"Oh? What would you know about that?" he teased.

Brenna's eyes widened. "I have experience, now," she murmured, rubbing her nose against his.

While her warm lips felt much more pleasant than the trumpet's mouthpiece, the practice chair strained under their combined weight. Garrick gathered her in his arms and stood, carefully carrying his wife around the corner and up the stairs.

"What are you planning to do with me?" she asked, her inflection an invitation.

"I have ideas," he replied. "You've been the subject of my imagination all day long."

Brenna smiled. "I like the sound of that . . ."

He sat in her favorite spot – a love seat by the window with an east-facing view. She leaned her head against his chest and curled into his embrace.

"Tell me about your day," he encouraged, enjoying the soothing sensation of her skin against his fingers, the

Secrets and Whispers: *Evidence*

weight and warmth of her body and the silky texture of her lengthening hair brushing his cheek.

She recited a list of unimportant events, sharing insight into her music students and expressing gratitude for the growth she witnessed in them. Garrick's listening ear and affirming whispers evidenced his devotion as much as his affectionate touch.

But he held his tongue when Brenna's monologue merged into complaints about the prejudices projected on her. This problem hounded her days, despite her quiet demeanor, no matter how kindly she treated others.

"I get frustrated having to put up with contempt of my colleagues," she admitted. "I'm sick of the men leering. I'm tired of their dirty jokes. None of the women are ever nice to me, and some of the parents are downright rude. I'm not expecting them to love me, but I'm weary of dealing with their harassment and negative attitudes."

Garrick knew that his wife found this ongoing and baseless hatred hurtful. "You're a mirror that reflects the soul of everyone you encounter," he told her.

"I know it's not fair, but people who only see your beautiful body reveal their own lust, envy, and insecurity. They can't evaluate your talent, good character, loyalty or any of the other excellent qualities that I find worthy of respect because they lack those traits, themselves."

She frowned, her brows raised and eyes widened. "You're amazing," she said, planting a kiss on his chest. "I couldn't handle all of this without you."

Garrick shook his head. "That's not true. You'd not have to put up with any of this crap if it weren't for me."

Holding him close Brenna said, "You're worth much more to me than their approval. Let them say what they will. As long as I have you, I'm happy. I'm sorry for venting." Then, shifting the focus to him she asked, "How did your meeting go with Dr. Bauer?"

Secrets and Whispers: *Evidence*

Garrick shrugged. "He thinks I've made good progress in the past few weeks, but he's still not willing to sign off on my return."

Hearing the disappointment in his voice, Brenna scowled. "I'm proud of how far you've come," she told him. "It won't be long before he'll see that you're ready."

He appreciated her support, knowing that recovery would have been much more difficult without her endless patience, effusive affection and – though he didn't want to admit this out loud – her persistent prayers. Garrick gently toyed with her hair, grateful for her longsuffering concern, her selflessness and loyalty.

His career had been haunted by disappointment from its outset. Among his many spectacular battlefield successes, failure featured more frequently than he cared to admit. During a training exercise at a place called Dysentery Ridge, his platoon had been abandoned by the acting commander on an isolated hilltop, leaving him with the choice to either surrender or call in a *danger close* artillery strike. At a nameless, dry lake bed in Kameron, he'd been surprised by attacks from well-coordinated rebel soldiers in three directions. His only option in that case involved ordering his men to run. And then, there was his first, terrifying night on the Saradon plateau a year hence. His outnumbered platoon fought all night with the pluck of the damned to survive, but too many had not . . .

In every instance, memories of Brenna had calmed him. Her constancy and trustworthiness inspired confidence that she'd always stand by him, always soothe away his worry and lavish his body and soul with comfort. That reality fueled his courage. Garrick found strength to face and overcome every obstacle in his path because he believed in the depth and breadth of Brenna's devotion.

But he didn't want to talk about Dr. Bauer. The judgement that rendered him unfit for active duty chafed

Secrets and Whispers: *Evidence*

in his soul, rubbing raw resentment into his thoughts with an automaticity that he knew affirmed the psychologist's judgment. "The truth is, I'm anxious to get back. Mariel told me that the new captain is a real piece of work."

"What does she mean?" Brenna asked, noting something in his tone that sounded judgmental.

Garrick didn't want to elaborate on his concern, fearing that she'd be offended. "The new captain's just not a good fit for Alpha Company," he said evasively.

Intrigued now, Brenna sat up. "Why? What's wrong? What's he doing?"

While he'd always found her intellect intriguing, sometimes Garrick felt weary of contending with her, especially when her emotions rose like this. "He's forcing prayers on the company," Garrick admitted.

"How does he get away with that?" Brenna asked, knowing that the Tamarian military had an officially neutral position in religious matters, a fact that protected her faith, especially during the early days of her service with the Expeditionary Force.

Relieved that she'd not been offended, Garrick shook his head. "Maybe everyone's afraid to complain. Making a fuss with a new commander can end a promising career."

"So they just complain behind his back, hoping that something will change?" she asked. "How does that help?"

"Obviously it doesn't," he replied. "If I was there and sensed that his behavior was impacting morale in a negative way, or if someone felt violated by the imposition of a particular view, I'd speak to the captain about it, first. But soldiers always complain. It's what they do."

Brenna returned to her more comfortable position. "And if the offended person was you . . ?"

This was dangerous territory. Garrick chose his words with great care. "Your prayers don't offend me," he

Secrets and Whispers: *Evidence*

began. "There's power in them. I don't understand how it works, but I see evidence of how it changes you, how it softens your heart and helps you forgive.

"No one who's watched you heal wounds can deny that there's an inexplicable force flowing through your lips when you pray. But with you it's a personal thing. It's never about you getting what you want. I've heard you ask for wisdom and understanding, so you can deal with ignorant and foolish people. You ask for insight into what lessons you can learn in your circumstances. You ask for patience and the discipline of longsuffering grace. You do this because you want to be an instrument of peace.

"I've listened to you pray for me. I've heard you pray for my siblings, your family, your students and the ungrateful people you work with. You pray in gratitude for beauty, music, friendship – even for the pleasure you experience in sex with me. There's an unselfish motive behind your petitions – they're always about helping other people, or asking how you can serve them better – and in all the time we've been together, you've never insisted that I think or believe as you do.

"But this guy is trying to impose his perspective on people who don't agree with him. There's nothing introspective about it. What he's doing is about power, and that's a fundamentally different matter."

Brenna didn't see herself in quite so positive a light, knowing the difficulty of her spiritual struggle in a way he could not. She knew the roots of her attitude, but she appreciated his affirmation, grateful that he'd always been remarkably supportive of her faith despite his disbelief.

Garrick lifted her chin with his finger, gazing into her lovely eyes. Drawn by the desire he recognized there, he leaned forward and kissed her slowly. "Can *The Twins* come out to play?" he whispered, nuzzling her neck.

Brenna smiled. "I've been waiting for you to ask."

Secrets and Whispers: *Evidence*

***

Vega watched her cousin putting on a pair of earrings, secretly afraid that the upcoming family dinner would involve an ugly confrontation about her faltering relationship with Willem. She'd only agreed to stay in town after Darren promised to exchange rooms with her, otherwise, Vega might have filed a complaint against Willem and returned to her own kin.

She'd had enough of his nonsense.

But Sikki had a different idea, entirely. "I'll bet that spineless husband of yours shot his mouth off to Bronwyn. She met with Arvid this morning while Irena and Tante Marla went to watch Algernon make a fool of himself in court.

"Irena spent the afternoon chewing the cud with our fat cow sister-in-law and her delinquent fiancé. Tante Marla's gone running with boobs-for-brains Brenna for the last two days, as well. I told Darren to get Willi under control before this whole thing gets out of hand . . ."

Vega felt nervous. She couldn't contend with Sikki and worried that her cousin might eventually figure out what she'd told Kira. "It may be nothing," she replied reassuringly. "I don't think Willi would betray us. He needs the money more than you do . . ."

Sikki scoffed. "Irena booked a private dining room and made it clear she expected our attendance. That sounds serious to me."

Stifling anxiety, Vega slipped into her shoes and picked up her purse. "Are you ready to go?"

Ignoring her cousin, Sikki touched up her lipstick and replied, "Do you have your gun?"

"No," Vega admitted. "I don't expect I'll need it tonight, so I put it in the side table drawer."

Secrets and Whispers: *Evidence*

Putting the cap back on her lipstick, Sikki turned. "Well, just don't forget about it," she warned. "You never know when it will come in handy."

The two women took the elevator down to the dining floor, where a porter directed them to a small private room where Irena, Arvid, Tante Marla, Darren and Willem awaited. Neither Bronwyn nor Algernon were present, and only two place settings remained unfilled. That could not have been an oversight.

Although they were the last to arrive, Vega would not sit until Darren and Willem changed seats. She noticed that no wine glasses stood at the table. Willem looked both pale and shaky.

He, however, wouldn't look at her.

The meal consisted of poached fish with vegetables, bread, cheese and a dessert of berries with cream. Even Sikki, who'd entered the dining room in a foul mood, seemed to enjoy the high-quality food served to her. However, the family's muted, strained conversation made Vega feel uneasy.

After the hotel staff served dessert, Irena stood at the head of the table. "It's come to my attention that we have a problem in our family," she began.

Darren remained stone-faced, while Willem rubbed his forehead with his fingertips. Sikki felt tension rising in her shoulders as Vega stared at her hands, afraid that she'd be exposed as a traitor.

"Maybe I should have said something earlier, but I've been wrestling with my own doubts and I've had to reconcile a lot of conflicting feelings. This has not been easy for me . . .

"But my own children have made matters worse. Before any of you start thinking that we're here to dissuade Bronwyn from her wedding plans, let me put that to rest. After careful consideration, I have decided to

Secrets and Whispers: *Evidence*

offer my consent to Bronwyn's union with Algernon. I sincerely hope that every one of you will support and love her as she begins this new phase of her life."

Arvid watched his sons carefully. Darren lowered his eyes, while Willem's expression betrayed bewilderment, as if his future had just been snatched from his hands.

Sikki leaned toward him and snarled in a whisper, "You stupid man!"

"I didn't do anything!" he spat angrily.

"Shut up, both of you!" Darren ordered.

Irena glanced at Arvid, and then her sister. She put her hands on her hips and scowled. "So, it's true. There's a conspiracy going on here."

Darren shook his head. "There's no conspiracy, Mother. You've expressed opposition to this wedding from the start. We're just trying to support you."

"That's not what Bronwyn thinks," Irena replied. "Both Kira and Brenna agree with her."

"You believe a suction queen and a Lithian bimbo with big boobs and no brains over us?" Sikki stated.

Marla grew a little angry. "Watch your mouth, Sikki!" she warned. "You're only making matters worse for yourself with that kind of talk."

Willem shook his head. "There's no point in pretending anymore," he argued. "Kira knows everything. She laid out the whole story for me in front of Bronwyn and Algernon this morning . . ."

"No!" Sikki insisted. "You had a guilt trip and spilled your guts to Bronwyn. I bet you were hoping for a little sympathy after Vega kicked you out of her bed last night!"

Willem stood, his chair falling over behind him. "I did no such thing! This was your idea, and you didn't think my sister would figure it out, but maybe she and her friends are smarter than you think they are.

Secrets and Whispers: *Evidence*

"We've all underestimated Bronwyn – every one of us. We've been treating her like she's a little girl. She was, a long time ago, but she's a woman now. She has her own mind, her own will, and all the while we've been trying to impose what we want on her. That's not right."

"Sit down, Willem!" Darren ordered. "You're making an idiot out of yourself!"

"No son," Arvid corrected. "He's speaking sense for the first time since we arrived."

"Sense?" Sikki countered. "He's up to his neck in gambling debt. That's why he wants the dowry money!"

"Shut up!" Willem shouted. "You have no shame, Sikki! No discretion, whatsoever!"

"I'm not leading a double life," she snapped. "You want me to start talking about your real secret, Willi?"

Vega stood. No matter how badly her husband mistreated her, she still loved him. "Enough of this!" she pleaded. "Why are we turning on each other?"

"Everyone needs to calm down," Irena commanded. "We have faults, but we're a family." She paused, waiting for Vega to sit and Willem to retrieve his chair. "Now that the dirty laundry is out in the open, we will wash it among ourselves. There will be no more talk of Bronwyn's dowry or inheritance. These are rightly hers, and if this marriage goes south, she's going to need the money to support herself."

Darren threw up his hands. "This family has far fewer problems than the Ravenwoods do," he argued. "My little sister wants to marry a pariah priest who's been kicked out of the Temple, to live in the same house and raise her children with his lesbian twin sister and all her wayward clients. Their brother is on the ragged edge of a mental health discharge, and you're okay with it?"

Sikki tugged on the front of her blouse. "Don't forget about bountiful Brenna," she added.

Secrets and Whispers: *Evidence*

"That woman is the only person in their family worthy of respect," Darren countered. "She's a saint, and you'd be a lonely widow scraping by on my pension if it weren't for what she did for me!"

"You just can't keep your eyes off of her!" Sikki accused. "I've seen it! Tell me you don't envy the lieutenant over his busty little bride . . ."

"Sikki, that's enough!" Marla spat angrily. "The only envy here is yours, and it's obvious every time you open your mouth. Brenna is completely innocent of any wrongdoing, while all the evidence points to you as the source of Bronwyn's mistreatment."

When Sikki took in a breath to respond, Marla stood and cut her off. "Did you not hear me?"

Though it proved difficult to do, Sikki backed down. "Yes, Tante Marla. I hear you."

Marla returned to her sitting position, allowing Irena to continue. "We'll leave Brenna and Garrick out of this," she stated. "I have my concerns about Bronwyn's choice of a partner and I've expressed them to her.

"However, I have also been watching the dynamic between them and I see no reason to presume that he would ever mistreat her. In addition, after witnessing what he does for exploited women in court, how the authorities respect the work that he and Kira do in this community, and after spending the afternoon in his company, I'm convinced that our anxiety concerning his past behavior may have, in fact, been misguided."

Darren groaned.

"Son, if you have something constructive to add, now is the time to speak your mind. But I'll not tolerate you engaging in criticism without evidence."

Darren tightened his lips and shook his head. He dared not cross his mother and quietly acquiesced defeat.

Storm Clouds

The prevailing wind changed overnight, bringing cooler temperatures, clouds and blustery conditions. After morning prayers and sharing a light breakfast, Algernon held Bronwyn's hand as they walked down the trail to the Augury Creek Service Road.

"Are you feeling better now?" he asked.

She nodded, but kept her counsel to herself. The roller coaster emotions of the past few days left her soul exhausted. Now that she'd secured her mother's blessing, the young woman worried that something else might ruin the happiness she believed she should be feeling.

While joy eluded her, an increasingly urgent fear arose in her soul. Rooted in childhood trust, anxiety that her mother might be right after all crept into Bronwyn's mind like an amorphous mist. She tried to rationalize the worry away – knowing that her mother had been fed a steady diet of carefully-selected stories intended to malign Algernon's reputation, but found herself powerless against its lure.

Meanwhile, desire stirred in her imagination. Fueled by late-night fantasy as Algernon slept on the floor near her bed, Bronwyn could barely control the longing for him that whispered seductively into her thoughts. She wanted to talk to someone about this, but it would be awkward to discuss the issue with Kira, and too much tension still existed with her mother for that type of honest confession.

Torn by these conflicting thoughts, the young woman felt herself carried along in the turbulent current of her imminent wedding. Above everything else, a growing sense of helplessness inspired emotions ranging from mild despair that she might be making the wrong choice, to giddy delight that she'd finally enjoy the full extent of Algernon's masculine attention.

Secrets and Whispers: *Storm Clouds*

For his part, Algernon struggled to discipline the desire that surged in his flesh. Just thinking about Bronwyn aroused him. While he honestly loved her for more than her body, he secretly obsessed over her unveiled form and what he might do to inspire her delight.

The thought simultaneously excited and terrified him. Algernon, who'd heard enough of his brother's intimate contact with Brenna in their next door guest bedroom, had long worried that his performance with Bronwyn would pale by comparison. He didn't know what to do, but couldn't bring himself to ask Garrick for advice. Algernon believed he'd be finished within 15 seconds of being inside his new bride, and that she'd forever feel secretly disappointed by his lack of lovemaking skill.

Glancing at his waist, Bronwyn noticed his arousal. "What's this about?" she asked, drawing near and sliding her hand down from his belt.

Algernon turned away. "Stop it!" he warned, his tone betraying embarrassment. "You're not helping!"

"Do you want to go back home?" she asked, presuming that it had to feel uncomfortable to walk around with an erection like that, but not sure of how to alleviate his arousal, as they'd both agreed to delay having sex until their wedding night.

"We'll be late meeting your mother if we do," he replied. "Just leave me alone. I'll be fine."

Bronwyn pouted. She felt a little hurt, as he'd never objected to being touched before. However, he had a point. After arguing heatedly with Kira the previous evening, Algernon hadn't slept well and had struggled to awaken in the morning. For that reason, they were running late and couldn't afford delays.

"When do the people in your family start arriving?" she inquired.

Secrets and Whispers: *Storm Clouds*

Algernon scrunched his brow. "Neither set of my grandparents can attend, so it may be limited to a cousin and maybe an aunt and uncle on my mother's side. If they come, they'll be on the train from Burning Tree tomorrow. It's Brenna's family that concerns me."

Puzzled, Bronwyn asked, "Brenna's family?"

Reluctant to say the wrong thing, Algernon hedged for a moment. "They're all attending," he admitted.

Bronwyn stopped, placed her hands on her hips and tilted her head to the right. An expression of annoyance evolved on her face. "So, she's coming too . . ."

"If by she, you mean Brenna's sister Cynthia, then yes," he stated.

"How long have you known about this?" Bronwyn demanded, anger rising in her tone.

"Garrick told me about it yesterday. We met for lunch after I'd finished in court."

"Why didn't you tell me earlier?" she complained.

"Because I knew you'd react this way," he replied. "I didn't want to make a scene in front of Kira, so I didn't say anything until now."

Bronwyn crossed her arms and scowled. "You were thinking about her, weren't you?" she accused. "Is that what your erection was about?"

"No," Algernon responded, reaching for her hand. "You're the one I need. You're the only one I want. I left her behind for you."

Despite seeing the sincerity in his eyes, Bronwyn struggled to believe him. "I don't want that girl at my wedding! Who invited her, anyway?"

"It's a Lithian thing," he countered. "Their families are very close and they consider marriage a means to strengthen relationships. Kira and I joined their family when Garrick married Brenna, and now her parents treat me as if I was their actual son.

Secrets and Whispers: *Storm Clouds*

"It would be really rude to not invite them. Besides, I've already caused enough grief in their family and don't want to make things worse."

"Algernon, I don't want that girl at my wedding!" Bronwyn spat. "I don't want to meet her. I don't want to see her, and I don't want you to, either!"

He dropped her hand and held both of his up. "Then talk to Brenna. I have no say in this, and I'm not going to fight with you over Cynthia Velez."

"You don't get it, do you?" she countered. "Can't you see how this makes me feel? You spied on that girl while she was skinny-dipping, and she had the temerity to tell her father that you wanted to court her. Brenna's family accepted that story like it was perfectly normal, even after she admitted she'd done everything in her power to turn your eye. How am I supposed to face her after that?"

"I understand," he soothed. "And I told Garrick it was a dumb idea for Thea to attend. But the social dynamic in Lithian families is a sensitive matter, and while their customs sound odd to us, they're loving people who deserve our respect. I know from living with them that they're as deeply committed to family as we are.

"Brenna's been isolated ever since she escaped from Shirak and hasn't seen her parents for a long time. She has a baby brother who was still nursing at her wedding and is probably running around by now. Tirra, her maid, desperately wants to see her again, as does Thea, who hasn't spent time with Brenna since she married, either.

"Then there's Jawara, whom I consider a true friend. He protected me and Astrid on our journey to rescue Kira in Kameron – and his wife, Niobe – whom Brenna hasn't seen since before the Azgar burned Shirak. Niobe has a son, whom Brenna has never met. Re-establishing those connections is very important, and our wedding is the first opportunity all these people have had for a reunion.

Secrets and Whispers: *Storm Clouds*

"In their eyes, our marriage brings you into their family. You'll become Brenna's sister. You'll be Lord Lynden and Lady Alexina's daughter. They see this as a time of rejoicing for everyone. I know they're going to love you, so please don't make this difficult for them."

"I don't care if they visit with Brenna," Bronwyn retorted. "They can see her all they want and have a grand party on their own, but I don't want that girl at my wedding. Promise that you'll support me!"

"I have neither need nor desire to see Thea," Algernon told her.

"Promise me!" she demanded.

Algernon nodded. "This wasn't my decision. I didn't invite her. The whole thing has taken me by surprise."

He wasn't sure that would be enough and worried about Cynthia's imminent arrival creating friction with Bronwyn, or providing more ammunition for her family members to subvert their union. Over and over again, he'd wished that he could go back to that moment when Thea's lovely form caught his eye and turn away from her, rather than approaching for a better look. That singular lapse in judgement had created a disproportionate burden of guilt in his soul, as well as betrayal and mistrust in Bronwyn.

The hurt that arose in the young woman's heart dominated every thought as she took Algernon's hand. Silence loomed between them as they walked together.

With the aroma of healthy soil wafting on a strengthening wind from the west, Bronwyn and Algernon passed fields of sprouting grain. Shrouding the northern ridge lines, dark clouds advanced in unbroken ranks, threatening to cool the mildly warm day with rain carried from the distant sea. Algernon glanced over his shoulder, then gazed at his beloved's face, pondering a gloom that cast its shadows over her hope of happiness.

Secrets and Whispers: *Storm Clouds*

While she wasn't as pretty as Thea Velez and quite a bit heavier as well, he'd stopped caring about all of that. In Algernon's mind, no one compared favorably to Bronwyn. His devotion to her risked creating a rift in the relationship with the Velez family he'd carefully cultivated, yet that possibility paled when compared to the potential loss of Bronwyn's devotion. He needed her to soothe away the lingering, internal wounds wrought by years of rejection. Bronwyn's selfless nature, her kindness and willing affection had already softened his anger. No one understood that fact as profoundly as did he.

Bronwyn clung to the hope that she'd found true love in Algernon. It seemed that everyone who'd presumed her too big and too plain to attract interest evaluated Bronwyn's engagement with skepticism. Their contempt, evident in body language, smug and condescending commentary, and their dismissal of Algernon as a suitable partner, eroded her self-esteem. They hinted that he had to have some flaw that made him undesirable to more attractive women.

But Thea Velez – if she looked anything like her sister, Brenna – put that doubt to rest in Bronwyn's mind. She'd felt desperate at the thought of losing him, and when he returned, she'd been determined to keep his focus fixed firmly and forever on her.

That's why she'd become more permissive with his touch, following Kira's earlier counsel concerning her brother's need for comfort. The influence of maternal rejection left an invisible, yet lingering scar. Kira knew him well, and she'd been right. Shortly after her boundaries loosened, Algernon stopped paying attention to other women. Understanding this little secret about her betrothed and personally witnessing the change it wrought in him, Bronwyn believed Algernon when he said he'd never laid a hand on Brenna's not-so-little sister.

Secrets and Whispers: *Storm Clouds*

Bronwyn had not invited Brenna's family to attend her wedding because she'd not considered them related. However, his explanation of the Velez family's interest in celebrating her nuptial ceremony made logical sense, and with so few of Algernon's kin willing to attend, Brenna's loved ones could bolster the ranks on his side of the banquet table.

Unwilling to hurt Algernon deliberately, Bronwyn didn't want to articulate her fear that she'd be upstaged by a prettier maiden who'd once captivated his attention. Bronwyn wanted to be the center of attention at her own wedding. Wasn't that how it should be?

She scowled at the thought because it sounded selfish, yet she couldn't help feeling threatened. Why did Brenna's sister have to show up? After finally winning her mother's support, Bronwyn felt overwhelmed by this new problem. She wanted to cry, but willed her tears away.

***

Kira, leaning on her cane, suppressed the expression of anguish she felt in her right leg. She'd been exerting herself too much and paid her bill with pain.

Irena, noting the subtle signs of Kira's discomfort, dared to put her hand on the younger woman's shoulder. "Are you okay, my dear?" she asked.

For a moment, Kira sensed in Irena the same sweetness she adored in Bronwyn. Her kindness disarmed any hostility Kira had previously felt for the woman. "It comes and goes," she replied, covering her affliction with a forced smile. "It's gradually getting better."

"Would you mind if I prayed for you?" Irena asked.

Taken aback by the request, Kira hedged. "Here? In the clinic?"

"Why not?" Irena countered. "I can be discreet."

Secrets and Whispers: *Storm Clouds*

Kira consented, listening to whispered words that conveyed concern and contrition for capricious judgment. Irena sounded sincere, but Kira's skepticism urged expression. "Thank you," she responded at the conclusion of the prayer. "But why are you blessing me now after being so critical about my friendship with Bronwyn?"

Irena pursed her lips. "Please hear me out," she urged. "Based on what I know of you, I have concerns. Bronwyn is my only daughter and in my heart I want what's best for her."

"If you're still worried, why the change?"

Given Kira's understandable reluctance to extend grace, Irena forged ahead with her social bridge building. "I've spoken to my sister and my husband," she admitted. "They bring a different perspective into their appraisal of you than did my source at the Temple."

"Priestess Alba forced my head between her thighs at a tender age," Kira retorted. "She took advantage of my vulnerability and turned me into a toy for her pleasure. She's hardly an objective source."

"You're right," Irena admitted. "And I've been wrong to judge you based on her testimony."

"Well, that's progress," Kira replied, stifling her anger. She didn't want to ruin anything for Bronwyn.

Irena evaluated the simmering rage behind Kira's grey eyes and had to think carefully about her response. She didn't want to stir a storm in this volatile young woman. "I'm sorry, and I hope you'll forgive me."

Kira's expression softened as she heard this. She paused for a moment as if thinking, evaluating the older woman to discern any guile that might lurk beneath her apology. Kira turned away, glancing at the serene scene of the river flowing beyond the clinic's window, then pursed her lips and shut her eyes before returning her gaze to Bronwyn's mother.

Secrets and Whispers: *Storm Clouds*

"Okay," she breathed. "I forgive you. But I still want to know why you've changed your mind."

The tranquil, steaming river also drew Irena's attention. She found it easier to look outside than to sustain eye contact with Kira. "My sister goes running with Brenna every morning," she began. "Marla's a keen judge of character, and what Brenna said about you and your brother sounded compelling to her."

"Brenna's the most noble woman I've ever met," Kira stated. "She's about as saintly as they come. Anyone who thinks otherwise is an ignorant fool."

That judgment stung a little, as Irena had been too focused on Brenna's appearance to accurately gauge her character. "Marla would agree with you," Irena concurred. "She says Brenna regards you highly and insists that my daughter would not associate with anyone of poor character. Marla tells me that Brenna's much smarter than . . . than people credit her, based on her looks."

"Brenna's mother is nothing short of brilliant," Kira insisted. "My sister comes by her intelligence honestly."

Irena nodded. "That may be so, but I've not had much contact with Brenna and can't speak to the quality of her mind. I'm basing my remarks from what Marla has confided to me, and I trust her judgment unquestioningly.

"My husband is generally slow to draw conclusions about people. He's not dull. He's methodical and careful. He came here with an open mind, intending to assess the situation with you, your brother and our daughter in an objective manner. Algernon favorably impressed him, and Arvid is not a man who is easily impressed.

"After watching your brother in court yesterday, I understand why he feels that way. I'd drawn all manner of conclusions about your ministry, not understanding how closely you work with the authorities in this town, and not appreciating the methodology of your approach.

Secrets and Whispers: *Storm Clouds*

"I'd made assumptions about your work with exploited women without bothering to learn of your motives, the comprehensive scope of your effort, nor did I inquire about the transformation of lives and the restoration of hope that lies at the heart of your public service. I was wrong, and I'm sorry."

Irena turned toward Kira again. "Algernon's performance in court amazed me. The way he conducted himself made me proud that Bronwyn has chosen him as her partner. I've badly misjudged both of you. That's why I've changed my mind."

Kira extended her arms and drew Irena into her lingering embrace. "Thank you," she whispered.

A moment later, a slender young woman wearing a forced smile called Kira and Irena into a consultation room that smelled vaguely of antiseptic and featured a picture window behind a large desk. "Please have a seat," she said. "Dr. Ecksted will be with you shortly."

After the receptionist closed the door, Irena posed a question that revealed some of her lingering concern. "When Bronwyn marries your brother, how will that work in terms of who runs the household?"

"It's my house," Kira replied. "But Bron is the best thing that's ever happened to Algernon. I'm not going to do anything to jeopardize their relationship."

Irena nodded. "And when children come along, will your ministry continue to shelter women who struggle with addiction and poor social skills?"

Kira finally sat down, stretching her right leg out in a rather unladylike manner. "Our initial intention was to bring the girls up to Superstition Mesa in order to get them away from their pimps and madams. But that hasn't worked as well as getting them situated in public housing here in the city."

"Why is that?" Irena asked.

Secrets and Whispers: *Storm Clouds*

"Part of it's the isolation," Kira admitted. "These girls need a social network, they're often addicted and require both counseling and medical treatment. Child care and the availability of honest work are essential to their recovery. We've discovered that the distance to our homestead complicates all of this, while the services these women need are more easily accessed here in town.

"We also find that having women in recovery living with us complicates our lifestyle, particularly our need for uninterrupted prayer and meditation. The turmoil created by having drug-addicted girls living in our house disrupts the simplicity of our lifestyle.

"Feeding additional mouths, supplying water and finding time for all of the chores necessary to keep the homestead running demand the balance of our time. It's hard to sustain that while conducting ministry in town."

"So, it's easier to house the young women here than shelter them at your homestead," Irena concluded.

Kira nodded. "That's what we've learned."

"But you have that Lithian lady living with you."

"Well, Ileana's a refugee. She's devout, she's gainfully employed and she doesn't have issues."

"Okay," Irena stated, broaching another of her concerns. "I'm happy with that, but is Bronwyn going to have any say in household decisions after she's married?"

Kira scrunched her brow. "Bron has always had a say in what we do. That's not going to change when she marries. Why are you worried?"

Irena didn't want to admit that she still felt uneasy, didn't fully trust Bronwyn's judgment, and secretly felt that her daughter should wait. At this point, however, she had no rational reason to object and shook her head. "It's every mother's burden to worry about her child," Irena admitted. "If I didn't care, I wouldn't be concerned."

Secrets and Whispers: *Storm Clouds*

"Set your heart at ease," Kira replied. "Algernon loves Bronwyn, and so do I. She's in good hands with us."

The older woman nodded, but couldn't find words to respond. No matter how hard she tried to push her doubts away, they gnawed at her soul.

Dr. Ecksted, a thin woman with an emotionless demeanor, finally entered. She'd pulled her waist-length hair into a tight ponytail that accentuated the rounded, northern features of her face. Pale eyes appraised the two women thoughtfully as she introduced herself.

"Miss Bronwyn and Brother Algernon are strong and healthy," she began. "Blood tests show no abnormalities, and the two physical exams I've conducted over the past six weeks revealed no venereal diseases present.

"They both self-report as non-sexually active. Miss Bronwyn's hymen is still intact, but that's not always an accurate indicator of virginity.

"Now," she continued, "which of you is the head of household for Brother Algernon, and what is the nature of your relationship?"

"I am," Kira stated. "He's my twin brother."

"Oh? If I may be bold, what happened to your mother?" the doctor asked.

"She got drunk and drowned in Broken Wing Lake a few years ago."

Dr. Ecksted's face remained passive. "That's unfortunate. Please initial these medical results and confirm that you're giving your consent to this union.

"By signing, you certify that your brother is of sound mind, has no history of mental illness and is engaging in this marriage of his own volition."

Kira nodded. "He's perfectly capable of speaking for himself. He doesn't need my permission."

"It's routine," the doctor replied.

Secrets and Whispers: *Storm Clouds*

After Kira signed the papers, Dr. Ecksted went through the same procedure with Irena. "Miss Bronwyn has elected to delay having a family," the doctor stated. "She's requested contraception. Do you object?"

Irena shook her head. "That's her decision to make."

"I understand she's your only daughter," the doctor continued. "There are risks of uterine perforation, infection, spotting between periods, cramping and backache. These are uncommon, but they happen. Given these facts, do you consent to the IUD insertion?"

Irena reached for the pen. "If it's what my daughter wants, then I support her decision."

"Very well," Dr. Ecksted concluded. "On behalf of the Ministry of Health, I certify Miss Bronwyn and Brother Algernon of sound body and mind. Congratulations to both of you. May their marriage be happy and fruitful."

***

Cold wind carried a reminder of the faded winter, and while Carlos de Sanchez had once nurtured fantasies of living in the exotic highlands of Tamaria, weather in the nation's capital never approached what he'd known as warm, even in high summer. Nothing in this place approached the heat of Kameron. On days like this one, with the temperature dropping quickly, he hated it here.

Scurrying up the stairs of the Kamerese embassy, Carlos presented his credentials to the guards on duty and headed to his office on the third floor. In the privacy of his office, Carlos adjusted the framed photo of his wife, smiled at her, and began writing notes.

In his tenth year as the Intelligence Liaison Officer of the Kamerese Crown, de Sanchez moved through Tamaria's capital with the ease of a native, but the loyalties of a foreigner.

Secrets and Whispers: *Storm Clouds*

Because his family originated in the frontier near the Tamarian border, he shared the tall, blonde-haired features common to his host country and spoke the local language fluently. All of this helped him blend in.

Carlos also maintained regular contact with Captain Mariel Hougen, of the Tamarian Expeditionary Force. He used her to pass on intelligence information that his government deemed useful to their foreign policy, and likewise, gained insight into military planning – especially as it related to Kameron – from her.

He'd resisted all efforts at seduction from the beautiful Tamarian officer, not only because he loved his own wife and committed himself to marital faithfulness, but also out of respect for Mariel's wit and ruthlessness. Absolute devotion to her nation's security characterized her approach to the Intelligence Service, and Carlos didn't want to wind up on the receiving end of her wrath.

With the notes he began composing, however, his career careened headlong into outright betrayal of his ally. These would form the second communique to the Foreign Service Secretary in Kameron City, and if Mariel Hougen ever learned of his duplicity, she wouldn't think twice about cutting his throat.

"I suspect my Tamarian contact has connected our group to the bombing. She's met with a colonel in charge of the investigation and presented her findings. Fortunately, the colonel remains skeptical of our involvement. We should provide additional evidence through third-parties that will sway opinion in our favor.

"The political mood in Tamaria's capital remains tense. While closed-door negotiating between the Tamarian Minister of State and the Nordan ambassador continues, factions within the Senate have begun clamoring for a more assertive posture than the Tamarian government has taken in public thus far.

Secrets and Whispers: *Storm Clouds*

"The Capital News – the best source of off-the-record reporting – contends that military readiness is increasing. While the paper offers no details, I have independently confirmed the rail shipment of ammunition and the pre-positioning of military stocks – including artillery tubes, transport trucks, aluminum spools and ethanol for fuel, as well as armored vehicles – at locations near the border to sustain operations once a deployment is ordered.

"We know that Tamarian Special Forces units have already been sent into the Kurian highlands, but these operations are not public knowledge and my contact remains tight-lipped about their role in the region. It is likely that they're providing Intel to senior military planners who advise the Queen on foreign policy.

"While our operations here have not yet resulted in a commitment for deployment from our allies, it is likely that the brute momentum of force-building along Tamaria's northwestern frontier will eventually result in the Queen sending her Expeditionary Force into Eastern Kurian. There are factions here that are pressing for a decisive victory from that branch of the military, as many Tamarians perceive that the Expeditionary Force has not performed well in their cross-border deployments thus far.

"That outcome would be favorable for His Majesty's government, potentially opening a secure rail corridor into the country for the overland transport of commercial and military supplies."

Once he'd completed his composition, Carlos called for an aide to supply a diplomatic pouch. He placed his correspondence into the secure envelope and sealed it before slipping the message into the daily dispatch to the Foreign Office in Kameron City.

***

Secrets and Whispers: *Storm Clouds*

In a café at lunch, Garrick could tell that his wife didn't like what she was hearing from Bronwyn. Shy Brenna typically kept her views on controversial matters private, but when it came to her family, the Lithian woman had no compunction about speaking her mind.

"What you're telling me is a reflection of your own insecurity," Brenna stated. "You've never met my sister, you don't know her, and beneath your strident opposition to Thea attending a family function lies an irrational fear that she's going to do something to upset your happiness. Nothing is further from the truth."

When Bronwyn looked to Algernon for support, having warned her of Brenna's strong will, he shook his head and shrugged. "I told you."

Struggling to constrain her anger, Bronwyn blew breath through her nose and tightened her lips. A pretty waitress sauntered to the table and asked for everyone's order, but Bronwyn no longer felt like eating. When the waitress departed, she turned toward Algernon. "I need your support in this!"

Brenna reached for Bronwyn's hand. "No one is going to do anything against your will," she soothed. "It was not my intention to create a problem by inviting my family to share in your happiness. But you need to know that snubbing my sister will not go over well with my parents. They have a long memory and won't forget a slight like that."

Bronwyn withdrew her hand, crossed her arms and sat back against the booth. "Are they so dull they can't understand how she slighted me?"

Garrick raised his brow. He glanced at Algernon, expecting his brother to say something wise and feeling disappointed when he didn't. "Algernon made a poor choice," he replied. "That's not Thea's fault."

Secrets and Whispers: *Storm Clouds*

"She admitted that she followed him up the hill and went skinny-dipping in a hot spring within plain sight of the trail," Bronwyn countered. "Don't tell me she had no culpability that day!"

"Still my choice," Algernon added.

Bronwyn shot him a judgmental glance.

"I didn't have to look," he told her. "That was my weakness, my lack of discipline. Blaming Thea for what I did solves nothing."

"We've been over this," Brenna replied. "Algernon chose you over my sister. Had he not done so, we'd not be having this conversation right now."

"Okay, that's fine," Bronwyn sighed, resignation in her voice. "I'll just go along and let her steal the show on my wedding day . . ."

Algernon tried to offer reassurance, but Bronwyn's body language warned him away.

Brenna shook her head. "Once you meet Thea, once you get to know her, you'll understand that she won't ever take anything from you. She's soon to be your sister, an ally, a friend you can always count on. Don't be afraid."

"That's easy for you to say!" Bronwyn retorted. "You're beautiful. Everyone falls all over themselves to be nice to you!"

That wasn't true and Brenna knew better, but she refrained from responding to that remark. "Please, Bronwyn. Just meet with her before you make a decision."

***

Torn between heeding Brenna's counsel and the nagging desire to call the whole wedding off, Bronwyn headed back to the Gold Leaf Hotel in Algernon's company. "You promised that you'd stick up for me," she complained. "Why didn't you say anything?"

Secrets and Whispers: *Storm Clouds*

"No need," he explained. "Brenna won't insist that you do anything against your will."

"So, if I say I don't want to meet Cynthia, you'll go along with that?"

"Are you changing your mind, now?" he asked.

Bronwyn sighed. "I went into this thinking you'd be my ally, that we could talk Brenna out of ruining our wedding. But you said nothing in my defense!"

Algernon stopped, tugging on Bronwyn's hand until she came close. "You don't need defending," he told her. "I want you, and only you. It's not going to hurt to meet Brenna's family. They'll shower you with more love and affection than your own siblings have, and if you're still convinced that you don't want them to attend, you can make that decision and no one will oppose you."

Bronwyn closed her eyes as he kissed her lips, the familiar sense of longing rising in her soul again. "It's not her parents that I mind. Only her not-so-little sister . . ."

"She has nothing on you," he assured.

"You said she was pretty," Bronwyn complained.

"Yes, but I prefer you to her."

That wasn't what Bronwyn wanted to hear. "You think she's prettier than me?"

Algernon struggled to avoid rolling his eyes. "She's different. That's all."

"What does she look like?"

"She looks like Brenna, but bigger."

Bronwyn's eyes widened. She thought Brenna was perfectly proportioned and beautiful. "Bigger boobs?"

That remark made Algernon laugh. "Yeah, they're even bigger than yours. What does that matter?"

Bronwyn scowled as he stood close. She turned her head away as he ran his finger along her collar bone, nearly daring to trace his touch further down.

Secrets and Whispers: *Storm Clouds*

"It's you who I want," he told her quietly, pressing his body close to hers, nuzzling her. "It's you I need."

"You're so sweet," she replied. "I don't deserve you."

Algernon shook his head. "You deserve better than me, and we both know it. I love you and I'll do my best to treat you well. I'll always stand by you, Bron. I promise."

After his failure to defend her at lunch, Bronwyn felt no reassurance. She really didn't want to meet Thea Velez, but suspected that Algernon didn't feel the same way.

***

"That stupid husband of yours ruined everything!" Sikki spat, leaning across the table at a bistro near the Gold Leaf Hotel. "If he'd not gone and spilled his guts to Bronwyn, none of this would have happened!"

Vega, who'd been long dominated by her cousin, felt too frightened to admit her role in foiling the dowry and inheritance plot. From the moment she'd heard the plan, Vega thought the idea violated moral principles, evidenced by the fact that Sikki didn't want to approach Irena with the idea. While Willem needed the money to pay his debts and it would have been nice to have some finer things, that money rightfully belonged to Bronwyn.

"Well, maybe it's for the best," she suggested meekly, hoping that Sikki wouldn't jump down her throat for saying so.

Sikki glared at her cousin. "Is that what you think? Well you're either dumb as they come or a sucker for abuse," she retorted. "That money would have set you up in a place of your own, far away from that drunken loser you married. Now that he's derailed your life again, what are you going to do?"

"I'll manage," she replied. "I'll find a way."

Secrets and Whispers: *Storm Clouds*

"I doubt it," Sikki said coldly. "You're trapped and you're deluded. You keep giving Willi chance after chance to get better and he never does. The fact that he's wrecked our plans proves that Willem is weak, and you're weaker still for tolerating his nonsense. You should never have married him."

Vega didn't think of herself as weak. She knew her husband's foibles better than anyone else and had always felt a quiet confidence that she was the stronger person in their relationship. Only she could stand up to him. Willi manipulated and used everyone else, and though he might rage and hit her on occasion, it took a very strong woman to deal with his anger, a strong woman to handle his many weaknesses.

"He didn't say anything to Bronwyn that she didn't already know," Vega responded.

Sikki put her tea cup down. "What are you talking about, dear cousin?"

"Kira came to see me after her fight with Heidelinde. She'd already figured out what we were doing."

Angrily, Sikki leaned forward. "You told her!"

"No!" Vega insisted, lying. "Underneath that hillbilly accent Kira's got more brains than you credit her. You need to face the fact that Bronwyn's friends are more clever than you think. Kira outmaneuvered you."

Sikki fumed. "There's no way that braless bimbo figured anything out. Once a whore, always a whore, and that girl is good for nothing but laying on her back and spreading her legs. The only reason Bronwyn hangs around with Kira is to make herself feel better about being fat and ugly."

"She's your sister-in-law!" Vega contended, growing annoyed with her cousin's critical attitude. "Why are you always running her down? What has she ever done to merit that kind of treatment?"

Secrets and Whispers: *Storm Clouds*

"Listen to yourself!" Sikki warned. "Your pretty face is sprouting wrinkles, and you struggle to keep your figure from falling apart. If you'd had children, it would be even worse! You've wasted the best years of your life on that loser husband of yours, so now you're living vicariously through Bronwyn, who – even now – doesn't hold a candle to your beauty. Wake up, Vega! Your life is slipping away and I'm the only one who cares enough to do something about it."

"Swindling an inheritance that rightly belongs to Bronwyn would benefit you more than anyone else," Vega replied, accusingly. "And there's no guarantee that you'd get so much as a farthing, anyway . . ."

"Don't be stupid. The only thing Bronwyn has going for her is a fat inheritance and an oversized pair of tits. Those Ravenwood boys are breast-obsessed, but time and gravity will put an end to that. There's nothing else about Bronwyn that's worth Algernon's attention. Once he gets what he wants from her, he'll be off bonking better-looking women. You'll see!"

Vega shook her head. "You know nothing about him. You're spewing invective because you're bitter. You've lost the game. The dowry and inheritance are going to Bronwyn, and there's nothing you can do about it.

"Whatever Algernon sees in Bronwyn is not our business. Arvid's right. We should be supporting her. This conspiracy of yours has turned a sweet girl against the people she loves. It's hateful. It's vindictive. It's not right."

Sikki shook her head. "You deserve him!" she spat. "You'll go crawling back, like you always do, and beg him to take you in. But when he hits you again, don't come crying to me for sympathy. I'm done with you!"

***

Secrets and Whispers: *Storm Clouds*

By the time Brenna finished dressed herself to meet her family, waxing wind pushed the towering redwoods near the music manse into a slow, sensuous dance. Garrick pulled his bride into a tight embrace just outside their door, relishing a final moment of close contact before they ventured into public where, in harmony with their mutual custom, they would not touch one another.

Yet their hands lingered together while they walked across the waterfall bridge and into the forested buffer that screened their home from a nearby residential neighborhood. They slowed, as if reluctant to step out of their private world and onto the pavement.

"Are you still sad?" he asked.

Brenna nodded. "I didn't want to hurt Bronwyn. She's so obsessed with Thea that she can't see what a blessing it will be for her to join our family. I don't think she appreciates how her fear puts me into an impossible position. What would my parents think if I'd not invited them to such an important occasion?"

Garrick, who'd never spoken to Algernon about his misdeed with Cynthia Velez, savored irritation whenever he thought of his brother's impropriety. "I don't blame Bronwyn for being upset. Your sister is a lot more attractive, and it'll take a great deal of courage to step out of that envy. Algernon's made a real muck of this."

"Yes, but he was honest and contrite with my parents," Brenna replied. "And in the end he chose Bronwyn over Thea anyway. That was the right thing for him to do. Pretty doesn't guarantee a good partnership, and Bronwyn's a far better fit for your brother than Thea."

"True," Garrick agreed. "Now we just have to hope that Bronwyn's good character prevails and she doesn't fall apart when she needs to be strong."

"I pray she'll find that courage," Brenna stated.

Secrets and Whispers: *Storm Clouds*

Nothing had returned to normal at the palace gate. The Defenders on duty seemed tense. Rumors of a second attack had been circulating among them, and an ominous new policy loomed in large letters above the entrance desk. It read, "No foreigners allowed."

After Brenna nudged her husband and lifted her chin toward the sign, prompting Garrick to ask the duty sergeant about the reason for the notice.

"Security," the sergeant replied. He jerked his head toward Brenna and continued, "She's okay, but no one else gets through. Colonel Scheer's orders."

"Her family is coming up for my brother's wedding in the summer garden," Garrick explained. "Will there be a problem getting clearance for them?"

"I'm afraid you'll have to take that up with the colonel, LT," the sergeant responded reluctantly.

In the weapons room, Garrick clipped his handgun into its concealed holster. Brenna slid her boot knife into its sheath. She looked at him with pleading eyes, her wordless expression communicating a host of worries.

"I'll talk to the colonel tomorrow morning," he promised. "I'm sure there's a way to get clearance for your family. It's for a wedding, not a political rally . . ."

Although she didn't question her husband's good intentions, Brenna quietly worried that the security issue would create yet another layer of complexity to an already convoluted situation. In the back of her mind, Brenna also fretted about Garrick's cousin, Gudrun, who'd once claimed that he'd fathered her son out of wedlock. She might attend, just to spite Garrick and make things miserable. Her father, Werner – the eldest of Garrick's maternal uncles – worked a cattle and horse ranch on the Saradon, where the teenaged Garrick had lived for awhile before joining the Junior Scouts.

Secrets and Whispers: *Storm Clouds*

Blustery wind intensified beyond the palace gate. The young couple huddled as close as they dared while waiting for the street car at the edge of Equality Park. When the trolley arrived, they instinctively headed for the rear benches after entering. People moved a row or two away, eyeing the Lithian woman with suspicion and muttering epithets just above the threshold of hearing.

Brenna ignored them, but Garrick glared back. He hated the ignorance motivating such commentary, but suppressed his desire to confront the bigotry out of respect for Brenna, who didn't want to make a scene, and didn't want to be defended.

At various stops along the way, boarding passengers headed toward the empty seats at the back, only to pause at the sight of Brenna and stop. Many preferred to stand rather than sit anywhere near her.

But a scruffy, blonde haired man who smelled like he needed a bath eased onto the bench next to Garrick. "I know who you are," he spoke in accented vulgate.

Finding it hard to take the man seriously, Garrick rolled his eyes. "I don't know you, but I'm in no mood for nonsense. Tread carefully . . ."

"Hear me out," the man admonished. "You're friends with an analyst, an intelligence officer named Hougen. The demon Kamerese are feeding her lies, and if she believes them, you're heading for war . . ."

The fact that the stranger knew Mariel's name changed Garrick's attitude. He noticed Brenna reaching for her boot knife, but he stopped her by gently putting his hand on hers. "What's this about?" he asked.

"It's always about money, isn't it?" the stranger replied, cryptically. "It's always about the powerful squeezing profit from the weak, taking things that aren't rightfully theirs. Your pretty little lover with the blade in her boot knows how it feels when that happens."

Secrets and Whispers: *Storm Clouds*

"Watch your mouth," Garrick glowered, unbuttoning his jacket and putting his hand on his weapon.

The stranger inched away and held out his hands. "No need to threaten me," he said. "I'm harmless to you. I'm trying to stop the madness before it begins . . ."

"Then tell me how I can help you," Garrick replied.

The scruffy man glanced from side to side before speaking. "Your pretty little lover has a sister whose *novio* is a trusted friend of King Alejo. Ask him about *"Los Patrones del Estado"* and then tell your analyst exactly what he says. Stop this lunacy before it's too late."

As the streetcar halted near the financial district, the stranger stood and hurried toward the exit. Garrick watched him vanish into a crowd as two fit men in suits boarded the street car, scanning faces until they reached the last row. One of them looked at Brenna in disgust before the other flashed a picture in Garrick's face.

"Have you seen this man?"

"I was just talking to him," Garrick replied.

"Then you'll need to come with me."

"No," Garrick stated flatly. "I don't think so."

With a nod to his partner, who headed to the front to stop the streetcar, the fit-looking man produced a badge from the Crown Intelligence Directorate. "Well, I do. This can either be easy, or difficult. The choice is yours."

***

Director Maia Sperger pushed a document across her desk. "You're the subject of a citizen complaint," she warned. "This type of conduct is unprofessional and reflects badly on our department."

Karin, red-faced, quickly scanned the paper. She grew angry and shoved the complaint back to her boss. "There's no substance to this!"

Secrets and Whispers: *Storm Clouds*

Mrs. Sperger sat back in her chair. "No substance? So you didn't trespass on her property?"

"I had evidence of her collusion in the case of the Wounded Heart Canyon Clan," Karin began. "That girl and her brother supplied the gwynling with tools and food, in direct contravention of Section 8 of the Wildlife Protection Act. I went to confront them with the evidence, and this is how she responds!"

"This took place on her property?"

Realizing she'd blundered into an admission of guilt, Karin paused to think. "I was on my way back to the office and thought I'd ask them some questions . . ."

"So you were on her property, then," Director Sperger concluded. "How did this confrontation occur?"

Trying to be careful, Karin hedged. "I knocked on the door, but no one answered."

"Were you looking through her window?"

"Nobody answered the door . . ."

"Answer my question, Karin," the Director insisted.

"No," Karin stated.

Maia Sperger shook her head. She opened a folder and produced a carefully created copy of hand prints. "So if I check your hands to these prints, they won't match?"

How did that wicked girl lift her prints from the window? Karin sighed. "How did she make those?"

"With baby powder, a make-up brush, tape and a lot more intelligence than you're showing right now," Director Sperger stated. "You've lied to me twice, Karin. That's not an effective way to impress me."

"I'm sorry ma'am," Karin said sheepishly. "I'm just trying to do my job."

"It's not your job to make accusations. We have an investigative division for that. Neither is it your job to trespass and peek into windows." Mrs. Sperger returned the prints to the folder on her desk. "As of this moment,

Secrets and Whispers: *Storm Clouds*

I'm placing you under indefinite suspension while we investigate your conduct in this matter."

"What about all the evidence I collected?" Karin objected. "You can't let these people tamper with an endangered species and get away with it . . ."

"That's no longer your concern," Maia stated.

***

Marla and Irena waited with Bronwyn and Algernon beneath the covered entrance of Marvic's Central Railway Station. Between rain showers and bouts of hail, they watched three streetcars arrive and discharge passengers.

"Where are they?" Irena asked.

"Something must have happened," Algernon replied. "It's not like my brother to be late like this."

"I hope they're okay," Bronwyn added, her tone expressing worry. She not only felt concern for the young couple, but also didn't want to meet Thea Velez without Brenna being there.

A long time later, in the midst of a terrific downpour, Garrick followed his diminutive wife as she emerged from a steamy-windowed streetcar and scurried up the train station stairs.

"Sorry for the delay," he announced, wiping rain from his face with a handkerchief. "We were detained."

Algernon wanted to know what was going on, but Garrick shrugged off his brother's concern. "It was a misunderstanding," he insisted. "Nothing to worry about. Let's go. They're probably here already."

Despite her small size, Brenna moved with impressive speed as she navigated through the crowded station. Everyone else struggled to keep up. After turning the corner near the ticket counter, her expression brightened. "*Umma!*" she cried, bursting into a sprint.

Secrets and Whispers: *Storm Clouds*

Marla watched an even smaller Lithian woman, whose delight radiated from her lovely face, run toward Brenna with open arms. Lady Alexina embraced her daughter with overflowing joy, holding her close, gently rocking side to side. The women exchanged a lip kiss and spoke in words that Marla couldn't understand.

Moments later, other Lithian people swarmed around Brenna, reaching for her until she relinquished her mother's arms and melded into theirs, one at a time. Tears, smiles and laughter flowed freely.

Lord Lynden, Brenna's strikingly handsome father, lifted his eldest daughter off her feet, twirling around with her like he'd done when she was a child. When he put her down, Brenna laid her head against his chest and embraced him tightly, while he stroked her hair and planted kisses on her head.

In the same order, Brenna's family moved from her to Garrick. He bowed his head in the presence of his mother-in-law until she lifted his face with both hands and kissed him like a son. He beamed in her affirmation, delighting in maternal affection long denied him.

His greeting with Brenna's father began with a firm embrace and strong hands that lingered on his shoulders and upper arms. Marla, surprised that Garrick could converse in Lithian, recognized a bond of mutual respect between the men that transcended spoken language.

On this went. Algernon, swept into a sea of smiles, became immersed in reaching hands and embraces. Brenna's three sisters – including Thea – kissed him, but Eren, her young brother – didn't like the noise and cried for his big sister to hold him. Other Lithian adults, whom Marla presumed were household servants, and the tall, beautiful, dark-skinned Abelscinnians who'd bound their fates with these warm-hearted Lithians, also joined in.

Secrets and Whispers: *Storm Clouds*

As Algernon reunited with his friend, Jawara, Brenna wept in the arms of Niobe, Jawara's wife. Among the Abelscinnians, affection between women was tolerated on occasions like this, but not so among the men – whose greetings were far more restrained – and forbidden by custom among members of the opposite gender. This was true even in families. Like Garrick and Brenna, Jawara and Niobe never touched in public.

Brenna met Osayande, Niobe's son – who looked nothing like Jawara – for the first time. He'd watched his mother embrace and weep with the Lithian woman, but he didn't know her and shied away. Similarly, when Thea brought Eren over to see Brenna, the child didn't remember her and clung to Thea's thigh.

All of her sisters kissed Brenna on the lips, and the Ravenwood brothers on the cheek. Marla figured this was their custom, so she watched carefully as Algernon introduced Bronwyn to each of Brenna's siblings.

Acacia – whom everyone called Cassie – was the prettiest of the bunch. She stood on her toes to kiss Bronwyn, who towered over the smaller woman. Jared, her white-haired, bespectacled boyfriend, followed, but kissed Bronwyn's forehead, instead. Camille, Brenna's youngest and most extroverted sister, had met Bronwyn on an earlier trip to Marvic. Delighted to see Algernon's bride-to-be again, her embrace lingered longer and she followed her kiss with a soft caress to Bronwyn's face.

As the moment she'd been dreading arrived, visibly nervous Bronwyn struggled to look Cynthia in the eye. She'd stifled an expression of jealousy when the Lithian woman kissed and embraced Algernon, and kept averting her gaze to avoid eye contact. When shy Cynthia lifted her head and pursed her lips to offer her sisterly kiss, Bronwyn pulled away and presented her cheek instead.

Secrets and Whispers: *Storm Clouds*

Algernon took in a deep breath. Dr. Caerwyn Yates, Thea's muscular and handsome Lithian boyfriend, also tensed in that moment. But Camille, ever sensitive and empathetic, laid her hand on Bronwyn's shoulder. "It's okay, my sister," she said in vulgate. "We all understand."

"Great God, you are beautiful!" Bronwyn rasped, trembling and teary-eyed as she appraised Thea.

Cynthia smiled sweetly, reaching for Bronwyn's hands. "And so are you," she replied.

***

The reunion moved Marla's heart and struck a deep chord in Irena, who fought back tears while witnessing the overwhelming joy among Brenna's loved ones. Secretly, she wished that her own children were as close and extended such love toward one another. In the taxi on their way back to the Gold Leaf Hotel, she remarked to her sister, "I've never seen such a tightly-knit family."

Marla agreed, but she'd noticed the tension in her niece when Bronwyn met Cynthia, the look of guilt in Algernon's eyes, and suspected that something had gone on between the two of them. Determined to find out, she decided to sit with Brenna at dinner and ask.

To avoid offending Tamarian sensibilities, Brenna's family took a back entrance into the hotel and a service elevator to the 12th floor. They'd reserved the entire level for the duration of their stay, but were required to avoid public areas and use the service stairwell, so as not to upset other guests. Since the 12th floor also featured a commanding view of the city and had its own dining room, Brenna's father consented to the arrangement.

But at nearly 800 sterlings for each night, the family's accommodations didn't come cheap . . .

Secrets and Whispers: *Storm Clouds*

Three chairs remained conspicuously empty at dinner that evening. Kira, despite wanting to see Tembe, went home in the early afternoon because she'd been dealing with pain and felt exhausted. Tembe sat at the table with Jawara, Niobe and the mischievous Osayende, trying to overcome his obvious disappointment by pretending to look happy.

Willem, who'd taken money out of Vega's purse after returning to the hotel with his brother, hadn't been seen since. Despite Darren, Arvid, and Algernon visiting every bar in the area, they'd been unable to locate him.

Vega had also vanished. Nobody knew where she'd gone. Sikki played coy about her cousin's disappearance, but when Darren returned to their room, he found that Vega's things were missing. She'd not gone out for a casual afternoon of shopping on her own. He wondered if she'd returned her room key and checked out of the hotel.

Arvid maintained the appearance of calm, but inwardly, he worried about his son and daughter–in–law. "I'm sure they'll turn up," Irena told him soothingly.

But their empty seats whispered into Irena's heart. With no power to do anything at the moment, she smiled and tried to ignore the gibberish of Lithian language arising around the table.

Intriguingly, Cynthia Velez sat at Bronwyn's right hand for the meal. The earlier tension between the two young women faded as Thea made a concerted effort to engage in, and sustain, conversation with the woman who'd once been her rival in romance.

"They seem to have overcome some friction," Marla told Brenna. "Their introduction was rather awkward."

Although she'd only sipped at her wine, Brenna felt comfortable enough with Marla to converse freely. "I knew my sister would try to make Bronwyn comfortable."

"Why would that be an issue?" Marla asked.

Secrets and Whispers: *Storm Clouds*

Garrick shook his head, embarrassed. "Do we have to rehash this old story again?"

"It speaks to the goodness of Thea's character," Brenna replied.

"Bronwyn's never met her before," Marla stated. "Why would there be any bad blood between them?"

"When my family fled from the Azgar," Brenna began, "they settled in a remote region of the Kamerese frontier. With no social prospects for a pious maiden in that place, my sister took an interest in Algernon during our wedding celebration. Naturally, this created a problem for Bronwyn, who'd stayed here to run Kira's ministry."

"That's a rather charitable explanation," Garrick added. "In my view, Algernon acted like an idiot."

Marla's eyes widened. Garrick didn't drink, so she couldn't attribute that admission to alcohol. He'd clearly held that resentment against his brother for a long time. Without anyone directly telling her, she deduced that Algernon had behaved improperly with Thea Velez. Yet Marla knew that Lithians mated for life, and Thea now had a handsome - and obviously Lithian – boyfriend at her side. "But your sister preferred the man she's with?"

Brenna shook her head. "No. Algernon came to his senses and realized he was better off committing himself to Bronwyn. He asked her to forgive him, and she did."

Marla felt stunned. Nobody in Bronwyn's family had believed she was attractive enough to compete with other girls, yet she'd managed to turn Algernon's head and lure his heart away from a far prettier woman.

"So, how did she meet the man she's with?" asked Marla, intrigued.

"Algernon introduced them," Brenna replied. "Like me and my mother, Thea struggled to find a suitable partner among our people. The isolation of our father's estate in Kameron made matters much worse for her.

Secrets and Whispers: *Storm Clouds*

"But Algernon found her a man who appreciates her beauty. Mother tells me that they respect each other and get along well. It looks like a good match thus far."

Across the table, Marla heard Bronwyn laugh. She'd relaxed and seemed happy for the first time in weeks. Algernon beamed with delight, his hand mingled with hers. Marla smiled at her niece, genuinely pleased that things finally seemed to be going her way.

***

With a hard rain pelting the homestead's metal roof, Kira hobbled to the door. With her brother and Bronwyn staying overnight in town, Kira and Ileana weren't expecting company.

Vega stood at the entrance with her suitcase in hand, soaking wet and shivering. "My cousin kicked me out," she said. "I have nowhere to go. Can I stay here?"

"Of course," Kira replied, beckoning for the older woman to enter. "Let me get you a towel."

Because she'd been raised in the north, the style of the homestead's architecture evoked memories from childhood. "Wow, this place is huge!" she remarked.

Kira limped to a closet for the promised towel while Ileana retreated to her room and closed the door. "Everyone says that. Algernon wanted to build a place big enough for our ministry, but it turns out that he'll be raising his family here, instead."

Vega accepted the towel with gratitude, following Kira to the central masonry stove and sitting in the chair the young woman offered to her. She rubbed her face and arms with the towel, then used it on her hair. "I'm sorry for imposing," she said. "I don't know where else to go."

"Tell me what happened," Kira encouraged.

Secrets and Whispers: *Storm Clouds*

"It's complicated," Vega began. "Willem sometimes gets violent when he's been drinking. It's happening more often now. Something changed a few weeks ago – he won't tell me what – but he started sliding into this pattern where his drinking binges are steadily worsening.

"Sikki helped me buy a gun to protect myself. When Willem tried to hurt me a couple of nights ago, I used it to scare him off. That's why he wound up here. I stayed with Sikki, while Darren moved in with Willi.

"Bronwyn met with Arvid that morning and complained about the inheritance plot to him. I figured you'd told her what I'd said, so I tried to stay out of it. But Irena called a family meeting to announce that she'd decided to support Bronwyn's marriage. Sikki blamed Willem for revealing the scam, and that was just wrong."

Kira raised her brow, understanding. "You stood up for your husband and Sikki threw you out?"

Vega nodded, shivering. "She said I should go crawling back to Willi and beg him to take me in. She'd like nothing better than to see me humiliated right now."

"How did you know to come here?" Kira asked.

"When I called the cab company, I asked if they knew where to find Superstition Mesa. The driver who picked me up said he knows you and Algernon. He brought me to the bottom of the hill and told me to follow the road beyond the gate. But I nearly broke the heel of my shoes walking up here."

With sympathy, Kira leaned on her cane and stood. She listened to Vega further explain her family's dysfunctional dynamics while preparing a kettle for tea. "So what are you going to do about all this?" Kira asked.

"I can't go back to Willem," Vega replied. "I have enough money in my savings account for a train fare. Maybe I'll go back to my family."

"Would they help you start over?"

Secrets and Whispers: *Storm Clouds*

Vega shrugged. "Nobody's wealthy in the north. The weather's cold and life is hard. I'm not so young anymore, either. I don't know what'll happen."

Kira had heard many sob stories in the course of her ministry and had become hardened to any tale told to elicit sympathy. Vega had some tough choices to make. There was no easy way out of her situation.

"Why don't you get out of those wet clothes," Kira suggested. "You can change in the guest room." She pointed to a door next to Ileana's room while waiting for the tea to steep.

With nightfall approaching, Vega turned the light on when she shut the door, hoisted her suitcase onto the bed and changed clothes. But then her face grew pale. "Where is it!" Vega shrieked in alarm.

Kira turned. "Where is what?"

Vega dumped her belongings onto the bed, rummaging through every compartment in the suitcase and spreading her clothes out. "It's gone!" she cried. "The gun I bought is missing. I know I packed it, but it's not here. It's not anywhere!"

Ileana emerged from her room, concerned.

"Were you searched at the gate?" Kira asked, knowing that security had become obsessive since the palace attack.

Vega opened the door, her body energized with tension. "No one gave me a second glance. They just let me through."

Kira, confident the weapon had been misplaced, remained calm. "Maybe you forgot it in Sikki's room."

Vega returned to the bed and put her head into her hands. "No," she insisted. "Sikki must have taken it. I'd hidden it in the night stand drawer for safekeeping and packed it beneath my leather jacket this afternoon. She probably took it from there while I was in the bathroom."

Secrets and Whispers: *Storm Clouds*

After thinking for a moment, Vega stood. "I have to go back," she announced. "If she gives that gun to Willi, there'll be trouble!"

Kira glanced out the window and into the gloom, where hard rain created puddles and flowed in ephemeral streams down the hill. "That's a really bad idea," she warned. "The Daystar's going down and there are dangers in the dark. Stay here tonight. Let the storm pass. You can deal with this in the light of day."

Desire, Doubt, Disappointment

Garrick's favorite time of day occurred during the moments between lying in bed with his bride and falling asleep. While listening to her talk about the challenges and triumphs she'd faced, the proximity of her quiet company, the silky sensation of her skin, the sound of her voice and the warmth of her soft body filled his soul with a sense of belonging.

Sometimes he acted on his desire for her, but on most evenings, the affectionate act of sliding his left hand over her hip, along her belly and to her breast satisfied his need for close contact. As he kissed her shoulder and let his body relax, he found comfort to soothe away every bad memory, every self-doubt, every fear about his future.

Garrick remembered the longing he'd felt for Brenna in the days before their wedding. She represented a prize and a promise for his patience, his personal restraint and his persistence. On that memorable night where he'd first expressed the full extent of his passion for her, he'd been nervous, exhausted and worried that the anticipation of loving her would eclipse the actual experience. Yet they'd grown together since then, and the more he learned about Brenna, the more he adored her.

No one else knew the secret way she laughed and smiled when they were alone, how her eyes expressed invitation when she rubbed herself against him, encouraging his touch. He'd learned about the sensual sound of her contented murmurs when she laid her cheek against his bare chest, and breathy prayers whispered in gratitude as her beautiful body, suffused with pleasure, trembled during sex. These mysteries, revealed only after he'd committed his life to hers, continually delighted him.

Garrick desired her with greater depth and passion since they'd married than he had during the months of

Secrets and Whispers: *Desire, Doubt, Disappointment*

constrained longing that followed their first encounter on a windy hilltop overlooking the Saradon. They'd grown so close since then, he couldn't imagine life without her in it.

In contrast, after watching Algernon at the table that evening, Garrick felt a bit sorry for Bronwyn. Thea certainly held out an olive branch to her rival, but the way her presence tugged at Algernon's attention inspired doubts in Garrick's mind that his brother wanted Bronwyn with the degree of devotion she deserved.

During his own wedding at the Velez estate, Garrick remembered how Algernon couldn't keep his focus away from Brenna's not-so-little sister. Even Kira had grown angry with her twin brother for behaving this way. While he'd shown far greater restraint in Bronwyn's company at dinner that evening, Garrick knew what his brother liked in a woman, and Algernon's best effort at concealing his fascination with Thea hadn't fooled him.

Had Brenna noticed anything that evening, she'd kept her counsel to herself. With Lynden and Arvid engaged in conversation, and Dr. Yates far too timid to challenge Algernon in public – even if he'd perceived the mutually-suppressed interest – the simmer of attraction remained constant over the course of the family gathering.

Noting that Brenna had completely relaxed and her breathing became shallow, Garrick slipped away. She made a quiet noise of disapproval in her sleep, but quickly settled as he arose and reached for his robe. With care to avoid making noise, Garrick tiptoed to the balcony and headed downstairs. He held onto the rail because the darkness of the stormy night made it difficult to see.

Algernon lay on the downstairs couch. He stirred as his brother descended and sat up. "What's going on?" he asked, mildly alarmed.

"I can't sleep," Garrick replied. "We need to talk."

Secrets and Whispers: *Desire, Doubt, Disappointment*

That sounded ominous. Algernon scooted over, leaving room for his brother. "What's on your mind?"

"It's about you and Bronwyn," Garrick said quietly. After pausing for a moment, he could think of no way to express his thoughts discreetly. "I'm worried. Are you sure you want to marry her?"

"What brought this up?" Algernon asked.

"I've never told you how ticked off I felt about your lusting after Cynthia at my wedding. You turned an event that should have been a celebration of committed love into an embarrassment."

"You can't make me feel worse about my behavior than I already do," Algernon countered. "I've regretted that incident since it happened, and I'm sorry that it spoiled your happiness. Will you forgive me?"

"I can't say that I want to," Garrick replied.

"Well, that's your problem, not mine," the priest stated flatly. "What does this have to do with Bronwyn?"

Garrick tensed. "I saw how you and Thea were looking at one another tonight," he accused. "I know you did your best to cover it up, but Bronwyn deserves to feel confident in your commitment to her."

"You're right," Algernon conceded. "I can't deny the attraction. Thea's lovely, and worse, she wants me too, but, I *can* control how I respond to her."

"Well, you didn't do that at my wedding. And tonight, you were on the ragged edge of composure."

"You have no idea how restrained I've been in Thea's company after the hot spring incident," Algernon told him. "All of this started when Astrid and I were first introduced to Brenna's family, where Cynthia caught my eye. After we rescued Kira, Thea went out of her way to be in my company, and never missed an opportunity to display herself for me. She knew exactly what I wanted."

Secrets and Whispers: *Desire, Doubt, Disappointment*

"Everyone knows what you like," Garrick replied. "That's no secret and I'm not saying it's wrong, but there's a right time, a right place, and a right person. It might have been okay when you first met Thea, but it wasn't at my wedding, and I can see that it's still a problem now. You're about to marry a good woman who deserves your full devotion. Your desire for Thea concerns me."

Algernon sighed. "I can't forget what I've seen. It got much worse after falling off the boat on the way home. When I wound up at the Velez estate again, Thea told me that God had sent me back to court her. Lady Alexina had just weaned Eren, and whenever Thea took care of him, she never stopped him from pawing at her, or lifting up her blouse. She'd sit very close and press against me. She'd run down the stairs whenever I was nearby.

"One early morning while I was stretching in the courtyard, I caught her watching me from her patio door windows, as naked as she'd been at the hot spring."

Garrick raised his brow, having never heard about this before. "What did you do?" he inquired.

"I turned away, but how can I forget a lovely sight like that? Lady Alexina and Lord Lynden knew that my heart was here, with Bronwyn, and they understood that their daughter was using her body as bait. Lady 'Xina scolded Thea for her behavior, but it didn't stop."

Garrick, who'd deployed to fight on the Saradon while this was going on, had no idea what Algernon had experienced. They'd never talked about the circumstances of his return to Kameron. Garrick's combat stress made communication difficult, and the threat against Kira's life further distracted him. This new information planted a more nuanced understanding of his brother's conflict in the fertile ground of Garrick's mind. He loved Algernon and wanted to feel confident in his brother's integrity. "If Thea was that interested in you, why did you come back?"

Secrets and Whispers: *Desire, Doubt, Disappointment*

"There was a time I envied your relationship with Brenna," Algernon admitted. "I wished I could have a stunning partner, and for a while I hoped that Cynthia might fulfill my desire. But the more time I spent in her company, the more I realized the folly of that fantasy. Bronwyn's the woman I need. She knows the good and the bad in me, yet loves me anyway. We share common faith, common language, common experience and common values. We share a ministerial focus, too.

"Bronwyn and Kira are the best of friends. I couldn't deal with friction between my wife and my sister. I lost Kira once and I swear that'll never happen again.

"I don't need a goddess. I need a kindly woman of noble character. That's Bronwyn. She's also excellent in the kitchen. Thea has none of that going for her."

"So, this is all about you?" Garrick inquired. "It's all about what you need? You're telling me that Bronwyn's little more than a cook and a wet nurse to replace Mom?"

Algernon shook his head and his tone hardened. "That's a really cold thing to say, Garrick. You know how Mom was, but she never hated you. She never tried to harm you the way she enjoyed wounding me.

"Bronwyn soothes that pain away, but don't think she gives without getting. She has her own issues, her own doubts and problems, but I've watched her blossom. I've seen her inner beauty emerge. She's attractive in ways that most people, even her family, consistently overlook."

Garrick wanted to believe his brother, but his doubt lingered. "Even though she's not as pretty as Thea?"

"I've already told you that doesn't matter," Algernon replied. "I have more discipline than you think. I walked away from Cynthia – though she's the prettiest girl I've ever seen – and chose Bronwyn, instead. I love her. I choose to not act on my attraction to other women, and I've always honored her virtue when we're alone."

Secrets and Whispers: *Desire, Doubt, Disappointment*

Hearing Algernon speak this way didn't surprise Garrick. Remembering how Brenna also would have given herself away before they'd married, a new respect for his brother's integrity arose in Garrick's heart. "I'm honestly proud to hear you say that," he stated.

"So to answer your question directly, I'm completely confident that Bronwyn is the woman I want. She's the woman I need. Thea has Caerwyn, and if she had Brenna's decency, she'd strive to make him feel as confident in her as you do in Brenna."

Garrick put his forearms on his knees and leaned forward. "She will, in time," he said, knowing a secret of Lithian biology to which his brother was not privy. "I'm happy for you, Algernon, but I want you to know that I'm watching. I'll help you in whatever way I can, but I'm also holding you accountable. If you have any second thoughts about marrying Bronwyn, it's better to back out now than after the wedding."

"Don't worry Garrick," Algernon assured. "I have no doubt that she's the woman for me."

***

Brenna had been right. Her parents and siblings showered Bronwyn with attention and affection, welcoming her into kinship with honor she didn't believe she deserved. After her own family – along with Brenna, Garrick, and Algernon – left for the evening, everyone else gathered in a conference room for a vespers that felt very different from any that Bronwyn had ever experienced.

Jawara and Tembe, who had beautiful and powerful voices, led unfamiliar songs that blended Abelscinnian worship traditions – where nearly every aspect of the service was sung – with the Lithian customs maintained by their lifelong friends. They had to shorten their phrases

Secrets and Whispers: *Desire, Doubt, Disappointment*

because of the thin air, but the altitude didn't dampen their enthusiasm for song and prayer, all sung or spoken in two languages that Bronwyn didn't understand.

Camille sat at her right hand, translating the gist of what was happening – an exhausting task. "We're praying for you," she said. "We're blessing your marriage."

The gesture moved Bronwyn's heart, but couldn't address her unspoken worries. She needed to talk to someone who might understand her anxiety, and the only person whom she thought might be able to offer wisdom, was Brenna's mother, Lady Alexina.

Since Camille had talked her into staying, rather than heading for an uncomfortable night on the couch at Brenna and Garrick's place, Bronwyn waited for the chance for a private moment with the Lithian woman. More than 30 minutes after Lord Lynden concluded the vespers with a brief homily and benediction, most people began drifting to their rooms for the night.

Thea brought Eren to his mother, bade Bronwyn goodnight and left her parents' room holding hands with Cassie, who smiled a lot, but seldom spoke. As Lady 'Xina held her son to her breast and rocked him, Bronwyn asked Brenna's mother for a few moments alone.

"Of course, my dear," the Lithian woman replied. "Is something troubling you?"

Bronwyn waited until Lord Lynden left the room and closed the door before continuing. "Did your parents approve of your marriage to Lord Lynden?"

Lady 'Xina smiled. "They didn't have much choice in the matter," she said. "I come from one of the wealthiest families in Illithia. I was the top student at Sacred Vimlitia and a star on my lacrosse team. My prospects for finding a suitable partner were rather slim."

Bronwyn's brow furrowed. "How can that be, when you had all that going for you?"

Secrets and Whispers: *Desire, Doubt, Disappointment*

"Everything I've told you significantly narrowed my prospects," Alexina said. "I had a few dates, but no one seriously wanted me before Lynden came along."

When Bronwyn looked away in disbelief, Alexina continued. "You look at me and think that I had every factor in my favor. I come from a people who are uniformly beautiful, yet I terrified my suitors. It was far easier for them to look elsewhere than contend with my intelligence. My family believed I'd never marry."

"I'd never have suspected that," Bronwyn replied. "I thought the boys would have been knocking at your mother's door for the chance to court you."

Evaluating Bronwyn's facial expression, Alexina asked, "Does my experience resonate with you?"

Bronwyn nodded slowly. "Was your mother happy with Lynden?"

With Eren drifting to sleep, Lady 'Xina leaned back in her chair and put the child's head on her shoulder, continuing to rock him gently. "I come from a pure blood family, and I'm likely to live much longer than my husband. In fact, I am likely to outlive my children. That was my father's primary concern, but it's a choice I made, and I will have to live with its consequences.

"The same is true of you," she continued. "At dinner your father asked us some personal questions about our son. We are not ignorant of his past, yet we are confident of his future."

"I'd like to think that way," Bronwyn stated, "but now I'm not sure. I don't want to regret marrying Algernon. How do I know if I'm making the right choice?"

Lady Alexina smiled. "There is no right or wrong in love, my dear. There is only a willingness to set self aside and work in partnership. Do you believe my son can do that with you?"

Secrets and Whispers: *Desire, Doubt, Disappointment*

"Algernon?" Bronwyn clarified, knowing that Lady 'Xina treated him as her own, though she wasn't actually Algernon's mother. "He already has. I've watched him grow less reliant on Kira. He's been letting go of his own sister to make room for me."

"Then what is your worry?"

Bronwyn paused, reluctant to admit how much her own mother's concerns meant to her. "Some of the things in Algernon's past have been frightening and violent. I remember the depths of his rage and how he terrified everyone at the Temple. I heard what he did to those drug-dealing thugs after Kira went missing. I've seen him take on a fully armored giant with his bare hands and prevail. It was both horrifying and fascinating. He's fierce, he's headstrong, but he's always been gentle with me. Yet Vega, my sister-in-law, hides bruises from the hand of my brother. Her life is a lie. I don't want to live that way."

Lady 'Xina felt her son finally fall asleep. "Have you prayed about this?"

Bronwyn nodded. "I have, but the Great God never answers me."

"What form would such an answer take, my dear? Were you expecting a message in the stars?"

"I don't know," Bronwyn replied. "Maybe a voice, maybe something that made me feel more confident . . ."

Alexina paused. "The rage in my son had its roots in his belief that he was not – and could not be – loved. That slender priestess who loves Kira turned him around."

"You mean Astrid?" Bronwyn offered, scowling.

"Yes, Astrid," Alexina affirmed, smiling. "That's her name . . . She was the unlikely sower who planted hope in his heart, a seed you have watered and nurtured.

"The change you've witnessed in Algernon is the good fruit of your work. Why do you doubt what everyone who knows him can plainly see?"

Secrets and Whispers: *Desire, Doubt, Disappointment*

As much as Bronwyn resented Astrid for mistreating her at the Temple and struggled to forgive the woman, Lady Alexina spoke truthfully. The change in Algernon began after he'd taken the perilous journey to find Kira in Astrid's company.

"Do you believe the transformation of my son's heart has been sincere?" Lady Alexina asked.

"He's completely gentle with me when we're alone," Bronwyn stated. "I feel safe in his company."

"So your tongue speaks a truth that no one else can know – a truth that should allay your fear – yet you still wrestle with doubt. How can this be?"

Unable to sustain eye contact, Bronwyn looked away. "My heart is not pure. My motives are tainted by lust, and a visceral longing clouds my judgment."

Alexina suppressed laughter for the sake of her sleeping son, but she smiled beautifully. "You're a lovely young woman. Algernon is handsome and well-formed. Allfather gave you the gift of desire and has provided a comely offering to satisfy your hunger. Refuse that gift at your loss."

Hope dawned in Bronwyn's expression. "So you think it's the right choice to marry Algernon?"

In harmony with Lithian values, Alexina didn't answer directly. "Does he love you? Is he gentle with you? Does he listen? Is he diligent? Can he provide for your physical and emotional needs? Is he trustworthy and loyal? Does he love children? Would he be a good father?"

Bronwyn nodded. "Yes, to all of those things."

"Then what else do you want? What else do you need? Are you expecting perfection from my son?"

"No, of course not," Bronwyn replied, the furrow returning to her brow. "I know I'm not perfect. I have my own problems, too."

Secrets and Whispers: *Desire, Doubt, Disappointment*

"And you must choose," Lady Alexina concluded. "Allfather has prepared my son for you. My daughter, Thea, wept because she couldn't dislodge you from his heart – no matter how hard she tried. I held her as she grieved. I soothed her soul. Should you reject my son now, I believe she'd turn her back on Caerwyn in the hope that Algernon might return to her. That burden would lie heavily on both men, and might – one day – come back to haunt you. Is that what you desire?"

"No," Bronwyn said. "I want him. I really do."

Alexina smiled as she arose. She carefully lowered Eren onto a cot and pulled a blanket over his body. "Then choose accordingly."

***

Very early the next morning, Bronwyn awakened to the sound of someone knocking. With the eerie glow of the Great Eye Nebula lighting the room from its large windows, she saw Camille – whose eyes gleamed in the UV radiance – sit up, and heard her call out in Lithian. A quiet female voice answered, prompting the slender young woman to quickly slip out of bed and unlock the door.

Cynthia, wearing a thin white robe, followed her youngest sister inside. Her dark hair lay in tangled strands over her shoulders and she looked upset as she sat on the edge of Bronwyn's bed. In the dim light, her eyes lacked the glint Bronwyn always found a little spooky in Brenna.

Camille put on her own robe, sat next to Bronwyn and held her hand. "My sister needs a word with you."

"What's this about?" Bronwyn asked, uncertain why anyone would come visiting at this hour.

Secrets and Whispers: *Desire, Doubt, Disappointment*

Thea exchanged some words with Camille in Lithian before turning back to Bronwyn. "Your brother's in trouble," she announced quietly, speaking in vulgate.

"What are you talking about?" Bronwyn demanded. "Which one, what kind of trouble, and how do you know?"

"I had a dream," Thea told her, anticipating skepticism and subsequently reading it on Bronwyn's face. "Men with guns came looking for Willem."

Since Willi had been absent at the previous evening's dinner, Cynthia hadn't met him. She'd probably heard his name during the course of the meal, but a dream didn't mean anything, did it?

"What did these men look like?" Bronwyn asked.

"They wore black uniforms with white piping, shiny boots and white forage caps that had a gold badge on the front. There were mountain flags on their epaulets."

Bronwyn's eyes widened. That description matched a military police uniform, details Thea would not have known without direct contact with the Tamarian armed services. "Why were these men looking for my brother?"

"I don't know," Thea replied. "I never see the end when I dream, but you and Algernon have to save him."

"What? How am I supposed to do that?"

Thea shrugged. "I wish I could say. I told my parents before I came in here, and *Umma* said I should waken you so you can pray."

Interrupting the stunned silence that followed, Camille asked, "Do you want us to pray with you?"

Having only considered Cynthia a rival for Algernon's attention, not realizing her attunement with the spiritual realm and having never experienced one of Cynthia's clairvoyant dreams, Bronwyn remained incredulous and skeptical. "No," she murmured. "I'd rather pray alone. Can you give me a few minutes?"

Secrets and Whispers: *Desire, Doubt, Disappointment*

Camille exchanged words with her sister that Bronwyn didn't understand. "We'll be in the room next door if you need us," she said.

Bronwyn accepted their sisterly kisses as they departed. Once the door latch closed, she brought her pillow to her face and let emotion spill down her cheeks. While she wanted to dismiss Cynthia's vision as the fanciful imaginings of a jilted suitor, the compelling narrative struck a chord of legitimacy in Bronwyn's conflicted mind and she wept in worry for her brother.

***

Algernon awakened to the sound of Brenna stirring upstairs. The disorientation of unfamiliar surroundings faded as memory ebbed into his consciousness. After a quick trip to the bathroom, he slipped into his robe, folded his blankets and carefully opened the back patio doors, seeking solitude for prayer and meditation.

Many months had gone by since he'd done this alone. The discipline required to maintain focus became elusive as the cool, redwood-scented air, the breathtaking views of Wounded Heart Canyon, Fallen Moon Lake – a full mile below – and the distant Angelgate Mountains distracted his attention. With the Great Eye Nebula setting, he savored the beauty of the moment.

Then he frowned, wishing he could share the scene with Bronwyn. Imagining the sight of her leaning against the railing – her brown hair hanging over her broad shoulders, her back outlined beneath a diaphanous nightgown that hung to mid-thigh, her lovely eyes glancing at him in invitation – would have made the setting perfect. The thought of her aroused his desire, but for the moment, he willed every competing thought – no matter how pleasant – from his mind.

Secrets and Whispers: *Desire, Doubt, Disappointment*

After prayers and meditation, he spent nearly twenty minutes stretching every muscle group in his fit and athletic body. He'd slowly reach with each arm and leg, twist his back in every possible direction, pushing until he met resistance. Concentrating on relaxing at the point of strain allowed him to gently and persistently flex a little further than when he'd started.

Next came the martial forms, routines the Nordans called *kata*. These choreographed patterns of movement served to build and sustain muscle memory. Algernon knew dozens of these, but he reviewed them faithfully. Like a musician working scales, the ongoing practice honed his reactions to rapid automaticity.

He'd not come to the Temple as a naturally gifted fighter. Algernon simply worked much harder at gaining skill than anyone else, and even after he acquired the capacity to defeat all but the deadliest among the Temple priesthood, his restless pursuit of excellence pushed him even further. Street thugs feared him. Even members of the Assassin's Guild respected Algernon's martial skill.

Initially, his desire had been fueled by anger. As a lad of slight build and sharp tongue, he suffered torment from bigger, more aggressive boys. He'd fight to exhaustion, but rarely prevailed – and then, usually because his adversaries feared what Garrick would do to them in retaliation. Yet as his rage faded into memory, discipline, fitness and survival evolved as major motivating factors. Once at the top, Algernon intended to stay there.

Every day, he pushed himself to improve. Every day, he honed every move closer to perfection. He knew that Kira – though she rivaled his martial expertise – needed his muscle to protect her ministry from the worst of the city's criminal element. Without doubt, ruthless mobsters and delinquents left her alone out of fear that Algernon would avenge any harm done to her.

Secrets and Whispers: *Desire, Doubt, Disappointment*

With the Daystar risen fully over the distant, eastern ridge lines and the clear sky filled with glorious light, Algernon completed his morning workout and returned indoors. The smell of breakfast wafted from the upstairs kitchen, stirring Algernon's hunger.

"Garrick!" he called. "Is it okay to come up?"

"Yeah," Garrick replied. "Brenna's not back from her run yet."

Ascending the stairs quickly, Algernon noticed movement in the bathroom and made eye contact with Solace, a teenaged girl whom Kira had rescued from the Opium Guild. She now lived in an apartment not far away, hiring out as a maid to sustain herself. The Queen's Office paid Solace to clean the music manse for Brenna, another ministerial success in Kira's ledger.

She smiled and waved before resuming her task of scrubbing the shower tiles. Algernon absent-mindedly returned the greeting as he sauntered into the kitchen. He'd have to wait until she'd finished before rinsing the sweat off his body, but he wanted to eat first, anyway.

Garrick, wearing only a tank top and shorts, stood over the cookstove. Although Algernon knew that Solace didn't like boys, he felt a little surprised that his brother hadn't dressed yet. "Brenna's not working today?"

"It's Planting Break," Garrick stated. He stirred eggs in a frying pan, oblivious to Solace as she worked in the bathroom. "She also canceled her private students so we can spend time with her family. I'll be leading another tour of the sights before the train arrives this afternoon."

The brothers ate breakfast together while Solace changed the bed sheets and cleaned the kitchen. They'd not been enjoying their meal for very long when the phone rang. Garrick rose to answer it. Judging from his brother's tone and the curt responses he gave, Algernon concluded that something had gone wrong.

Secrets and Whispers: *Desire, Doubt, Disappointment*

"Corporal Soehn . . ? What about him . . ? Yes, my brother is getting married to his sister . . ."

Algernon could see the telltale flicker of eye movement indicating dishonesty.

"How would you expect me to know . . ? We've had dinner with the family, but . . . Under what charges . . ? But I just spoke to his lieutenant a few days ago . . . Yes, I can do that, sir . . . Thank you for calling."

"Trouble?" Algernon asked.

"Absolutely," Garrick replied. "That was the Military Investigation Command. They're looking for Willem."

Algernon scowled. "We don't know where he is."

***

Willem awakened with his head pounding. Desperately thirsty, he staggered to the bathroom for water, but his hands trembled so fiercely he dropped the glass into the sink where it shattered. Cursing violently, he cupped his hand beneath the faucet and slurped water from his palm.

Every muscle felt sore. He couldn't remember when he'd stumbled into the empty room, calling fruitlessly for Vega and then collapsing on the bed. Sleep failed to sate his sense of exhaustion, and the morning light spilling through the curtains intensified everything.

After relieving himself, Willem returned to bed. His world spun around him until the vertigo turned to nausea. Reaching for a nearby trash can, he retched and coughed until his belly ached and his teeth were etched with bile.

Where was Vega when he needed her?

They would come, he knew. Once they found out where he'd gone, they would come. They'd drag him away

Secrets and Whispers: *Desire, Doubt, Disappointment*

to rot in a cell for being different, for not being one of them, for having the courage to act on his true desire.

Betrayed, he would face the injustice alone. A dishonorable discharge, five years of imprisonment with forfeiture of pay awaited him. The gambling debt proved his guilt. Willem knew he was trapped. They'd say he presented a security risk to his unit and his country. No amount of honorable service would change any of that.

His rank made everything worse. The craving that condemned him looked like it had been inflicted from a position of power. It didn't matter that Mischa had also wanted him. Charges of abusing rank would aggravate what they called *unnatural relations*, and there was no mercy for any of that. It would be better to die . . .

Willem heard an urgent knock on the door. Dreading that the fateful hour had come, he wanted to hide. But Sikki's voice beckoned from the hallway.

"What do you want?" he called.

"Open the door!" she demanded.

"Where's Vega?" he asked.

Sikki sighed impatiently. "I have something she wanted me to give you, but you have to let me in . . ."

Willem pushed himself upright, his reward a spasm of pain between his temples. He groaned on his way to the door and when he opened it, Sikki scowled, wrinkling her nose and trying to wave the unpleasant smell away with her hand. She shook her head at his appearance, disgusted and disappointed.

"Where have you been?" she asked. "Arvid and Darren were looking for you."

"I went out," Willem replied. "Where's Vega?"

"I don't know," Sikki replied, speaking truthfully. "If you hadn't ruined everything in a drunken stupor, if you'd not spilled your guts to Bronwyn, you could have paid off your gambling debt and maybe your pretty wife would

Secrets and Whispers: *Desire, Doubt, Disappointment*

have stayed with you. But you're such a loser, you couldn't even manage that!

"It's too late to go back now. You have no hope to mend the mess you've made, so be a real man and put us all out of your misery."

"What do you mean?" he asked, unable to solve riddles in his current condition.

Sikki handed him a cigar box. "This is from Vega," she announced. "Take it and do the right thing."

Willem took the box from her and she promptly scurried down the hall. It felt heavy. Turning back into his room, Willem brought the box to his bed and opened it. Inside, he found Vega's weapon.

***

"Who are these clothes for?" Vega asked. Anxious to get back to the hotel and retrieve her gun, Vega had been pressuring Kira to hurry since arising an hour earlier.

Kira, freshly out of the shower, turned her head. "Oh, Heidelinde picked out that stuff for Bronwyn. I bought them for her, but she wants me to return them."

Without asking, Vega rummaged through the shopping bags Kira had left by the front door. From the feel of the fabric to the excellent stitching and expensive hook enclosures, she concluded that these garments lay beyond the means of most Tamarian women.

"These are lovely!" Vega remarked, holding a pinstriped blouse up to the light. "Why doesn't Bronwyn want them?"

Limping into her room to dress, Kira stated, "She's a modest woman. Bron doesn't like calling attention to herself by wearing expensive things."

Secrets and Whispers: *Desire, Doubt, Disappointment*

Vega folded the blouse and put it back. "Too bad they don't fit me," she replied. "I'd love to wear nice things like these!"

As Kira stuffed her own blouse hem into the skirt she'd chosen for the day, the telephone rang. After Kira hurried to answer the phone, Vega watched the platinum-haired woman's expression change from slightly worried to one of surprise.

"Yes, I am . . . She did what . . ? Unbelievable!" Kira reached for paper and a pen and proceeded to write down an address, which she dutifully repeated for clarification. "This afternoon, then . . ? Okay, thank you!"

Stunned, she put the earpiece back on its hook. "I've just inherited a house," she said, disbelievingly.

"What?" Vega inquired, concerned that something bad had happened. "Have you had a death in the family?"

"No," said Kira reassuringly. "It belonged to Mrs. Bergen, sister of the former High Priest Volker. She died the day you came to town. Algernon stayed at her bedside, which is why he was late for dinner that night."

Vega lowered her voice. "I'm sorry for your loss. I didn't know and I meant no disrespect."

"It's okay," Kira said, limping back into her room to pick up a note she'd written to herself. "I have to sign papers in town this afternoon. That's one more thing I have to do now . . ." She added the new task to a list of details she needed to complete before the wedding. These included coordinating delivery of the marriage bed she'd bought for Bronwyn and her brother; checking in with the catering firm; paying for Bronwyn's hairdresser; confirming delivery times for the floral arrangements; picking up the legal documents that former High Priest Volker, Algernon and Bronwyn would sign; making sure that Bronwyn's dress and shoes wound up at Brenna's house; returning the clothes she'd bought for Bronwyn to

Secrets and Whispers: *Desire, Doubt, Disappointment*

the vendor; and finally, meeting with relatives who were scheduled to arrive by train late that afternoon.

But then, the phone rang again. Kira hissed in frustration as she reached for the ear piece. Vega watched her expression transform as she accepted the call.

"Why?" Kira asked. "What's wrong . . ? But they had nothing to do with that . . . Can't Brenna talk to the queen . . ? A diplomatic mission . . ? So, we can't use the venue . . . Ugh!" Kira swore in a manner that lifted Vega's brow. "Don't worry about it. We'll go with Plan B . . . Okay, I'll see you this afternoon . . . Love you, too!"

With a scowl, Kira hung up the phone. "What else!" she groaned.

"What's going on?" Vega asked.

Kira shook her head and shuffled back into her room. "The Defenders posted a new policy refusing to allow foreigners into the palace complex," she explained. "My brother spoke to Colonel Scheer, but she won't allow any exceptions because she's worried about security."

Still not understanding how this impacted plans for Bronwyn's wedding, a puzzled expression arose on Vega's face. "Why is that a problem?"

"We planned to hold the ceremony in the Summer Garden near the palace. Brenna's family are Lithian, and her friends are all Abelscinnian. Now the Defenders won't let any of them in, but I've already made arrangements for the flowers and food. Now we'll have to use a different location for Bron's wedding."

"Maybe she should postpone it," Vega suggested. "With all the turmoil going on, that might be wiser."

Kira shook her head. "Not a chance. I've spent too much money on this to back out now. If we have to celebrate in a public park and host our dinner on the street, then that's what we'll do."

"What will Bronwyn say about that?" Vega asked.

Secrets and Whispers: *Desire, Doubt, Disappointment*

Throwing up her hands, Kira replied, "I don't know. I doubt she'll be happy, but we're running out of time and we'll have to improvise."

***

Algernon lingered under the hot water. At home, with a limited supply, he typically showered quickly. But with heat from the Honeywater offering unlimited luxury, he loitered under the warm stream for a long time.

When he finally stepped out of the shower, the sound of raised voices alarmed him. After returning from his last deployment, Garrick had become moody, difficult to understand, and prone to arguing with everyone – even his beloved Brenna. With time, he'd returned to a demeanor more typical of his character, but he could still be volatile and required patience. Algernon didn't want to walk into a dispute between the two lovers, so he prayed for them while toweling dry and dressing into his robe.

Yet as he stepped out of the bathroom, it became clear that Brenna was the one who was upset. Her agitation wasn't directed at Garrick, but at his admission that the Defenders refused to allow her loved ones and their friends behind the wall for Bronwyn's wedding. "How am I supposed to explain this to my family?" she complained. "They had nothing to do with the bombing. What is it with you Tamarians? This attitude is arbitrary, xenophobic, mean-spirited and altogether too common!"

Garrick drew her close, gently caressing her shoulders and resting his head against hers. "I tried reasoning with the colonel," he soothed. "but she won't make exceptions for anyone aside from you. I've already talked to Kira. She told me she has a backup venue, but she'll have to notify the caterers, musicians and florists."

Secrets and Whispers: *Desire, Doubt, Disappointment*

"What's Bronwyn going to think when she hears about this?" Brenna continued, crossing her arms. "Tomorrow's her special day, and every time she turns around, she's facing another problem. I had a hard time convincing her to let my family attend. What's she going to say now?"

"Leave that to me," Algernon offered. "I'll talk to her on my way to see Willem."

And as Brenna leaned into her husband's embrace, Algernon – anxious to respect their privacy – scurried downstairs. He gathered his rucksack from the couch and waved farewell to Solace, who was busy cleaning the floor near the grand piano. As he shut the outer airlock door, the serious nature of the task laying before him weighed on his heart. Algernon felt obligated to protect his brother, whose career would suffer if the Military Investigation Branch ever discovered he'd been less than completely forthright with them.

Anyone warning Willem about the call could be cited for obstructing justice, but neither Algernon nor Garrick wanted an ugly scene involving one of Bronwyn's family members the day before her wedding. That desire presented an ethical problem Algernon struggled to reconcile. He could shut down questioning by claiming priestly privilege, but doing that violated his vow to speak truthfully and also made him look guilty.

The Defenders at the palace gate always treated Algernon with a deference he didn't believe he deserved. Saintly Brenna's parents certainly merited more respect than he did, but the posted prohibition against foreigners excluded them for reasons based in fear, not fact. As he departed the gate and walked across Equality Park, Algernon brooded over how he might break the bad news to his beloved.

Secrets and Whispers: *Desire, Doubt, Disappointment*

With Brenna's family occupying the entire 12th floor of the Gold Leaf Hotel, security staff disabled elevator access to the area and locked the stairway to avoid the *racial mixing* feared by the hotel's administration. Algernon had to explain his business and acquire permission from the shift manager to use the service elevator.

When Bronwyn called him into her room, he found her saddened demeanor and posture troubling. She'd curled up on the bed – still in her nightclothes – holding a pillow close. "What's wrong?" he asked worriedly.

Bronwyn discarded the pillow and reached for him. "Willi's in trouble," she lamented.

Finding it strange that she would know this, Algernon kissed her and pulled her soft body into his embrace. The strength of her arms testified to the intensity of her emotional state. "Who told you?"

"Brenna's not-so-little sister had a dream," Bronwyn replied, still struggling to discard her previously conceived, less-than-optimal opinion of a sweet-dispositioned young woman who'd been nothing but nice to her thus far.

Algernon sighed, knowing of Cynthia's clairvoyance from personal experience. "Well, she's right. Military investigators phoned Garrick earlier this morning. They have a warrant for Willem's arrest. We need to find him before they get hold of him."

"What good will that do?" Bronwyn complained, her voice lacking its characteristic optimism as she looked away. "Where can he go? If they don't find him before the wedding, they'll arrest him at the ceremony. Then everyone will forever associate the day we married with the day Willem wound up in the brig."

"Maybe we can work something out," Algernon soothed. "Garrick knows how to deal with military people. He doesn't think they're interested in making a scene at anyone's wedding. It's not good for public relations.

Secrets and Whispers: *Desire, Doubt, Disappointment*

"What's more important is that Willem is vulnerable right now. It's up to us to help him."

A chill ran down Bronwyn's spine. She knew Algernon hadn't spoken to Thea, but Brenna's sister had mentioned that detail in particular. "What can we do?"

"The first thing is to make sure your brother's safe," he told her. "We have to find out what's really going on before we can decide the best course of action. But he took off yesterday and no one knows where he's gone."

"What if he's left town?" she asked.

As scenes of his father's bad behavior cried out from the prison of his memory, Algernon shook his head. "That's unlikely. It requires a plan, and people who drink excessively don't plan well. The first place we should check is his room. In all likelihood, he staggered back late last night to sleep off a hangover."

Bronwyn nodded and slid to the edge of the bed, pleased that he shared her concern. "Then let's find him."

Algernon reached for her hand. "There's something else I have to tell you," he admitted, fearing her disappointment and bracing for her response. "We can't have our ceremony at the palace. The Defenders won't let any foreigners – other than Brenna – through the gate."

"Ugh!" she groaned in frustration. "That's so stupid! Brenna's family are really nice people. They're not going to hurt anyone . . ."

"I know," Algernon replied. "It's not fair to them, and it's not fair to us, either."

"Why are we having so much trouble?" Bronwyn complained. "I'm sick of all this! Every day it's something else. I just want you. It's not complicated . . ."

Her eyes, full of desire, drew him close until their lips met and lingered. "Kira will handle everything," Algernon assured. "You won't be disappointed."

Secrets and Whispers: *Desire, Doubt, Disappointment*

***

They heard shouting before they arrived at the floor where Willem and Vega had been staying. A grim-faced military police officer stopped them from going further. "You can't come in here," he warned sternly. "We have a situation. Please return to your floor."

Glancing around the policeman's shoulder, Bronwyn saw armed men pointing their weapons into her brother's room. "Don't hurt him!" she cried, fearing for Willem's life. "Please! Don't hurt him!"

"Miss, you have to leave now," the MP insisted, one hand on his gun, the other pushing Bronwyn's shoulder with greater force than Algernon thought was warranted.

"Just wait," the young priest encouraged, wedging into the space between his beloved and the officer. "We know about the warrant . . ."

Shouting continued. "Step away!" the officer warned. "I don't want to hurt you, but I will if I must!"

"Who are you to threaten me?" Algernon demanded, confronting the cop directly. "How dare you!"

Having never used his priestly privilege before, Algernon wasn't sure how the MP would respond. Noting the indecision in the officer's eyes, he placed his hand on the MP's arm and said gently, "Let me talk to Willem."

"He's got a gun," the officer admitted.

"Tell your commander that I'm here. It won't hurt to let me through. If you keep doing what you're doing now, someone's going to wind up dead . . ."

Bronwyn began to cry. The policeman ignored her and shouted over his shoulder, "Captain, I have a priest who wants a word with the accused."

The shouting continued without respite. In a move too quick to counter, Algernon disarmed the MP, tossed his gun aside and stormed ahead. "Let me through!"

Secrets and Whispers: *Desire, Doubt, Disappointment*

At this, the captain drew his sidearm and pointed it at Algernon's chest. "Stop right there!" he warned. "Turn around and go back!"

"Are you going to shoot me?" Algernon asked, pausing and holding his hands out to the side. "I'm unarmed. I'm no threat to you or anyone else."

"Did you not hear me?" the captain shouted, agitated and nervous. He didn't want to fire at a priest. *Why won't this idiot just go away?*

"I'm here to save life," Algernon replied. "Tell your men to stand down and let me in."

"He's got a gun," the captain warned, sternly.

"So do you," Algernon replied. "Do I look like I'm afraid? Let me through!"

Knowing he was at an impasse with the accused and witnessing Algernon's determination, the captain relented. He ordered his men out of the room. "If he gets away, I'll arrest you for obstruction," the captain warned.

"Don't worry," Algernon assured quietly. "I've just saved your career . . ."

How much of that was true he couldn't be certain. In the hush that settled over the scene he heard Bronwyn praying between her sobs, and though he'd seldom invoked the divine when facing danger in the past, with her in his life, Algernon had far more to lose. "Great God, help me!" he murmured, stepping inside.

The room stank of vomit, stale sweat, bad breath and alcohol. Willem – sweating and trembling – sat facing the door, pressing Vega's .25 caliber gun into his temple.

"You can put the gun down," Algernon offered.

Willem shook his head. "What are you doing here? What do you want?"

"I'm here to tell you that we love you."

Secrets and Whispers: *Desire, Doubt, Disappointment*

Willem swore. "The hell you do! You just don't want me to wreck the wedding. What kind of honeymoon would you have if Bronwyn's brother blew his brains out?"

"It would be sad because you hadn't been at the ceremony to share our happiness. We want you there."

"It's too late for that!" Willem countered.

Algernon calmly sat in a chair by the window. "Not so," he said. "I know things look dark to you right now, but as long as you draw breath, you have hope."

"What do you know?" Willem shouted. "You've seen nothing in your sheltered life! You just want to bonk my sister and don't want me to ruin everything. Well, I hate to disappoint you, but no one cares about her happiness."

"I'm not here to talk about Bronwyn," Algernon replied. "I'm here to talk about you. How does putting a gun to your head solve your problems? How does it reconcile you to your wife?"

"Vega doesn't care about me!" Willem contended.

"Not true," Algernon stated. "No woman stands by a man she doesn't love, and she's stood by you for years."

Willem wanted to believe she still did, but he was struggling to think rationally. "Then why isn't she here now? Why did she leave me?"

"You threatened her. You've beaten her. You're responsible for your own behavior. Everyone makes mistakes, brother, but real men make things right. You can still do that. You can put the gun down and start rebuilding relationships. That's in your power right now."

"I'm not like you," Willem spat. "I'm different. No one will ever think you're immoral for bonking the daylights out of my sister, but I'm not allowed to act on who I am. So spare me your platitudes. You don't love me like I need to be loved. Just get out of here and let me get this over with in peace!"

Secrets and Whispers: *Desire, Doubt, Disappointment*

Algernon shook his head. "I'm not leaving you. It's not your place to tell me how I can and can't love you. That's my choice, not yours. If you end your life now, you'll never know the comfort of your wife's embrace again. The love and affection of your family . . ."

"Shut up!" Willem roared. "No one in my family gives a damn about anyone but themselves. Your sister's right. We were going to swindle Bronwyn out of her dowry and inheritance. That's what my loving brothers wanted to do!"

"Bronwyn loves you," Algernon replied. "She's crying in the hall right now, praying for your safety. Your mother and father love you, as does your Tante Marla. I know your wife loves you, too. Why throw all that away for money? If you need Bronwyn's inheritance, why haven't you asked her for it? She'll never want for anything."

"What are you talking about?" Willem retorted, finally lowering the gun. "Why would she give me anything that's rightfully hers?"

"Why do you presume she wouldn't? The fact that you believe she's selfish and greedy proves that you know nothing about her."

"You don't know what you're talking about!"

Algernon raised his brow. "She's lived in my company far longer than in yours. Bronwyn is the kindest, most giving person I've ever met. The only reason she hasn't helped you is because you haven't asked."

"So, you're telling me that if I'd come to her wanting money, she'd have given it to me?" Willem queried.

"Without question," Algernon replied.

Willem's mind raced. "You're a priest, and she wants to marry you. But you've taken a vow of poverty, and now you're saying that my sister is in a position to help me financially? You have no money and neither does she. You're out of your mind!"

Secrets and Whispers: *Desire, Doubt, Disappointment*

"If that was true, then why bother with your elaborate disinheritance plot? The lot of you have made assumptions about your own sister that reflect your values, not hers.

"But more importantly, you're presuming that money has greater merit than relationships. I know your sister loves you, no matter how different you may be. The same is true of your parents. I can't speak about your brothers, but I know it's true of Bronwyn . . ."

Willem fought back his emotion. "I've screwed this up. Sikki's right. Vega hates me. I've ruined everything!"

"Wait a minute," Algernon interjected. "Sikki put you up to this?"

"Vega told her to give me the gun," Willem admitted. "She said I should be a man and do the right thing. Well I'm trying!"

"Vega wouldn't say that," Algernon countered, remembering what Kira had told him. "You have relational work to do with her, but you're a soldier. You stand against what the enemy throws at you. Don't listen to what Sikki says. Be the man you know you are."

"What, a faggot? A queer? An abomination? You're a priest. You know what *Gottslena* says about men like me!" Willem muttered. "I can't change who I am!"

Algernon shook his head. "You're not defined by your sexuality any more than I am."

"That's easy for you to say. You're not going to prison for bonking Bronwyn. You've probably never set foot in a cell in your whole, sheltered life. Do you know what they'll do to me in there?"

"You're likely to face nothing worse than a dishonorable discharge," Algernon replied.

"What do you know about that? You're a priest, not an advocate, not a soldier."

Secrets and Whispers: *Desire, Doubt, Disappointment*

Algernon shook his head. "I know how courts work, and courts martial are not that different," he began. "But the very worst they'll do to you is still better than a self-inflicted bullet to the head.

"I'm worried about you, Willem. I hear the pain in your voice. I hear you doubting yourself, and while I don't know how that feels, you're my brother and I don't want to lose you. I don't want you to die. I can't make it any more plain than that."

Something subtle changed in Willem's countenance, a small step away from despair. "They're going to arrest me," he stammered fearfully.

"Yes," Algernon nodded. "And when they do, I'll go with you to make sure they treat you well."

Willem shook his head. "How can you do that?" he muttered. "You're a priest, not a soldier."

"You have the right to priestly counsel," Algernon reminded Willem. "And my brother has connections."

"Your brother . . ." Willem hissed. "Why would he bother with me?"

"He will, because he loves Bronwyn like she's his own sister. In time, he'll love you like a brother, too."

"They'll drag me through the lobby and make a scene. It'll be ugly . . ."

Recalling the arrangement that Brenna's family had to endure, Algernon countered, "I'll have them take us through the service elevator and out the back. I'll stay with you the whole time. No one else will have to know."

After a moment of contemplation, Willem relented. "Okay," he whispered, tossing the gun to the edge of the bed. "I'll go."

***

Secrets and Whispers: *Desire, Doubt, Disappointment*

Anxious to spend time with her family, Brenna showered and dressed with unusual urgency. She slid into a modest, pale-patterned blouse and knee-length skirt that veiled her lovely form from Garrick's admiring eye and imploring hands. She resisted his affection with a persistence that none of his charm could overcome.

"They'll have eaten and finished morning worship by now," she told him, a little less patiently than warranted. "There's no need to make everyone wait for us." When she noticed disappointment in her lover's eyes, Brenna's demeanor softened. "I'm sorry, Garrick," she said quietly. "I want you too, but can we wait until we get back?"

Although mildly disappointed that she'd brushed him off, Garrick held his tongue and restrained his desire. He knew that Brenna, who placed a high value on family relationships, had not seen her parents in many months and Niobe, Jawara's wife, in years. Her longing for close connection had always been integral to her character, and on a deep level, Garrick understood that Brenna's prioritizing of her parents in that moment did not diminish her devotion, passion, or commitment to him. He honored his wife's wishes without a second thought.

A bright and beautiful day awaited them outside the sheltering walls of the music manse. Garrick held Brenna's hand as they walked through the forest. They talked about the imminent wedding and Bronwyn's dysfunctional, familial opposition to her union, while leaving unspoken their shared disappointment arising from the strident resistance of Garrick's mother, prior to their own marriage. Then, as they reached the residential area just beyond the forest, their fingers mutually released and Brenna quickened her steps.

Unaware of his brother's interaction with Willem and distracted by imagined complications, Garrick hustled to keep up with his fleet-footed bride. While the sensuous,

Secrets and Whispers: *Desire, Doubt, Disappointment*

rhythmic motion of her skirt and billowing hair swishing from side-to-side would normally fan the coals of his desire, his heart was instead hastened by her energetic stride and sweat-inducing pace.

By the time they arrived at the Gold Leaf Hotel, no trace of the military police remained. Alone in the service elevator, Brenna pressed her hips into her husband's thighs as their lips met, as she breathed in the scent of his skin, and felt his strong hands caressing her. She smiled, unspoken promise in her eyes that lingered in her touch as she took his hand in hers. Here, among family members, Brenna feared no repudiation. Among her loved ones, she felt free to express affection to her beloved.

Within reason . . .

The sound of children playing greeted them as the newlywed couple stepped out of the lift. Osayande, son of Niobe, rolled a ball to Eren, Brenna's two-year-old brother, under Niobe's watchful eye. Brenna knelt to kiss her sibling, but he backed away fearfully.

Disappointment flashed in her eyes. Niobe, with her brow knitted in concern, picked up the child and spoke to him in Lithian. "This is your big sister," she soothed. "She loves you . . ."

And in Niobe's arms, Eren permitted Brenna's lips on his cheek, but the young boy remained doubtful of his relationship to the woman with the badly scarred neck.

"Where is everyone else?" Brenna asked.

"They're praying in the conference room," Niobe replied. "The woman who marries tomorrow came upstairs in deep distress. She said her brother has been arrested by the military police.

Brenna's eyes widened and her right hand went to her lip. "That's terrible!" she stated.

"Where's Algernon?" Garrick asked.

Secrets and Whispers: *Desire, Doubt, Disappointment*

With Osayande tugging at her skirt, Niobe set Eren back down on the floor. "He went with the brother," she replied. "I don't know where."

Moments later, Brenna and Garrick wandered into the lounge, where tea cups and bread plates lingered on the side tables of couches surrounding the fireplace. Tembe, the handsome engineer who'd taken a fancy to Kira, stood to greet them.

"*Nwanne* Blynn," he greeted, using the Abelscinnian word for "sister" that Garrick had heard from him before.

"Why aren't you praying, too?" Brenna inquired, clasping her hands together over her heart, in the manner of his people.

Tembe looked a little embarrassed. "Bronwyn called your home, but you'd already departed. She came upstairs thinking Kira would come looking for you. I decided to stay out here and wait . . ."

Brenna struggled to avoid rolling her eyes as she glanced away from Tembe. She squeezed Garrick's hand as her brow raised and her tone softened. "I'll go in with my parents. Will you wait for me?"

Garrick – who did not pray – agreed, letting her fingers slip away from his once more. He watched his wife scurry toward the conference room with concern lingering on his face. His plans for touring the town with Brenna's family would have to wait.

A few moments later, Tembe interrupted his reverie. "Do you think I can see your sister today?"

Garrick, who'd maintained a high opinion of Tembe in the past, caught a glimpse of the self-absorbed attitude from the young man that Brenna frequently criticized. He shook his head. "Bronwyn and my brother are getting married tomorrow," Garrick replied. "I know you've come to see Kira, but she's very busy right now."

Secrets and Whispers: *Desire, Doubt, Disappointment*

A pained expression crossed Tembe's face. "I'm not wishing to control her time," he said a little sadly. "I would just like to see her again. That's all. I worry that she doesn't wish to see me."

Remembering the chronic uncertainty he felt about Brenna while they were dating, Garrick put his hand on Tembe's shoulders. "Don't worry," he assured. "Be patient for now. I'm sure Kira will find time for you soon."

After a few minutes of awkward silence, waiting on the couches, Garrick turned at the sight of Jared, Cassie's fiancé, on his way to the conference room.

Garrick stood. "I need a word with you," he said. "Can you spare a few minutes?"

Jared invited Garrick into his room. Although the two men did not know each other well and had very little in common, their ties to the Velez family created cordiality between them. "What's on your mind?" Jared asked.

"Do you know anything about *Los Patrones del Estado?*" Garrick responded, getting straight to the point.

With widened eyes and a lowered voice Jared replied with another question. "What brought this up?"

"A stranger approached us on the streetcar before we met you at the train station. He knew that you're a friend of King Alejo, and he wanted me to ask you about *Los Patrones.*"

"Tread carefully," Jared warned. "Those are very dangerous people."

"I've never heard about them before," Garrick replied. "Why do you say they're dangerous?"

"*Los Patrones* are a shadowy organization of elite Kamerese who have a history of involvement in political killings and international intrigue," Jared began. "They're ostensibly loyal to the king, but they answer only to themselves. Anyone who opposes them tends to disappear. It's wise to stay clear of those people."

Secrets and Whispers: *Desire, Doubt, Disappointment*

"Would you be willing to share information about them with Crown Intelligence?"

Jared shook his head. "My family lives in Kameron," he reminded Garrick. "So does Lord Lynden and his kin. We are guests in that country, and what you're suggesting could be considered treason by native Kamerese. Who was this person who approached you?"

Garrick didn't want to lie, but he'd been ordered to get information from Jared and didn't want to shut the conversation down. "I don't know," he replied.

"So, why are you asking me?" Jared asked, his eyes narrowing. "You come looking for information, yet you're unwilling to speak the truth. How is that fair?"

Suppressing shame at being caught in a falsehood, Garrick shrugged. "The man spoke in vulgate, but looked Kurian and had a coastal accent. He says he's trying to stop a war and made uncharitable remarks implying the Kamerese government was involved in a terror attack."

"Did he offer proof?" Jared asked.

Garrick shook his head. "He talked about Cassie. He knew that she's Brenna's sister, and that you are friends with King Alejo. Those are details that couldn't be known without a lot of careful digging."

Jared's complexion grew ashen. "What did he want with me?"

"Nothing," Garrick replied. "He said you'd know about *Los Patrones del Estado*, and that I should report your statement to an analyst who works for the Expeditionary Force . . ."

"Dr. Hougen," Jared responded, remembering her from Brenna and Garrick's wedding. He had a very sharp mind for details. "But she's just a captain. What can she do about anything?"

Secrets and Whispers: *Desire, Doubt, Disappointment*

Garrick knew that Mariel had been asked to help with the investigation of the palace bombing, but he didn't reveal that to Jared. "Maybe he knows something I don't."

Jared shook his head. "You're not a good liar, dear brother. If I examined you under oath, it would be a simple matter to shred your testimony . . ."

"I'm not at liberty to tell you everything I know," Garrick said in his own defense. "I'm just a soldier, and I doubt I could offer the truth you desire, anyway."

"For the sake of my beloved and her family, I implore you to act with wisdom in this matter," Jared encouraged, speaking as much of a warning as his culture permitted. "*Los Patrones del Estado* is a dangerous group with a lot of money and deep connections in very dark places. They're rumored to be involved in the overthrow of governments. Some have even suggested they're funding another insurrection among the Abelscinnians. They probably have more money in dirty international dealings than your entire government's budget for espionage.

"I know you love your country and think you're doing the right thing by talking to me about this, but I doubt that even the most highly connected people in your espionage service have a solid idea how wide the sticky webs of *Los Patrones* reach."

***

Late that afternoon, Kira sat on a bench in Marvic's massive train station with Tembe and Bronwyn, waiting for passengers arriving on the train from Burning Tree. Garrick and Brenna walked up from the arrival deck together, with no one else accompanying them.

Kira felt disappointment rise in her soul and shook her head as her eldest brother approached. "It figures!"

Secrets and Whispers: *Desire, Doubt, Disappointment*

"What's wrong?" Tembe asked, attentive to the change in her demeanor.

"No one showed up," Kira stated. "I even offered to reimburse their train fares, but not a single person in my family bothered to come for the wedding."

"It's for the best," Garrick replied, putting a positive spin on the situation. "You know how they can be . . ."

"We must have the most dysfunctional family in the country," Kira complained. "Even cousin Inge couldn't be bothered to celebrate with us."

Bronwyn, still afflicted with sadness over the arrest of her brother, crossed her arms over her bosom. "I don't think your family is anywhere near as demented as mine. At least none of your kin are in custody . . ."

Sympathetic to Bronwyn's aching heart, Kira reached for her friend's hand. "We'll find a way to get Willem back," she promised. "Algernon's good at solving problems like this."

Suppressing tears, Bronwyn squeezed Kira's hand. "My parents are furious with Sikki right now, and my mother's an emotional wreck. How are we supposed to have a wedding celebration when everything's going wrong like this?"

Brenna, hearing Bronwyn say this, knelt down and put her hand on the younger woman's knee. "Love covers over all wrongs," she said. "Have faith, my sister."

Bronwyn nodded. "I love my family," she admitted. "I just don't like some of them right now."

Garrick didn't see the point in lingering at the train station when he had more urgent matters on his mind. He reached for Brenna's hand and pulled her to her feet. "Why don't we go home?" he suggested. "Let's end a disappointing day on a happy note."

Brenna smiled, desire illuminating her eyes. "That sounds like a great idea . . ."

Hurt

"How could we have been so blind?" Irena asked in a despairing tone. She sat on her bed with maternal anguish furrowed on her face, grasping a tissue in one hand. Her attention wandered from the hotel room window, to its wall, and then into her lap before returning to her sister, Marla. Irena shook her head, still struggling to accept the reality of a wicked secret – the contempt her children held for each other – finally and fully revealed. "And worse, how could Sikki turn on my son like this?"

Pity evolved in Marla's eyes. She felt sorry for Irena and had worried as she watched her sister pick at her breakfast. She also thought that Irena looked tired. "The nature of a conspiracy demands secrecy," she said reassuringly. "Sikki manipulated everyone, especially Darren. Giving Willem the gun was a way to deflect responsibility away from herself. That behavior is a reflection of her character, not yours."

Arvid glanced up from the newspaper he wasn't actually reading, noting his wife's pained expression. He quietly agreed with his sister-in-law's comment, but held his counsel to avoid inflaming a volatile situation.

"I raised them better than this," Irena countered.

"You had nothing to do with Sikki and Heidelinde's upbringing," Marla corrected. "Your boys will do anything to please their wives. You shouldn't be surprised that they are so easily led astray."

"That's a terrible thing to say!" Irena replied.

Marla didn't back down. "Do you have a better explanation?" When Irena couldn't find words to respond, Marla continued. "Now to Darren's credit, he was also trying to help Willem, who he said has a large gambling debt he has no way of paying back . . ."

Secrets and Whispers: *Hurt*

"That's not why the military police arrested him," Irena said, sadly.

Willem's sexuality had long been a sore spot with Arvid. He'd found it hard to accept his son's orientation and struggled to love him with the same intensity he lavished on his other children. He'd hoped that Willem's marriage would change his preference and resolutely denied that it hadn't.

Arvid had steadfastly refused to consider that Vega's frequent bruises reflected a breakdown in her relationship. Though he didn't admit this out loud, he also blamed himself for Willem's trouble and secretly believed that if he'd been tougher as a father when Willi was young, everything would have turned out differently.

Marla, who was better educated on the topic, approached the subject with sensitivity. "The rules that govern conduct in the military reflect a need for absolute control," she explained. "If Willem expressed his sexuality in a way that undermines discipline, then the environment is not suitable for him."

"They're going to throw my son into prison," Irena lamented. "How are they going to treat him there? Do you think he deserves punishment for acting on his natural inclinations? Is that justice? Is that right?"

Not knowing how best to reassure her sister, Marla fell back on Bronwyn's counsel. "Algernon is with Willi," she said. "We've seen him in court. If anyone knows how to defend Willem, it's Algernon."

Struck by the irony that her hope now rested on the radical priest whose marriage to Bronwyn she'd strongly opposed, Irena could not fully suppress her tears. She dabbed her eyes with the tissue in hand and glanced at her husband, whom she knew was only pretending to read the newspaper. "How am I going to function at my daughter's wedding while my son is under arrest?"

Secrets and Whispers: *Hurt*

"Be strong, smile, and support Bronwyn," Marla replied. "This is her day to celebrate, and the girl deserves to be happy."

***

During one of her explorations of Superstition Mesa, Karin stumbled upon the abandoned cabin that Bronwyn and Algernon had been using when they wanted privacy. Its hidden location suited Karin's clandestine purpose. The suspended wildlife officer brought bedding and food to sustain herself at the cabin while conducting her own investigation into the case of the missing gwynling.

This monotonous work had thus far uncovered nothing unusual. The garden showed signs of neglect. She'd seen Algernon head to the well at Lookout Point to fetch water twice. An older woman who stayed inside a lot had been visiting. A slender and very pretty Lithian woman routinely left in the early morning and returned in the late afternoon. Aside from her, no one else maintained a predictable schedule.

In the midmorning of her fourth day on watch, Karin concealed herself in the trees that grew on a ridge behind the homestead. After hours of fruitless waiting, she finally saw movement near the garden beds at the back of the property. Excitedly, Karin fumbled for her notepad. She'd been recording the times and direction of travel of anyone leaving the house, looking for patterns that she hoped would be incriminating. Karin reached for her binoculars to get a closer look.

It was the big girl, the one with brown hair, who lived with the pariah priest and his wicked sister. Karin scowled at first. This had to be the priest's bride-to-be, who – despite living at the homestead – wasn't on the suspect list.

Secrets and Whispers: *Hurt*

As the husky female moved away from the house, the wildlife officer became curious. "What are you doing?" she wondered aloud, following the woman's movements until she disappeared on a narrow uphill path, near the homestead's wind turbine.

Karin put her notes and binoculars back into a satchel that she hoisted onto her back. Moving westward, through the trees, she paralleled the buxom girl's heading, then stopped when she encountered a strangely well-worn path leading north. For a wild place, Superstition Mesa had a lot of these trails. Karin followed it unthinkingly.

As the trees thinned near the edge of the ridge, Karin paused. She could see the brown-haired maiden in the distance stop near a hot spring and unsling a bag she'd carried over her shoulder. Quickly, Karin pulled out her binoculars to have a better look. The woman unloaded her bag, unbuttoned her blouse and slipped out of her skirt. Karin groaned. This was not what she'd hoped to see. "Ugh! You came here to take a bath? Who does that?"

Annoyed, the wildlife officer put her binoculars away and trotted back up the unfamiliar trail, intending to return to her lookout position. Moments later – feeling disoriented – she had a feeling that she'd gone too far. Something about the smell in her surroundings sounded a warning bell in her mind that she chose to ignore, and one fateful step forward forever changed her life.

***

"You're out of your mind if you think this crazy idea of yours will work," Advocate Justin Piers told Algernon in a secure, armed forces holding facility. "You've never had legal training, and you think that a cursory glance through the Military Code of Conduct qualifies you to speak on behalf of Corporal Soehn? Get over yourself!"

Secrets and Whispers: *Hurt*

Exhausted from a long night divided between intensive reading and talking to Willem, Algernon gestured dismissively with his left hand. "The only evidence against the corporal is the testimony of a soldier who claims he was coerced into an affair. That's hardly compelling."

Advocate Piers didn't relent. Not much older than Garrick and easily a match for Algernon's intelligence, he anticipated a long career and didn't want his chances for promotion ruined by a hopeless case like this. "You're only a priest. In my view, it's ridiculous that the rules permit you to consult and counsel in military justice.

"But let me give you a dose of reality, Brother Algernon . . . Cases like this go badly for the accused. It's not just a matter of one soldier's word against another. Corporal Soehn signed a debenture to take responsibility for Private Metzger's gambling debt. He's admitted that he did this – in his words – *out of love.*

"When this matter goes before the Chief Military Bench, it's not going to play well. The armed services do not approve of relations between soldiers in the same unit, much less of same-gender sexuality. In our lingo, that's *Voluntary Disregard and Disobedience of Orders and Regulations, Abuse of Authority, Dereliction of Duty,* and *Conduct Unbecoming,* among others. Corporal Soehn is looking at administrative penalties – the least of which is dishonorable discharge – and criminal penalties which will land him in prison for a long time."

"I'm not dismissing the serious nature of the charges against him," Algernon countered. "My point is that all of this is based on the testimony of one man. The only thing that will actually stick in court is the debenture, and I'm not worried about that."

Advocate Piers, whose stern expression morphed into surprise, cocked his head to the side. "You can't just make that go away," he insisted. "Where is Corporal

Secrets and Whispers: *Hurt*

Soehn going to come up with more than nine hundred sterlings on a non-com's salary? That's a lot of money for just about anyone. In case you didn't know, it's nearly fifteen months' wages at his pay grade. Or are you – a humble priest – going to pay that on his behalf?

"The debenture proves his guilt. No non-com in his right mind would take responsibility for the gambling debt of a soldier in his unit. Private Metzger asked to be transferred into the Expeditionary Force to get away from his corporal. That's a matter of record."

"It's blackmail," Algernon contended, shaking his head. "Private Metzger seduced Corporal Soehn and threatened to expose the affair if Willem didn't sign off on the debt."

"That doesn't matter," Advocate Piers insisted. "In either case, homosexual activity took place. Both men admit it. That's grounds for dishonorable discharge."

"According to the Code, it should be grounds for discharging both men," Algernon corrected, "unless Private Metzger can prove that he was coerced."

Advocate Piers put his hands on his hips. *What was with this stupid priest?* "The only thing that matters is the asymmetry in rank. Corporal Soehn had authority over Private Metzger, ergo, the affair is the fault of the corporal, not the private."

"I'm sure I can get Private Metzger to drop the charge," Algernon replied. "He has to know his career in the military is finished over this, so why would he insist on pressing the charge?"

"That doesn't matter," Advocate Piers countered. "It's a clear-cut case that your future brother-in-law will lose."

"Not if I can get on the base to interview Private Metzger. All you have to do is get me through the gate."

Secrets and Whispers: *Hurt*

"This is a fishing expedition," the advocate complained. "It's a desperate effort to pervert the course of military justice."

"Not true," Algernon responded. "It's a way to ensure that justice is done without anyone getting hurt."

***

Her laughter healed his wounded soul. The same smile that revealed perfect teeth also showcased her steadfast commitment, a faith in the goodness of his character that remained undimmed, despite what he'd seen and done as a soldier. Brenna cast bright light into the darkest recesses of his memory, and Garrick felt he could never adequately repay her for the restoration his broken spirit experienced under her affectionate care.

He gazed at her, rested his forehead against hers, nuzzled her cheek and kissed her lightly. "You are so beautiful!" he whispered, admiringly.

Brenna nuzzled into his embrace, willing her halter top to loosen as she pressed her yielding flesh into her husband's strong body. The Lithian woman admired him with longing in her eyes, her desire bolstered by unspoken reluctance. Conflicted by a yearning for delay in preparing for her role in Bronwyn's wedding and a quiet acceptance of her responsibilities, Brenna's sensuality signaled a shifting balance toward the former.

Sensitive to this, Garrick lifted her chin and responded with a soft, extended kiss on her lips. "You promised that you'd cut my hair," he reminded her.

Breathing a sigh, Brenna's hand wandered from his chest to his abdomen, then dared move where only she had the right to caress. His arousal inspired hope that he might be willing to make time for her, rather than preparing for a wedding she didn't want to attend.

Secrets and Whispers: *Hurt*

Although she fanned the smoldering coals of his desire, and as much as he wanted her in that moment, Garrick took a step away. "We'll never be ready in time if you want sex right now."

"The ceremony is hours away," she replied, her dark eyes pleading for his attention.

Garrick tilted his head to the side. "Bronwyn's counting on your support," he stated. "We have a lot to do before the celebration starts."

"We could be quick," she suggested, her rising inflection revealing hope.

"And that would please you?" he countered, knowing the answer to that question in advance. Once they started down the path of intimacy, they'd tend to become consumed in their mutual delight and lose track of time.

Brenna let her gaze wander from his face to his belt, which she tugged at twice before crossing her arms. She didn't respond, but her facial expression and body language conveyed frustration.

He drew near again, bending to kiss her ear and whisper affection reserved for her alone. "I'll love you all night if you want," he promised. "I'll fill you with delight until your prayers overflow with the gratitude of a satisfied soul, then I'll hold you in my arms until you drift into the slumber of a saint . . ."

Anticipation rose in her brow. Brenna's heart beat a bit faster. He did not *believe* as she did, but on occasion he spoke in support of her faith, revealing acceptance, not just tolerance, and nurtured trust in his devotion. Words like these made her feel warm inside. "I'd like that," she murmured, slipping her arms around his back and rubbing her bosom into his belly.

He smiled. "Me, too."

Brenna pressed her hips into his. "It would be a shame to waste such lovely arousal . . ."

Secrets and Whispers: *Hurt*

Garrick raised his brow. "There's plenty more where that came from, beautiful wife," he replied, kissing her brow and caressing her neck with his left hand. "You stir my passion and I love you with all my heart, but your reluctance to get ready isn't about pleasing me, is it?"

A guilty look flashed across Brenna's face. She shook her head, her eyes averted.

Concern knitted into his brow. Sensitive to her shy demeanor, Garrick's keen intuition honed into the source of her dismay. He knew his wife very well. "You don't want to wear the jingle dress, do you?"

Again, she shook her head. "I didn't know what I was getting into when I agreed to it," Brenna admitted. "I'm supposed to follow Bronwyn around wearing this ridiculous dress with bells under my bosom. With every move I'm making noise, attracting attention I'd prefer to avoid. Given how you Tamarians are so worried about modesty, I'm stunned that it shows so much skin . . ."

Garrick, who thought she looked terrific in the dress, knew that saying so wouldn't help. His smile betrayed the delight that her feminine form inspired in his mind. "You always look lovely, and the dress is modest compared to the clothes you wore when we first met."

"I was a maiden," she reminded him. "But now we're married, and no one but you should be looking at me."

Garrick understood how she felt. Her natural beauty attracted undesired attention, but she'd known this from the day she first set foot in Tamaria. Brenna needed reassurance, not commentary on the uncomfortable reality that men typically didn't bother restraining their lust and many women openly simmered with envy in her company. "The ceremony will be private," he soothed. "Only High Priest Volker, Bronwyn's family, your family and your friends will be there. Everyone knows you're with me."

Secrets and Whispers: *Hurt*

While she appreciated her husband's support, Brenna frowned. "It's the community meal that worries me," she complained. "It's a wonderful idea to feed the hungry, but the Paradise District is home to every lowlife, thug and thief in the city. The leering will be intense."

"I know how that makes you uncomfortable," he replied sympathetically. "Maybe you can bring a sweater along to cover your shoulders while we're serving."

Brenna quietly acknowledged his wisdom, but scowled anyway. "I'd rather not wear the thing at all."

"Bronwyn isn't intending to cause you any grief," he replied. "In our wedding traditions, we honor the woman chosen to wear the jingle dress as the personification of moral purity. Everyone will respect you for that reason alone. It means a lot to me that Bronwyn selected you for that role. It illustrates how deeply she respects you."

His ability to listen gave him the skill to respond with tact and care. Brenna had talked Ileana into sewing a bandeau into the bodice of the jingle dress to cover its daring décolletage, but she still felt nervous about wearing the garment in public. "Okay," she assented. "Just promise that you'll stay near me."

"I promise," he replied. Then, noting the decline in erotic tension between them, he stroked her cheek with his index finger. "Will you cut my hair now?"

She reached for his face and nodded. "You need a shave, too. Then we can go out for lunch. The hairdresser will come after Kira and Bronwyn arrive. That would be a good time for you to fetch your dress uniform from the dry cleaners. The families will arrive in midafternoon, which means I have to be in that silly gown by then."

He brought a chair and towel into the bathroom as she reached for her scissors, a comb, and razor. Brenna's voice took on a sultry tone as he sat. "If you don't want hair all over yourself, you'll have to take off your shirt."

Secrets and Whispers: *Hurt*

"That sounds like an excuse for you to stare at my body," he teased.

Brenna's eyes glistened involuntarily as his broad, muscular chest and fit shoulders emerged from beneath the garment. She never tired of looking at him. "Absolutely," she replied, "and the memory of looking at you will sustain me until we're alone tonight . . ."

Swift and confident with her ultra-sharp Lithian scissors, Brenna completed Garrick's military-style haircut in a few minutes, trimmed the back of his neck with a razor, then moved on to shaving his face. When she'd finished that task, Brenna pulled his head back and dried his cheeks with the towel he'd earlier draped over his broad shoulders.

"You are so handsome!" she beamed, running her hands down his neck, driving her fingertips into the hair growing on his chest, caressing him with her thumbs.

"Not fair!" he protested, tickling and then chasing his shrieking wife out of the bathroom. She pushed him onto their bed, feigning helplessness as he playfully took hold of her arms and rolled her over on the mattress. Ever so slowly, Garrick lowered his head to kiss her, blowing breath on her skin and inspiring a burst of sputtering laughter between them.

Bits of cut hair settled on her face and she scowled. Squirming out of his grasp, Brenna arose and pointed at the bathroom. "The shower is over there!"

Garrick grinned at her, selected his clothes without complaint and swept the floor before entering the shower. He hadn't been beneath the water for very long before the phone rang. Reticent Brenna hated answering, but reluctantly, she picked up the receiver.

"Kira, for Big Brother or Wifey," the operator said.

Secrets and Whispers: *Hurt*

Brenna had never liked Kira's nickname for her, but in the interest of familial harmony, the Lithian woman didn't complain. "This is Wifey," Brenna replied. "I accept."

When the operator connected the call, Kira sounded anxious on the other end of the line. "Do you know where Algernon is?" she asked.

Brenna's brow wrinkled with concern. "He didn't come home last night?"

"No," said Kira. "Bronwyn told me he went with Willi when the military police took him away. We thought he might have stayed late and wound up at your place. I figured he'd call, but he hasn't."

"He wasn't here and we haven't seen him," Brenna admitted. "He's probably still with Bronwyn's brother."

Kira sighed. "Bron's worried. I forgot to fill the water heater, so she went to the hot spring for a bath. It'll be my turn as soon as she comes back and we'll be leaving after that. I don't have time to deal with this today. Can you ask Garrick to find out what's going on?"

"I will," Brenna promised. "And if we find Algernon, we'll have him come here."

After the call, as she put the receiver back on its hook a wicked thought entered Brenna's mind. She remembered Algernon's interest in Thea, recalled his misconduct during her wedding celebration, and worried that he might now be having second thoughts. Maybe he'd wandered off to be alone somewhere . . .

The Lithian woman put her head into her hands and quietly prayed for Allfather's influence to prevail. "Please don't let anyone get hurt," she breathed. "Bronwyn's already suffering needlessly. Let love prevail in this family."

***

Secrets and Whispers: *Hurt*

But it was Bronwyn, not Algernon, who quietly struggled with doubt. Immersed in steamy water to her chin, she closed her eyes and wished she could flee from all her troubles. The fantasy of nuptial bliss – the delight of which no one in her family seemed to think she would ever experience – the excitement of having Algernon bond his life to hers, and the joy she expected to experience faded in the harsh reality of her siblings' disinheritance plot, and the arrest of her brother. She'd never imagined enduring so much anxiety and stress on her wedding day.

Vega had spoken to Bronwyn the previous evening, outlining Sikki's plan and revealing the scathing contempt of Heidelinde, who referred to her sister-in-law as "brown bovine Bronwyn who belongs in a barn." That derisive language brought painful memories of teasing at the Temple to mind, where acolytes and initiates would moo to mock Bronwyn's bountiful and rapidly developing body.

Misty-eyed and sniffling, Vega begged Bronwyn to forgive her for going along with the siblings' conspiracy. "I'm not strong," she admitted. "I'm not brave, either. I can't stand up to my cousin, and Heidelinde despises me for lacking the courage to leave Willem . . ."

It all made sense now. *Mutti* had always been careful to investigate the people she entrusted to make the family's wealth grow, and since she'd been successful as an investor with that strategy, she naturally wanted to find out everything she could about Algernon and his family. But she hadn't relied on her usual methods, which involved meeting with the people involved, asking questions, and checking public financial records. Bronwyn, who'd known nothing about Irena's previous relationship with Sister Alba, felt betrayed to learn that her mother accepted the testimony of someone outside the family over that of her own daughter.

Secrets and Whispers: *Hurt*

Sikki, who'd been trying to get her hands on *Mutti's* money for years, had carefully crafted the disinheritance plot, assigning roles to each of her co-conspirators. Confident in Bronwyn's resolve to marry, she and Darren funneled news articles to Irena that confirmed her a priori view that Algernon was an unsuitable partner.

"The day after you announced your engagement, Sikki called me and Heidelinde over for dinner," Vega explained. "She had this idea to get the money by driving you away from the family. After she learned what happened with Brenna and Garrick, Sikki figured that if you felt bad about yourself, you'd be impulsive and run off to Kameron. She didn't admit that part to your brothers. She just encouraged them to treat you like a small child having a tantrum for not getting your way, all the while doing everything she could to undermine your relationship with your mother."

"Why would you agree to such a wicked plan?" Bronwyn asked, angrily. "I don't care about the money, but my relationship with *Mutti* is sacred!"

"Sikki promised she'd split the inheritance three ways," Vega replied. "I have no way of earning money to support myself. You know that Willem drinks too much. He's become more violent over the past year, and I thought that if I had a little money, I could leave him."

Bronwyn felt irritated hearing Vega blame her brother for their dysfunctional marriage. However, when Vega explained that she was still a virgin, after being married for more than ten years, sympathy stirred in Bronwyn's heart. The irony of being physically rejected, despite being pretty, struck her as a terrible burden to bear. Bronwyn, who'd wistfully watched Kira manipulate men with her charm, and who'd quietly envied beautiful Brenna, understood that Vega must have been deeply hurt by Willem's repudiation.

Secrets and Whispers: *Hurt*

"I know all about my brother," Bronwyn said. "His sexuality has been an unspoken secret in our family for as long as I can remember. My father was convinced that once he married someone as pretty as you, he'd . . . well, you know . . . get over his attraction to men."

Vega shook her head. "That goes against his nature. Even before we married, I had a feeling his heart wasn't in it. He didn't make me feel wanted. When I hear you talking about Algernon, I envy you. I'm a fading flower. No one will ever love me like he loves you, no one will ever want me like he wants you, and no one will ever treat me with the kindness and respect I've seen him give you.

"It's so unfair! Part of me wanted to hurt you, and that was wrong. When Sikki convinced us that you'd run off to Kameron and live in a hermitage with Algernon, I figured you'd be poor, but at least you'd be happy."

"You can see that this house is far from a hovel," Bronwyn replied defensively.

"Of course," Vega replied. "But none of us had ever heard anything good about Algernon. Our family is conservative. We support the Temple, but his reputation and choice of ministry raised everyone's eyebrows. Darren thought you were desperate for the first guy who showed any interest. When we heard that Kira and Algernon had been kicked out of the Sacred Community, we thought their ministry might be a ruse for running a whorehouse. Harold even made bets with his buddies about that.

"It's wrong, and I'm sorry for not defending you," Vega concluded. "If I'd done the right thing I would have spared you a lot of pain."

In the end they'd embraced. Bronwyn had promised to forgive, but the walls of resentment in her soul loomed high and impregnable. She'd fallen into a restless sleep, dreaming about Algernon, longing for him, craving him and feeling disappointed to wake up alone.

Secrets and Whispers: *Hurt*

He hadn't come home. He hadn't called, either.

Why had all of this happened? *Gottslena* writings taught that bad people attracted negative energy, that negative actions created negative outcomes. Willem's behavior served as a classic example of that dynamic, but Bronwyn loved her brother and his arrest wounded her soul. It hurt because she cared about him.

And though she wanted to hate Darren and Harold for their role in the disinheritance plot, the bonds of sibling attachment between them remained too strong. She felt angry about their actions, but didn't want to see them punished for their wrongdoing.

Sneaky Sikki and Heidelinde the Horrible were a different matter. Neither of those women had ever bothered being nice, and when Bronwyn heard Vega confirm that their constant critiquing of her weight and appearance had been rooted in disbelief that she'd ever find someone to marry, anger stirred in her soul. Despite her prayers for the willingness to forgive, the grace to offer magnanimity eluded her.

Bronwyn immersed herself in the warm water until her toes touched the rocky bottom of the hot spring. She washed her hair and stepped ashore, toweling off her body before getting dressed. She left the spring toying with the notion of abandoning her inheritance and running away, the very thing her siblings had expected her to do.

But she didn't want to give them that pleasure.

***

Disoriented and overcome with panic, Karin struggled against the net that enveloped her. A disgusting smell forced a retching reflex that she couldn't suppress, spewing the remnants of breakfast out of her mouth.

Secrets and Whispers: *Hurt*

Dust and leaves swirled and settled. A bouncing, twirling sensation amplified her terror. Rising and falling, twisting, then hitting something hard, Karin heard the swishing sound of dirt racing to the bottom of her prison, the creak of straining wood and the stretching of rope. Gravity finally settled the net that bound her into equilibrium in the center of a 10 foot pit.

She tried crying out for help, but bile etched her throat and choked her voice. Karin fell into sobs of helplessness for a long time. As her tears tapered off, she began to accept her circumstances and gradually relaxed.

Above her, blue sky rose over the tree canopy. A stout branch held her aloft, high enough that if it broke, the ensuing fall would most certainly cause serious injury. Below, sharpened spikes rose from the pit's floor, threatening death if she cut herself free of the net.

Who would do something like this to her? It had to be those horrible Ravenwood people. They were hiding something – they had to be – and they wanted her out of the way. No other explanation made sense. But they didn't know about the cabin. They didn't know about her rifle. She could, and would, defend herself. And once she got out of this mess, Karin swore that she'd extract revenge. She'd double their trouble, and it would hurt!

***

Algernon wearily stumbled through the front door, slipping out of his shoes in the airlock vestibule before entering. When Vega raced into the living area with a worried, rapid-fire interrogation concerning Willem's well-being, he replied a little impatiently, "Don't worry. I'm working on it."

Secrets and Whispers: *Hurt*

He'd not intended to snap at her. Vega, whose sense of self-worth had taken a beating over the past few days, couldn't contend with him and retreated. Ileana, peering out of her room, said something along the lines of, "That was rude!" in Lithian, but he didn't understand.

The banter stirred Bronwyn, who'd been trimming her eyebrows. She arose and scurried to their bedroom door where she met her soon-to-be husband with a strong, lingering embrace and a slow kiss brimming with promise of a lifetime's affection. His hands slid down to her backside, which he firmly pulled into his hips, and she made no move to stop him. "I was worried about you," she said quietly.

He looked exhausted. Dark circles had formed beneath his bloodshot eyes. His hair felt greasy, he needed a shave, and his breath smelled foul. "The guards wouldn't let me call," he replied. "By the time I got out of there, I figured it was best to just come home."

"Have you eaten anything?" she asked, holding her breath. "I can get you some food . . ."

Algernon declined. "There's something I need you to do, first." He gently pushed her back into the room, shut the door and spoke in a lowered voice. "This is just between you and me, okay?"

Uncertain of his intentions, Bronwyn merely nodded.

Earlier that morning, Vega and Ileana had moved Bronwyn's single bed out of the room and into the loft, in anticipation of the marriage bed that Kira had bought and scheduled for delivery the following day. With only the chair from her vanity available for sitting, Bronwyn didn't want to rest while her weary fiancé stood. "Okay," she agreed. "What's this about?"

"I wanted to surprise you, but our situation has changed. Remember when you told me that your mother promised to disinherit you if we married?"

Secrets and Whispers: *Hurt*

Bronwyn nodded. She'd first read that threat in a letter from her mother a few months earlier. Later, when she returned to Marvic after visiting her family, Bronwyn planned to get pregnant in order to subvert her mother's intent. However, Algernon's restraint in their private conduct prevented that from happening.

"I promised that you'd never have to worry about money," he continued. "You probably figured I was talking about Kira, but I wanted to make sure you didn't have to depend on my sister's good will."

Puzzled, Bronwyn hedged. "What's this about?"

Algernon turned toward their closet, moved a box of workout gear to the side and pulled up a floorboard. He arose with a pouch in hand, which he offered to her.

The leather sack felt heavy and smelled mildly unpleasant. "Is this a joke?" she asked.

"Open it," he encouraged. "Count the coins inside."

Bronwyn dumped out its contents on her dresser. Knowing of Algernon's vow of poverty, her eyes widened as 16 silver sterlings rolled out. "That's a lot of money!" she exclaimed. "Where did you get this?"

"My brother and Brenna took a pair of these from giant chieftains they killed on their journey to Marvic, just after the war with the Azgar." Algernon explained. "Knowing that I'd need money for the journey to find Kira, Garrick gave his to me just before I left for Kameron.

"Now, put the money back, then take a couple of the coins out." When her brow wrinkled in perplexity, he said, "Just trust me."

After she withdrew two coins, he asked her to set them aside, then dump out the contents again. To her amazement, Bronwyn counted 16 sterlings in addition to the two she'd already taken out. She dropped the bag to the floor. "What kind of wickedness is this?"

Secrets and Whispers: *Hurt*

Algernon shook his head. "It's from a repository of plunder hoarded by giant kings for over a thousand years," he replied. "The money comes from wealth stolen from our people and neighboring nations. No matter how much you take out of the bag – as long as you don't empty it completely – it always contains the same amount of money that you started with. It came in handy when I had to buy Kira back from the slave broker."

"This is not right," Bronwyn stated, fearfully. "This is an evil thing!"

"Not so. There's no evil in it," Algernon corrected. "Lady Alexina explained how it works. The device itself has no will of its own. All it does is shift matter from one dimension to the next in whatever currency is in use, wherever the device happens to be located.

"Despite their great strength, the giant kings of old couldn't carry all their wealth with them. Gold and silver are heavy and can be stolen. To protect their horde they forced a mage to cast an enchantment that moved their riches into another dimension for storage.

"This bag has a tiny portal to that place. It carries enough for a king's daily use and won't run out until all the plunder is gone. But I've taken a vow of poverty, so it's not right for me to have this thing. That's why I'm giving it to you. As long as you have the pouch, you'll never be in want. This is why I said you don't need your parents' inheritance."

Wide-eyed, bewildered, and a little afraid, Bronwyn shook her head. "I don't want that thing! Give it to Kira."

"My sister doesn't need it," Algernon replied. "She inherited seed capital from the sale of our parents' property rights and, like your mother, has learned how markets work. She's invested her funds and now has more than enough to be financially independent.

Secrets and Whispers: *Hurt*

"Once Lady Alexina's superconducting motors and generators come into production, Kira's investment royalties will make her very rich."

"But I'm a modest woman," Bronwyn insisted. "I have everything I want and don't need more. What about Brenna? She could do more good with this than I can."

"She already has one," Algernon replied. "That's why she spends money like she does. That's why she has an expensive wardrobe, and why Garrick always looks like a prince on a lieutenant's salary."

"So Garrick knows what this thing does?"

Algernon nodded. "My brother has always looked after us. But this isn't about Garrick. This is about you. I want you to be confident about our future together."

Uncertain of how to respond, Bronwyn picked up the pouch and put the two extra coins back in. When she dumped it out, she counted only 16 sterlings again. "Why didn't you tell me about this earlier?" she asked.

Algernon's eyes reflected an endearing vulnerability that Bronwyn adored in him. "I wanted to surprise you," he admitted with a downcast gaze. "I also needed to know that you were willing to marry me for love, not money."

Disbelief flashed onto Bronwyn's face. "How could you ever think such a thing?" she asked, drawing near, pressing her body against his and stroking his face in a maternal manner. "Don't you know that I love you? Don't you know that I'd do anything to make you happy?"

"Of course I do," he replied. "And I love you too. But your brother's in trouble, and you have an important role to play in helping him out."

Bronwyn remembered Thea telling her that she had to help save Willem without mentioning how it would happen. But how could the Lithian maiden dream about something like this in advance? Bronwyn's eyes widened as a shudder raced down her spine. "What do you mean?"

Secrets and Whispers: *Hurt*

"When you told me about your mother's threat, I set up a bank account in your name," Algernon explained, pursing his lips as if expecting her disapproval. "Every time I've gone to town, I've taken fifteen sterlings and deposited them on your behalf. Right now, you have twelve hundred sterlings in savings."

Bronwyn stepped away. "What?" she exclaimed in shock. "Why? I don't want your money!"

"I understand," Algernon replied. "But after your mother's threat, I wanted to protect you. Because of my vow of poverty, I can't have a bank account. I've been making deposits, but you're the only person who can arrange a withdrawal, and you need to act now."

After a moment of reflection Bronwyn sighed and shook her head. "I've never had that kind of money in my entire life. What am I supposed to do?"

Algernon leaned against her dresser, wishing he could sleep. "I want you to help your brother. I spent all night talking to him, reviewing his case, and reading through military law books. Early this morning I found a way to keep him out of prison."

Hope stirred in Bronwyn's heart. "How?" she asked.

"The charges against him stem from the testimony of a soldier who claims that Willem imposed a homosexual relationship on him," Algernon explained. "There's no evidence to support the accusation except for a Note of Debenture that Willem signed."

Bronwyn scowled. She'd believed her brother was clever enough to successfully hide the truth when it really mattered. "So, how much debt are we talking about?"

"Nine hundred and thirty-seven sterlings," Algernon replied, unfazed by the large sum.

"That's ridiculous!" Bronwyn exclaimed. "Why would he do a stupid thing like that?"

Secrets and Whispers: *Hurt*

"The man who made the accusation was a private in Willem's platoon. When he learned of your brother's orientation, he seduced Willem and then blackmailed him into signing the debenture."

Bronwyn crossed her arms, joining Algernon in leaning against the dresser. "How did this guy wind up owing that much money?"

"Willem says it's gambling debt. Micha, the man with whom your brother had the affair, feared for his life because the gambling syndicate took out a contract with the Black Blade Assassin's Guild to get their money back.

"He got Willem to sign under threat of exposing the affair, then quietly asked for a transfer out of Willem's unit into the Expeditionary Force. When his commander demanded to know why, Micha told her about the affair with Willem."

"What a mess!" Bronwyn exclaimed. "But you said you figured out how to help. What are you going to do?"

"First off, the only evidence supporting the allegation of the affair is the debenture. Your brother was quite clever about keeping everything covered up.

"I talked Advocate Piers into interviewing Micha at Fort Aeolus, under the condition that he give me a few minutes alone with the man. I told Micha that I have contacts in the Black Blade Guild, and that if he dropped the charge, I could arrange to pay the debt and cancel the contract on his life."

"He believed you?"

"No," Algernon replied, shaking his head. "He thinks it's too good to be true. But he knows nothing about me. Only a handful of people know that I was the only one who visited *The Shadow* before his execution. The Black Blade respects my integrity, but he worries that the assassins will kill him if he sets foot beyond the base."

Secrets and Whispers: *Hurt*

"That's a reasonable concern," Bronwyn concluded. "Nine hundred sterlings is a lot of money to owe, and everyone in the country – aside from you – is terrified of the Black Blade."

"I'm no less afraid of them," Algernon asserted. "They're ruthless, but they're also keen on preserving honor. They've promised me that once the debt is paid and their fee is covered, they won't follow through on the killing. They have no vendetta against the man."

Bronwyn shuddered. "How do you know this?"

"I met with *Dark Whisper*, their current leader, just before I came home. He told me that the Guild is grateful that I looked after *The Shadow* while he was in prison. That doesn't matter to me, but it's a big deal to them, and they want to return the favor."

To Bronwyn, the idea that Algernon was even talking to Black Blade assassins inspired unspeakable fear. She didn't want to lose him. Yet his ability to make peace with his enemies evidenced a personal integrity beyond anyone else she knew, aside from Brenna. "What if this Micha fellow doesn't drop the charges? What if he decides to ruin Willem's life out of spite?"

Algernon had thought of that. "I warned him that if he didn't drop the charge after I'd proven the debt was paid, I'd make sure the contract stayed active."

Bronwyn's eyes widened. "You threatened him?"

Algernon shrugged. "It's all I could think to do. He's terrified of setting foot outside the base. It was the only solution I could imagine."

"What about the charges against Willem?"

"Once they're dropped, a senior officer – likely his battalion commander – will make a ruling. Advocate Piers thinks the men will receive dishonorable discharges."

"Poor Willem!"

Secrets and Whispers: *Hurt*

"That's far better than a prison sentence," Algernon soothed. "Advocate Piers told me the military doesn't like the publicity from a case like this. They'll want to settle the matter quietly. It's not ideal, but it's the best I can do. This way, Willem has a fighting chance to start his life over again."

Bronwyn turned toward Algernon, took hold of his hands and kissed him, despite his bad breath. "Thank you," she whispered. "After everything my family has done to run you down, it's noble of you to help us like this."

"Your family is my family," he replied. "Willem is going to need counseling for his drinking problem and relational help if he's ever going to make things right with his wife. He has a long road ahead of him."

"Vega won't take him back," Bronwyn stated. "Willem's hurt her and begged forgiveness too many times. She's had enough. She wants to leave him."

***

Just before Garrick and Brenna left to eat lunch at their favorite bistro, the doorbell rang. Annoyed, Garrick scurried downstairs and found himself confronted by Agents Froese and Wenzel of the Crown Intelligence Directorate. The men, both fit and handsome, displayed their badges and insisted on entering.

"This is really not a good time," Garrick stated.

"National security is more important than your schedule," said Agent Froese.

Garrick shook his head, standing in the doorway to prevent the men from coming inside. "I have nothing more to tell you."

"That's for us to judge," Agent Wenzel retorted.

Secrets and Whispers: *Hurt*

Aware of his citizen rights, Garrick's demeanor hardened. "Then ask your questions here and now. You're not coming inside."

Wenzel shot Froese a glance, then smirked. "You've been in contact with a Kamerese agent, a Jared Hohner."

Garrick rolled his eyes. "Jared is Lithian, not Kamerese, and he's not an agent either."

"We know he's associated with the inner circle of King Alejo," said Froese. "He's an advisor to the king."

Steadily losing his patience, Garrick crossed his arms. "The two men are similar in age, they share common interests and they get along well. Where I come from, we call that friendship."

Neither agent found that dismissal relevant. "You were seen entering and departing the Gold Leaf Hotel yesterday," Wenzel stated. "The staff report that you used the service elevator to access the secure floor where Mr. Hohner is staying. We understand that during the time in question, you contacted Mr. Hoehner at the hotel."

"I spoke to him at the request of your agency," Garrick replied. "And I phoned your office yesterday afternoon to report the scope of that conversation."

Froese wasn't impressed. He stepped forward and lowered his voice. "Subsequent to your visit, Mr. Hohner made a phone call to a number in Kameron . . ."

Moments passed. Garrick expected some kind of definitive statement about the call, but the agent remained silent, as if Garrick should draw some kind of conclusion with national security implications. "His parents live there," Garrick said at length. "Has it occurred to you that maybe he wanted to talk to them?"

"We don't appreciate your tone, lieutenant," Wenzel continued. "We're just conducting inquiries."

"I don't appreciate you wasting my time," Garrick retorted. "I've cooperated by reporting the details of my

Secrets and Whispers: *Hurt*

conversation to your office yesterday. There's no need for this interrogation right now. Are we done?"

"No," Froese insisted. "One more question. Did Mr. Hoehner suggest or imply knowledge of your contact with the Kurian spy known as Rathdurm?"

Garrick shook his head. "He outlined what he knew about *Los Patrones del Estado*, explained that they're very dangerous people, and warned me to stay out of this."

Wenzel gave Froese a knowing glance before returning his attention to Garrick. "If you remember anything else from your conversation that may aid in our investigation, we expect you to contact us."

"I've told you what I know," Garrick insisted.

"It's nothing personal, lieutenant," Froese replied. "We're just trying to keep people from getting hurt."

***

The fact that Bronwyn hadn't wanted an elaborate wedding suited Kira. She'd changed the venue to a sheltered place called *The Old Mill*, which stood upstream of the palace wall. Kira had been praying that she could manage the ceremony, procession, community dinner and street dance without incident. She wanted her best friend to have a happy day. Bronwyn deserved it.

On her way back from bathing, Kira could have sworn she heard a woman's voice crying for help. She paused, her heart racing. Confident that the only women on the mesa were at the homestead, she feared that a glacier gull might be nearby. These huge, predatory birds could kill a person with a single kick and made an eerily similar cry when hunting. Glacier gulls typically did not stray far from Fallen Moon Lake and were unlikely to think of her as food, but Kira quickened her pace anyway.

Secrets and Whispers: *Hurt*

With the heat of the day building, the Tamarian woman descended from the narrow canyon that led from the hot spring, passing near the homestead's wind turbine and noting – with some dismay – that her garden needed attention. Her plants would have to wait, however, as more important tasks clamored for her attention.

Kira entered through the back door, where the aroma of stir-fried vegetables and fish brought a scowl to her face. She was about to chastize Bronwyn for wasting time when she noticed Algernon at the table.

"I was worried about you," Kira told him, hobbling forward to kiss her brother's cheek in gratitude for his safety. When his abrasive stubble pressed against her lips, Kira wrinkled her nose. "You need a bath and a shave."

"You didn't fill the water heater," he replied. "I'll have to use the hot spring when I'm done eating."

"There's no time for that," Kira announced. "We have a hair appointment and have to get dressed. Take your things along so you can shower and shave at Brenna's place. We need to go."

Ileana dressed in a pretty gown she'd made for the occasion. Vega, who'd been reluctant to attend after admitting her role in the disinheritance plot, agreed at Bronwyn's insistence. She and Ileana would head to the Gold Leaf Hotel and stay with Bronwyn's family.

Algernon took his ceremonial dress robe, another gift from Lady Alexina, along with an overnight bag he'd share with his new bride for their brief stay in the honeymoon suite at the Gold Leaf Hotel. Both Bronwyn and Kira remained in their street clothes, as Kira had taken their dresses to Brenna's home the day before.

After Kira called a cab, Algernon and the four women went down to the farm service road and waited to be picked up for the ride into Marvic. Overcome with exhaustion, Algernon slept against Bronwyn's shoulder for

Secrets and Whispers: *Hurt*

the entire ride into town, in the street car as they headed to the bank, and again on their way to the palace gate. A headache settled in as the young couple passed through the tightened security. By the time they arrived at the music manse, his pain had blossomed substantially.

Oddly, Kira answered the door. She'd not yet dressed, she'd wet her hair again, and looked unhappy. "Let's get you into the shower," she recommended, glancing at her brother. "The hot water will do you good."

Brenna remained in a halter top and shorts, which would have annoyed Bronwyn, had she not been so concerned about Algernon. But Brenna's gentle face showed concern as she evaluated her brother-in-law's lack of sleep and discomfort. "Let me get you some medicinal tea," she said. "You'll need a lift to get through the day."

With Algernon in the shower and Brenna busy with her analgesic-stimulant tea concoction, Kira spoke to Bronwyn in a low voice. "Crown Intelligence Officers took Cassie's boyfriend, Jared, in for questioning this morning. They think he's a spy."

Bronwyn sighed. "What next? Why now?"

Kira shook her head. "Garrick and Captain Hougen are trying to sort it out. Brenna doesn't want to put on her dress until he's back."

Worriedly, Bronwyn asked, "Did he say when that would be?"

"He was already gone when I arrived," Kira told her. "The hair dressers will be here any minute."

"Why is everything going wrong?" Bronwyn exclaimed. "What have I done to deserve this?"

Brenna watched Kira soothe Bronwyn's anxiety with sympathy rising in her heart. She turned back to her tea and whispered a revision of her earlier prayer.

***

Secrets and Whispers: *Hurt*

Sikki had packed her things and vanished. Two hours after lunch, Darren sat in the lobby with his father, making excuses for his wife. Arvid, however, didn't let his eldest son persist with justifying her absence. "What you have done is reprehensible!" Arvid scolded in one of his very rare displays of anger. "Restoring your relationship with Bronwyn should be your highest priority right now, not rationalizing a conspiracy to steal her inheritance!"

"Yes sir," Darren acknowledged. He'd been caught up in the belief that Sikki's plan would work – that their financial stress would finally end – but now that the plot had been exposed, he could think of no face-saving way to avoid his father's wrath, aside from contrition. "You're right. I should never have agreed to it."

After that brief exchange, Arvid fell into silence. The men waited in the hotel's lobby for Irena, Marla and Vega to join them. Arvid had blamed Vega for her childless marriage, yet she was the only one of his daughters-in-law who'd stayed for Bronwyn's wedding. That fact represented a glimmer of good news in an otherwise dark situation.

Irena, whose heart had been pierced by her children's unspeakable behavior, wept for a long time in her sister's arms before she felt sufficiently composed to put on makeup and get into her gown.

Vega seemed unusually timid. She struggled to make eye contact and kept fidgeting with her hands when she joined the sisters, just before Marla had finished her hair. While Vega's presence stirred tension in the room, Irena touched the younger woman's upper arm and said, "Thank you for staying. It means a lot to me, and it will mean a lot to Bronwyn, too."

Unsure that her mother-in-law was being forthright, Vega put on a brave face and nodded. "Let's go. They're waiting for us."

Secrets and Whispers: *Hurt*

Since the hotel manager refused to allow Lithians into the lobby, Irena led her small entourage around the back of the hotel and stood under an overhang with Brenna's family and friends – along with Ileana – waiting for their conveyances to arrive.

The two families mingled well. Irena struck up a brief conversation with Lady Alexina until their dialogue was interrupted by the arrival of five parade carriages, each drawn by a team of magnificent, white draft horses outfitted in fine show harness. A detachment of armed, mounted Defenders in polished dress uniform served as an escort for the entourage.

Irena openly wondered how a hick from the hills like Kira had arranged all of this. Marla, seated to her left in the lead carriage, responded to that sentiment by speaking quietly into her sister's ear. "Brenna's on good terms with the queen," she said. "Also, being a Heroine of the Republic entitles her to a military escort at public functions. She told me on our run this morning that she's nervous about wearing the jingle dress at the service dinner, so this retinue is probably her doing."

That made sense. Irena also felt reassured by the presence of trained soldiers, as she'd been told they'd be venturing into Marvic's most dangerous district for the post-ceremony events. Tamarian brides usually served the service meal in their own neighborhoods, but Bronwyn wanted to feed the hungry where she and Kira did their work, rather than the rural environment where she lived.

A sergeant assigned people to each carriage in harmony with a list that Kira provided. Once everyone found their seats, the procession turned onto University Way and headed toward the palace. This brief journey felt surreal in Irena's mind. Despite the wealthy trappings and pomp of this procession, she worried that Bronwyn would forever struggle with want for the rest of her days.

Secrets and Whispers: *Hurt*

None of the citizens who pressed against windows, or poured onto the street to watch the carriages and soldiers in their stately march had any idea of the pain that preceded this moment. Their wonder at witnessing the procession would, at best, feature in dinner discussions forgotten not long afterward.

Irena, swept along by the inertia of careful planning and lavish spending, held her husband's hand, astonished at her passive role in the spectacle.

She knew nothing of Jared's detention and Cassie's sorrow. She didn't know if her son, Willem, would ever feel the wind of freedom against his face again. She had no faith that her children would reconcile with one another, a belief that inspired deep distress in her soul.

Yet as the carriages turned onto Victory Street and headed down the broad avenue to Equality Park, Irena determined to set her own hurt aside and focus on Bronwyn's happiness.

***

Even after showering, shaving and drinking Brenna's tea, Algernon couldn't stay awake. He slept through the hairdressing appointments and heard nothing while the women put on their gowns.

Finally, Brenna awakened Algernon. "Your hair's a mess," she warned. "Would you like me to fix it?"

He tolerated Brenna's fussing, mildly amused by the tinkling of bells that accompanied her every move. He'd trained himself to focus on her face – as Brenna had a distracting figure – noting the conspicuous absence of her smile and the gentle manner that went along with it. She wore neither makeup nor jewelry, as she was naturally beautiful and didn't like attention, anyway. Her hair-repair task ended abruptly as the front door opened.

Secrets and Whispers: *Hurt*

Garrick called from below and ran upstairs at the sound of his woman's voice. She embraced her husband with longing as he relayed news of Jared's detention. "Mariel got them to release him," he told her. "Jared held his own under questioning, and they couldn't find reason to charge him. Mariel pressured the team into letting him go, rather than holding him until tomorrow."

Brenna sighed with relief. "Cassie will be happy."

Garrick kissed her. "He's gone back to the Gold Leaf to clean up and change into wedding clothes. I arranged for a cab to pick him up and take him to the venue."

Algernon wished he'd had similar success in getting Willem released. It would have pleased Irena and Arvid to have their son walk free, but clearing him of the charges would take time. Since the allegations against him were serious, Willem's commanding officer had to review the case, and could still recommend courts martial proceedings if warranted by the evidence. However, that outcome seemed unlikely. Algernon had done his best to advocate for Willem, though he doubted anyone in the family – other than Bronwyn – would express gratitude for his effort.

As soon as Garrick changed into his dress uniform, a phone call from the hotel notified him that the wedding party was on its way. He, his siblings, his bride and Bronwyn, left the music manse for the palace gate, where they would meet the rest of the wedding party.

In harmony with custom, Bronwyn and Algernon led the procession. Garrick pushed his sister in a wheelchair he'd borrowed from the Defenders at the security checkpoint, while Brenna walked beside them with her hand on top of his, her gown jingling with every step.

"You seem quiet," Algernon said to Bronwyn as they crossed into the shade of the redwood grove growing on the far bank of the Honeywater. "Are you sad?"

Secrets and Whispers: *Hurt*

Bronwyn shrugged. "I'd always imagined this would be the happiest day of my life. I had this fantasy about how things would be, but the reality is disheartening."

Her tone and body language concerned him. "Have you changed your mind about me?"

"No!" she insisted. "Don't think like that. Don't ever think like that! I love you. I want you, and maybe my longing is the reason we're having all this trouble."

Recognizing the root of Bronwyn's worry in a manner of interpreting *Gottslena* – where people were believed to attract retribution for evil and honor for goodness – he responded from a perspective he'd first heard voiced by Thea Velez. "Your desire is pure. Your willingness to share yourself with me moves my heart and quiets my soul. Everything else is outside of that desire, and has neither influence, nor meaning on the love you lavish on me."

Bronwyn blinked back tears. His support and tireless confidence inspired hope. She believed that with him at her side they could overcome any adversity. His willingness to accommodate her views, his ability to listen and his oft' stated – frequently poetic – affirmation of her intelligence and character made her feel highly valued. This is what her family would never understand. They would never know the goodness she experienced from him.

For Algernon, the unspoken terror that Bronwyn might back out at the last minute, that his dream of living with and loving her might somehow end before it began, inspired anxiety. His heart raced in the knowledge that even now – should Bronwyn reconsider her commitment to him – he remained very vulnerable to getting hurt.

***

Secrets and Whispers: *Hurt*

Tamarian weddings involved a simple set of traditions and very little ceremony. Elements common to all marriage celebrations included the color of the bride's dress – red, for passion, or purple for fidelity – a procession of the wedding party, a selection of herbs carried by a maid or maiden, a pious woman wearing a jingle dress, a private exchange of vows between the couple, the maternal tying of hands, a blessing by a priest, and a communal meal.

As the wedding party walked across Equality Park to the waiting carriages, Bronwyn's appearance in her burgundy gown, the simple golden tiara glittering on her forehead in the afternoon daylight, and the sound of Brenna's jingle dress lightened the mood among family and friends waiting in the carriages.

Cassie wept joyfully when she heard that Jared had been released. Both Marla and Irena shed tears at the sight of Bronwyn walking arm-in-arm with handsome Algernon. Vega forced a smile, while secret envy of her sister-in-law filled her soul. Tembe, who'd been waiting all day long for his chance to spend time with Kira, beamed a beautiful, welcoming smile as she approached.

The carriages and military escort traveled a short distance to the north, stopping at the edge of Equality Park where a narrow, flagstone-paved passage leading between the trees and rocks opened into a tree-shaded courtyard. Here stood the roofless remains of a long derelict flour mill.

High Priest Volker, who'd retired shortly after Algernon left the Temple, welcomed the wedding party and beckoned first for Bronwyn, and then Algernon. "Are you willing to proceed?" he asked each of them privately. With their mutual assent given, he gestured to an open portal in the old stone building. The couple went inside to pray and utter vows each had written for the other.

Secrets and Whispers: *Hurt*

Algernon trembled. He'd struggled with rejection for many years, desperately hoping that someone would finally recognize his worth, his capacity for love. When it came his turn to speak, he trembled nervously.

Bronwyn held his head against hers and rocked him gently while he whispered his devotion to her. His eloquence, his endearing vulnerability and the beautiful words he spoke filled Bronwyn's heart with confidence in his sincerity.

"Tonight, I want you to love me," she said to him. "I won't let you stop until I know all of your passion, all of your strength, all of your desire. What you need is mine to give, and I will lavish my gifts on you forever . . ."

They remained in a firm embrace for awhile, then prayed for each other. As their guests enjoyed cold apple and pear juice in the courtyard, Bronwyn and Algernon walked back to the portal.

High Priest Volker smiled. He raised his hand and the guests grew quiet "Have you spoken your vows to one another?" he asked.

In unison the couple responded, "Yes, we have."

"Let the family matrons come forward," the high priest commanded with a beckoning gesture.

Irena took Kira by the arm so she wouldn't need her cane. They accepted a silky cord from the high priest, and at his invitation, the two women tied Bronwyn's right arm to Algernon's left arm – a symbol of unity they would wear until they were alone in the honeymoon suite of the hotel.

With their task completed, the women made way for Brenna. She stood on the portal and offered a prayer for the couple in Lithian that neither of them understood. Later, she'd give them a framed parchment, carefully translated and written in gold calligraphy, of her words. It became a prized possession they displayed over the headboard of their bed.

Secrets and Whispers: *Hurt*

After this, the old man stood with Brenna behind the young couple and placed his hands on their shoulders. He offered a blessing in the name of the Great God on their union, for their commitment and for their future family.

Garrick raised a toast to his new sister-in-law, everyone drank to their happiness, and the formalities ended with much applause, cheering and embracing.

***

By twilight, Karin's body felt stiff and numb. Hunger gnawed at her belly, she'd wet herself and felt ravenously thirsty. Despite her best effort, she'd not been able to wriggle free from the trap. As despair deepened in the fading light, a shadow fell across her face.

That foul smell intensified. Birds cried in warning. The ground trembled. Suddenly, some powerful force lifted the net, swung her around and dumped her on the forest floor. Karin struggled to escape, but a massive and powerful hand smacked her down.

It hurt. Her head felt like she'd been hit by a train. Dizzy and reeling from the blow, Karin curled into a fetal position and cowered beneath the net. She felt that huge, strong hand reach inside and yank her out.

With her will broken, unable to resist, Karin whimpered in terror. When she dared glance up at her massive captor, the Tamarian woman nearly fainted.

The giantess appraised her prisoner in disgust, snorting mucous from her nose. "You are not the fork-tongue!" she spat. "You are not the brown girl, either."

"I'm a wildlife officer!" Karin squeaked, hoping that the official title might intimidate a humanoid four times her size and weight.

Secrets and Whispers: *Hurt*

"You are my slave," the giantess announced. She pressed Karin's face into the ground, cut off her clothes with a large, obsidian knife, then bound the Tamarian woman's hands with a cord. "Now you will know the pain of your ancestors," she promised. "If you try to escape I will track you down. I will hurt you if you disobey."

***

Kira felt relieved to see that the pavilions she'd rented for the community meal hadn't been damaged, vandalized or stolen. She should have known better, as her ministry was well-regarded in this neighborhood and everyone who lived here really liked Bronwyn. Local citizens cheered as the big horses pulled the well-dressed wedding party into a public plaza in the heart of the Paradise District.

Tembe helped her down from the carriage for the second time – a courtesy she'd have scorned had she been able to walk normally – and lingered at her side while she greeted her many clients, though he never touched her with affection. Bronwyn and Algernon joined her as the wedding party climbed down from the carriages and prepared to start serving.

The Defenders dismounted, tied their horses to a nearby rail and took up their positions. Their presence had a calming effect on the gathered crowd and ensured that the celebrating remained appropriately restrained.

Brenna's family and friends sat at an honored table near the front and were the first to enjoy the meal. Since few Tamarians would accept food offered to them by Lithians, Lord Lynden, Lady Alexina, their children and servants would serve the wedding party after the street people had gone through line.

Secrets and Whispers: *Hurt*

Irena and Arvid offered slices of cake and cookies, while Kira, Tembe and Vega served hot drinks. Brenna, who'd put on a blue sweater for the sake of modesty, joined her husband in passing ceramic bowls to the newlywed couple.

Bronwyn and Algernon dished out a poultry, sticky rice and vegetable medley to a lengthy gathering of vagrants, pensioners, thieves, prostitutes, addicts, poor families, seamstresses and day laborers, who – like most Tamarians – ate using their fingers rather than cutlery. It took well over an hour to feed the assembled crowd. Bronwyn and Algernon's commitment to this community earned sincere gratitude from these often neglected and scorned people for the hot food and blessings to the serving family their generosity.

A handsome man with a black dagger tattooed on his right wrist passed through the line and winked at Bronwyn. She shuddered, but Algernon smiled and thanked the man for joining the celebration.

"I wouldn't miss it," he said.

All the street lamps came on at dusk. As the caterers moved the empty bowls and tables away, a big band arrived for the celebratory dance. The Defenders formed a wide circle. Their sergeant announced, "Make way for Brenna Velez, Heroine of the Republic!"

Garrick led his wife into the spotlight for the traditional dedication dance as the crowd fell silent. Once the music began, the obvious devotion between them broke down the prejudice of the assembled guests, whose polite applause made Brenna blush. She endured their unwanted attention with an embarrassed smile as Garrick twirled, dipped and led his petite lover in a graceful display of adoration. For a glorious moment, it didn't matter that she was Lithian. Everyone watching witnessed a delighted and pious woman dancing with her beloved.

Secrets and Whispers: *Hurt*

Bronwyn and Algernon took to the floor after this. He looked visibly exhausted and unusually slow on his feet, but the newlyweds completed their obligatory dance and said their farewells to the crowd amid whistles, clapping, stomping feet and loud cheering.

A small carriage conveyed them to their destination in the wealthy University District across town. Algernon could hardly believe his good fortune. His admiring gaze wandered from Bronwyn's dark eyes, down her neck, lingering longingly where he'd dared only glance before, and then rising again as he took her hand in his.

"Are you excited?" she asked.

"I can hardly wait," he admitted. "I just wish I wasn't so tired."

She noted that his signature on the hotel's register looked sloppy. Worried about his need for sleep, Bronwyn helped him into the elevator, wishing there was no attendant present because she thought that arousing her lover with a bit of foreplay might help him stay awake.

When she closed the door to the Honeymoon Suite, Algernon untied the knot that bound them, unwrapped the cord and took her into his arms. With anticipation rising in his eyes and stirring in his loins, he took off her tiara and unzipped her gown. "I've wanted you since I first laid eyes on you," he admitted.

"I'm yours now," she whispered, her fingers working the buttons on his dress robe. "And you're mine."

As their long anticipated moment of intimacy arrived, Algernon trembled with the uncertainty of inexperience. Bronwyn, anxious to please him, didn't take the time to guide and encourage him in the art of arousing a woman. As he'd feared, their first encounter lasted a very short time, and worse, he'd not anticipated that loving her would hurt.

Regret

Clouds and cool air descending from the distant mountains brought a refreshing overnight rain that inspired shivers and raised gooseflesh on Marla's bare arms and legs. The scent of evergreens and the early morning bird songs wrought a sense of the wild to Marvic's university district. Concrete slick with moisture; grass sparkling with water droplets that glimmered in the early morning light; small puddles and rivulets draining water from higher ground saturated a landscape that had already painted Marla's running shoes in a wet sheen.

Brenna, her face fixed with a far-off smile, waited at her customary place near the university's stadium. Marla thought she looked happier than usual, as the hint of sadness she often detected in the Lithian woman's dark eyes had been vanquished by quiet joy. Brenna smiled as Marla approached, her expression revealing the delight of friendship that had developed between the women.

"Why don't you set the pace this morning?" Brenna suggested, faithful to her cultural reluctance to command. "We can cover as much or as little ground as you like."

Marla nodded, though her lips bent downward into a tiny frown. This would be her last run with the Lithian woman, the last time she'd enjoy Brenna's pleasant company, her wit and the intense loyalty she extended to the people she loved. "Okay," the Tamarian woman replied. "Let's go."

With much longer legs, a slender physique, her heart, lungs and blood finally acclimated to the high altitude, Marla had the chance to demonstrate her champion speed; yet she set a moderate pace during their warm-up lap around the university athletic track. She didn't want to hurry. She didn't need to impress anyone.

Secrets and Whispers: *Regret*

Brenna's ponytail swished back and forth in rapid rhythm. The Lithian woman maintained excellent, upright posture and a stride that minimized vertical movement. She appeared to glide over the ground, almost noiselessly landing on the ball of her foot with each tread, her shoulders and arms relaxed. Brenna's natural strength and stamina had developed to the point where running fast seemed effortless.

The women left the spongy stadium track, running on gravel as the path followed the edge of the university's boundary. Here, beyond the shelter of the stadium, wind from the west swayed tall grasses on either side of the trail and bit into Marla's sweating skin with sharp teeth. When the route turned to the west, the champion runner bent her brow against its force, occasionally glancing up to see Brenna's hair fluttering eastward like a frayed flag of black silk.

Descending into a canyon, roughly a mile later, Marla felt relieved to get out of the wind. With gravity amplifying the downward force on her body, Brenna slowed and shortened her stride. Slender Marla had no difficulty with the slope and easily pulled ahead before the trail flattened through a lengthy stretch of mature forest. Moments later, she heard her fleet-footed companion catch up. Brenna glanced at Marla and smiled. She wasn't even breathing hard . . .

Running demanded mental discipline, self-control and physical toughness, traits the Lithian woman revealed every time she took to the track. Marla, who'd spent many years developing these characteristics in herself, had let prejudice concerning Brenna's apparent youth, ethnicity and physical form influence her attitude toward the Lithian woman when they'd met at the family dinner. Knowing she'd been completely wrong, Marla regretted her early condescension.

Secrets and Whispers: *Regret*

She'd been wrong about Algernon, too. Initially, Marla accepted Irena's concerns as meritorious. Having watched the young man endure insult with patient grace, witnessed his advocacy for exploited women in court, heard that he'd talked Willem out of committing suicide and stayed with her nephew after his arrest, Marla realized that he truly honored his priestly vows.

While reluctant to admit she'd been swayed by rumors of the Ravenwood family before actually meeting them, the obvious love between the siblings had changed Marla's view. She'd disdained both Kira and Algernon for their unusual public service, only to develop respect for the scope of their ministry and discover the widespread tarnish of her own family's piety. The secret treachery of her nieces and nephews revealed a spiritual rot that belied the family's devout reputation. Marla believed that Irena and Arvid genuinely exemplified moral conduct, but the veneer of their family's integrity had proven thin.

Marla had also quietly shared the presumption common in her family that while Bronwyn was undeniably sweet, the young woman seemed unlikely to marry. Yet despite her husky size and dark skin, Algernon treated her with respect and effusive affection. Additionally, Bronwyn showed much more maturity in dealing with her siblings than they'd been willing to extend to her, and far greater loyalty to the family than she'd received from any of them, aside from her father.

These secrets and whispers haunted Marla's memory as she labored up Heartbreak Hill with Brenna at her side. While listening to the patter of shoe soles on gravel, the whistling of wind over the nearby city wall, her rhythmic breathing, and by enjoying the mild euphoria of her own strength and speed, Marla set all regret aside. Nothing could be done to change the past, but greater wisdom would inform her future.

Secrets and Whispers: *Regret*

***

Algernon awakened with Bronwyn at his side. He traced the bones of her spine with his finger, then slid his hand around her waist, snuggling close, worried that she'd been dissatisfied by their first nuptial encounter.

She rolled over to face him, clutching his hand to her breast with the hint of a smile on her lips. "Did you sleep well?" she asked.

Wordlessly he nodded, gazing into her brown eyes and placing a soft kiss on her lips.

"You're trembling," she remarked with concern. "What's wrong?"

Algernon pulled away from her and stared at the ceiling. "I'm sorry I disappointed you," he said quietly.

Propping herself up on her elbow, Bronwyn reached for his cheek with her right hand. "Honey lamb, how can you say such a thing?"

Reluctant to explain in explicit detail, Algernon tightened his lips. He worried that failing to delight his newlywed bride like his brother did with Brenna had proven true. Rightly believing that she would be offended if he said this, Algernon hedged.

"Go on, love," Bronwyn urged. "Tell me what's troubling you."

He didn't want to talk about Bronwyn's illicit encounter with Kira, either. Algernon had long worried that he'd pale in comparison with his sister's apparent skill as a lover, and felt secretly terrified that Bronwyn would contrast his sloppy performance with her previous experience. "If sex is supposed to be such a wonderful thing, why does it hurt?" he inquired.

"I was a virgin until last night," she reminded him. "It'll take time for my body to adapt to yours."

Secrets and Whispers: *Regret*

Algernon wanted to believe her, but the difference between his expectations of intimacy and the reality he'd experienced with his wife stirred anxiety in his heart. "Were you disappointed?" he asked.

Bronwyn worried that he might be comparing her to someone like Brenna's not-so-little sister. "You were so tired, I knew you needed to sleep." Evaluating his tone and sensing concern that tapped into her own self-doubt, she asked, "Do you wish you hadn't married me?"

The young man shook his head. "Never!" he insisted. "I just want you to be happy."

She let him hold her for what felt like a long time. Having never witnessed anything but complete confidence from him in the past, Bronwyn felt a little frightened to hear him express self-doubt like this. "We'll get better at this love thing," she promised. "We'll take our time. I'll teach you how to please me, and you can show me how to please you."

Algernon furrowed his brow. "I don't want to hurt you," he admitted. "I don't want to cause you pain. I don't ever want you to regret binding your life to mine."

The sympathy in Bronwyn's eyes transformed into longing. Terrified at the thought that he might leave her, she sat up and leaned into a kiss. "It'll be okay, my love. We'll work this out. Just don't give up on me."

***

Weary of Bronwyn's family drama, worried about a sharp exchange she'd witnessed between Brenna and her sister, Cassie, Kira felt responsible for stirring up trouble. After arguing with Tembe at the end of the evening, she'd left the wedding clean-up duties to others and returned with Ileana to Superstition Mesa by cab.

Secrets and Whispers: *Regret*

With the morning wind tossing her platinum locks eastward, Kira sat on a stool in her garden while pruning vegetable vines. A pile of weeds and sucker growth destined for the compost bin awaited the electric shredder. This task, which typically took no more than a quarter hour, extended well beyond that due to many days of neglect. Kira had been too involved in Bronwyn's wedding to work with her plants and missed this quiet time, alone.

A sense of mild discontent arose in her mind. The frenetic planning and spending of the past few weeks, culminating in a happy celebration for Bronwyn, should have filled Kira's heart with satisfaction. Garrick had even embraced and kissed her, telling his little sister how proud he felt that she'd orchestrated such a wonderful event. That praise brought tears to her eyes, as her eldest brother's approval meant a great deal to her.

Yet she couldn't stop the melancholy feelings that shadowed her soul. It made no sense. Algernon, though exhausted, would finally benefit from Bronwyn's intimate delights. At the wedding, Bronwyn triumphed over the low expectations nearly everyone projected on her.

Kira knew they made a strong pair. Bronwyn's gentle nature nicely balanced Algernon's intensity. Her industrious complimented his confidence and keen skill at solving problems. Kira knew how desperately he needed Bronwyn's comfort, and she understood that Bronwyn desperately needed Algernon's affection and fierce loyalty.

Garrick had faithful Brenna, who'd patiently nurtured goodness and healing in her traumatized husband following his last deployment. Kira witnessed a gradual return to normalcy in her eldest brother. Although Brenna said he'd never be the same again, at least Garrick was no longer viewing every situation through the lens of threat analysis.

Secrets and Whispers: *Regret*

Growing up with Algernon had led Kira to expect that she'd always be the most important person in his life. Gradually and wistfully, Kira had sensed her twin brother turn away from her – his trusted confidant, the one to whom he quickly turned for counsel – and toward her best friend. Bronwyn blossomed under this change, but Kira felt increasingly left behind.

This was natural, wasn't it? This was the nature of men, who always left their mothers and flung themselves into the arms of another woman. Kira, who'd shared the womb and long history with her brother, who knew his strengths and secrets more intimately than anyone else, had been eclipsed. She had to let him go.

Even though she understood that Algernon would never find the fulfillment he needed in their sibling relationship, Kira felt devalued. It hurt. She found no other way to describe the feeling that spilled from her grey eyes and trembled through her soul in the darkness.

Her secret envy of Bronwyn had likely informed a relationship-ending exchange with Tembe. She'd been impatient because he refused to touch her, aside from offering her a hand in and out of the carriage. He'd been upset and offended when she wanted a good night kiss, the event which finally brought her anger to the surface.

"I'm not asking you to bend me over for a good bonk!" she snapped. "But I can't take you seriously when you're so afraid of skin to skin contact."

"I wish to honor you," he'd countered. "I want what is best for you, what is right and noble. There is no guile in my conduct."

"There's no passion in your conduct," she corrected. "You listen to me talk, but never have anything to say, no matter how hard I try to engage in meaningful conversation. You sit near me, but you'll move away if I so much as bump my shoulder against yours.

Secrets and Whispers: *Regret*

"I'm not demanding grand displays of devotion in public, but you won't even hold my hand. I'm not asking you to fondle my tits in private either – though that would be nice for a change. This is not about morality. It's normal for relationships to progress beyond platitudes of expressed interest. I just can't believe you actually want me when you don't make me feel wanted. If you never express your desire, if you recoil from my touch, how do you expect me to respond?"

"The time for that will come," he cautioned. "The only way I can prove the honorable nature of my intentions is to control my conduct. Why are you so impatient? Don't you want me to respect you?"

"I want to be wanted," she replied. "I need to be needed. If you can't offer that much to me, then this relationship is a waste of my time."

"Maybe my father was right," he replied, his face reflecting disgust. "You're a whore at heart."

She'd slapped him hard for saying that. When he tried to retaliate, Kira stepped into a martial stance. Her fierce glare, reputation as a skilled fighter and a quick intervention by Jawara and Lord Lynden restrained his response, preventing an even uglier scene. "Oh, so it's okay to hit a woman, but you can't caress one?" she taunted. "Where's the morality in that?"

Caught by the truth of her accusation, Tembe let the other men lead him away. Kira watched him sulk over to the table where Jawara's wife, Niobe, was sitting, and she'd left the festivities with Ileana shortly thereafter.

It had seemed right at the moment, but in retrospect, Kira regretted her impulsive behavior.

***

Secrets and Whispers: *Regret*

Unfitness for Service was the technical term for military discharge that Willem faced. It carried a stigma that would complicate his life outside of the armed services, making it much harder for him to find work. Willem knew that he could apply for a hearing board to appeal the inevitable ruling, but doing that would expose him to an investigation, questioning, and possibly a recommendation for confinement in a military prison.

Squinting in the bright daylight, Willem left the secure compound – a nondescript building in Marvic's industrial district – in need of a shower, a shave, and a rehab program, none of which he wanted at the moment.

They'd given him runny eggs and toast for breakfast, as well as a half sterling – plenty of cash to cover the cost of a phone call, a streetcar anywhere in the city, with money to spare for lunch. He could have called his mother at the Gold Leaf Hotel, knowing that the family would be leaving Marvic by train that afternoon. She would have quietly looked after him, but a deep and intense desire compelled very different behavior.

Willem wandered along a one-way street leading east. Light industrial buildings gave way to a book store, barber shop and hair dresser, convenience stores and small food markets. Climbing uphill, clothing outlets, tenement housing and pawn shops dominated the environment. Litter, graffiti, and alleyways that reeked of urine became common as Willem ascended. He passed a broken-down sign that read *Welcome to Paradise.*

"Looking for a friend?" a woman asked.

She'd have been considered pretty a few years earlier, but a life of many regrets transformed the echo of promise into long despair. Her tight blouse and very short skirt left little to the imagination and might have been alluring to many men, but her feminine features did nothing for Willem. He shook his head and walked on.

Secrets and Whispers: *Regret*

Two blocks later, he caught a glimpse of his desired destination. Willem's heart pounded. His step quickened in anticipation. A familiar feeling of imminent relief trembled through his fingertips. He raced for the front door, wide-eyed and panting to regain his breath in the thin air.

Glass containers whispered to his soul. Willem scanned the various brands, checking prices, looking for a deal that represented the best bargain for the money he had. Drinking would help him forget. Drinking would soothe away all of his pain and regret.

***

Feeling light in her soul, the euphoria of a vigorous run bolstering her mood, Brenna breezed over the stone bridge leading to the music manse she shared with Garrick. She could hear him struggling with the trumpet again as the roar of the nearby waterfall diminished with distance. Just outside their front door sat Captain Mariel Hougen. The woman stood as Brenna approached.

"What brings you here so early?" Brenna asked, accepting the much taller woman into her embrace.

"I need a word with your husband," Mariel replied. "But when I came through the gate, you hadn't checked in yet. He doesn't like me coming around when you're not here, and when I heard that awful racket in there, I decided to wait 'til you arrived."

One of the many things Garrick did to instill confidence in Brenna was his reluctance to spend time alone with other women. At times his role as an officer required this, but in that context propriety was expected. In the looser realm of social interaction, Garrick behaved with great care in order to honor his wife.

Secrets and Whispers: *Regret*

Mariel, and the women under Garrick's command, respected him for consistently behaving this way. Even her exotic beauty and considerable talent for seduction proved impotent against the strength of the lieutenant's devotion to his wife. Mariel had long envied the little Lithian woman for so completely captivating his attention.

"Please come in," Brenna said, opening the front door, haphazardly removing her running shoes and unzipping her workout sweater. "I'll send him down."

Garrick heard the door open and paused, carefully setting his instrument back into its case. He greeted his bride with a strong, lingering embrace that nearly took her breath away. "Tembe has been calling for you," he said, relinquishing her.

Brenna scowled. "I warned him. I told him that his infatuation with Kira would end badly, but he didn't want to hear what I had to say."

"Are you going to call him back?" he asked.

"No," Brenna replied flatly. "He didn't listen to me, so why should I bother listening to him?"

Garrick raised his brow. Brenna had little patience for Tembe's entitled attitude. This was not the way she typically treated other people. "He seemed pretty upset."

Brenna turned to her dresser, pulling out freshly washed undergarments for the day. "Then he should have stopped acting like a dead fish in Kira's company. We knew she wouldn't put up with that."

"He was only trying to be honorable," Garrick said in Tembe's defense. "You were impressed with my restraint when we were dating . . ."

"You were careful. You respected my virtue, but you weren't cold," she reminded him. "I never doubted that you wanted me. And the moment I encouraged your touch, you were more than happy to make yourself acquainted with *The Twins*.

Secrets and Whispers: *Regret*

"Tembe has been a spoiled brat since birth. He's never had to work for anything in his life and expects everything to go his way, on his terms. That alone would never fly with Kira, and I told him so. He's also terrified of his own libido. Tembe believes that winning a woman's heart requires absolute denial of all his desire.

"That's flat-out wrong. I've told him so, but he's never been willing to take advice. I don't blame Kira for slamming the door on a pointless relationship."

Garrick, who sincerely longed for his sister's happiness, didn't share his wife's perspective. He held Tembe in high regard, precisely because the young man treated Kira with dignity, whereas others, who'd come before him, had been quick to exploit her passion. Kira's growing maturity enabled a steadily increasing ability to function as the head of the family. Her chaste relationship with Tembe seemed like a natural result of personal growth that Garrick wanted to affirm.

Yet Brenna had a point. Kira's maturity had not moderated her hot-blooded, foul-mouthed and impulsive nature. Pious Tembe was not a good fit for her. Brenna had even gone so far as to suggest that Tembe might only consent to sex for the purpose of reproduction, and then insist that it take place in the dark, beneath the sheets, so that the angels couldn't watch.

Because he'd not replied, Brenna presumed that her husband had nothing further to say on the matter. She began to undress – which always drew his attention – and smiled in approval of his appreciation. "Captain Hougen is waiting for you," she said.

Garrick ran his hands down her arms, pulling her close from behind. Though her skin felt sweaty, he caressed her affectionately and planted little kisses on her neck before she giggled and he reluctantly let her go.

Secrets and Whispers: *Regret*

Heading downstairs while Brenna went into the shower, he noted that Captain Hougen had draped herself across the downstairs love seat. "Can I get you some water?" he inquired.

She declined. "I had tea not long ago." Then, with a raised brow she cleared her throat and added, "I'm sorry. It sounds like I interrupted the two of you."

Garrick ignored her innuendo, knowing that Mariel enjoyed teasing him about his amorous relationship with Brenna. "What brings you here this morning?" he asked.

"Apparently, you've earned a place at the center of the investigation into the palace bombing," she stated.

"I was quite nearly a victim of the attack," he replied, taking a seat on the couch adjacent to her. "So, how can that be?"

Mariel shifted in her seat, leaning her forearms onto her knees. "Why would a Kurian spy track you down?" she asked. "Why would he risk his life coming all the way up here to pass information on to you?"

Feeling uncomfortable with the tone of her inquiry, Garrick narrowed his brow. "Are you questioning my patriotism?" he asked.

"Never!" she replied. "I didn't say you were involved. I think you're being used."

"How so?"

Mariel paused, allowing tension to rise between the two of them. "How credible is it that a total stranger approaches you on a streetcar with knowledge of who you are, of your wife's family, and of me?"

Garrick scowled. "The Crown Intelligence agents have already interrogated me about this!"

"They had it backwards," Mariel assured. "I can't see you contacting a foreign spy. That Kurian agent had been briefed on you. The question is, by whom?"

Secrets and Whispers: *Regret*

"I have no idea," Garrick said. "The guy approached us on the streetcar. I'd never seen him before."

"How could a Kurian national have any knowledge of a Tamarian Expeditionary Force lieutenant?" she asked. "A man like him wouldn't have access to that information.

"Ergo, either we have a double agent in our midst, or someone with excellent intelligence resources has funneled information to a two-bit spy who is in way over his head."

Garrick narrowed his gaze. "A traitor like that would have to know me pretty well," he replied. "That's probably why the Crown Intelligence was interested in Jared."

"He's squeaky clean," Mariel replied, shaking her head. "But he's not the only one who might know about you and your family connections. An allied government would have the requisite assets to know who you are, but why were you selected as a point of contact?"

"I live behind the palace wall," Garrick replied. "My wife and I are your friends, and Brenna's sister happens to be engaged to a man who is well acquainted with King Alejo. Crown Intelligence thinks that makes me a target.

"The foreigner who contacted me felt confident that I'd share his information with you, and must have known that I'd pass it to our own intelligence people."

"That's why I suspect someone in the Kamerese government leaked that information to manipulate us, or the spy is a double agent," she concluded.

"Okay," he continued. "But that's completely speculative at this point."

"Not exactly," Mariel clarified. "My contact in Kameron's Foreign Service Directorate got very nervous when I related the story you told me. He promised to look into the matter, but I've just learned that he's been called back to Kameron . . ."

Secrets and Whispers: *Regret*

"That's inconvenient," Garrick replied. "But why would our allies become involved in a plot to bomb the palace gate? That's an act of war."

"I don't think the Kamerese government was directly involved," Mariel clarified. "I think that certain actors in King Alejo's court are trying to tangle us in their conflict with the Nordans. Those people have undercover relationships with terrorist organizations, like *Los Patrones del Estado,* who likely arranged the attack."

"It's still an act of war," Garrick insisted. "If the Kamerese government was involved, that would have serious implications for our relationship with them."

"Yes," Mariel agreed. "That's why my contact at the Foreign Service began feeding me misinformation. The only scenario that fits all the evidence is that *Los Patrones* arranged for the attack, using Kurian nationalists to carry it out. This was paid through back channels leading to the Kamerese court, who instructed their Foreign Service to cover it up. But their story began to unravel when I started asking uncomfortable questions . . ."

"That would mean this Rathdurm fellow who found me was telling the truth," Garrick concluded.

Mariel nodded. "The double agent scenario makes the most sense of what we know. If he was working for both the Kurian separatists and the Kamerese intelligence community, he could access information on you and me with relative ease. That's what made my contact at the Foreign Service so uncomfortable.

"Prior to that revelation, the Kamerese government had plausible deniability over the attack. But if the links to the king's court can be verified, that all goes away."

"That's a very serious allegation," Garrick stated. "We're an important trading partner and a critical, strategic ally for them. It doesn't make sense that they'd want to damage that relationship."

Secrets and Whispers: *Regret*

"It's a risk that certain elements may have been willing to take," Mariel concluded.

Garrick shook his head. "If you're right, I hope they live to regret it!"

***

Unaccustomed to admitting fault and feeling that he'd been singled-out for culpability in the disinheritance plot, Darren struggled to look his little sister in the eye. It didn't help that Algernon, who always had his hands on her, sustained a glare hot enough to melt glass. "I've wronged you concerning your inheritance," Darren stammered. "I've also ignored the fact that you're a grown woman and treated you like a child. There's no excuse for my behavior, and I don't know how to make it right."

Bronwyn's face reflected a longing to restore her sibling relationship. As a girl she'd admired Darren from a distance, as the age gap between them ensured that he usually had better things to do than to bother with her. Nonetheless, Bronwyn arose, put her arms around her eldest brother and kissed his cheek. "I forgive you," she promised. "Everything is okay."

Her affection amplified his discomfort. "Don't be gross!" he warned. "There's no need to be gushy about it."

"Son, she has every right to be very angry at you," Irena reminded him. "Don't dismiss her magnanimity."

Arvid watched the scene in silence. He'd already said his piece to Darren, and while he questioned his son's sincerity, the older man understood how socially difficult this attempt at conciliation had to be for an older brother. At the very least, Darren was making an effort. Harold had run away before any of this had come to light, and nobody knew where Willem had gone.

Secrets and Whispers: *Regret*

Eyeing the bags packed in readiness for imminent departure, Irena felt pressured to conclude family business. She reached into her purse, pulled out an envelope and held it in her lap with nervous fingers. With pursed lips and tension in her voice she announced, "We need to discuss the matter of the dowry . . ."

"*Mutti*, I don't need it," Bronwyn replied gently.

Irena tried to be patient. "Honey, this is a practical matter that deserves consideration. I know you don't need the dowry to set up a household, since you're already living in a functioning home, but we thought it wise to hold the funds in trust for your children."

Bronwyn shook her head, pushing away the envelope that Irena offered. "I'm serious," she said in a stronger tone. "We'll never need it."

Irena's face took on an expression that blended desperation with condescension. "Darling," she began. "I know how you feel, but you never know what you're going to need in the future. This is a hedge against trouble. Even if you never use it, one day you'll have a daughter, and you can pass it on to her."

Glancing at Algernon for support, Bronwyn steeled her nerves. "We have a different idea," she began, opening her own purse and pulling out a piece of folded paper that she spread on a coffee table. The neatly-written ledger allocated her entire inheritance – including her dowry – in trust to her brothers.

Arvid scowled. Irena shook her head in disbelief. "Why would you do such a thing?" she asked. "We've set this money aside for you since birth. Your brothers tried to swindle what is rightfully yours away, and you intend to reward them for their dishonesty?"

"It's not a reward," Bronwyn replied. "It's a way to ensure they each have an independent future."

Secrets and Whispers: *Regret*

"Honey, you need to think about this," Arvid counseled. "We know you live in a lovely home. We know that Algernon's sister is a wealthy woman, but he is a priest, and you need to think about your children."

"What about my brothers?" Bronwyn replied. "All three of them have devoted their lives to serving the Republic, but their pay is barely sufficient for them to survive. Harold will be okay as long as he stays with Heidelinde, but she's the most selfish and cold-hearted woman I've ever met. He's completely at her mercy. What will he do if she leaves him?

"For all we know, Sikki has run off with whatever savings Darren has set aside all these years, leaving him flat broke. Lydia will have nothing for her dowry when she marries," Bronwyn added, referring to her niece, the only daughter born to Sikki and Darren.

"And then there's Willem. Vega's sick of his violent temper and I don't blame her. No woman should tolerate being beaten. Their marriage is a total sham, and she's told me she'll never take him back. Willi's on his own.

"The best he can hope for is a dishonorable discharge for sleeping with another man, and on top of that, he's got a serious drinking problem that needs treatment whenever he's ready for that step. He doesn't need criticism, condemnation, or disapproval. How is he going to overcome all of this if we don't help him?"

With her parents stunned into silence, Bronwyn continued. "Let's stop pretending we don't have problems in this family. Let's accept that Willi's sexuality isn't like ours. Let's act like we love one another.

"Since the inheritance is rightfully mine, I have the right to decide where to invest it. I choose to stand with my brothers." Bronwyn tapped the ledger sheet forcefully. "This is where the change begins!"

Secrets and Whispers: *Regret*

Darren, struggling to cope with strong emotion, arose and walked out of the hotel room. Arvid let out a deep sigh, shaking his head. Irena blinked back tears. "Okay darling," she assented. "I just hope you don't live to regret this."

***

Being alone had never ranked high on Kira's list of favored experiences. The extroverted young woman enjoyed the company of other people, and when left by herself for extended time periods, she typically felt restless for companionship. She'd kept herself busy through the morning by catching up on neglected chores, gently stretching – which always made her right leg feel much better – finishing a decorative basket she'd started weaving for Bronwyn, and soaking in the hot spring.

The new bed she'd ordered for the newlyweds arrived in the early afternoon. After arranging their bedroom, adding flowers from her garden to a porcelain vase on top of Bronwyn's dresser, putting on a fresh set of sheets and changing all the towels in the bathroom, Kira finally glanced at the clock. Brenna and Bronwyn's parents would be boarding the train to leave the city, but she'd deliberately not gone to the station to say goodbye.

That's when she heard a knock on the door. Worried that it might be Tembe, she checked her appearance in the mirror, fiddled with her hair, steeled her nerves, and hobbled to the entrance.

Sheriff Gant took off his hat and bowed his head respectfully. "Miss Kira," he said in greeting.

She smiled beautifully in response. Kira could dial up irresistible charm, particularly with men, whenever she needed it. "Welcome, sir! To what do I owe the pleasure?"

Secrets and Whispers: *Regret*

Because she was alone, Kira didn't invite him in. The sheriff declined her offer of refreshment and chose one of the chairs on the porch. "It's a missing persons matter," he told her. Reaching into a satchel, he produced a photo. "Have you seen this woman recently?"

It was Karin, from the Wildlife Office. Kira's eyes widened. "She was poking around here several days ago. I filed a complaint against her for voyeurism, but I've not seen her since. What happened?"

The sheriff took back his photo. He already knew about the complaint. "She's been reported missing . . ."

That triggered Kira's memory. "Yesterday morning, on my way back from the hot spring, I thought I heard a woman scream. I worried that it might be a glacier gull, so I hurried home."

"About what time was this?" the sheriff asked, pulling out his notepad.

"Midmorning," Kira replied. "I called for a taxi shortly thereafter. If you contact the cab company, they'll have a time stamp for that phone call."

Sheriff Gant appreciated Kira's cooperation. He'd always liked this pretty young woman and trusted her testimony, despite the fact that the most serious trouble in his jurisdiction over the past couple of years had been centered on her homestead. "Can you show me where you heard the scream?"

"Of course," Kira replied, rising from her seat with the help of her cane. "Come with me."

***

As Thea Velez watched broad, verdant fields slide past her window, she leaned her head against the glass in wistful silence. Though Caerwyn sat to her left, Cynthia's imagination drifted toward her longstanding fantasy of

Secrets and Whispers: *Regret*

Algernon. He would forever be the one who got away. She'd been able to turn his head for a little while, but in time, Bronwyn's hold on his heart had proven too strong.

She believed that the envy rising in her soul was wrong. In her private prayers, Thea confessed feeling hurt by the fact that a heavier, plain-looking woman won out in the contest for Algernon's attention. After meeting Bronwyn, Cynthia recognized the sweet character and gentleness that Algernon adored in her. Thea knew that he needed someone like that, yet it still didn't seem fair.

She'd kept a tight rein on her emotions, hoping no one would notice the pain and regret wrenching her soul, yet her keenly-perceptive mother knew better. Lady Alexina had held her tongue until Thea was ready to talk, her eyes projecting sympathy and her touch reassurance.

"I did my best to treat Bronwyn with kindness," Thea told her mother while they waited on the platform.

Alexina had smiled and nodded. "Your conduct was above reproach. Your desire to ensure another woman's happiness reveals the nobility of your character."

But Thea didn't feel noble. She'd chosen to act in the way she knew was right, despite a rising sense of compelling desperation that clamored for attention in her soul. Overcoming this demanded discipline, but first, she had to find the desire to leave her fantasy of Algernon behind, a goal proving oddly elusive.

She'd wanted to sit down with Brenna, who'd pushed aside her long-time friend, Woodwind, in favor of Garrick. However, after Cassie's fiancé was arrested, Thea's older sisters engaged in a vigorous debate best left for them to resolve. Cassie, who'd resented Tamarian bigotry toward her family and felt outraged by Jared's detention, did not often argue with anyone – let alone her willful and formidable sister.

Secrets and Whispers: *Regret*

Their quarrel ended with a long embrace and sisterly kissing – which was how their sibling disputes always concluded – edging out any opportunity for Thea to bare her soul to Brenna before leaving for home.

That meant she had to handle her regrets in silence, a process Thea had never done with any skill. She'd always been sentimental, prone to intense introspection, and sensitive to the emotions of anyone whom she loved. These traits made Cynthia an ideal vessel for her clairvoyant gift, yet it did not serve her well when she tried to conceal her turmoil from Caerwyn.

He sensed great tension in the tenuous influence his affections held on Thea. He'd once served as chief geologist on the *Cupitor Mineralis*, an Azgar research boat whose rescue team had saved Algernon from certain death in the Desolation River. A brief friendship between the two men floundered when Algernon introduced the Lithian scientist to Thea. Caerwyn sensed the chemistry between Algernon and the beautiful young woman, who'd transferred her interest from him only after it became clear that Algernon intended to return to Bronwyn.

Caerwyn watched Cynthia accept her young brother, Eren, into her arms. Thea treated the child in a manner that edged on the maternal, holding him against her breast and gently rocking from side to side.

She would not disclose her obvious turmoil. If Thea found comfort in snuggling with her brother this way, Caerwyn voiced no objection. Their relationship had survived what he considered a serious threat, and now that Algernon was finally out of contention for Thea's heart, all Caerwyn had to do was wait for their wedding. He knew that once she'd experienced intimacy with him, her longing for another man would fade away. They would be devoted to each other for the rest of their days, and she would never regret becoming his wife.

Secrets and Whispers: *Regret*

***

Alone in her hotel room, Vega brushed her hair while contemplating the direction of her life. Staying in Marvic, rather than returning to Feral Springs with Willem's family, had been her choice. With the urgent need to sustain herself looming in the immediate future, Vega faced the hard prospect of finding work, with neither practical skills nor experience to offer.

She'd been a fool to heed Sikki's advice, first in marrying Willem – who'd only agreed to their union in order to conceal the reality of his sexual orientation – and second, in participating in the disinheritance plot. It had been humiliating to beg Bronwyn's forgiveness, no matter how easily her sister-in-law extended grace.

Vega couldn't remember the last time she felt in control of her own life, yet the idea that being accountable to no one but herself – which should have inspired the joy and laughter of liberation – wrought anxiety, instead. It also inspired anger, as she concluded that she'd wasted the best years of her life living a lie.

Tamarian culture valued community, a sense of connectedness and belonging that enabled everyone to find a unique place in which to contribute to the overall good of society. Yet Vega had never felt fully accepted among the Traugotts. Irena, whose success as an investor commanded respect, whose piety inspired friends and neighbors to honor her devotion, represented a lofty standard by which everyone measured the three younger women who'd married into her family.

Isolated in Feral Springs, Vega quickly and painfully learned that Willem would only touch her in anger. Among the Traugotts, she functioned as a pretty ornament to distract everyone from Willem's homosexuality. Irena and Arvid wanted no one to know about that, insinuating in

Secrets and Whispers: *Regret*

public that Vega's inability to have children stemmed from some mysterious, physical flaw. She'd endured this humiliation for years, acting as the dutiful daughter-in-law, honoring the deception for the sake of fitting in.

Yet after meeting Kira – who'd been abused and enslaved, who'd first worked as a stripper and then a *strichmadchen* – Vega found hope. Kira's tightly-knit family nursed her through opium withdrawal, an unwanted pregnancy and subsequent miscarriage. They'd stood by her as she began and sustained her unusual public service. Her brothers vigorously defended her from every threat, allowing the young woman to capitalize on her self-discipline, determination, intelligence and exquisite charm.

Nobody in Irena's family had ever offered Vega that kind of support. Nobody had ever encouraged her to explore her dreams and talents, either. She'd been expected to play the role that Irena determined, and nothing more.

Unlike Irena's imposed and inflexible obligation, Kira offered options. She'd agreed to help Vega with housing and help her get on her feet. While it wouldn't be easy to face Bronwyn on a regular basis, Vega planned to take control over her life. She could no longer tolerate being dominated by her older cousin, her abusive husband, or her well-meaning, but misguided mother-in-law.

In the interest of easing tension between Vega and Bronwyn, Kira promised to pay for another night at the Gold Leaf Hotel. The following day, Vega would move into the former residence of Mrs. Bergen and care for the property in lieu of paying rent. Kira intended to use that house as a transitional haven for battered women.

The telephone shocked Vega out of her reverie. She accepted a call from a police station in the Paradise Precinct, where an officer named Weber was looking for the wife of Willem Soehn.

Secrets and Whispers: *Regret*

"This is Vega Soehn," she affirmed.

"I'm sorry to inform you that your husband has been arrested for public drunkenness and assault. He'd like you to come down and post bail on his behalf."

Vega's tone hardened. "I regret that I'm unable to help him," she said. Without another word spoken, she put the receiver back on its hook.

***

Once word got out that Bronwyn and Algernon had married, many people on the streets of Marvic stopped to offer congratulations. The Defenders who worked at the city's main gate raised over 200 sterlings for the Veteran's Widows Charity in honor of the newlywed couple.

This outpouring of goodwill felt overwhelming to Bronwyn, who'd never before experienced being the center of attention. She accepted hugs and kisses on her cheeks from elderly people and turned beet red when the Defenders stopped their work to chant a cheer for her.

Algernon responded with broad smiles and blessings. Affirmed and vindicated by this community support, the self-doubt that often haunted his steps melted away. In its place arose a serene sense that his ministerial efforts had been making a positive difference, and that even people who didn't know him recognized this as fact.

Yet his euphoria did not dampen the sensitivity he'd long maintained concerning the emotional well-being of his new bride. Noting her facial expression and quiet demeanor, he took her hand in his just beyond the city gate. "Are you okay?"

She nodded, but didn't immediately reply. A few steps later she said, "I just wasn't expecting things to end like this with my family."

Secrets and Whispers: *Regret*

"It's not over," he replied. "Damage has been done, but that doesn't mean your relationships are ruined beyond repair."

"*Mutti* is worried sick about Willem," Bronwyn stated. "I don't know why he'd run off, rather than going home after being released from custody."

Knowing a harsh reality from experience, Algernon took a deep breath before responding. "Alcohol is a very tough drug to quit," he told her. "Your brother has likely gone on a bender and will wake up under a bridge."

"That's a terrible thing to say!" Bronwyn cried.

"Yes, it is terrible," he agreed. "But it's truth. Recovery is not going to be an easy road. Even if he wants it badly, he'll have setbacks. I've lived through episodes of rage and remonstrance with my own father and I know that the only control Willem has is to not drink at all. I've said this to him, Kira's said this to him, and so has Garrick. He may wake up and regret what he's done, but until he decides to never drink again, he'll struggle."

They walked down the ramp in silence, with Algernon carrying their overnight rucksack on his shoulder. His dress robe and her wedding gown shared a garment bag, which he'd draped over his right forearm. The distance from this point to Kira's homestead could be covered in less than 20 minutes via the Augury Creek Farm Service Road, which ran along the heavily treed, western scarp of the mesa, following a narrowing valley dotted with market garden farms and small ranches.

The ill-maintained trail that traced through Wounded Heart Canyon – the narrow, rocky gap between the mesa and the promontory upon which Marvic stood – cut that time by a third. This was the way Algernon typically took when traveling to and from the city, despite its steep and extended incline.

Secrets and Whispers: *Regret*

When he paused at the trail head, Bronwyn sensed that he had more than one reason for wanting to go this way. Glancing around to make sure no one could observe, her demeanor changed into one she reserved for her husband, alone. She drew near, pressing her body into his chest, turning her head for a kiss. Then, stepping back, she willed her Lithian halter to relax. "You want to go to the cabin?" she asked, suggestively.

He nodded, captivated by the sight of her.

Bronwyn smiled. "Well then . . . Follow me!"

He didn't need any more encouraging. Although she'd grown tall and broad, Bronwyn exercised regularly, maintained a training regimen similar to Kira and Algernon, and could move with surprising agility for a woman of her size. Whenever Algernon reached for and squeezed her backside, she nimbly skipped away, or returned the favor. They laughed, pausing to kiss before moving onward.

Free to express the full extent of her sensuality, the young woman sustained her husband's interest with affection spiced with a promise of something more. She lured him to the top of the slope, where a broad meadow stretched across the summit of Superstition Mesa.

Her devotion also earned his trust. Algernon matched her pace and breathlessly kissed her at the edge of the meadow. Bronwyn encouraged his touch, her desire rose in tandem with his and threatened to escalate. "Honey lamb," she breathed. "Let's get to the cabin."

With a smile he assented. They walked across the meadow, playfully bumping hips. Wild grasses, thriving where barley and oats had once been planted, stretched into the encroaching forest. Young, pioneering pines stood like advancing soldiers in a field where nature reclaimed territory long ago lost after human settlers abandoned their dreams on the mesa.

Secrets and Whispers: *Regret*

Algernon loved living up here. He felt grateful that Bronwyn had chosen to join him and accepted the inconvenience of a homestead lifestyle.

A few minutes later, they arrived at the overgrown trail leading up to the hidden cabin. Bronwyn scurried up the slippery stones that served as crude stairs, turning to embrace her husband at the entry. He pressed her against the door, showering her with affection and murmurs of appreciation as she pulled him close and basked in his affirmation. Moments later, he lifted the halter off her shoulders and paused in admiration.

"You are so beautiful!" he breathed.

She pulled off his shirt and with a smile, ran her hands down his strong, sculpted chest. "Let's go inside."

As Algernon rotated the door handle, opening the portal with a loud creak, the amorous mood between the two lovers evaporated. Bronwyn instinctively covered herself and froze. Algernon moved her to the side before entering the small, single room.

Bedding, a stack of clothes, a small pair of boots, food tins, a lamp and a cookstove told the tale of recent habitation. Algernon noted a rifle leaned against a corner, next to a box of 30 caliber ammunition. A diary and a pen lay by the sleeping bag. In a paper box next to the bedding, Algernon found a woman's menstrual cup, which he showed to his wife.

Bronwyn wriggled back into her halter and buttoned up her blouse. What did this mean? She watched her husband leaf through the diary as a familiar and dangerous anger hardened on his face. "Honey lamb, what is it?" she asked.

"That slavering gobermouch!" he spat. "She's been spying on us!"

Bewildered, Bronwyn reached for the book. "Who?"

"That pillock of a Wildlife Officer!" he replied.

Secrets and Whispers: *Regret*

"The one who left her lipstick on the mug?" Bronwyn asked, careful to avoid an accusing tone that might inflame her angry husband.

"Yeah. Look at this diary of hers. The last entry came from two nights ago."

Bronwyn's voice hardened as she scanned the words. "How long has she been watching us?"

Algernon pointed to the last entry, his brow narrowing. "At least five days," he replied. "Sheriff Gant should have a look at this. She's harassing us, and I want her to regret it . . ."

***

The sound of a baying hound stirred Kira from the kitchen. She'd been expecting Bronwyn and Algernon to arrive any minute and wanted to surprise them with a meal they both enjoyed eating, but the sound of the dog called her away from the black bean and vegetable dish she was cooking.

Watching the deputy and his tracking dog head south, she fruitlessly banged on the window. Moments later, she hobbled onto the patio and yelled as powerfully as she could, "That's the wrong way!"

But the bloodhound urged its handler onward, lunging at its leash. His keen senses detected the desired scent and excited him to the extent that Deputy Schlossberg struggled to keep the beast under control. Focused on his task, the young man couldn't hear Kira over the howling.

Sheriff Gant trotted up the path. Noting Kira's distress, he paused at her front porch stairs. "We have a garment that belongs to our missing woman," he stated. "The hound has clearly picked up her scent."

Secrets and Whispers: *Regret*

Kira shook her head. Knowing nothing about the cabin, but suspecting that giants still lived in the area, she genuinely worried for the meddlesome Wildlife Officer. If Karin had been taken prisoner, that might mean a lifetime of torment for her. Despite having caught her spying on the homestead, Kira felt a bit guilty for her role in getting the woman suspended from her job.

Remembering her dinner on the stove, Kira limped back into the house. "No!" she cried, noting the smoke rising from the skillet. She dashed to the stove as quickly as her lame leg allowed, pulled the pan off the fire and dumped it into the sink – dousing the growing conflagration with water from the tap. She swore, then slumped against the cabinet. Feeling overwhelmed by all the change occurring in her life, and the weight of feeling unworthy of love, she began sobbing.

***

When Algernon heard the hound, his protective instinct prompted him to move in front of Bronwyn. She could take care of herself, but any creature that posed a threat to her would have to get by him, first. He felt her hand rest on his shoulder as he stopped on the dirt path leading toward the homestead.

But his caution proved unnecessary. Deputy Hans Schlossberg, who kept the dog under his firm control, recognized the young couple as he turned a corner. He could tell, from the tension on the lead, that his animal felt confident he was nearing the source of the scent.

Thinking it strange that the dog had become focused on Algernon – whom Hans considered above reproach – the deputy wrinkled his brow.

Secrets and Whispers: *Regret*

"What's this about?" Algernon asked as the bloodhound raised onto its haunches and began sniffing his overnight rucksack.

"Drop the bag and open it," the deputy commanded.

Algernon complied. "Our clothes are in here," he complained. "My wife's undergarments, too . . ."

"Everything in there belongs to you?" Deputy Schlossberg clarified, respecting Bronwyn's privacy.

"No," Algernon replied. "We found a diary in a nearby cabin."

"Pull it out," Hans demanded. When the bloodhound sniffed the book, jumped up and placed his front paws on the cover, Hans took it away from Algernon. "Whose is this?" he asked.

"It belongs to a snoopy Wildlife Officer," the young priest replied.

"Where did you find it?"

Algernon zipped his rucksack up again. "Come with me and I'll show you."

By this time, Sheriff Gant arrived. Bronwyn, seeing that she wasn't needed, chose to go home. She took the rucksack and the garment bag from Algernon, kissed him goodbye and bade farewell to the sheriff and his deputy.

The dog led the way back to the cabin while Algernon explained why he and his wife had gone up there to the policemen. He also complained that Karin had been spying on them.

"She's gone missing," Sheriff Gant told him. "Your sister thought she heard a scream yesterday. If the woman was staying here, she's likely nearby."

At the deserted cabin, it didn't take long for the dog to find her scent on a narrow track that led further uphill.

"What's up there?" the sheriff asked.

"It's a deer trail," Algernon replied. "Giants were using it while they were hunting the local gwynling."

Secrets and Whispers: *Regret*

The dog seemed anxious to climb. "Is it safe?" the deputy asked.

"I know the way," Algernon replied. "I've used it to get across the ridge."

The three men followed the hound, with Sheriff Gant taking up the rear. Rather than turning north on the track, the dog wanted to go south. Less than a hundred yards later, Deputy Schlossberg had to pull hard on the leash to prevent his animal from falling into a large pit.

That's where they found Karin's clothes and the notebook with her neatly-written record of all the comings and goings at Kira's homestead. Noting that her clothing had been cut off, and examining the construction of the pit trap, Sheriff Gant shook his head ruefully.

"I need to contact the army again," he said. "I regret that we may have to call another evacuation."

***

Algernon returned home to find his twin sister sobbing into Bronwyn's shoulder. Uncomfortable with her display of emotion, he struggled to respond in a way that would help, rather than hinder.

Kira moved her eyes toward him, then pulled herself upright using the counter top. She sniffled, then opened her arms to her brother, beckoning him into her embrace.

Bronwyn stood and kissed Kira on the cheek. "Don't worry, darling," she encouraged. "I'll work on dinner."

"What's wrong?" Algernon asked.

The strength of Kira's embrace worried him. While he'd known her affection for as long as memory reached into the past, this felt different. He sensed a desperation in her that he'd never witnessed.

"Promise you won't leave me!" she sputtered.

Algernon shook his head. "I'm right here."

Secrets and Whispers: *Regret*

"Do you love me?" she asked.

"With all my heart," he replied.

Kira gradually relaxed and withdrew. She sniffed and wiped her eyes. "Sorry for making a scene. I should be leaving the two of you alone."

Algernon watched her shuffle to her room, shut and lock the door. He turned toward Bronwyn and gently squeezed her soft shoulders. "Did she say what's wrong?"

Bronwyn nodded, speaking quietly while she began working on dinner. "She's sad because she feels that everyone around her has a partner, but the one person who expressed interest didn't love her enough to show affection. She's worried that she's ruined her chance to find love, and that she'll spend the rest of her days alone, never having sex again."

"I like Tembe, but I never thought he was a good match for my sister," Algernon replied. "She needs to be accepted for who she is, not for the wild fantasy someone imposes on her."

"And she's a hot-blooded girl," Bronwyn added. "Kira needs a partner who can handle that."

Algernon put his arms around his wife, reaching for her bosom from behind. He felt the weight of her breasts fall into his hands as her halter loosened in response. "Are you a hot blooded girl?" he asked.

Bronwyn smiled. "Only for you," she replied.

Kira, sensing that the newlyweds needed to be alone, sat on her bed and gazed out the window. She'd already shed enough tears to cope with her regret.

***

The next morning, Kira awakened to the sound of her brother running water in the bathroom sink. That wasn't unusual, as he was typically the first person to

Secrets and Whispers: *Regret*

arise, but instead of making tea, she heard her brother head back into his room and shut the door.

Moments later, Kira could hear breathlessness overtaking Bronwyn's voice. Knowing where this was heading, Kira pulled a pillow over her head and tried, to no avail, to fall asleep again. It was hard to hear other people engaging in intimate contact when she felt she'd been doomed to loneliness.

Fortunately, Algernon and Bronwyn were nothing like Garrick and Brenna in the lovemaking longevity department. A few minutes later, they were quiet again, permitting Kira to drift back into a shallow sleep.

A ringing phone awakened her. Kira wanted her brother to pick it up, but the phone kept ringing. Annoyed, Kira slipped out of bed and limped over to the kitchen just before the operator gave up on the call.

Algernon heard his sister talking to someone she knew. A few moments later, she hobbled to the door and quietly knocked on it. "Are you guys decent?" she asked.

"Come in, sweetie," Bronwyn replied. "It's okay."

The room smelled mildly stuffy and vaguely like sex. Kira wrinkled her nose and glanced at the window, where the last glimpse of the Great Eye nebula had begun slipping below the horizon. Thinking it would have been rude to open the window and ventilate the room, she leaned on the doorframe rather than coming inside.

Kira found it hard to see her twin brother curled up with his bride in bed. His muscular shoulder lay next to hers with his arm vanishing beneath the sheet as he held her close. The reality of his good fortune stung Kira's heart, but she pushed her envy aside. He deserved his happiness and her problems were not his.

"That was Vega," she said. "The cops found Willem drunk yesterday. She didn't want to bail him out, but now she's feeling guilty. Can you go?"

Secrets and Whispers: *Regret*

***

Hangover symptoms hammered in Willem's head. He felt exhausted and irritable. A terrible thirst parched his mouth and clutched his throat as nausea rumbled in his belly. He suspected the jail guards took sadistic pleasure in making loud noises and keeping the lights on, too.

The mere sight of breakfast made him feel sick, but the thought of being stuck here until his trial date felt terrifying. Why had he have to get drunk? Why couldn't he stop after the craving went away? Why had this become such a problem?

Why had Vega refused to help him?

Willem cursed her when the guard told him what she'd said, but in the dead of night, he'd mourned over the suffering she'd endured at his hand. Deep in his heart, Willem knew that she'd been a far better woman than he deserved.

He just didn't want a woman. The sight of her body repulsed him, and as sweet as she could be in public, Willem knew how whiny and relentlessly critical she behaved when they were alone. She'd get him angry when she thought he'd had too much to drink, and he'd often hit her, only to feel overcome with regret, afterward.

Algernon spoke truthfully, and Willem knew it. Accepting counsel from someone younger – especially a priest with a bad reputation – proved hard to take. Yet the key factor in nearly all of Willem's trouble related directly to his addiction. Where Vega nagged him about drinking too much, Algernon spoke with conviction.

"Your whole life will turn around with one decision," he'd said. "You're in control as long as you choose to not drink. But the moment you put that bottle to your lips, it controls you."

Secrets and Whispers: *Regret*

Willem had sworn at him like an erupting geyser, but Algernon remained unfazed. No threat forced him to back down. Willem had never met anyone so fearless in his entire life.

Yet now, as the gravity of being abandoned weighed on his soul, Willem knew that if he continued down his current path, he'd wind up all alone with no one to help. The change had to be radical. The change had to be permanent. The change had to happen now.

Lost in his thoughts, Willem didn't hear the guard arrive at his cell. "Get up, hangover boy! Your sister posted bail on your behalf. She and your brother-in-law have come to pick you up."

Trembling, Willem arose. He felt dizzy and weak. His head throbbed as the guard led him through the hall, waited at the secure gate to be let through, and then paused in the waiting area.

Bronwyn rushed forward, accepting her brother into a strong, soft, motherly embrace. She held him for a moment then backed away, her face reflecting concern. "Are you okay, Willi? You look terrible!"

"I can't do this anymore," he told her. "I should have pulled the trigger when I had the chance."

Algernon arose from the bench where he'd been sitting. He put his hand on Willem's shoulder. "Nonsense! Let the end be a new beginning," he encouraged.

"I'm a drunk. I'm a failure. I'm a . . ."

"You're none of those things," Algernon corrected. "You're my brother now. Leave the past behind and come home with us. You won't regret it."

Epilogue: *Secrets and Whispers*

When Carlos de Sanchez boarded the train for Kameron, he suspected that operatives from the Crown Intelligence Service were following him. Every time he turned his head, a well-dressed man happened to be sitting nearby, standing in a passageway, or enjoying a meal in the dining car.

At Desperado Falls, the only place in Tamaria where the local rail network linked with Kamerese train traffic, Carlos gathered his luggage with the ever-present agents shadowing his every move. When he walked to the Customs Office, intending to present his credentials and leave the country, the operatives stopped any pretense of discretion and followed right behind. He heard one of the Tamarian agents say, "That's him!" in Kamerese.

Two men wearing dark glasses and expensive suits came out of the customs office. After presenting badges from the King's Guard one of them announced, "Carlos de Sanchez, you'll be coming with us." The men quickly hustled him away from the crowd.

Carlos spent a long time in an interrogation room. The King's Guard agents questioned him for hours about his connection with Eduard Campillo, the Foreign Service Secretary, and *Los Patrones del Estado.*

"We know about the money trail," an interrogator stated. "We have your phone records and intercepts from the diplomatic pouch . . .

"You lied to that analyst contact of yours, but she figured out that you were involved in the plot. She showed your photo to the suppliers who sold the bomb-making materials. The agro-chemical vendors confirmed that you paid for the ammonium nitrate and kerosene in cash."

"She's a liar!" Carlos claimed.

Epilogue: *Secrets and Whispers*

The interrogator shook his head. "Not so. Unlike you, she's a patriot. She loves her country. She's not a traitor with blood on her hands. She's nothing like you!"

"I was acting under orders!" Carlos insisted. "I had no idea where the money came from. I just arranged the payments that came through the embassy . . ."

That story, however, had no basis in fact. Carlos knew this. The cover-up he and the Foreign Service orchestrated when Captain Hougen began piecing the mystery together led the King's Guard to the truth. She'd given her notes to Jared Hoehner, who subsequently passed them on to King Alejo by secure courier.

Under relentless questioning, deprived of food, water and sleep, Carlos couldn't keep his story straight. "The Foreign Service wanted to accelerate deployment of Tamarian forces to the Kurian highlands," he admitted. "The operation was approved at the highest level . . ."

That wasn't true, either. Two days later, Carlos de Sanchez, Eduard Campillo and three other men – all bound in chains – appeared in the throne room of the palace in Kameron City. A retinue of King's Guard and Tamarian Defenders stood at attention around the room.

King Alejo sat on his throne. To his right sat ageless Tamar, Queen of the High Land. She did not speak, but her presence signified cooperation with her closest ally.

A Crown Prosecutor read the names of the accused and the charges, which included Terrorism, Falsification of Documents, Conspiracy to Defraud, and Treason. All of these merited the death penalty.

When the prosecutor finished, King Alejo let silence weigh heavily on his captives. "You are not worthy of a lengthy speech, but I will make one promise you can take to your graves. When I am done dealing with your secret *Los Patrones del Estado,* people will only mention that cursed name in whispers, and with great fear."

Thank you for reading "Secrets and Whispers," the seventh novel in the Deveran Conflict series. Other titles include:

The Edge of Justice

The Long Journey

Crisis

Ceremonies and Celebrations

Dreams and Missions

The Inquest

All books are available in paperback and electronic book formats

Additional stories from the author include:

The Girl in the Game

Four Days to Freedom

The Hollow Solitude

www.newadventure.ca